GIMCRACK

BY RICHARD LAWS

for Harry and Rory

My sincerest thanks go to Linda Cronk, Mike Dunn, Claire Dickens
and Pat Grant for their invaluable editorial advice.

Also by Richard Laws:
The Syndicate Manager

First published 2019 by Five Furlongs

© Richard Laws 2019
ISBN 978-1-9164600-2-7 (Paperback)
ISBN 978-1-9164600-3-4 (Ebook)

Published by Five Furlongs 2019

One

Laya was sure her set had gone well. The smoke filled working men's club had remained quiet enough to allow her to perform without interruption and the hundred or so punters had provided a ripple of polite applause following each of her songs. A few pockets of onlookers had even stood and clapped appreciatively at the end of the performance. She took that as a huge positive. They could be a tough midweek crowd at this venue and weren't beyond booing an act off the stage. Being a female singer didn't confer any special treatment; they knew what they liked in Yorkshire and wouldn't be shy in expressing their displeasure for a below par performance. She thanked the audience with a genuine broad smile and a quick little inclination of her head. As she exited the stage the applause died and she found herself wondering whether she was *finally* starting to win them over.

Once in the wings she removed a change of clothes from the cloth guitar case that she'd stowed before going on stage and carefully replaced her instrument, the most expensive item she owned. She glanced at her wristwatch. It was nine minutes past ten, a minute earlier than she was due off stage. She bit her lip, hoping the club manager wouldn't dock her fee for her mistake. She stood in the wings of the small stage for half a minute, listening to the audience scraping their chairs behind the chipboard façade, before tapping on a thin painted door in the back wall of the stage. There was a scuffling noise and it opened inward a crack before bouncing shut. Laya could hear a man swearing behind the door's wooden panels as he struggled with the spherical door knob; she watched it turn viciously left then right, followed by rattling as he pulled in vain.

Taking care not to knock anything over in the tight space behind the curtain, she backed off a few paces. Eventually, and awkwardly, the door swung inward to reveal a putty-faced, overweight man in a three-piece suit and bow tie. He was still muttering expletives as he tried to push his mass through the doorframe, eventually having to edge out sideways.

'Now then love,' he offered in a gruff, heavy Liverpool accent as he sidled past the good looking, conservatively dressed black girl with a guitar case in her hand. 'Is there a mic in the wings here or is it stage only?' he asked without making eye contact, scanning the area, a lit cigarette bouncing around in the corner of his mouth as he spoke.

'Over there on the wall,' she replied quietly, pointing at a small hook at shoulder height. 'Hold the button down to speak.'

With his back to her he growled 'Cheers, love,' before lumbering over to the hand-microphone and picking it off the wall with a small, fat hand. He wheezed while clearing his throat, phlegm still crackling as he held the microphone button down to announce his own arrival on stage.

Laya didn't wait. She darted into the changing room and closed the door quietly behind her. She knew the comic's brand of comedy and didn't want to listen to any more than she had to.

The changing room consisted of a grubby looking chair, a narrow desk with a full ashtray and a full-length mirror leaning against the wall. It stank of cigarettes. A single un-shaded light bulb hung from the ceiling, sending a fierce glare onto whitewashed walls which had long since lost their lustre. The entire room was a shade of nicotine smudged yellow.

The comedian had left various bits of himself around the room, including a coat with what appeared to be a spare hairpiece hanging out of one pocket. It was more corridor than changing room, however, Laya worked quickly. Swapping her silk shirt for a jumper, she pulled on a pair of tight jeans and squeezed the skirt she had been wearing on stage into her guitar case. She scooped up a pair of white pumps from the instrument's side pocket and her stage shoes were carefully tucked under her guitar and the whole lot zipped up.

The muffled sound of male laughter came through the stage wall as she headed to the stone steps at the end of the 'Turn's Room' as the club manager had described her dressing room the first time she had played there two years ago. Despite the drab surroundings, she was grateful for the extra money her singing brought in, and on top of riding out for a couple of racing yards it meant she and her son Harry could keep a roof over their heads, even if it was just a one bedroom flat which backed onto the railway track.

A'laya Bolt had bought a one-way plane ticket from Barbados to Manchester nine years previously, in search of her unborn son's father. There was no family left for her in Barbados. Instead, she'd came to Britain to create her own. She travelled on a train to Malton, Yorkshire using her last few pounds and walked the final four miles from the station to the outskirts of Norton where she found Willie Warcup's training stables. She was eighteen, three months pregnant and had expected to fall into the arms of her sweetheart. Instead, Laya confronted her first love at the stables. The young man concerned promptly drained of all colour and love, leaving the town a day later without a goodbye or a forwarding address.

After spending two nights crying herself to sleep on the sofa in a static caravan shared by two other stable lads, A'laya - quickly shortened by everyone she met to 'Laya' - had been taken in hand by Annie, the trainer's wife, and was given light stabling duties. A week later she astounded Willie by readily jumping on the back of a headstrong three year old gelding and proceeded to tame her mount's fiery temper.

'Where did you learn to handle a horse like that, lass?' Willie had asked the young girl as they walked the horses back to the yard.

'I rode in races at the Garrison back home.'

Willie had scratched his head. 'So what did your fella do over there then?'

The girl had furrowed her brow. It seemed she thought the answer was rather simple. 'What he did here. He cleaned out stables, Sir.'

'That probably accounts for why he was such a terrible rider,' Willie had muttered rather too loudly to himself.

'You'll ride the next lot. And I'm the Guv'nor, not a Sir... yet,' he'd added with a nod and given Laya his trademark twinkling smile.

She had ridden out three lots a day for the next three months and Annie had seen to it that Laya was provided with a desk job for the last three months of her pregnancy. She found friends, a flat and settled into a new life in Malton.

Laya climbed two steps at the back of the club, pushed down on the fire escape bar, and poked her nose out into the cool autumn air, peering around the car park. It was twenty past ten when she sidled between the parked cars, passed the dimly lit railway signal box and turned onto Church Street. It wasn't freezing, but there was a definite nip in the air. It was the sort of night where you maintained your pace and looked forward to getting back home and in front of a warm fire.

It had been raining that afternoon so the road and pavements looked greasy. Small puddles were still dotted around where the aging pavement slabs had sunk, providing an uneven ridge between them for rainwater to pool. She shivered, wishing she'd brought her coat, but it was only a five minute walk home. Wrapping both arms around her chest she walked with her head down, guitar bobbing up and down on her back, trying to avoid stepping in the larger puddles. Her watch said ten twenty-five; she could just about make it home to her eight year old, Harry, and relieve her babysitter before ten thirty.

She headed away from the railway line, hurrying down Church Street toward Commercial Road, the main street in Norton. There was hardly anyone around. An elderly man with a small dog ambled along on the opposite side of the road. The only other person on the street a disgruntled looking woman, standing on the pavement opposite the railway crossing. She switched between inspecting her watch and peering up the street. As Laya hurried past the woman issued an irritated sigh, tapping a high-heeled foot onto the pavement with tinny clack. When Laya stole a glance back at her seconds later, the woman had melted into the darkness.

Even the petrol station was closed, a single dim light behind the cashier's counter the only sign of life. A couple of cars passed her, headlights dazzling, sending wild shadows onto the buildings around her. Still with her head down, Laya skipped over a few badly broken paving slabs before getting her bearings. She slowed and looked up and down the road. The road was empty of traffic, the dog walker was about to disappear

4

over the railway crossing now and the impatient lady had melted into the shadows. If she were to cross the road, her flat was only fifty yards away.

Laya looked right again and saw a set of headlights turn onto the road, travelling quite slowly. She considered whether to quickly scoot across the road before the car arrived, but decided against such a rash move, her guitar wouldn't stand too much jostling. Waiting impatiently by the kerb, she looked up and shielded her eyes from the car's bright full beams. The vehicle seemed to slow further, coming towards her, almost *for* her. It indicated and pulled right up onto the pavement, bumping up the kerb in front of Laya. She stepped back against a hairdressers shop window, believing the car could be set to do a u-turn, yet the headlights still blazed at her. Straddling the path and the road at a jaunty angle the vehicle came to a halt a few yards in front of her. The passenger side window was wound down and a head bobbed out.

'Any chance you could give us some directions, love?' asked a pleasant male voice.

Laya approached cautiously and bent to answer, still a yard or two from the car window. The young man's face looked ghostly at the open window and suddenly she recognised the danger in the situation. As soon as her facial expression changed from helpful to concerned, the back door nearest the footpath burst open. A tall, wiry figure wearing dark clothes emerged from the back of the car. Laya straightened and set to run, but he was on her quickly, easily gripping both arms, forcing her backwards hard against the hairdresser's window. She winced at the splintering noise from the guitar slung over her back as it became crushed against the window.

They remained in this pose for only a second, Laya too shocked to respond, staring into the young man's pockmarked face. Pinpricks of perspiration broke on her forehead, and she tried twisting her wrists in order to break free, but he was strong and his grip didn't slacken.

Laya shuddered. There was another man, someone she hadn't noticed, right beside her. His sudden presence jolted her and she half screamed, her voice catching as she gasped for breath. He was breathing in her right ear, sniggering first, then some broken speech. He was babbling incoherently, close up to her ear, so much so, she couldn't help but thrust her ear to her shoulder and screw her face up.

A sharp prickle of pain flowered from the base of her neck, just above her collarbone. It only lasted a couple of seconds.

Before Laya could contemplate a defensive or attacking move she was inexplicably released, being pushed backwards into the window one last time by her assailants. She bounced off the glass pane and ended up on her knees. Two dark figures walked back to the car. They were casual, swaggering with testosterone inflated egos. One looked back, just for a second, grinning at her. Laya shuddered and suddenly felt angry. Doors slammed and as if underscoring their arrogance, the car stood for a while and took time to indicate, then pulled slowly and unobtrusively onto the road and trundled down the street.

Laya watched incredulously as the car retreated leisurely away from her. Her heart was racing and she sucked in deep breaths. As her thumping pulse started to settle she became aware of a sharp stinging sensation at the base of her throat. She fingered what felt like a wasp bite. It almost touched her collarbone. A smudge of blood coloured her fingertip upon inspection under the street light. She shook her head, bewildered by the events of the last minute. She just wanted to be home, safe with Harry.

Shivering, she hugged herself. A wave of uncertainly washed over her, leaving her feeling vulnerable and strangely ashamed. She regained some composure, told herself she was fine, there was no harm done, well, apart from her guitar; she'd need to inspect that later. They were just some idiot teenage boys trying to frighten her.

Laya watched the boys' car travel another few yards into the distance. When the brake lights flashed red she didn't wait. She set off across the road at a run and quickly reached the corner of the small lane that led to her home. She could see the door to their flat now.

Twenty-five yards from her front door Laya started to lose her balance. She tottered drunkenly from one side of the alley to the other, desperately trying to reach her goal of getting to safety, to get home. Her legs suddenly refused to respond to her urgings to carry her forward and she fell to her knees, still trying to shuffle onward. Her thoughts became dull, her head felt heavy, she could hardly hold it up.

'Harry!' she shouted, pleading in her voice. Then consciousness swung away from her control. It spiralled in a wide arc, taking her completely and she toppled forward, striking the damp paving slabs outside her flat with a sickening crack.

A'laya Bolt's eyes twitched momentarily and then she died, ten yards from her front door.

Presently a light flicked on and her flat door opened. An eight year old black boy stared out from the doorway, his shock of tightly curled hair casting a distorted, shadowy image of himself over his mother's prone body.

Two

August, present day.

Findlay Morrison coped well with being taken out of his comfort zone; it was a trait which had helped him become renowned in his line of work. However, his experience today had taught him there were deeper and darker levels to be plumbed when successfully intimidating someone.

He had been impressed with the professionalism displayed by the two men and one woman and deeply disappointed in his own staff's performance. They had been dealt with... he searched for suitable words, idly running his tongue over a newly chipped tooth... ah, yes... with *malicious zeal*.

He wasn't too surprised. His expansion up and down the east coast had probably been too rapid and inevitably he had trodden on a few toes. Apparently these people weren't convinced his brand of sudden pressure should be applied to their digits. However, this little group of extremely dangerous people hadn't killed him, which was surprising. Had the roles been reversed, he'd have had no hesitation. In fact they were being exceptionally careful to keep him alive, albeit on a very fine edge. Now that *had* to be a positive.

Findlay had also been impressed with their use of a trained medical man. He'd received a full check-up after being used as a punch bag. Now *that* showed a level of professionalism currently beyond the capabilities of his own organisation. If he was able to live through the rest of today there would be a range of improvements to be made to his business. An ex-army trained field medic might come in useful...

In his early teens Findlay had worked the streets of Seaham and had come to the conclusion that if you didn't overly value your life, were driven by greed and a need for self validation, and then combined these traits with a complete moral vacuum, plus an added streak of malevolence, organised crime was a doddle. It helped that he was intelligent; however, he accepted being well read was low on the list of requirements of a wannabe crime boss. His innate ability to understand what drove the people around him, and use of this skill to manipulate them, was of far greater value. He'd left school at the first opportunity and happily ensconced himself in the dangerous and dirty world of drugs and protection at the sharp end until the opportunity to seize control of his own slice of illegality had come along. After that, it was just a matter of controlling the growth.

The travelling car hummed quietly and he tried to slowly raise his head to see where he was. A powerful hand pushed his head firmly back down. He'd been in Sunderland that morning but had been immediately knocked unconscious as soon as they had overpowered his people, so he could be anywhere by now. Come to think of it, he wasn't too sure when *now* was. He considered the state of his beard, scratching his stubble against the course cloth bag on his head; it felt like the same day. He would be *very* impressed if they'd bothered to shave him whilst unconscious. His watch was gone but there had been a suggestion of sunlight when he'd been roughly deposited in the back of the car.

The sound of other engines reached him and the car began to stop and start; they were in traffic. Then a hand pinched the back of his neck and suddenly his eyes were assaulted with painful light and blurred colour as his hood was whipped off. Once his eyes began to adjust, he examined the car and found one of his assailants beside him on the back seat, the woman was in the passenger seat, and the other man was driving. Land Rover logos filled the inside of the car.

'Don't move, Mr Morrison,' the young gorilla of a man to his left instructed as the thick black tape wound around his wrists was expertly slit open with a knife.

Findlay considered. He determined he was either going to be dumped on the street or presented to someone. The latter looked more likely. He recognised the street. He was in Newcastle, almost in the centre.

'Sit still and do as I say. Give me an excuse and I can drain your blood from you where you sit,' hissed the man on his right.

'I don't doubt it,' replied Findlay without a hint of sarcasm.

The car came to a stop, the woman got out and the back door was opened from the outside.

'We're walking, Mr Morrison,' the gorilla instructed, grasping Findlay's right wrist in a vice-like grip and pulling him across the back seat. Just as he planted his feet on the pavement, a hat was handed to him.

'Put it on.'

Findlay regarded the black hat; it was the wide brim which interested him. Christ, they were thorough. His face must look like a dog's dinner, the Fedora would mask the worst of the beating he had taken. Clever.

Getting gingerly to his feet, he looked around from under the brim of his newly acquired hat and found himself in the centre of Newcastle; just off Grey Street. The gorilla faded into the furniture of the street and, instead, the sharply dressed woman from the passenger seat stepped forward.

'Mr Morrison. Let's get a coffee shall we?' she said in an authoritative Geordie accent.

'Certainly. And you are?'

The woman was in her late twenties with a lithe, fit frame, wearing a pencil skirt that accentuated her curves. She wore her brown hair very short and Findlay could just make out a set of long lashes behind a dark pair of small round sunglasses. She didn't reply, instead gesturing to a small cobbled alley down which the two of them walked about twenty yards before she guided him into a small Italian restaurant with a closed sign hung on its door. She followed him in and indicated a table which had clearly been reserved for the two of them in the middle of the deserted restaurant. An iPad tablet sat propped up on the table.

'You're probably wondering why you're not dead, Mr Morrison,' she said in a mildly amused tone as soon as Findlay had managed to bend his aching body into the basic wooden chair.

Findlay fought his natural urge to be flippant. It might not work to be cocky with her. Instead he gave a non-committal grunt.

Two coffees arrived at the table brought by a nervous young female waiter. Findlay couldn't disguise a smile when he recognised his favourite hot drink in front of him. He noted that it was always the small touches which impress most.

The cool brunette continued, 'We have been following your progress in the last sixteen months, Mr Morrison. Your incorporation of Middlesborough and in particular Gateshead has been… impressive, although its execution was a little ham-fisted. Nevertheless, you are making waves and affecting our business.'

'And your business is…?'

She paused, removing her sunglasses to reveal an incredible pair of huge deep brown eyes. 'We are cleaners, Mr Morrison.'

A flicker of understanding in his eyes, even for that split second, betrayed him and the woman gave Findlay a cold smile, her eyes becoming black slits.

'I believe you may have heard of us?'

'I believe I have,' he answered quietly.

'Then you will understand that this is not a negotiation. You've seen how we operate, and I'm sure you will appreciate that we had to…,' she flicked a hand with blood red nails through her fringe. '… *convince you* that your participation is now necessary.'

Despite a cacophony of constantly crashing cymbals in his head and most of his muscles singing with pain, Findlay Morrison's ego received the biggest boost of his life. He'd become important enough for 'Halo' to come calling. The biggest money laundering operation down the east coast of Britain wanted his business. Drug pushing, theft, blackmail, intimidation, and fraud were relatively easy, it was how you turned your revenue into usable currency that took the time and effort, and Halo was a hallowed name among criminal circles. It was said they came calling once you were of interest to them – and you didn't say no. He allowed himself to bask in his newly found success for a few glorious seconds, extending the moment by taking a slug of his coffee.

Membership to this club was by request only. These bruises and this headache were the registration papers, which had been filled and filed.

9

However, he was getting a strong impression that this woman wasn't the real power base. The fat lady still hadn't sung.

'I'm intrigued,' he offered.

'I'm sure you are.'

'So when do I meet your boss?' he asked eagerly.

She leaned back and crossed her legs, forcing her skirt to unmask the shape of her legs. 'He's been here all the time,' she replied, leaning forward and lightly tapping the tablet on the table. It immediately sprang to life and a man's face appeared. He was grinning.

'Mr Morrison, I'm so pleased to meet you. My apologies for our rough little game earlier, we needed you to understand we were… *serious*. I'm sure you understand?'

Findlay nodded his head, his Fedora's brim sucking up the sudden pinpricks of sweat which had formed on his forehead. He cleared his throat to answer with a weak, crackly, 'Yes.'

'Your exploits on Teesside have been devious, amoral and… commendable,' continued the face on the tablet, 'However, it's time to take you to the next level. It's time you joined our enterprise.'

The bearded man was now smiling so broadly a ring of perfectly sculpted upper teeth shone through his thick, bushy beard.

'You have completed your initiation; however, there is something else we will require from you… a small request.'

The man raised his palm to his forehead, lightly striking himself. 'Oh! Forgive me, Mr Morrison I'm getting ahead of myself, we haven't been introduced!' he added playfully.

'I'm…'

Findlay couldn't help himself. He'd recognised the man instantly and now he mouthed his name in unison with the disembodied head on the tablet.

'… Benedict Manton.'

Three

It was too dark for the early morning mist to display itself in any depth. Instead, a grey cloud swirled around Harry Bolt's stout figure, waiting for that first refraction of sunlight to give it some substance. His wheelbarrow cast wisps aside as it crossed the stable yard, the leading edge of the barrow becoming wet from the fine prickles of water. Harry smiled. Ordinarily he was a happy soul, however today he was surpassing this; he was filled with joy, although he knew he had no good reason to feel that way.

Harry's march down the stable yard ceased mid-step, his gumboots making a hollow rubbery sound as they scraped to a halt, the wheelbarrow emitting a tinny clink as he dropped it carefully onto the concrete. He blinked to clear his vision and stared up his top yard. It consisted of two lines of ten stables which faced each other. The area between them was concreted, slightly concave with a shallow drainage channel running down the centre. Just beyond the last stable stood three deer, facing him, the white flecks in their ears standing out as the mist swirled around them. They turned toward him, statuesque, regarding Harry dolefully. Then, as one, they turned and disappeared at a trot into the paddocks beyond. He tracked them until all he could pick out were bobbing white tails, which eventually dissolved entirely into the misty darkness.

He smiled broadly after them and considered: a doe and her two fawns. Jill, his wife for the last ten years, entered his thoughts. He had left her sleeping in the farmhouse, enjoying a lie-in of sorts. Being a trainer's wife meant rising at seven o'clock counted as an indulgence. Could he see Jill with two offspring? Of course he could. His smile grew even bigger at this thought. He'd have to mention it to her, they'd not talked about children for months, if not years…

Harry knew he had a reputation as a quiet, cheery sort, and some people got him and others simply didn't. He didn't spend too much time wondering why people didn't take to his positive approach, however racehorses were another matter. He'd never met a horse he hadn't been able to get along with. And he'd encountered plenty in his thirty-two years.

His thoughts were interrupted by the start of the dawn chorus. The stable's resident blackbird had taken up his favoured perch on the tiles at the apex of the stable block roof to announce how really pleased he was about another day starting. Harry listened to the first three choruses, nodding along with the song, sighed, took up the barrow and continued his trudge to the nearest stable door.

He really didn't mind getting up at daybreak. It was a time of day just for him and the horses. He'd check each of them over, give them their first feed and connect with each of them once again. The words of the first horseman he'd worked for at the age of fifteen came to him, as they did many times a day.

'They can't speak, you know,' Willie Warcup had told him fifteen years ago, nodding sagely toward a young bay filly standing in the back of her box and fixing the then sixteen year old Harry with a look which was both appraising and critical, 'but it doesn't mean you shouldn't listen.'

He'd beckoned to Harry and the two of them had edged across to the yearling who had cowered slightly as they approached. The old man had murmured to the filly, gaining her confidence then expertly ran his hands down her legs, down her back and across her chest before carefully checking her feet one by one. He'd shown Harry a small cut to the sole of the filly's foot and said quietly, 'She told me there was something niggling her. Want to know how?'

'Yes please, sir,' Harry had whispered back.

'She spoke to me lad,' Willie had answered with one eyebrow raised, trying to determine whether the boy understood. Harry hadn't at first, but it didn't take long around legendary trainer, Willie Warcup before he did understand – about listening to horses, and a whole lot more.

Harry smiled at the recollection as he unbolted the door to the first stable of the six racehorses he currently had in training. The bay gelding was already knocking into him before he got over the threshold, begging for his breakfast. Harry shushed him, pushing the half a ton of horse gently backwards before checking him over. Magic Jewel continued to nod his chin gently into the top of Harry's shoulder and then into his head as he looked him over. The six year old was a box walker, so Harry had placed a steel mirror on one wall of his box to try and get the horse to admire himself and not pace around. Harry finished looking Magic Jewel over and caught himself in the dusty, smudged mirror. Riding most days still kept him relatively fit at thirty-two. He examined his broad face, with its fine cheekbones, flat nose and chiseled jaw, something he was proud to put down to his mother. His extremely short, jet-black hair matched the colour of his skin. Born in Yorkshire, Harry Bolt was one of only a small number of black racehorse trainers in Britain.

Harry smiled at his reflection, then stuck a large tongue out and laughed at himself. The gelding snorted his derision and Harry returned his attention to him. This chap was known as 'Paste' in the yard because far from being a jewel in the crown, Magic Jewel was adept at throwing his races away. From forty-four runs to date, he had managed to win once and be placed second a further eighteen times. He was rarely out of the first few home in his races, but stubbornly refused to realise his true potential.

Satisfied that Paste was in good order, Harry returned to his barrow and scooped up the six year old's breakfast. As soon as the feed touched his trough, Paste had his head buried, slurping happily.

'If only all of them ate like him,' Harry moaned to himself as he re-bolted the stable door and moved on to the filly dwelling in the next stable.

The five minutes with Paste had allowed the September sun to add a dash of colour to the morning sky and Harry could see a line of horse's heads over their stable doors, looking down the line in anticipation of their own visit from him and his feed bucket. He picked up his wheelbarrow and moved down the four yards to the filly called 'Smashing Lass', known as 'Smasher' in the yard.

'Is it Mr Bolt by any chance?' asked a slightly wavering, gentle voice close behind him.

Shocked, Harry lurched forward, a surge of fright running through him which seemed to vent through the top of his head. He spun round, one hand clasped to his chest.

A small, wrinkled man leaned lop-sided on a walking stick no more than a yard in front of him. The old man peered up at him through thick, round, horn-rimmed glasses. He blinked at Harry, shifting slightly so his bifocal spectacles enlarged his eyes. Harry tried to stifle an audible reaction to seeing the bug-eyed man so close up, but a small whimper still got out.

'Mr Harry Bolt?' the man asked again in a mangled Yorkshire accent, frowning ever so slightly.

Harry took a breath. 'I'm so sorry er… Sir, I didn't hear you come into the yard. Yes, I'm Harry Bolt.'

Allowing his heartbeat to tumble back to normality, Harry took the chance to examine the man in a little more detail. His tweed suit and matching waistcoat were placed under pressure by a rotund waistline and his ensemble was topped off by a cream coloured tie pierced by a pin headed with a small ruby. His brogues looked well worn and Harry wondered if this could have contributed to the fact he hadn't heard the man approach across the concrete surface of the yard. He had a doughy face, with extended jowls and a number of thin lines across his forehead, but a constantly upturned mouth helped him radiate some warmth. A crescent of silver-flecked brown hair ran around the back of his head, from ear to ear. Harry noticed the man's right ear had a flesh-coloured hearing aid carefully secreted, almost out of sight. He tried to place the man's age and found conflicting evidence; he could have been anything from late forties to mid sixties.

'No, no it is I who should apologise,' said the stranger gently, still standing motionless. 'I believe I must have caught you in early morning thought. I've always done my best thinking early in the day. Please, let me introduce myself, I am Thomas Redblood.'

The visitor leant a little more on the stick in his left hand and extended the other towards Harry. He took it and enjoyed a dry, vigorous handshake from the stranger. As Harry was about to let go, Redblood gripped his hand tightly and pulled him down toward him with surprising strength.

'I'm looking for an honest man, Mr Bolt. An honest man to train horses,' he insisted, fixing Harry with another stare, but this time it came with a warm smile which revealed a set of upper teeth which were almost certainly dentures. They looked far too perfect and regimented.

Redblood held Harry's hand for a few seconds in silence, still looking into the younger man's face, examining him, and in return demanding examination of himself. Harry got the sense the old man was assessing whether he was being taken seriously. Redblood blinked, broke eye contact, and released Harry's hand, taking a deep breath as he did. Then he cast his gaze down the line of stables.

'Please feel free to keep feeding,' Redblood suggested, gesturing with his eyes to the line of horses. 'I would be interested to observe.'

Harry scratched his head and then slid his hand down the side of his face, trying to weigh up how he should respond. Redblood's upturned face held an expectant expression, which turned into a frown and then enlightenment in quick order.

'Ah, I sense I've been a little too forward,' he said, casting closed eyes to the ground and shaking his head slightly. He tilted his head back up to lock his bespectacled eyes with Harry once more.

'Let me explain. I am interested in becoming an owner of racehorses and I am led to understand that you are the right person for this particular job,' he announced.

Harry gave a tight-lipped smile and nodded. 'That's fine... well perhaps we could go into the house and discuss...'

The little man shook his right palm at Harry. 'Oh, no. No need. I really would rather we talked while you work, if that would be acceptable?'

Harry shrugged, nodded back and unbolted Smasher's box, pushing the filly back as he entered. Redblood didn't seem to be any sort of threat, and whilst he couldn't place his accent, there was a definite Yorkshire twang every now and again. Besides, there wasn't any law against being a little bit eccentric, and this Redblood character had an interest in having a horse trained by him. After all, he was *supposed* to be a racehorse trainer, although the present lack of horses in his yard was clear for anyone to see. Harry currently had twenty-two boxes without an inmate and his yard was at its lowest ebb since he and Jill had begun their lease at Pickering Farm Stables two years previously.

The two men spent the next twenty minutes moving along the line of stables, Harry checking the horses over for heat in their joints, inspecting feet, eyes and mouths. Redblood entered each of the boxes and leant up against the wall beside the stable door, watching in silence for the bulk of the time. Harry would finally add a splash of feed into the manger, direct Redblood to exit the box and leave the horse alone to eat its breakfast. Although a little stilted at first, the two of them finally fell into amiable conversation. Harry warmed to his subject once the old man fed the trainer's enthusiasm for his horses with what appeared to be a genuine interest, along with a smattering of knowledge about racing.

After bolting the sixth stable door, Harry indicated his wheelbarrow. 'I'm due to get rid of this in the feed room and I'd usually get a cup of coffee in the kitchen around now, before my stable lass, Zoe, comes in. Want to join me?'

'Absolutely,' Redblood replied enthusiastically before going on to ask about paddock space and turnout for the horses.

The two men headed down the corridor of stables, still chatting, Harry being careful to pace himself so as not to leave the older man behind. Once they were walking in a straight line he noticed that Redblood walked with a pronounced limp, his left leg appearing to be bowed. His stick was a requirement then, not an affectation.

Harry was expecting to see a car parked beside the farmhouse, but when they walked round the front of the house the three spaces for visiting owners were empty.

'You haven't walked here have you, Mr Redblood?' Harry asked with a laugh.

'Not at all,' Redblood replied, raising an eyebrow. 'My helicopter is in that field over there.'

'*Really*?' Harry said in mock astonishment, flashing a brilliant white smile at the same time.

'No. Not really. I came in a taxi. It dropped me at the top of the lane.'

Harry helped Redblood up the steps to the back door and lifted some old newspapers off a chair to allow him to plant himself in front of the already lit wood burning stove. The kitchen table was littered with old copies of *The Racing Post*, well-thumbed fixture booklets and copies of *Owner Breeder* with letters and junk mail mixed in with discarded mugs. A large square tin of biscuits with a tartan motif sat in the middle of the plain, six-seater wooden table.

As Harry flicked the kettle on, Jill walked into the kitchen in her dressing gown and a thick pair of slipper socks. She sat down at the table as she did every morning at this time, looking bleary-eyed and oblivious to anyone else in the room. Slightly smaller than Harry at five foot six Jill huddled, head down, appearing even smaller. Her un-brushed shoulder length blonde hair lay slab-like down one side of her face in an unruly mess.

'Tea?' asked Harry, unclear how to deal with the situation.

Jill yawned expressively, extending both arms upwards. 'Mmmm… please.'

She opened her eyes at the end of her stretch, rubbing them with the heels of both hands. Waiting a few seconds for her focus to return properly, she suddenly jumped up, sending her chair scraping backwards over the stone floor.

Harry winced. 'Ah yes. Jill, this is er… Thomas…'

'Oh my… I didn't realise you were…' Jill mumbled before bolting back out of the door she'd entered, holding her dressing gown tightly to her chest with both hands.

To Harry's relief, his guest chuckled quietly and nodded appreciatively at Harry, before turning back to the warmth of the stove. Five minutes later Jill rejoined the two men in the kitchen, a hand and half a face appearing around the side of the kitchen door first before she quietly entered again, fully clothed and hair brushed back this time. She'd even added a touch of make-up.

'I'm so sorry about that. I had no idea Harry was meeting someone,' she said in apology to Redblood after being introduced. Then she turned to Harry and added 'I *wasn't warned* was I!'

'Dear lady, the fault lies entirely with myself for calling so early in the morning. You have nothing to apologise for,' Redblood smoothly assured her, before suggesting she pull up a chair beside him.

Jill sat down at Redblood's elbow and the two of them traded small talk for the next ten minutes, the old man sipping his tea slowly and warming his hands around the mug. It wasn't cold inside or out but it seemed he was in need of some warmth. It was convivial and positive, Harry allowing Jill to lead the conversation. She was good at that, making up for his lack of confidence in that department.

Realising they had talked almost exclusively about themselves and the yard since Redblood had sat down, Jill tried to switch the focus of the conversation.

'So what is it you do, Mr Redblood?'

Redblood contemplated inwardly, rolling his hand over the nub of his walking stick for a few seconds 'I've recently become retired,' he replied, pausing to stroke the top of his stick. Again, their guest fell silent and Jill could sense her husband was about to speak, to fill the vacuum. She held up her hand and Harry caught himself and remained silent. He stood, leaning up against the kitchen sink and allowed his wife to continue. Jill was always much better at working people out. He tended to be too trusting, something which had caused him to make bad decisions in the past regarding potential new owners. She seemed to be able to see through and into people.

Redblood rolled his eyes around the room and eventually they came to rest on Jill. He took another sip of his tea. 'I have unfinished business with racing and with Malton, and in fact, Pickering Farm.'

Jill's eyes narrowed slightly. She fought the urge to ask another question and instead nodded for the older man to continue.

'I grew up in this farmhouse. Of course it was one large farm then, not as it is now, being sectioned off into… well, I don't know how many racing yards.'

Having stunned his audience into silence, Redblood let out a weak chuckle. 'You know, about forty years ago I used to play with toy soldiers on this kitchen floor as a boy.'

Redblood turned to Harry. 'I knew your mother when she worked for the Warcup's.'

The strange little man was suddenly stony faced, clearly waiting for a reaction. Harry stared back at him, unbalanced. His dark brown eyes searched the man's features intensely for a confirmation of truth.

Jill looked up at her husband in bewilderment then back to the man warming himself beside the stove. 'You knew Harry's mother?' she repeated slowly.

Redblood paused to warm his hands on the stove, before turning back to her. 'Oh yes, she was a beautiful young thing and certainly made her mark around here when she arrived with Harry. She was quite the breath of fresh air in Malton. It was a terrible thing that happened to her…'

'You knew my mother… well?' Harry interrupted. 'I…' he found he couldn't continue, with a dry lump at the base of his throat stemming further speech.

Redblood looked strangely pleased, still minutely examining Harry's reaction and raising one corner of his mouth a fraction; a hint of mischievousness, perhaps? It evaporated and he nodded gravely at Harry.

'Yes, I knew her. Your mother and I enjoyed a passion for music.'

'You sang with her?' Harry queried with deeply furrowed eyebrows.

'Oh dear me, no!' he exclaimed, a warm smile hanging on his face for longer than seemed natural. 'I played jazz trumpet and backed her with a few other musicians – only for a short time.'

Silence descended on the kitchen as this information sank in.

'She never stopped talking about her Harry you know,' Redblood added wistfully. He turned and smiled at Jill.

'I know the value in dealing with honest people and if your husband is anything like A'laya he will be an honest man. Perhaps, too honest,' he noted with a theatrical wink.

Jill studied the man. He seemed genuine enough. There was a niggling doubt tugging at her though, something she couldn't quite fathom. She responded with a half-hearted 'Thanks.'

The temperature in the kitchen seemed to drop a dozen degrees and silence settled onto the three occupants of the room. Redblood's unexpected knowledge of his mother and the weirdness of the man didn't sit easily with Harry. He tried not to stare at Redblood, sliding his gaze to the floor and batted away the painful recollections of his mother which were trying to engulf him.

Millie, Harry's West Highland Terrier trotted into the kitchen at this point, her claws making a clicking noise as they tapped the tiled floor. She stopped stock still, entranced by the stillness. Millie was twelve and tended to snooze until nine or ten o-clock most days, so she must have been interested in the new voice in the farmhouse to bother investigating. She unknowingly provided a welcome distraction, as every face in the kitchen turned her way. She trotted over to Redblood and wagged her tail, placing one foot on the man's shoe in the hope he would either have a snack or start scratching her.

Redblood broke his gaze with Millie, looked to the ceiling, and sighed expressively. He had fulfilled his objective from this meeting and had no need to take it any further. Harry was his mother's son, which was plain to see. He should have the same resolve. His wife was a bit of a bonus, she was the clincher.

'Well, that was a nice cup of tea, but I must be off now,' he stated positively, passing his mug to Jill and struggling to his feet. Millie's tail whipped between her back legs and she darted away.

Jill stood too, shooting a worried glance at Harry as she guided their potential new owner to the back door and held it open for him. Redblood thanked her but stopped before going over the threshold. He drew himself up an extra inch or two to stand straighter and slowly turned to face Harry, his walking stick making sharp raps on the tiled floor as it aided his shuffling feet.

'I'd like to see you as the first trainer from Pickering Farm to get a Group winner. You've the skill and drive. You just need the ammunition,' Redblood stated.

Rather sullenly, Harry raised his eyes to Redblood but didn't speak. The initial shock of meeting someone who knew, or even remembered his mother was subsiding, however he had too many conflicting emotions to converse with him. He found himself biting the inside of his lip and tensing the muscles in his cheek. He managed a quiet agreeing grunt and dropped his eyes to the floor.

'Your mother deserved better son, and so do you,' Redblood said, turning. 'You'll be hearing from me.'

Redblood nodded curtly at Jill and after carefully descending each of the kitchen steps one at a time, entered the bottom yard and walked jauntily round to the front of the farmhouse. Harry watched his potential new owner make his way slowly out of the yard's front gates before pointing his walking stick to the right and setting off down the single lane track to the main road. He lost sight of the old man behind the horse walker belonging to his next-door neighbour.

Four

'I shouldn't let it affect me,' Harry told Jill as together they swept the walkway between the two lines of stables in the top yard later that morning. They worked side by side, leaving the white concrete spotless behind them.

'You're allowed to be sensitive about your mum.'

'Maybe. He wasn't to know that, though.'

Jill stopped sweeping the dust, straw and muck and stood leaning on the yard brush with both hands. Millie, who had been sniffing around a stable door looked up, sensing the work might be over, which invariably meant breakfast.

'I thought he was a bit flakey anyway. He didn't say *how well* he knew your mum, just that he'd met her and played some music with her. Besides, I think he did it for effect. It wouldn't have taken much research. And what on earth was he doing turning up at five forty-five in the morning? That's not normal.'

Harry maintained his brushing. Jill waited. Her husband was never talkative, but she had learnt to leave a few seconds between statements, just in case…

She continued. 'So what did he talk to you about before I made my entrance with such panache?'

Harry stopped sweeping and looked at his wife, sparks of playfulness in his eyes for the first time since Redblood's visit. 'I think your performance amused him.'

'Really? You think I wowed him then?' she kidded.

'Certainly! Showing a bit of ankle at six o'clock in the morning is more than enough to get an old man's pulse racing!'

They both laughed and went back to finishing off the yard.

'So, come on, what did you talk about?' Jill persisted.

'Just the horses.'

'And that was it?'

Jill's tone of voice demanded a fuller explanation, so, reluctantly Harry stopped sweeping and met her gaze.

'I explained about each of the horses as I fed them. He seemed interested in how I checked them over. He asked why we only had six in at the moment and I explained about Billington and how he'd taken his bunch away last month.'

'What did he say to that?'

'Nothing much I can remember. He kept close to the door of each box and was quiet for much of the time.'

'I can't see Mr Redblood being a replacement for the Billington bunch,' Jill said sadly.

Harry resumed sweeping. 'Something will turn up.'

'And what if it doesn't? We can't run this place on six horses.'

The loss of Daryll Billington's eight horses the month before had impacted their small business in a big way and Harry was still smarting from the fallout he'd had with his most important owner.

Harry had refused to run a couple of Billington's young two-year-olds through fear of breaking them down, as they were quite unfurnished and backward. An argument had ensued, lasting for a few weeks and resulted in the middle-aged scrap metal merchant switching all his horses to another Malton-based trainer. Harry had been sorry to see the horses go, but not the man. Billington was a self-made man, blunt at the best of times and like an anvil the remainder. He liked a gamble and constantly pushed Harry to set up his horses for betting coups, which he'd managed on a couple of occasions, but the physical stress on the horses and mental stress to the trainer had taken their toll. Truth be told, Harry wasn't too disappointed to see Billington's business leave the yard, regardless of the financial issues he and Jill would now have to face.

'I can always play a few extra nights on the piano. I can ask Emma and Pascal.'

Jill considered. It was how she had met Harry; his piano playing. She could see him now, as an eighteen year-old, bent over an old upright piano in the backroom of the Black Bull in Malton. He'd been an apprentice jockey at that time, looking a touch emaciated, but she'd discovered every fibre of his flesh was taut muscle. The pub piano had sat unopened for years, used as a drink shelf, leaning post or even a seat by the youngsters playing pool. Harry had opened the old thing up one Friday evening and started playing and within minutes people were singing along and dancing. Jill had walked in to what was usually a bustling pub, to find eighty percent of the clientele squeezed into what had become a piano karaoke-cum-dancehall. The young black boy was playing Hangover and Street Boogie by Lux Lewis, Jimmy Yancy numbers and adding in a smattering of current pop songs, given a jazz-blues makeover.

Laya had recognised and then nurtured her son's musical talent from a young age, firstly with opportunities to sing at school and then local town choirs and bands. At the age of six she had found him perched on a piano stool in the town hall, aping the chords he'd seen the resident pianist, Nigel Wears, playing a few minutes before. It had been amateur production of The King and I, and Harry had amazed the cast by making it through the first half dozen bars of 'Getting to Know You' with only a little prompting from Mr Wears. He had offered to give the boy lessons on the spot and a year later at the age of seven played him 'Chicago Breakdown' by Big Maceo after which Harry became obsessed with boogie woogie piano.

Jill hadn't been the only girl that night to take note of the good-looking, always smiling piano player, the fact that he was a jockey only added to the fascination. The Black Bull was the favoured meeting place

20

for the younger stable staff around Malton in those days and Harry had suddenly been swamped with all manner of offers from women who became entranced with his skill as a musician and his quiet nature.

Theirs hadn't been a love at first sight. Instead it was a relationship where both of them were tentative and when they finally did get serious, it had endured. They were loosely part of the same group of friends, but given the lifestyle of stable staff and jockeys, there were many transient friendships as young, free singles moved stables and around the country. It took a year from their first meeting in the Black Bull for Harry to ask the blonde-haired, almond faced racing secretary out on anything resembling a date. Even then, the first half dozen times they were together it would be as a foursome or six-some with other couples; usually along with Harry's best friend, Rory Lewis.

As a teenager Jill had loved a good time, as her work as a racing secretary for one of the bigger yards in Malton kept her chained to a desk most days. She lived at home with her rather one-dimensional parents, so any sort of excitement created by the vibrant young stable staff, jockeys, and trainers in the town was a welcome distraction. She had originally been drawn to Rory, and he had welcomed the interest, the two of them dating for a few months, but Jill had soon found Harry's quiet, cock-eyed way of looking at the world starting to fascinate her.

Rory had played a big part in them getting together. He had realised Jill's interest in him was waning and ended their relationship himself, with their friendship still very much intact. Rory was also the perfect foil for Harry's quiet, affable nature. He had manufactured their first half-date, seeing the suitability of the match a long time before the two of them. Rory had been an apprentice jockey too, and was a socially uninhibited live wire who managed to pull Harry into all sorts of scrapes. Somehow, the two of them managed to extricate themselves before any serious harm came their way. There was a strong bond of trust between the two of them and it had continued right into their thirties. Whilst Harry's battle with his weight meant he gave up race riding once he rode out his apprentice claim at nineteen, Rory managed to retain a steady eight stone five, had an excellent racing brain and was able to rise up the ranks to become stable jockey for one of the biggest yards in the town.

Jill once asked Harry what it was about his relationship with Rory that made is special. Harry thought hard before coming up with an answer he felt did justice to the subject matter.

'If I really needed help, Rory would come running,' Harry had told her with a serious face. 'No second thoughts, no excuses. He would come.'

She'd asked if he would do the same for Rory and Harry had immediately replied, 'Of course, absolutely,' then she'd asked why.

'He has no family,' Harry had explained. 'We had a lot in common when we were young.' That was it. He'd left the explanation ambiguous for many more months and slowly Jill came to understand that the bond Harry and Rory had begun building as eight year olds was unshakeable.

Jill and Harry walked into the smaller bottom yard which was now devoid of any equine residents. As if to underline the lack of horses, weak shards of sunlight were starting to cut through the mist, giving the seven empty boxes a sense of abandonment and even a ghostly presence. Millie's claws made a tinny clicking noise as she followed them in, accentuating the lack of life around them.

'We need to bring a couple of the horses down from the upper yard,' Jill said with a shudder, 'I hate the bottom yard looking empty when I walk out of the kitchen door.'

Harry nodded but said nothing. The fact was, they needed horses in every one of the twenty-five boxes they had sitting empty. Even though it was Jill who sorted all the finances and kept the books straight, Harry knew what feed, rent and rates cost and the billing for six horses wouldn't cover their costs, never mind pay them a salary. Something would surely turn up, Harry told himself. It always had up until now.

They entered the back door and Jill bustled around the kitchen, flicking the kettle on and getting a breakfast of toast and jams organised, while Harry started tapping on the *Racing Post* app on his phone. Millie circled his feet in anticipation of a scratch behind her ear or even a dropped speck of toast.

Harry had one of his two remaining two-year-olds running in a seller that afternoon at Beverley and noted with a grin that 'Tuppence' was quoted at a double-figure starting price. He occasionally had a few pounds on his own horses but he wasn't a gambler; he really couldn't bear losing. It was the same when one of his horses didn't run to his own expectations. No-one had to shout or scream at Harry Bolt when their horse didn't perform, he was always his most critical judge and had been known to still be brooding over the reasons for a poor run many weeks later.

While waiting for the toaster to pop up Jill turned and faced Harry. 'The money from your playing would help in the short term I guess, but it's not really the answer. What we need is to fill the yard with another fifteen horses, each with owners that pay their way.'

Harry looked up from his newspaper and managed an 'Mmm...'

'Oh, and Billington still owes us for a month and a half of keep for his seven horses. We need the money,' she added, biting her lip.

Harry shot a desperate look at his wife and sighed. 'Any chance you could do the chasing phone call? I don't think he'll be keen to speak with me, and you're so much better...'

Jill rolled her eyes and murmured her agreement. Harry had been unusually blunt with Billington when he'd arrived to take his horses. It hadn't helped that their destination had been a trainer with a reputation for breaking young horses down.

'Did he run the Bated Breath filly yesterday?'

'Yep, she finished last at Ripon. Hated the undulations on the track, was green as grass and finished down the field as a result,' Harry replied irritably, adding, 'Mark my words, they'll ruin her. She would have won nice races for him as a three year old, but he has no patience. It's all about the gambling.'

The two of them settled glumly into silence, Harry buried in his phone and Jill staring absently at the toaster. When the slices popped up, Jill took a deep breath.

'Perhaps you should have a talk with a few of the venues you used to play… it might help with a few bills.'

Harry looked up, surprised. Jill had never suggested this before.

'It's just possible we could have some unforeseen expenses,' she said, placing a slice of toast and a coffee in front of him.

'Well, I guess so, but it'll mean I'm out more nights.'

'It's no different to night racing!' Jill scoffed gently.

'Hmm… yes, I suppose so.'

Jill was about to say something else, but she watched Harry sit upright in his chair and lift his head back, his eyes narrowing as he focused out of the kitchen window. Then he got up and moved to the back door.

'What?'

'Police,' Harry said simply.

'At half past seven in the morning? Oh God, I hope my parents are okay!'

A few seconds later there was sharp rap and Harry opened the kitchen door to a tall police constable in full uniform.

'Morning, Sir. Apologies for the early call but…' announced a young looking man, his voice tailing away when he looked down at Harry, a hint of recognition in his eyes.

'You want to come in?' Harry offered.

'No thank you, Sir,' the young man responded, his cheeks visibly reddening as a silence developed. He collected himself and continued 'We're doing house to house calls because there's been an incident at the end of your lane. There's a man we need to identify.'

Jill relaxed a little, her worries regarding her parents quashed.

'We just wanted to know if you had seen this man recently?' continued the officer, holding up a mobile phone with a photo of a man's head and shoulders.

Recognition registered on Harry's face immediately.

'Yes, that's Thomas Redblood. He was here this morning. You might catch him – he was walking back into Malton.'

The officer swallowed with some difficulty and wet his lips with his tongue before attempting to reply.

'I'm sure we won't Sir. He's dead.'

Five

The young constable had been camped out in their kitchen for an hour by the time a more senior officer parked her car in front of the farmhouse. The lanky young lad had proved to be quite talkative until he heard the car draw up and recognised the bulky woman struggling to extricate herself from her small car.

He was currently peering through the kitchen window, his eyes bulging. He downed the remains of a cup of tea in one gulp and wiped his mouth with the back of his hand.

'DI Mary Gwent,' he stated mournfully to the kitchen.

'She's your boss?' Jill asked quietly, standing on tiptoes trying to get a closer look at the woman.

'My boss's boss,' he replied, getting ready to greet Ms Gwent by straightening his clothes and wiping a hand through his hair.

It turned out that the constable was called Anton Preston. He was only twenty-one and he'd pointed out at length that Mr Redblood was his first dead body. He'd been called out after a trio of work riders had noticed a man sitting cross-legged, head down on the grass verge where the lane to the four training yards met the main road. Redblood had keeled over when they'd tried to shake him awake.

Anton had recognised Harry when the door opened. Not from his racing connections but from having seen him play piano at one of the pubs in the town. He was a fan of blues music, so the last forty-five minutes had been spent chatting with Harry about his music, the dead man at the end of their drive being largely ignored. However, they did manage to press the boy into revealing that in his opinion Redblood had died of natural causes, probably a heart attack. He'd left an ambulance crew and another couple of constables beside the main road, having been nominated to do the house calls on the four yards branching off the lane.

'You may be the last people who saw Mr Redblood alive,' Anton had explained 'So I need to stay with you until a DS or DI arrives.' Apparently, it was the latter of the two options that was about to land on their doorstep.

The constable opened the kitchen door to a heavy set, pasty-faced woman in her mid fifties, who looked as if she'd thrown her clothes on blindfold that morning. Jill shook the Inspector's hand and looked closer at her face, in no doubt the woman hadn't found time to put any make-up on this morning or comb her collar length, straggly hair.

'Okay Preston, you can finish the house calls and then get back to the road,' Gwent growled in a deep Hull accent.

'Contact me if you find anyone else who saw or met him.'

Anton looked relieved in return, accepted his instruction with a sharp nod and quickly disappeared.

Once he was gone the woman's demeanor altered markedly, becoming far less officious. After admitting she was gasping for a cup of coffee, she peeled off a light grey, calf length raincoat and planted herself on a kitchen chair in a flurry of skirt, handbag, and hair. Jill caught Harry grinning and shot him a warning look.

After a few minutes of preamble consisting of Gwent getting herself settled, digging various tools of her trade from a voluminous handbag and slurping the first few gulps of coffee, she fixed Harry with an appraising eye and asked the first of her questions.

'So, Mr Redblood was here this morning.'

Neither Jill nor Harry replied, assuming this was a statement of fact.

'So Mr Redblood was here this morning?' Ms Gwent repeated as she sipped her very milky, sugary coffee, adding the query inflection this time around.

'Yes, he came to talk about placing a horse with us,' replied Harry patiently.

'Ri…ght.' Gwent confirmed, elongating the word as she looked down at her notepad on the table, ballpoint pen twiddling between her teeth. She continued asking questions in this vein before Jill finally cut her short during another Ri…ght.

'I'm sorry to interrupt, but we only met Mr Redblood this morning, and although it's awfully sad he's died, we really didn't know him well. To be honest, I found him a bit creepy. It's just that we have a runner this afternoon and Harry needs to get the horse ready to go to the races. Will this take much longer?'

Gwent, hunching over the table and slightly tensed, stared belligerently at Jill for a few seconds before answering. 'Did the young officer tell you how Mr Redblood died?'

Harry and Jill nodded in unison. 'Heart attack,' Harry confirmed.

'Mmm… ' Gwent murmured. 'Well the reason I'm here is because he died alone and until we do a post mortem we can't assume anything,' she stated flatly.

Gwent's eyes flitted between the two of them. She had hard, sharp eyes. Harry felt them penetrate him, peeling back the layers as she watched their reaction to this development. Jill shivered and moved closer to Harry. Sensing her discomfort, he put his arm around her.

'As you two were probably the last house call he ever made, I'm afraid it means I need to ask a few more questions.'

'That's absolutely fine,' Harry said quickly. 'We're more than happy to help.'

Jill nodded her own agreement, although she couldn't help crossing her arms in what Gwent took to be a sign of mild frustration.

'Ri… ght.' the Inspector answered. 'Only, am I right in thinking your mother was A'laya Bolt?

'Yes, that's right.'

'And her death was suspicious?'

Harry nodded this time, keen to understand where Gwent was going with this line of questioning.

'That's fine. I just wanted to confirm that was the case,' Gwent stated matter-of-factly, making a short note on her pad.

'She died from an insulin overdose didn't she?' asked Gwent, looking up into the two young faces and arching an eyebrow.

'Yes,' answered Jill before Harry could react.

It was ten-fifteen when Gwent finally departed, three cups of coffee and half a pack of chocolate digestives later, promising that she would need to speak with the two of them again. She'd asked about their movements for the next few days and just when Harry thought the inspector was finally leaving she dropped in a parting remark.

'When you have time later today, can both of you nip down to Malton police station and provide a full statement. Basically just regurgitate everything we've just talked about. Ask for Martin, he's good with paperwork.'

Harry murmured his agreement through gritted teeth. He forced a smile as the Inspector scooped up her purse, two notepads, two pens (the first having run out during the discussion), various tissues, and her two mobile phones from the kitchen table. She absentmindedly deposited them into her handbag, appearing to be unfussed with where they landed.

Gwent pulled on her coat with some difficulty, struggling with one arm, and was still trying to straighten it out as she walked out of the front gate, leaving her car parked in the yard.

Jill slumped into a chair and let out an irritable sigh, holding a finger and thumb to her temple.

'That woman has given me a headache.'

Jill refused Harry's offer of a painkiller, instead helping herself to a chocolate biscuit. 'Did you get the feeling she was weighing us up, you know, whether we had anything to do with Redblood's death?'

Harry grimaced, flopping into a chair beside her. 'Yes. For certain. Forget a horse to train, it looks like the only thing Redblood is going to bring us is a load of hassle. I've no idea when we're going to find time to visit the police station, I've got to leave with Tuppence in about half an hour.'

'You best get on with it then,' Jill responded, slapping her husband's thigh playfully. 'Get to it, Tiger, we need the prizemoney!'

Immediately brightening, Harry jumped up and strode to the kitchen door, a checklist of what he needed for the trip to Beverley already running through his mind.

'Worry about the statement after you've won the first race at

Beverley,' she called after him as he closed the kitchen door.

Once Harry had gone, Jill grabbed another biscuit, taking small bites and munching through it thoughtfully. After brushing a few crumbs off her stomach she allowed her hand to stay there.

'Don't worry, we'll tell him when he's not got so much on his mind,' she whispered.

At the bottom of the lane Gwent watched the ambulance crew go about their work. She supposed it wasn't suspicious enough to warrant too much messing around. Waiting until the ambulance crew were finished packing Mr Redblood away, she approached the two paramedics.

'Anything on the body, you know marks or bruises?'

A fresh faced young woman looked horrified that she'd been asked anything, but the older crewman jumped off the back of the ambulance and took Gwent to one side.

'Off the record, there weren't any visible signs of struggle I could see, but he wasn't a well man by the general look of him. I'd guess it was some sort of degenerative disease. Also, he's recently had an injection.'

Gwent raised an enquiring eyebrow. 'What, in his arm?'

'Well that's just it,' the paramedic answered with a shrug. 'It was a puncture just above his collar bone. Not exactly a likely place for testing blood or administering a booster jab.'

'No,' Gwent agreed thoughtfully.

She spotted Preston loitering just beyond the hedge and waved him over. The poor boy looked positively pale. She supposed he was still recovering from his first encounter with a dead body. As the lad approached, she detected nervousness in his eyes.

'Did you find a syringe beside the body?' she asked before he'd had time to say anything.

'No, Ma'am.'

'So you've scoured the area with a fingertip search around the perimeter of where the body was found?' Gwent enquired.

'Er… no, Ma'am. I just sort of, looked around.'

'Guess what you're doing for the next forty minutes constable.'

Six

    Beverley racecourse was bathed in sunshine when Harry pulled his ageing two-horse transport into the stables car park. The morning mist and nip in the air had been transformed into a fine autumn day and he and Mike Dunn went through the process of getting Tuppence off the transport and booked into a stable with well-drilled precision.

    Mike was Harry's race-day driver, lead-up, helper, and all round go-to man. He'd originally had a small share in a syndicate horse when Harry first started training; however the Malton based retiree had soon become a firm friend. The sixty-eight year old had offered to help out driving the horsebox on a day when Harry had been short of staff and since then Mike had become an invaluable member of his part-time staff. Mike had a quiet way with the horses and had learned quickly. Harry could trust him with any horse and any owner. Being a retired civil servant in the tax office, Mike's life had been sedentary and one-dimensional, until he'd been presented with a small share in a racehorse by his wife one Christmas. Right from the first moment he walked into the Bolt yard, he had been entranced. He seized the chance to be more deeply involved with Harry's horses, and would regularly tell the trainer that there was no need to pay him, often informing owners, 'This is so much better than playing golf!'

    Shining Brass, known as Tuppence to the stable staff, was only in her racecourse stable for ten minutes before Mike and Harry returned with her saddle and tack for the race. The two year old bay filly was running in the opening selling race and the morning delays had meant everything had become a little rushed. When the filly stepped across the car park and into the pre-parade ring, Harry began to relax a little. Led in by Mike, the filly joined seven other two year olds walking around the ring and Harry positioned himself in the centre of the oval of green grass to measure them all up against his own runner.

    Tuppence was a likeable sort because she would put her head down and try hard. She was moderate but had managed a couple of placed efforts in similar races earlier in the season. Harry had told her owners she was capable of winning a moderate race even before she went to Catterick for her debut, which they had accepted with good grace. She hadn't been expensive, only three-thousand pounds at the Goffs Silver Sale at Doncaster the year before, so he'd always set their expectations at a reasonable level. Despite her lack of top class ability, the lads who owned her admitted to thoroughly enjoying her run of placed efforts and the fact that she was competitive each time meant the filly was great value for her small up-front cost.

    After three turns around the pre-parade ring, Mike led the youngster into the chute beside the track on his way to the parade ring and Harry turned, intending to spot his owners in the small crowd which had built up beyond the white railings. He immediately had to shimmy right to avoid walking straight into his brother.

'For crying out loud, look where you're going will you.'

Andrew Warcup spat the words at Harry, with no attempt to conceal his contempt for the younger man. A small circle of owners standing a few yards away stared over at the two of them for a few seconds, hurrying away once Andrew shot them a cool look.

'Andrew,' Harry said levelly, regaining his composure and standing arms crossed and legs planted. 'I'm sorry, I didn't see you looming there,' he added with a touch of sarcasm.

Andrew bowed his head closer. 'Be as clever as you like. You won't be beating ours today. Not with your filly. She looks like two boards strapped together. Can't you afford to feed them?'

Harry looked up into his brother's face and saw a sneer raging there. Andrew had the features of his father; eyes close together, thin nose and ears that stuck out ever so slightly. However the resemblance stopped there. At thirty-five his hair was receding at an alarming rate. A dome of forehead sat above his non-existent eyebrows and only wisps of hair were left on his crown. He wore a tired looking woollen suit with a cream shirt underneath; no tie and a beaten-up set of riding boots finished off his working trainer look. In comparison, Harry's dark suit with yellow tie looked sharp. The two brothers' attire seemed in keeping with their relationship; completely at odds with each other.

Harry hissed, 'Yes, I'm more than capable of affording feed. I'm using the thirty-thousand pounds our father left to me to pay for it.'

As soon as these words left his mouth, Harry was agonising over their delivery. However, he remained steadfast; gazing into Andrew's face and watched anger contort his brother's features.

'Watch your step you little shit,' Andrew spluttered. 'You burrowed your way into the affections of my mother and father, but you're nothing to me. I'll never forget what you did and I'll make sure you don't either.'

Before Harry could reply Andrew gave him a serious, frosty stare while balling his fists at his side. His stance suddenly reminded Harry of when Andrew had been a bowler for the local Malton cricket team. He'd spent many Sunday afternoons watching his older brother play at the local ground, in younger, happier times.

Andrew scowled and took a step forward, smacking one fist into an open palm in front of Harry's face. However this stab at intimidation didn't elicit the flinch he was after. Well versed in his brother's childish scare tactics, Harry remained stoic and regarded him sardonically. Then he watched as Andrew spun round and stalked off up the chute after the runners.

Harry rocked back once Andrew was out of sight and composed

himself. He wasn't proud of himself for fanning the flames of the spat and bitterly regretted the comment about the money. It didn't reflect well on either of them. He could have handled the whole conversation better. Thank goodness Jill wasn't here to witness his performance; he thought, she'd have died inside. The childlike taunts and counter attacks were almost ingrained now. The two of them had been having the same arguments for the last three years and Harry hated it, yet it was hard to break the cycle. Harry hugged himself whilst inspecting the pre-parade ring's pristine green grass, wondering whether either of them would be able to calm down long enough to make their relationship workable. He doubted it.

The world had been much simpler at the age of eight. Willie and Annie Warcup had taken him into their home after his mother died, Laya being close to Annie, and young Harry having been a real favourite of Willie's. In their late fifties they had already been acting as a surrogate Aunt and Uncle to Harry and at the age of eight it seemed natural to go and live with them, now his mother wasn't around.

The Warcup's had eventually adopted him and for the next twelve years he had shared their lives; their triumphs, failures, good times and bad. Andrew had been sixteen when the eight-year-old Harry moved into the big farmhouse with them and he had treated his new younger brother as a Warcup right from the start. Harry had managed to push the pain of losing his mother deep within himself and got on with growing up, counting himself lucky that he'd been taken in by such a loving family. That was until the day at Carlisle races.

'Harry!'

Harry snapped back to the moment, pushing the pain of that day to the back of his mind. He looked over to the pre-parade rail and saw one of Tuppence's owners beckoning to him. He jogged down the chute and jumped over the rail to join Peter McGuiness, the manager of the small syndicate.

'Hello Peter, sorry about that, I just zoned out for a while,' he explained, as the stout Irishman with watery blue eyes pumped his hand up and down in greeting.

'Ah, there's no need to be sorry Harry. I saw your brother there. It can't be easy.'

'Oh, you did?' said Harry, his smile evaporating.

'Never mind that,' dismissed Peter, moving the conversation on and placing a hand on Harry's back to guide him into a walk toward the parade ring. 'I've some excited owners waiting for you over there.'

Andrew was standing with his own connections when Harry walked into the immaculate parade ring, studiously ignoring his brother. Andrew trained the favourite for the race, a gelding called Sky Larks. Peter accompanied Harry over to a small circle of owners he'd got to know quite well from their attendance at previous runs that season.

After a round of hand shaking he told the group, 'The filly could go close.'

Prompted by Peter, Harry expanded 'She's been working better than ever at home and I think this is weaker than the last race where she finished third. We've a decent apprentice on board giving us a weight advantage and, most importantly, she's got the stall one draw with the favourite beside her. That's really important here over five furlongs. It may become a contest between the two of us.'

Seamus Thorin, a Malton based apprentice jockey strode over to Harry and raised his whip handle to his forehead. Peter and his six owners enjoyed a few minutes of race tactics talk with him before the 'Jockey's please mount' announcement was made over the public address system.

Harry rated Seamus. He was an intelligent seventeen-year-old who had a bright future if he could maintain his weight in the next couple of years. Harry gave him a leg up onto the filly, which started jig jogging a little until Seamus found his stirrups. Harry joined Mike to walk the young filly the final circuit around the parade ring, giving last minute instructions to his young jockey.

'We've only got Andrew's gelding to beat so make sure you get her out of the stalls sharpish and grab the rail. If you end up leading, just ease back after a furlong and let the gelding give you a lead on the outside. He'll end up doing the work for you.'

Seamus nodded his understanding down to Harry. 'Is this one important to you Harry?' he asked as they closed in on the exit to the parade ring.

'They all are at the moment!' Harry called after him as Mike let the filly loose on the course. She bounded off down the Beverley hill, clearly pleased to be allowed to break into a canter after fifteen minutes of walking in circles.

The Tuppence syndicate were golfing buddies from the local course at Malton. Harry joined them in the small area reserved for owners, while Mike stayed close to the racecourse gate in order to be ready to collect the filly after the race.

Harry's heart thumped in his chest when he noticed Andrew, together with Sky Larks owner, climbing the large steps that led up to the private owner's area of the stand. The race was almost ready to be off, nevertheless he cast his eyes down the track and tried to put the situation with Andrew out of his mind. Thankfully, a few moments later the race-day commentator called the race under starters orders.

Seamus anticipated the stalls opening, and halfway through the starter's call of 'Jockeys!' he squeezed his heels into the filly's belly and she tensed. As soon as there was a crack in the starting gate Shining Brass kicked forward and got a flyer out of her stall one position and onto the inside running rail.

Pushing the filly for the first four strides, she was quickly prominent, and Seamus was able to put his hands onto the bottom of the filly's neck and allow her to bowl along at the front of the field. Up on her left flank, the favourite, Sky Larks, had also jumped well and Seamus could hear the snorts coming from the gelding's nose in regular bursts. He was dimly aware of another couple of horses further out in the middle of the track, but they were a length or more down on his filly.

Tuppence was travelling well and loving the ground, which had just enough cut to allow her to get her toe in. The four furlong pole came up after only thirteen seconds, but with the filly going so well, Seamus allowed her to simply bowl along for another five or six strides. As per Harry's instructions, he gave the faintest tug on his reins, albeit over three furlongs out instead of four, and the filly slid back, changed her legs to his command and Sky Larks immediately took a lead of a neck on her outside.

With two furlongs to run both leaders came under pressure and their riders started to become active in their saddles. Sky Larks jockey was the first to give his gelding a flick of his whip, but Seamus continued to ride vigorously with hands and heels only. Sky Larks went half a length up.

In the stands there was a huge roar as the favourite struck for home at the furlong pole. Harry wasn't shouting though, he was waiting. Seamus hadn't asked the filly yet, but now was the time…

Seamus saw the one pole zip past to his right, drew his whip through to his left hand and crouched lower in his saddle. He shouted 'Come on girl,' in the filly's ear, simultaneously giving her a flick of his whip and within two strides he was level with his only competitor, the rest of the field flailing three lengths in rear. Sky Larks responded for a stride and then started to wander off a true line, away into the centre of the track, as his jockey resorted to giving him a couple of back-handers.

As soon as Tuppence picked up under Seamus's drive and they drew level with Sky Larks, Harry already knew the result and started to make his way down the stands steps. By the time he reached the bottom and started to jog over to the winners enclosure, Shining Brass had gone on to win by a length and a half with Andrew Warcup's gelding in second and the rest of the field fighting for the minor honours some way behind.

On his way to meet the horse Darren Hawker, another Yorkshire based trainer caught up with him, asking 'You want to sell her in the auction, Harry?'

'No, she's a keeper hopefully.'

'No problem, I'll leave her alone,' Darren responded and melted into the crowd behind Harry.

Seamus came back in with a big smile on his face and the filly received a decent round of applause, when Mike, also smiling maniacally, led her into the centre of the winners enclosure reserved for the winner. She'd won at odds of eight-to-one, the third favourite, beating Andrew's even money shot. Peter and his entourage of beaming owners quickly surrounded Tuppence, huddling around Seamus and Harry, excitement written across their faces.

In a moment of clarity amid the celebration Harry caught Andrew's gaze in the runner's up spot a few yards away. Andrew was trembling with what Harry could only assume was rage. He radiated hatred. His face and forehead were beetroot red and he glowered at Harry and his owners. Their eyes locked for a moment and Harry knew he was in trouble when Andrew cracked a smile. It was the sort of smile Harry knew only too well.

Twenty minutes later in the winning owners' celebratory room the members of Tuppence's syndicate sat in stony silence watching the replay of the race. All the excitement was gone, replaced with a hollow feeling of loss. Once the filly had crossed the line and the commentary halted abruptly, silence descended.

'We don't blame you,' Peter said for the third time in as many minutes. 'But we couldn't go any higher; it was becoming... well, crazy.' Harry cradled a small glass of champagne in his fingers, but didn't feel much like drinking alcohol.

'I know,' he replied. 'I'm only sorry that my family feud has meant you've lost your horse.'

The owners had formed a semi-circle around their trainer and on the whole were taking the loss of their filly in the post-race auction very well. Peter, doing his best to placate the syndicate was keeping the atmosphere as light as possible.

'To be fair, we've lost her for twelve thousand pounds, which is more than she was worth,' he pointed out. 'And I'm sure these guys will want to replace her with another for next season.'

There were various nods and murmurs of approval from the group.

Harry managed a weak smile and thanked them all again but he knew this was a hollow promise if he had correctly anticipated Andrew's next move. Almost to order, Peter's phone buzzed in his pocket and momentary look of astonishment flashed across the syndicate manager's face.

'Er... apologies, I need to take this,' he said, accepting the call and heading to the door.

'Say hello to Andrew from me,' Harry called after him.

Peter turned, plainly shocked that Harry had known who the caller was. He shrugged, an uncertain smile playing on his face and went to leave the room.

'Don't buy her back for more than eight-thousand. And limit him to thirty-five pounds a day training if you have to keep her with him for the next twelve months,' Harry shouted disconcertedly to Peter's receding back.

The other six members of the syndicate looked at each other uncertainly as Harry got up and deposited his untouched champagne on the small, thin bar. He smiled at them and methodically shook each of their hands. The last of them, a lively man in his early seventies screwed his face up and shook his head. 'What's going on Harry?'

Harry had started to walk to the door but stopped to explain, it was the least he could do.

'Andrew Warcup has just bought your horse for twelve-thousand pounds. It was a selling race, and he had the right to do so. However, he is now offering Peter your horse back. I would imagine he will want ten thousand for her, at least that's where he will start. However, to take your profit on the deal you will have to agree to keep her in training with him. If Peter is a sensible syndicate manager, and I'm pretty certain he is, he will negotiate and take the deal, because it's a way to get your filly back and pay for her training expenses for the next four months.'

Harry nodded sadly to his ex-owners. 'I wish you the very best of luck with her,' and exited before they could respond.

He found a forlorn looking Mike waiting outside, leaning up against one of the white posts that ringed the weighing room. He jumped to attention and dropped into stride with Harry.

'That man is unbelievable,' Mike growled angrily under his breath. 'You know he's talking with your owner now!'

'It was a selling race,' Harry re-iterated. 'Andrew had every right to bid for her. He was willing to pay more than my owners could afford and so she went.'

'What he did had nothing to do with the filly, or good sense,' Mike said quietly.

Harry quickened his pace and crossed the pre-parade ring. He waited until they were outside the racecourse and walking towards the stabling area before he answered. As he did, the commentator announced the start of the second race.

'I know Mike. But it's of my own making… sort of. I shouldn't have wound him up before the race.'

Mike's eyes narrowed and he tilted his head. 'You really think that's all it was?'

Harry shrugged his shoulders and kept walking. This day was just getting better and better. Now he had lost another horse and a decent set of owners. He was down to five horses in the yard, the income from which wouldn't even cover his monthly lease on the stables.

The journey back to Malton in the empty horsebox was a strained affair. Harry brightened a little and entered his standard 'Everything will work out' mode of being, while Mike desperately tried to prick the trainer's bubble with the stark realities of his situation. Every time the box went around a corner, the lack of weight in the back of the transport reminded them both that they'd lost a moderate, but nice filly who tried really hard.

The conversation dwindled in the last few miles and Harry jumped when his phone buzzed in his suit pocket. It was Jill.

He answered immediately in an upbeat voice, 'Now then!'

'Where are you?' she asked.

Harry detected worry in his wife's tone and he instantly felt a wave of concern crash over him.

'We're only five minutes away. Why, what's wrong?'

There was a pause on the line which seemed to Harry to go on longer than in any conversation he'd ever had with his wife. He actually heard her swallow before she answered.

'Inspector Gwent has been in touch,' she managed eventually. 'We have to go down to Malton police station straight away. Anton... er, constable Preston is here to take us.'

'O...kay.' Harry answered slowly, 'Why this sudden rush?'

Again Jill paused, pouring further fuel on the fire of concern already raging in Harry's head.

'Harry. I don't want you to worry...'

'Please, Jill,' Harry implored. '*What is the matter?*'

'It's Mr Redblood. The police now know how he died. It wasn't a heart attack; well it was, just not by normal causes. He was injected with a massive dose of insulin... just above his collar bone.'

Harry Bolt froze, dropping his phone. It clattered into the cab's foot-well and lay in the debris of mud, straw and discarded sweet wrappers at his feet. The phone lay face up, illuminating the underside of the dashboard in a greenish glow. Jill's far-off tinny voice could still be heard, desperately calling his name.

Harry didn't hear her. He was eight-years old again, stood at the front door of their flat, watching his mother die in front of him.

Seven

Inspector Gwent rubbed her eyes again and collected the pages of Harry's statement together. She tapped them straight on the table in front of Harry and yawned expressively.

Harry watched in fascination as the Inspector's mouth opened wide enough to deliver him a view of two groups of fillings at the back of the woman's mouth. She made no effort to cover her yawn, and when a dollop of saliva dripped off her bottom lip and splashed onto the table she dutifully mopped it up with the palm of her hand displaying no sign of embarrassment.

'Ri…ght. That's enough for now, Mr Bolt. Sign here and we'll call it a day.

'Where's…'

'Your wife is waiting for you,' interrupted Gwent, impatiently tapping the location she wanted Harry's signature to land.

'And that will be it?'

The Inspector stared hard at the trainer who was still sitting behind the desk. She'd been working for fourteen hours straight now and all she wanted was to get out of this pokey room and get into a hot bath. How could this racehorse trainer who claimed he had met Mr Redblood at five-thirty this morning *still* be so lively?

'That will be it. Until I need to *question you again*!' she replied; only barely disguising her irritation.

Harry read the situation, smiled sweetly, and signed.

Gwent watched from her second-floor office as Harry and his wife shared a hug and a quick conversation before disappearing down the station steps. Neither of them struck her as the sorts to be inflicting any damage to an old man. But the similarities with Bolt's mother's death were striking. Both of them had reacted with what appeared to be genuine shock when confronted with the details of how Redblood had died by the same means as Bolt's mother. Harry had been quiet after he had learned this, his wife just concerned for her husband. Gwent thought there was more to Harry Bolt than met the eye, but a pre-meditative killer? She shook the thought from her head.

She had a suspicious death on her hands. Gwent was waiting for the Laya Bolt file to be retrieved from the archive but everything looked like a carbon copy. The injection was in the same place, it happened in the same town and there was the Bolt family link. But looking on the bright side, it was certainly more interesting than chasing arrogant young drug dealers around the streets of Hull.

She glanced at her notes, allowing the facts to coalesce. Without being aware she started to click her tongue against the roof of her mouth. Gwent had a nose for the irregular. She toyed with various possibilities before becoming befuddled due to tiredness. The Redblood file was tossed back onto her desk into the 'Pending' tray.

****

By the time Harry and Jill arrived back at Pickering Farm a crescent moon was high in the night sky. Jill had started yawning from the moment she settled in the passenger seat and Harry's eyes were heavy too. They were both usually in bed and in a deep sleep by now.

They sat in the stationary box and didn't move. Jill broke the silence. 'I know it's weird and worrying, but it could just be coincidence, you known, the insulin thing.'

'I don't think so. How many people die from a massive dose of insulin being injected into them? It can't be many, and for two to happen and be linked to me…'

'Even so, we *have* to leave it to Gwent,' Jill insisted. She took his hand and squeezed it. 'Please don't worry.'

Harry squeezed his wife's hand back and gave her a tired smile. 'I'll try.'

Mike must have heard the box drawing into the yard as he was coming out to meet them. He too looked tired, but as he approached the driver's door there was agitation present in his face as well. He indicated a parked car further up the yard.

'He's been waiting in his car since I got back. That was seven hours ago. He wouldn't shift. Been waiting for your signature,' Mike explained, shielding his speech behind his hand.

Harry stepped gingerly out of the cab of the horsebox and signalled wearily toward the car. The man pushed his door open, approached and asked if he was Harry Bolt. When Harry answered in the affirmative, the man produced his mobile phone and switched on its flashlight, which he proceeded to point in Harry face and then down to the papers in his hands. Harry realised the delivery driver was comparing him to a photo.

'Look, I'm Harry Bolt for heaven's sake! It's late, we have work to do and there's a bed in that farmhouse we should have jumped into three hours ago.'

'That's fine, Mr Bolt. Sign here,' said the man, seemingly happy with the comparison of likenesses.

Harry signed his name on official looking paperwork for the second time in the space of fifteen minutes and a small jiffy bag envelope was handed to him. The courier strode away and left immediately.

'He disappeared sharpish,' commented Mike conversationally as the courier's car disappeared down the lane. 'Seven hours and he's hardly said ten words to me. He's just sat there playing on his phone.'

'Can't imagine why it was important for him to wait for a

signature,' Harry replied, inspecting the envelope. 'Horses okay, Mike?'

'Yes Guv' all's well. But if it's okay I have to get off now. My missus has been calling every fifteen minutes, wondering when I'm due home.'

Harry stuffed the envelope into his suit pocket and thanked Mike for doing the afternoon and evening feed, upon which the retiree responded with, 'No problem! Enjoyed it!'

As Mike aimed his sensible family car down the lane, Harry walked up the yard to check on his five remaining horses. He returned to the farmhouse a few minutes later, walking in on Jill who was already sat down at the kitchen table holding a mug of hot chocolate in both hands. Another steaming mug sat waiting for Harry.

He removed his suit jacket and with an animated groan sat down heavily. He picked the mug up with two hands, enjoying the heat it transferred into him before taking a deep draft of the sweet milk. He allowed the liquid to penetrate his chest and then his stomach before speaking.

'That tastes good,' he admitted, speaking slowly and expressively while smiling over at Jill.

'You're welcome,'

She returned a similar, tired smile, and the two of them sat quietly, enjoying the silence of the farmhouse. Even Millie was caught in the moment, deciding to flop onto her side with a tiny sigh, resigned to a long wait.

Two minutes passed before Jill finally decided to jolt her husband into action.

'So are you going to open it?' she asked, allowing her impatience to creep into her voice.

Harry shot her a questioning look and she nodded at his jacket.

'Oh, right,' Then after a pause he added 'Or should I say Ri…ght!'

Jill giggled, waving a limp hand. 'Just open the darned thing.'

Harry pulled the small package from his jacket pocket and tore the seal. A packet of Marlboro cigarettes fell out. Harry popped the lid, frowned, and shook the contents out onto the table. A few cigarettes dropped from the box. Then a small key bounced out and skittered across the tabletop, coming to rest beside a copy of *Owner and Breeder*. A folded credit card sized piece of paper also fluttered to the table.

Jill picked up the paper while Harry shook the Marlboro carton some more and then checked inside. 'Nothing else, except some more cigarettes,' he reported.

She read the piece of paper, screwed her face up and then turned it around so Harry could read it too. The words 'Yorkshire County Bank, Malton' were written in capitals. Underneath a nine digit number was printed in large letters and underneath the words 'Please quote to cashier.'

Harry took the piece of paper and turned it over in his hands 'This is all too weird. I really can't take it in, what with everything else that's happened today. Redblood dying like that, the same way that my mother...'

'Let's go to bed,' Jill interrupted. 'Come on Tiger, we're too tired for all this. Lock up and meet me up there.'

Harry nodded and did as he was told.

Eight

Harry turned the keys in the horsebox ignition and the rumbling transport fell into silence. He and Jill looked over the high street towards the Yorkshire County Bank.

'Should we be doing this?' Jill whispered.

Harry shrugged and continued to stare at the imposing building with large, double oak doors.

'Gwent told us to report if anything out of the ordinary happened. Should we tell her before we... well, before we try to use a key that turned up in the post?'

'What? This was your idea!' retorted Harry.

'Yes, but I'm allowed to change my mind, or at least question what we're doing!'

'So we should just go home and sit looking at a mystery key – from a bank?'

Jill squirmed in the passenger seat. 'No... but it's not *our key* is it.'

'Look!' Harry said, pointing across the road. 'The bank's just opened. Come on, let's find out if it's our key or not.'

It turned out that it was their key, or at least Harry's key. After a little confusion at the young teller's window, an elderly man was summoned from the back office and he took one look at the piece of paper and the key, asked for proof of identity from Harry and suddenly doors were opened.

The Bolt's were ushered through a security door and down a corridor and finally to an oak door. Once unlocked, the aged bank clerk asked them to enter and make themselves comfortable, as a Mr Smith would be along to deal with them. The room could have featured in a period drama, boasting a high ceiling with an ornate rose at its centre, oak panelling around the walls to head height and high-backed, leather clad furniture. A large stone fireplace with a semi-circular beveled mirror hung over the mantle. The room had a faintly musty quality and the two of them selected a pair of identical armchairs which exhibited the least amount of dust. Harry breathed in the stale air and got the distinct impression the room hadn't been opened for some time.

About twenty minutes later, a small, neat man who looked to be in his fifties, entered the room and quietly clicked the door shut behind him. His receding silvery hairline was marked by two rows of deep worry lines up his forehead, but the skin itself had a bright, newly washed sheen to it. He wore a polo shirt and a pair of dark blue slacks and Jill wouldn't have been surprised to hear he had just walked off a golf course.

'Hello there, Mr and Mrs Bolt, I'm David Smith,' he said brightly. 'I would offer you a coffee or tea, but I imagine you will want to view your security box straight away?'

Harry cast a look of bewilderment at Jill. Ignoring him, she immediately turned to Smith and answered with an air of normality that flummoxed Harry.

'Yes, that would be fine, Mr Smith. Please lead on!'

He nodded and cracked a plastic smile toward the two of them before skipping to the door, waving encouragingly for them to follow.

Smith beetled down a few corridors, turning left and right so many times Jill and Harry were both confused as to where they could be in the building. They followed a few paces behind, looking around at ancient woodchip wallpaper, dado rails filled with thin plates, questionable art and heavy dark wooden doors embossed with gold letters and numbers. A minute into their tour, Smith slowed.

'It would be best if you follow me in single-file now as the basement vault is a bit of a squeeze,' he called over his shoulder.

A few seconds later Smith stopped at a rather narrow wooden door which looked like it had been wedged into the middle of the corridor as an afterthought. He checked the faded gold number painted on its thick layers of paint and produced a large set of blackened keys on a copper ring from his trouser pocket. He tried two before finding the correct key, the bolt finally pounding loudly into the doorframe after a number of unsuccessful attempts. When the oak door was pushed back, a set of sharply descending stone steps were revealed which disappeared into blackness.

'Down we go!' Smith announced with what appeared to be genuine enthusiasm. He reached inside and flicked an old-fashioned Bakelite switch, which stood proud on the whitewashed wall and the entire staircase was lit up by five light bulbs spaced every few yards as the steps descended. Their guide appeared to be thoroughly enjoying himself.

Jill looked down the long, steep, and very narrow flight of steps and could see a small landing and another door about twenty yards below them.

'Claustrophobia and vertigo all in one neat package!' she whispered conspiratorially to Harry whilst watching Mr Smith's bald patch bounce down the steps in front of her. There was no handrail so they each used the walls to steady their progress. As they descended, the smell of damp became increasingly pungent and walls started to become slightly tacky to the touch.

The door at the bottom of the steps was quite different from those in the rest of the building. It was made of steel, and had a small wheel in its centre. Two metallic disks protected the keyholes. They had apparently reached the vault. Smith inserted two keys, yanked the wheel to the right, and then pulled so hard, Harry and Jill both heard him grunt with exertion. The steel door was a good four inches thick and opened outwards, revealing another black space.

Smith stepped into the darkness, feeling for a switch. There was a click and suddenly the small room was momentarily lit up by an ancient and dusty strip light on the ceiling. It flickered, went dim and then slowly intensified, revealing an almost bare steel room of about twenty feet square. Inserted into the back wall was a single line of steel boxes numbered one to ten. The only other items in the vault were two rickety wooden chairs under a small table pushed into a corner.

Jill hugged herself 'This is really weird. I'm not kidding about the claustrophobia; it's like a cell down here.'

'We stopped providing a safety deposit service about twenty years ago,' explained Smith, producing his handkerchief and wiping a thin coating of dust from the vertical line of boxes. 'The gentleman who provided you with your key was a particularly important customer and so the bank allowed him to retain a couple of boxes, at exorbitant cost of course!'

'So you know the person who sent us Harry's key?' Jill asked.

'Oh, yes, of course. I've never actually met him face to face, but he was a very active customer from the mid-nineties right through until recently.'

Smith paused, a faint smile on his face, apparently being transported back in time for a short while.

He continued 'Yes, he was our top customer considering our little branch was just a regional office. I dealt with all his business – a very shrewd man indeed.'

'…And his *name*?' Jill prompted.

'Oh, I do apologise, I just assumed… his name is Thomas Redblood.'

'What!' exclaimed Harry. His voice reverberated around the steel box and up the stairs. Smith blinked at him and looked perplexed. His bright complexion had diminished in the vault and the sheen on it gave him an almost ghostly appearance under the old fluorescent light.

'Yes Mr Bolt. Thomas Redblood requested these specific deposit boxes in this vault from us a year ago. He gave very specific instructions that only you and your spouse could be allowed to enter the vault and open your box, and only when you had the key in your possession.'

Jill found Harry's hand and drew herself closer to him. He recognised her nervousness, so smiled reassuringly, and gave her hand a squeeze. She was right, this *was* weird.

Smith continued, 'Mr Redblood was insistent that we kept his box right here in Malton instead of York. I just assumed you knew…'

'Perhaps we should get on and use the key Mr Smith,' Harry interjected.

'Ah well, then I should leave.'

'Really, couldn't you stay?'

'Oh no, whatever business you have with Mr Redblood is between the two of you,' Smith countered. 'I will wait in the corridor at the top of the stairs until you are finished. Call out if you need any help.'

With that, he nodded to the two of them and disappeared out through the vault door. Jill fought the urge to follow him out in order to make sure they weren't locked in. She was relieved when she heard his feet reach the top of the stairs and the lights remained on. She listened for the creak of a door closing or the sound of a key turning in a lock, but instead there was an eerie silence.

'This place is giving me the willies. I can't make any sense of it,' she told Harry in a low voice. 'What do you think?'

He remained silent, and held up the small silver key. 'I guess it won't make sense until we open the box, and even then...'

'Oh, get on with it then!' she urged. 'The quicker I get out of here the better.'

Harry inserted the small key into the oblong box with a number one etched into its steel surface. It turned easily and the box slid out of the wall. He carried it over to the little table in the corner and carefully set it down.

He and Jill looked at each other, Harry bending both shoulders forward in an expressive shrug of confusion.

'Go on, it's your box,' said Jill.

Harry recognised a twinkle of excitement in her eyes. He, on the other hand, felt no real anticipation. Had the strange events of the last couple of days dampened his predilection for being positive? He lifted a small steel lip on the top of the box and the lid came away, providing them both with an instant view of the entire contents of the box.

'Well that could have been a little more exciting,' Harry remarked sardonically.

Inside the brushed steel interior of the box was a solitary white and red packet of Marlboro cigarettes.

'Obviously a smoker,' Jill observed, disappointment showing in her voice.

'Either that or a practical joker.'

Harry picked up the packet of cigarettes. It had been opened, the cellophane was still intact around the bottom of the box, but had gone from the top. He noted it must be an old pack though, as there were no photos of diseased organs or huge warnings on the packet. So he flipped the lid. Inside were sixteen cigarettes... and a memory stick.

Two minutes later, they emerged from the vault to find Smith standing waiting for them in the corridor. Jill sucked in a deep breath through her nose and was sure the air tasted sweeter. She found she had a sudden craving to see some real sunlight as the corridor was simply a line of oak doors and walls.

Smith nodded at them both 'Mr Redblood instructed me to have audio visual equipment ready for when you came out of the vault. Would you like to use it?'

Harry looked at Jill, wondering whether they should just leave and then investigate whatever was on the memory stick at home. She was looking a little pale, something Smith must have noticed too.

'Perhaps Mrs Bolt would like some refreshment and a seat for a little while?'

'That sounds wonderful,' Jill agreed, meeting her husband's concerned gaze. 'I could really do with a coffee and I suppose we may as well see what this memory stick has on it.'

Harry put an arm around her. 'Is that okay?'

'Certainly!' Smith confirmed, wheeling round far more lithely than a fifty year old had any right to. 'Please follow me and we'll get you all set up.'

Back in the waiting room a television, laptop and a tablet had appeared and were set out in front of four armchairs. On a small table sat a large, steaming cafetiere and coffee making accessories.

Smith indicated a seat for Jill and after a struggle, managed to open one of the ancient sash windows. The stillness in the room was immediately eradicated by the sound of the town outside. Jill sipped her strong coffee and the combination of fresh air and caffeine immediately flooded her cheeks with their usual rosy glow. She watched the light breeze catch the bottom of the net curtains, making them billow then deflate. Lost in her thoughts for a moment, the nets reminded her of the house she grew up in. She really needed to find a moment to tell Harry, but the last few days had been so stressful…

'Shall we try the memory stick?' asked Smith in an enthusiastic tone.

Harry studied Jill's face again and was relieved to see her colour returned. 'Yes, let's get it read, or listened to or… whatever it is Redblood has in store for us next.'

Smith seemed to find Harry's comment amusing, pouting slightly as he took the box of cigarettes from Harry and nimbly crossed the room. Jill idly wondered if Mr Smith had a wife and children. She somehow doubted it.

The bank manager extracted the memory stick from the Marlboro packet and plugged the small device into one of the television's array of connectors. A small group of filenames appeared and after some playing around with a remote control a blue screen appeared followed by the easily recognizable head and torso of Redblood. Harry shuddered at the sight of the man. He was looking tired and was sat in a deep, plush armchair. Harry shuddered again when he realised it was the same armchair he was currently occupying. He checked again. The video had been recorded in this room; one of the pillars of the huge fireplace was clearly showing in the background.

Smith paused the playback. 'Would you like me to leave?'

Again, Harry deferred to Jill and she shook her head.

'No, you may as well stay.'

Smith nodded appreciatively, crossing over to the window to close it and draw the curtains.

'We can't be too careful,' he explained. 'Mr Redblood was always one for security.'

He returned to his armchair behind Jill and Harry, pressing the button on his handset as he settled. Thomas Redblood started to speak.

'Harry!' Redblood exclaimed in greeting from the wide screen. *'I must be dead!'*

He had an incongruous smile plastered across his face. Harry swallowed, a dryness having developed at the back of his throat and he shrank back in his seat at the dead man's obvious pleasure in greeting him from the grave.

'Don't bother being sad, I had my time. However, I've taken a keen interest in you for some time and I have a proposition for you.'

Redblood paused, possibly for effect. Harry ran a hand down his face, rubbing his eyes. Being spoken to directly by a recently deceased man was proving to be a little surreal, especially when the dead man had spent the last hour and a half of his life with you.

'I want you to train a group of horses for me with the goal of winning one race, one very specific race for me. In return, you will be well rewarded.'

The video altered its view for the first time, cutting to a closer, half profile view of Redblood's face, his round glasses becoming prominent. The whole feel of the presentation suddenly changed. It transformed from a jerky home movie to something far more professional.

'I want you to win The Gimcrack Stakes for me!' announced Redblood in a triumphant tone, a huge grin allowing his bright white dentures to show for the first time.

The television picture suddenly cut to several shots of York racecourse and then to horses Harry recognised from the last few years – all of them passing the York winning post. Redblood's voice continued in voiceover as the winners of the Gimcrack Stakes continued to cross the winning line in increasingly quick succession.

'The Gimcrack Stakes. A Group Two contest for two-year-old colts and geldings. It is held during the famous Ebor meeting at York in mid August each year. It's worth about a hundred thousand pounds to the winner. A race which is certainly valuable, but it holds an important extra bonus for the winning owner.'

The shots of winning horses abruptly stopped and the view switched back to Redblood, who had replaced his toothy grin with a far more serious stare. Harry wondered whether Jill saw the same hint of sadness in the man's eye. It was bordering on… desperation. An involuntary shiver started at the top of his spine and travelled into his skull and down to his thighs.

Redblood continued *'The winning owner of the Gimcrack Stakes in August is always invited to speak at the annual Gimcrack Dinner. The dinner is hosted by the York racecourse executive in late November or early December and all the great and good of the racing industry are invited. The speeches at the dinner are widely reported and in recent years some of the speakers have sparked debate lasting for many weeks or months afterwards.'*

Redblood stopped speaking and the shot was cut to a new view where he was staring ahead. In what could only have been a well-rehearsed motion, he theatrically swung around and looked directly into the camera. Such was the intensity of his gaze both Harry and Jill involuntarily sunk lower into their armchairs.

'I wish to make that winning owner's speech!' Redblood announced excitedly.

The close up of Redblood's face covering the entire screen now broke into a rather ugly grin. Jill was relieved when the video cut to another long shot of Redblood, sat unmoving in his armchair. The garish grin had gone. Instead he wore an amused expression, one eyebrow raised. It was as if he expected his audience to be discussing his declaration. After a short pause a timer appeared at the bottom of the screen, counting down from thirty seconds. As it did, Redblood sat in his chair making childlike ticking gestures with his index finger.

'This is crazy. He's bonkers if he thinks I can just go out and buy a Group Two winner just like that…' said Harry to the room.

Jill picked up the thread '…more to the point, why on earth does he want to make a speech at York… and how?'

'I'm sure Mr Redblood will explain,' Smith suggested quietly from his chair behind them.

Jill grumbled something under her breath which neither man could fathom. Harry didn't worry, Jill could never keep anything under her hat for very long, it was one of the things he loved about her. She was always straight up and out with any issues or wrinkles which were tugging at her mind. She didn't play games, and he loved her for that.

The three of them cast their eyes back to the screen and once again became transfixed by the inane figure on the screen. Silence returned as Redblood ticked away the seconds and the countdown reduced to single figures.

'Now then,' continued Redblood, his strange Yorkshire accent suddenly becoming broader. *'I have no doubt you have a large number of questions. I will answer the primary ones straight away.'*

Again there was a cut to a new view of Redblood, this time he was still in the same room stood beside a blackboard, an inch of white chalk in his hand.

'Mr Smith will confirm that I am lucky enough to be a wealthy man. I realise that buying quality bloodstock does not come cheap, which is why you will have two and a half million pounds at your disposal to find me my winner.'

He wrote '£2.5m' onto the blackboard.

'You only have one season to find my Gimcrack racehorse...'

He shuffled over, dragging his left leg as he went, adding the word 'bloodstock' to the board.

'...and of course all of your training costs will be paid, in full at the end of each month. If you manage to pull this off I will pay you a handsome bonus: I will pay you a further two and a half million pounds.'

As if to emphasize this point, he added a '+£2.5m' to the '£2.5m' and underscored it three times, motes of chalk dust being spun from the board from the pressure his fingers applied. Redblood turned back to deliver his next instruction to the camera.

'There are a further two videos and also various pieces of paperwork on this memory stick, which hold all the details of my requirements.'

Jill looked over to Harry and found him, eyes bulging and staring open mouthed at the screen. Behind them Smith attempted to stifle a chuckle which he converted into a cough.

Redblood paused before continuing, as if predicting Smith's reaction.

'So, why am I willing to spend so much of my wealth on what to most would be such a frivolous goal?'

Redblood was now in close-up, his spectacles enlarging his eyes as they burned with what Jill read as fervour.

'Well, here is the reason: Mr Benedict Manton.'

Redblood's manner subtly altered. He stood a little rigid and put his hands behind his back.

'My reasons are very personal. Manton and I have history. Put simply, I have a little score to settle with Benny Manton.'

The scene changed once more and Redblood was back in the armchair, his elbows on the armrests and hands steepled in front of him.

'Mr Manton and I worked together for some time. Sufficed to say, we didn't see eye to eye. Unfortunately, I was unable to challenge him like this when I was alive, so I intend to do so in death.'

Redblood paused before continuing. He sucked in a deep breath and looked away off camera, blowing the air out slowly and finishing with a sigh.

'As you will probably be aware, Manton is an entrepreneur; a self-

made man. However, his consuming passion is horseracing. He is a prodigious racehorse owner and he has won several high profile races.'

Now Redblood formed a grimace, hooking his fingers together.

'He has very recently become desperate to land the Gimcrack Stakes. A win would afford him the platform his fantastically bloated ego desperately desires; a stage upon which to pontificate whilst cementing his position at the top table of the racing fraternity. He will be buying at least half a dozen horses this autumn expressly for the purpose of winning this race next summer.'

Now the camera went to another close up and Redblood's eyes were blazing. 'Imagine if we were able to beat him to it!'

He laughed, not quite maniacally, but pretty close, and again Jill and Harry's eyes locked momentarily in an anxious embrace.

'So, Harry, will you take on the challenge? Will you buy me the racehorses, train them, win the Gimcrack and earn me an invite to speak on that stage at the Gimcrack Dinner – even though I'm dead?'

Nine

The day after the extraordinary meeting at the bank, Jill decided to tell Harry she was four weeks pregnant. She'd chosen to tell him after the horses had been ridden, washed down and the three fillies had been released into the paddock for the afternoon. Then she'd made his lunch and waited until he'd eaten.

She was now starting to feel dizzy. Harry circled around the living room at Pickering Farm, bumping into the magazine rack and coffee table. Hands around her thin waist, Harry spun and wheeled the two of them lightly around the living room. He was dancing so enthusiastically, Jill's hair had fallen over her face like a golden curtain.

'Please stop, Harry. I can't see!'

'No way. This is just brilliant.'

'No really... '

Her change of tone brought Harry's twirling to a gradual stop after which the two of them fell in unison, still holding each other, onto their favourite old sofa; their first purchase as a couple.

Harry covered his wife's face with gentle kisses, eventually stopping to lie nose to nose with her.

Quietly, and trying to contain his excitement, he said 'We're going to have a baby!'

Jill nodded, minutely watching his face. She seemed pensive.

Harry's eyes hardened slightly 'What's up?' he whispered.

She swept her hair from her face but stayed up close, holding him to her. 'I've been waiting for the right moment since last Friday, but with everything that's happened...' Her voice trailed off, however Harry remained quiet.

'I'm so glad you are pleased, and excited, I just hope it's the right time. Everything seems so messed up at the moment. We have to make a decision about Redblood and...'

Harry had slipped his hand between them and put his index finger gently to her lips. Jill looked directly into his eyes and watched the points of light dance as they spiralled around his rich brown irises.

'You realise we'll need that revenue from Redblood now, don't you?' she queried.

'Yes.'

'And you know I'll be useless for about four months at least?'

'I'm used to that,' he answered deadpan.

She bit her lip, raising an eyebrow in comic rebuke. 'Watch it, Tiger.'

Harry touched his nose to hers once again. 'Yes, boss.'

Jill studied him once again, then stiffened and sat upright, leaving Harry lying alone on the sofa.

'You were going to say yes, anyway, *weren't you?*' she said, appearing slightly agitated.

Harry propped himself up on his elbows, pursed his lips and fixed his wife with what he hoped was a conciliatory look.

She frowned for a second, but couldn't hold it. 'You want to buy all those gorgeous horses don't you!' she said, her mock anger being replaced with a wide smile. She started to tickle the side of Harry's stomach. 'Actually, I really don't blame you; the yard deserves a chance with some really nice horses.'

Harry took her hand and held it to his chest, 'I know it's a risk. But given what you've just dropped on me I think it's a risk we have to take. Besides, what's the worst that can happen?'

Their tryst was interrupted by three staccato raps on the back door. Both of them sat up on the sofa and they looked at each other.

'I'll go,' Harry sighed, stalking off to find out who was calling in the middle of the afternoon, the middle of their free time when they weren't racing. However his thoughts were full of the future and by the time he'd swung the door open to the visitor his irritation at being disturbed had vanished.

David Smith stood there, hands in his brown corduroy pockets, looking nervous, and his eyes darting around. He had a backpack slung over his shoulder and removed it once the door was answered.

'Hello, Harry. Could I have a quiet word with you and Jill?' Harry nodded and showed Smith into the kitchen and called Jill through.

'I wanted to bring this paperwork around as soon as I had it printed off the memory stick,' Smith remarked once he'd deposited the sheaf of papers on the kitchen table. 'This is the important one, the contract,' he indicated, pointing to a single page with one paragraph of writing. 'I've looked it over and it's quite straightforward. There are two copies to sign, one for yourself and one for me to lodge in the bank.'

He paused, hope filling his shiny face. 'Have you decided yet?'

Without hesitation Jill responded, 'Yes. We're going to accept the offer thank you very much.'

Harry raised both eyebrows and smiled at her.

'Yes,' he said turning back to Smith. '*We* have decided to go ahead and accept Mr Redblood's kind offer.'

He studied the one page contract for a short while before accepting the offer of a pen from Smith. Jill noticed Smith looked relieved as Harry signed the contract. Perhaps a little *too* relieved?

'You think we're doing the right thing. In your capacity as a representative of the bank, I mean?' Jill queried.

'Oh, yes. Certainly. It's a great opportunity and Mr Redblood, whilst being a little eccentric, has always been honest and straightforward to deal with. But I must explain: I'm actually a retired bank manager now.

I only deal with Mr Redblood's business as a favour to him, as he was such a good customer to me and the bank. I promised him I would see through any instructions he had after his death, should it be required. I was just as surprised as you at the er... *extent* of his plans.

With that, he sat down heavily into a chair, rubbing his hands over his face and then his bald patch.

'I assumed he was just going to leave you some money, but it looks like I will have up to two years more work,' he said with a faraway look. Harry thought the man looked ten years older all of a sudden.

Outside in the yard a car honked its horn twice. Harry could see the driver hanging out of his window, peering towards the farmhouse.

'Forgive me if I seem slightly flustered, I need to catch a train back home from York to London, and I'm running a little late. I have a taxi waiting for me.'

Smith lifted a thumb over his shoulder to indicate the taxi which was parked with the engine running out in the yard.

'Will we still be dealing with you with things concerning the sales, the horses and racing?' Jill asked.

As if he anticipated this query Smith was already gesturing to the second document he had produced from his backpack.

'It's all in there: bank account details, contact numbers and then, of course, Mr Redblood's instructions for horses. Again, there's one or two of his requests which may seem rather strange, but nothing which will affect the way you wish to train his horses.'

Harry picked up the group of stapled papers. It seemed Redblood had something to say on a range of topics, each capitalized in bold and running to three sheets. He read the first, under the heading 'Jockey Silks'.

'Arrange for four sets of colours to be made. My jockeys will always wear them, without any advertising. The body is solid red. The cap is also red with a single white hoop around the centre. They are already registered with Weatherby's...'

The next section was entitled 'Racehorse Naming' and Harry read with increasing bewilderment Redblood's requirements.

'The first eight horses to race will take the following names: Five Four, Nine Two, Nineteen, Twelve Five, Eighteen Twelve, Fifteen Four, Nine Fifteen and One Twenty-Two. Any further horses can be named by H Bolt.'

He briefly flicked through the rest of the list, noting that the instructions entitled 'Horse Sales' was by far the most in-depth section.

'Well it seems to be straightforward enough,' he admitted whilst still scanning the instructions.

'Good. Then I will be off to catch my train,' Smith said, clearly wishing to wrap up the conversation. He got up from his chair. 'I'll be in touch once a week by phone or email to make sure everything is going smoothly, otherwise, it's down to you…' he added, nodding curtly.'

Smith scooped up the signed copy of the contract and grabbed his backpack. 'I'll let myself out,' he said on his way to the door. However, before his hand reached the doorknob he stopped suddenly and spun round.

'There is one more thing… in the contract it states all the horses will race in the names Mr Redblood has chosen and the owner will be listed as 'The Revenge Partnership'. However it also says that you must not reveal to anyone other than family who is behind the name in the racecard until the day of the Gimcrack dinner otherwise the contract is void and the horses will be removed. As I have said before, Mr Redblood was always very concerned with security, so please, don't mention his name or our arrangement to anyone. I wouldn't enjoy taking this opportunity away from the two of you.'

'We understand, Mr Smith,' replied Jill, trying to inject an air of professionalism into her words. Behind her, Harry added his own nodded confirmation. With nothing more than a tight smile, Smith was out the kitchen door and skirting around the farmhouse.

The two of them watched the comic little man scurry across the yard and down to the yard gate where his taxi was waiting.

'We have made the right decision haven't we?' Jill queried uncertainly.

'Of course. Like I said, what's the worst that can happen?

'Well, it does look like Redblood was a bit loopy. Then there's the fact that he died at the end of our street and he knew your Mum. Oh, and the guy we have to deal with when we're spending millions of pounds on bloodstock is another weird little chap, who we've just discovered lives three hundred miles away.'

Harry's smile broadened with every one of Jill's words. He took his wife up in a dancing embrace, only for her to pull away.

'Oh, no, not again,' she warned.

Harry stuck out a bottom lip, but then he visibly brightened and rushed out of the kitchen. Half a minute later the old upright piano in the living room was pounding music through the farmhouse and out into the yard. He started with 'Baby's Coming Back', followed by 'Be My Baby' after which Jill lost track of the baby references Harry was building into his musical tribute to her condition.

She left him to play for twenty minutes as she did the washing and cleaning in the kitchen, smiling to herself as he sang at the top of his voice over a bluesy accompaniment. Stopping work to listen to a lullaby Harry now sang in falsetto, she considered whether to remind him he was playing a gig tonight and shouldn't strain his voice. However, as the lullaby finished and Harry picked up the rhythm of another up-tempo blues number, Jill couldn't stop a genuinely joyous smile from creeping across her face.

Ten

DI Rosemary Gwent finally struggled through the turnstiles at the grandstand entrance to Haydock racetrack and scowled at the member of staff standing waiting to clip her badge on the other side. He aimed a blank stare to some point in the distance behind her, not wishing to make eye contact with the woman.

Giggle and I'll give you something to clip she thought, fixing the aged ticket puncher with a withering look. Her handbag hadn't helped, managing to get wedged between the bars of the turnstile, effectively trapping her midriff and causing a queue to form behind her, but having DC Poole with her had made it worse.

A lanky young man, with closely cropped hair and a constant expression of astonishment on his face, followed her into the racetrack.

'Where to now, Ma'am?' he asked, looking up and down the concourse, assessing the back of the grandstand. He knew better than to mention the issues his boss's bulk had caused a few moments earlier and purposefully didn't catch her eye.

Despite the track being busy for a weekday meeting, strolling around the course was still relatively easy. It was a fine autumn day, but a brisk wind tugged at the flags flying on the top of the stands, and advertising sails dotted along the walkway billowed as the gusts took them. Gwent pulled her voluminous camel raincoat around her and set off.

'Follow me,' she rasped irritably and kicked off at a strong pace, leaving Poole to roll his eyes skyward and then skip to catch up with his superior.

They bore left, around a betting shop and several food outlets and then the course opened up to reveal a large parade ring containing several mature trees, allowing sunlight to dapple the weed free grass. There were a greater number of race-goers milling around here, and Gwent turned her nose up at the vista.

'Nope, not here.'

She dug in her coat pocket and produced a small notepad, flicking through to reference a few words on one page.

'We need to be inside the stands. He's in a suite or box… thing,' she stated uncertainly. 'Find us a way in.'

Poole turned his face into the breeze and the sides of his suit started flapping. He stood still, hands in pockets and looked toward the nearest stand but couldn't locate any sort of entrance.

'Come on Mr Dynamic,' Gwent grumbled. 'We'll walk around to the front.'

A few minutes later they were being whisked to the top of the Centenary Stand. When the lift opened at the premier suite level, they stepped out and were met by a dark, burly young man who was bursting out of his suit.

'I need to see your identification.'

Gwent didn't move a muscle and simply stared up at the swarthy youngster. He stood his ground.

'I beg your pardon?' Gwent replied, spitting the words out.

Unfazed, the man tried again, but after catching the look from Gwent tacked a 'Please?' onto the end of his request this time.

Gwent and Poole both flashed their warrant cards and the big man blinked a few times before instructing them to wait where they were. He turned and headed to the bottom of the corridor, knocked quietly on a door and disappeared inside.

Gwent murmured, 'Come on, Poole,' out of the side of her mouth and trotted down the corridor with the younger officer in her wake. She tried the handle of the suite, which twisted open easily, and strode into a lavishly decorated rectangular room. Several antique looking pieces of furniture were scattered around and the far wall consisted of floor to ceiling glass which looked out over the racecourse finishing post.

She scanned the room. She'd done her homework and checked the records on Manton for his known associates. It appeared she'd struck lucky; his entire team was present. There were four men in the room, the youngster they'd already met, Gavin Loretta, was facing her, looking like he was ready to launch himself at her on command. Interestingly, there was a hard-faced man on a sofa against the left wall who had started to reach a hand down to the top of his boot and nip at something below the leather. Gwent provided him with an expectant gaze and he started nonchalantly brushing his calf as if the eradication of fluff was his immediate reaction once a policeman entered his presence. She calculated this must be Pete Warren.

Beside Warren was another man Gwent recognised from her file on Manton, Charlie Doyle. He was a tall, almost gaunt figure wearing a dark suit which hung off him, and a brash red tie. Doyle was leaning back in a relaxed position, arms across the back of the sofa, his thin facial features drinking in Gwent and Poole. He wore an amused expression and for some reason Gwent suddenly felt slightly vulnerable. In retaliation she gave each man a stare lasting three to four seconds, telegraphing how deeply unimpressed she was with them.

There was an older looking, bearded man sitting in an armchair on the other side of the room looking out over the racecourse. He faced away from them, so Gwent could only see him in profile, his torso being hidden by the high arms of his chair. Still, she recognised him immediately; it was Benedict Manton.

Standing behind Gwent, Poole felt pressure to say something. The silence following their entrance was intense and had been hanging there for far too long. Gwent still said nothing and he unconsciously hid behind his boss's ample frame. He knew enough to keep quiet though, she didn't appreciate anyone who babbled. His heartbeat was banging so loudly he wondered if the people around him could hear it thumping.

'Ah, I assume we must have guests,' the man in the armchair finally stated without looking around.

Gwent cleared her throat. 'Good afternoon, gentlemen. I am DI Gwent, this is DC Poole. Please continue to enjoy the racing. However I do need to speak with Mr Benedict Manton. I believe he is here?'

The taut youngster facing them relaxed and balefully turned his head toward the armchair.

Weakly waving a limp hand in her direction, the man in the armchair answered, 'Guilty, Inspector, please come over and have a seat with me.'

He turned his head to survey Gwent as she moved through the room.

'Oh, and your friend too,' Manton added with a smirk, as if seeing the six foot plus Poole for the first time.

'You are a difficult man to pin down, Mr Manton,' said Gwent, sitting down opposite the heavily bearded Manton on what turned out to be a lumpy, saggy sofa. She squirmed a little when her heavy frame sank into the furniture, giving Poole a nudge with her elbow when he joined her to ensure he didn't sit too close and end up sliding into her.

'Am I?' Manton mumbled with surprise. He picked up a glass with a generous measure of whisky and took a tentative sip.

'We've been trying to speak with you for ten days.'

'Well, I am *very* busy,' replied Manton, replacing his drink and opened his palm in order to swing it to the left and right. 'As you can see.'

On the opposite side of the room, Pete Warren had joined Charlie Doyle in treating the police intrusion with levity, sniggering quietly to his colleague.

Gwent considered the man in the armchair. He was in his late forties, but looked older. She decided it was the perfectly trimmed one-inch beard making him look older. Where the beard didn't reach, his face was pitted. Most likely the remnants of a skin condition in his youth she ventured, which could explain why he wore a full set beard. He was slumped in his armchair, probably a little overweight if the small hillock of a tummy was anything to go by, but otherwise seemed fit and well with a full head of silver-flecked mousey hair, which matched his beard. His cold blue eyes were set just a little too far apart in their sockets to rate him as handsome.

Ri…ght,' Gwent breathed.

'Well, you've caught up with me now Inspector. However, I must warn you that I have a runner in the two-thirty, so I will need to leave in about fifteen minutes to brief my trainer and jockey.'

'*You'll* be briefing them?' Poole queried, rather glibly in Gwent's opinion, but she let it go.

'Of course. I own the horse. I determine where and when my horses' run and how they are ridden.'

Manton responded with an air of courtesy, but it felt like there was a sharp edge to his answer. He took a short breath, aiming to start elaborating but Gwent quickly fired a question at him.

'Do you know a man called Thomas Redblood?'

Manton altered his position in his armchair, languidly crossing his legs and she could sense he was using his movement to create time, judge her and determine where to pitch his answer. She imagined him as a young man; certainly more vibrant, probably ruggedly handsome without the beard. But he would certainly wish to be in control, or at least *appear* to be in control. There was a constant flicker of petulant anger behind his eyes and an element of bravado in his performance which jarred slightly, as if there was something missing, perhaps a skill or ability he didn't possess which was being masked, or compensated for.

During her twenty-two years in the force she'd investigated a number of people with his type of underlying menace. It was almost a criminal cliché; allowing your anger to bubble under a serene exterior, bringing it out for impact when it was required. In her experience some of the men and women with these character traits were honest. Most were not.

Her problem with this case was Redblood himself. She had no one to identify Redblood's body, apart from the young racehorse trainer the deceased had visited only a few minutes before he died, which was far from ideal. Gwent had needed to cast her net further. Upon investigating Redblood's tax returns, she had been pleasantly surprised to discover he had been employed by one of Manton's companies for most of his life. In fact, he had taken early retirement only a fortnight before he died.

Manton had grown up in Malton and was something of a local hero; from a working class background he had risen in the business world and done well for himself. He wasn't quite *Sunday Times* rich list standard, however, a decade ago he had warranted a mention as a possible entrant in the future.

A self-made man and law-abiding for decades, he had racked up a number of charges between the age of sixteen and twenty-one, all drug related apart from one instance of actual bodily harm which ended up never going to court, the recipient of the beating having refused to give evidence at the eleventh hour; not so unusual.

The other part of Manton's police record wasn't a matter of public knowledge. He kept some shady personal company and had been quietly investigated three times over the last twenty years under suspicion of being involved in organised crime. No hard evidence was ever found in any of the investigations, even though a few tentative links existed. It appeared that Mr Manton was adept at being a couple of places removed from any serious wrongdoing.

Thomas Redblood's record was unblemished. He too had grown up in Malton and attended the same school as Manton. He had also worked as an accountant for a small marketing company Manton had bought out in the late eighties; one of his first acquisitions which set him on a path to business riches.

Manton had been a low-level public figure thanks to his commercial success. However, his wider notoriety had come from his television work in the late noughties. He'd been on the original team of four business angels who offered their cash as investments in the popular ITV television show 'Funding Feud'. His performances on the show had received praise and derision in equal measure for the way he rode roughshod over the generally young and wet-behind-the-ears entrepreneurs who asked for his investment. He had lasted just the one series before dropping out. The official reason released to the press had been a need to re-focus on his commercial interests, although there had been a series of sniping columns in the tabloids which had suggested a good proportion of the hopeful entrepreneurs handed his investment cash had found it impossible to work with him due to his tyrannical management style. Gwent noted that the same subtle undercurrent of menace he used to reduce hapless would-be businessmen to tears in the show was also in evidence today.

'Certainly I know of Mr Redblood,' Manton replied smoothly, breaking into a hideously plastic smile.

'Oh really. How?'

'Oh come, come, Inspector, I'm sure you will be aware I was at school with him and I employed him… indirectly of course.'

'So you would recognise him?'

Manton leaned forward to place his whisky glass on the coffee table between them.

He's playing for time again thought Gwent. Christ he's a slippery one. She waited patiently for him to lean back, re-arrange himself on the seat, and look up at the two policemen.

'I can't have seen him for… oh, fifteen years or so I'm afraid. We grew up in the same town and I knew him quite well in my early twenties actually. But again, I think you already know that, *don't you?*'

Gwent felt her hackles start to rise and caught herself before betraying any reaction to her interviewee. Not only was he slippery, he was playing games with her. Poole, once again unbalanced by the silence which had descended on the conversation found himself speaking, rushing in to fill the void.

'So you wouldn't be able to identify his body for us?' At this, Gwent shot a look of contempt at her colleague and he visibly crumpled.

Manton allowed one end of his mouth to curl up in amusement before he answered.

'I'm so *sorry,* Inspector, can I intimate from DC Poole's question that Mr Redblood has died?' Manton's response was delivered with a certain amount of surprise, although Gwent doubted it was genuine. He broke eye contact with them and stared off through the window to the racecourse, his fingers gripping both sides of his armchair.

'That's such a shame,' Manton added quietly, his bushy eyebrows diving toward his nose as he pondered the news.

'So would you be able to… identify him?' Poole repeated.

Manton sucked in a big breath and turned back to them. 'I'm afraid not. I simply wouldn't b e any use to you. I would imagine he's changed hugely over the last twenty or so years.'

'In…deed,' Gwent said, studying the man intently. 'Would it surprise you to know he didn't die of natural causes?'

Manton feigned surprise once more. 'Really?'

'Yes, *really.*'

'I do remember being informed he was suffering from some sort of disease, oh, some time ago now,' Manton said, waving a couple of fingers back and forth in a vague manner.

'No,' Gwent replied firmly. 'He was injected with a fatal dose of insulin.'

Gwent's gaze never left Manton's face. Every micro-movement of his eyes, every twitch of his facial muscles she intercepted and analysed.

'I'm very sorry to hear that,' Manton offered blankly. 'I'm shocked.'

He delivered this statement in a flat tone, but did so whilst continuing to lock eyes with Gwent. The words themselves didn't intimate shock, nevertheless there was a distinctly wintery essence to their delivery. Gwent sensed her time was running out. She'd try again, and perhaps try to cut a bit deeper.

'He was found in Malton, close to a racehorse trainer's yard. The yard belongs to Harry Bolt.'

In the background the hard-faced Charlie Doyle uncrossed his legs and stood, clearing his throat. This prompted Pete Warren to do the same. The youngster Gavin Loretta remained standing at the door where he had been throughout the conversation, but his hand now went to the doorknob.

Manton took up his whisky glass once more and downed the last two fingers in a single gulp. He smiled and in doing so, his beard parted and revealed unnaturally rouge lips, presumably a result of polishing off the remains of his whisky.

'Apologies, Inspector, it is time for me to visit the parade ring for my race. If you have any further questions please feel free to send them into my office and we will answer by letter, or email, whichever you prefer.'

Manton gripped the arms of his chair and gracefully lifted himself to a standing position and Poole started to follow. Gwent remained rooted in her sitting position.

'Would there be any colleagues of Redblood's we could speak with?' she asked, looking up at Manton.

He shook his head. 'Again, I'm going to disappoint you Inspector. He always worked alone, from home I would assume. He was something of a recluse you know, preferred his own company I believe.'

Manton crossed to the door which was being held open by his young beefy colleague, drawing to a halt before exiting.

'But I understand he was a mighty fine accountant,' he called over his shoulder. Then he and his three-man posse were gone.

Gwent, still sat down, looked up at Poole, and sniffed.

'Help me out of this nightmare of a sofa will you?' she asked, awkwardly rocking backwards and proffering her hand to him.

Five minutes later the two of them stood on the top level of a small gantry looking over the parade ring as a dozen racehorses were being led around. Gwent watched Manton in the ring, standing beneath a tree, surrounded by a small group as he held court with grand gestures. His audience consisted of his associates from the premier box, a small man dressed in country clothes who Gwent guessed was the trainer, and a jockey in almost while silks save for a black hoop on his cap.

Poole consulted his racecard. 'Manton's horse is this one here,' he told Gwent, nodding toward a chesnut colt which was jig jogging past them. 'It's called 'Splendid Manton'.'

Gwent sniffed impassively. 'How very self-deprecating of him.'

'Many of his horses have his name in them,' Poole added.

'You're allowed to advertise a business as part of a horse's racing name?'

'Oh, yeah, lots of businesses do it. I guess it helps when writing the cost off as a business expense,' Poole explained.

'You're a racing fan then?' enquired Gwent.

'No not really, just the odd bet. I go to York and Beverley races a couple of times a year. That's all.'

Gwent sensed the lad was being a little defensive. There was no need for it, she didn't gamble herself, but could see that a little punt or a day at the races could be enjoyable. She was a drinks and dance girl herself.

'Still, you know more than me, and I've worked around Malton for the last twenty years,' she pointed out.

They fell into an easy silence as the call for the jockeys to mount came over the public address and one by one the horses were united with their riders and led out onto the racecourse. Gwent watched Manton share a final short conversation with the trainer before he marched purposefully out of the ring, closely accompanied by his minders. The four men crossed the public area of the enclosure and disappeared into the back of the Centennial stand.

The crowd around the ring started to filter away toward the stands and Gwent and Poole allowed themselves to be carried along with the river of people until they peeled off and stood on a grassed area opposite the winning post.

'What's this worth to the winner?' Gwent asked Poole as they waited for the race to start.

Poole dug the racecard out of his trouser pocket and thumbed through to the right page, duly reporting that just short of fifteen thousand pounds would be collected by the winning owner.

'Is that normal for a race?'

'No, this is a Listed race, so the winning prizemoney is higher. The average sort of level for a race these days is about four thousand pounds to the winning owner.'

'And what's it cost to train a racehorse?'

Poole shrugged. 'I'd be guessing, but between twenty-five thousand to forty thousand pounds a year, depending on which trainer you place your horses with and how many times it races.'

Gwent raised an eyebrow, staring past the hundreds of heads in front of her, all of whom were focused on the large screen in the centre of the racetrack. She was only faintly aware of the race having gone off, continuing to consider other matters.

There was something nagging her about Thomas Redblood. He had died alone and it appeared he'd lived life as a loner. No friends, no colleagues, and no family. His rented, compact two-up-two-down terrace in Malton had been clean and basic, lacking virtually any personal touches. There was a small amount of food in the fridge and cupboards, but on the whole the house felt neglected and soulless. It was a house and not a home. Whether or not Manton was telling the truth about how well he knew Redblood, Gwent doubted the man had worked from home. There had been no papers, files or even a writing desk anywhere in the house.

His neighbours had been no help either. She had spoken to families living on both sides of Redblood and came away trying to imagine a life where even the people next door couldn't say for certain you had lived there, let alone identify you.

Yes, all in all, Mr Redblood was proving to be more of a conundrum with every passing day. He'd moved through his life causing so little resistance he'd hardly been noticed. His will hadn't helped either. The conservative amount of money he had in his single current account was left to the Racing Welfare charity in Malton. It seemed that Mr Redblood had saved his one significant impact on the world until the very last moment.

The crowd around Gwent was still concentrating intently on the large screen and only the odd shout went up as the course commentator described the changing shape of the race. Contrary as ever, Gwent chose that moment to turn and look up into the top of the Centennial stand, trying to pick out Manton's box.

She was also pretty certain Manton knew more about Redblood than he was letting on. He had tried a little too hard to know nothing when learning his long-term employee was dead. His reaction had been… interesting. Every fibre of her being was pulling her towards this case even though she was already under pressure from her boss to dump it and get on with other more pressing matters. He thought it was most likely suicide. Did Manton realise that her real reason for the visit today was because he figured in Redblood's life, a life which was strangely blank?

Amid a cacophony of shouts, screams and bellows as the race entered the last two furlongs, Gwent peered up into the top tier of the stand and caught sight of Manton standing impassive as the race reached its climax. She could hear the horses' hooves thumping the turf as they passed behind her. Manton scowled as the commentator's voice stopped calling the race and he disappeared from the balcony into his private box.

'Where did his horse finish?' she demanded of Poole.

The DC fumbled with his racecard, but his input became redundant as the result started to be broadcast over the public address system a few moments later.

'Third,' Poole offered quickly, just before the announcer confirmed the finishing positions.

'Do the owners get a chance to speak with their jockey and trainer afterwards?' Gwent asked.

Poole shot a look of amused disbelief at his boss. Mixed with his default setting of astonishment, it helped prompt a tart response from Gwent.

'Well? Am I somehow embarrassing you, DC Poole?'

'No. Ma'am, not at all,' he blustered, blinking rapidly in an attempt to blank his face of any emotion.

'Show me,' she demanded.

Poole led her back to the parade ring where the first three horses home were now being unsaddled at one end under very large numbered poles. Manton was back in the ring, involved in an animated conversation with his trainer and jockey. Gwent watched with growing amusement as the discussion became increasingly heated, reaching its conclusion when the trainer threw his hands up and stalked off towards the stabling area. The jockey stood in glassy-eyed silence, being chastised by Manton for a further minute before touching his forehead with a semi salute, trotting across the parade ring and up the steps to a building Gwent assumed was the weighing and changing rooms.

There was definitely more to Manton than met the eye but Gwent resisted the urge to accost him for the second time that afternoon. Instead, she and Poole followed him and his three associates out of the racecourse at a distance and watched them leave in a blacked out Range Rover which had been parked in a private bay close to the entrance.

Within the blacked out interior of the car the two men in the front seats bent their heads down slightly and shared an anxious glance as Manton hurled expletives around the car. He was holding a phone conversation which currently consisted of short, yelled sentences. Doyle sat in the back seat with his boss and remained statuesque, his eyes closed.

'I don't care what he's doing, *put Deacon on,*' Manton hissed menacingly.

After a short pause, a new voice came through on the car's hands-free loudspeaker. The man spoke with a faint Birmingham accent, sounding educated and succinct.

'Hello, Sir, yes, I do understand, but what you're suggesting is highly improbable.'

'I don't care what you think. Listen carefully. I've had the police asking bloody stupid questions today and I need to be sure. You will complete a full forensic analysis on our network, Redblood's old workstations, his rooms, and the entire Money Tree. Turn it upside down and inside out.'

'Really Sir, I can assure you Redblood's couldn't have…'

'Make sure,' Manton cut in.

'There's no way…'

'Shut. The hell. Up,' interrupted Manton, forcing the words through gritted teeth, his anger palpably growing. The car returned to silence. Finally a deferential voice rang through the car's sound system.

'No problem, Sir, we'll start the work now.'

'Good,' Manton replied forcefully, only partially placated. 'If Redblood got anything out or accessed anything iffy before he died I want to know about it.'

'And Deacon…' Manton added as if calling a child in from play. 'I want to know *how the hell* he could be dead when your men left him at the hospital and alive enough to die again a week later!' Manton dropped the call with Deacon halfway through another placating apology and turned to Doyle.

'He was supposed to be found dead in Scarborough, what the hell happened? How did he get to Malton a week later to be injected with insulin? You get the relevance of how he died don't you, Charlie?'

Doyle wasn't looking at Manton. With eyes closed he held his hands together and rested both index fingers on his chin, apparently in deep thought.

'We need to find Billy Redblood and tie that loose end up first. Has Morrison made any progress yet?' continued Manton.

Doyle said nothing for a few more seconds but then slowly opened his eyes and turned to Manton.

'You're right. With Redblood dead, his brother needs to be… dealt with...' Doyle stated slowly, carefully pronouncing his words.

'And Laya Bolt's son….?' Doyle added with a questioning arch of an almost invisible eyebrow.

Manton inspected Doyle's expression. He leaned back into the sumptuous leather car seats and considered for some time, before finally replying.

'It seems our past may be trying to catch up with us. You of all people must understand why this can't be allowed to happen… whatever the cost.'

Doyle nodded sagely and cast his gaze out of the car window, catching his reflection in the glass rather than the view beyond. He examined his contorted, sour features playing on the glass before answering.

'I understand,' he replied softly.

Doyle closed his eyes and sank back into his seat, his upper lip peeling away from his teeth and nostrils flaring as he produced a mirthless grin.

Eleven

'Look Fin, there's so little to go on. I'm not saying it's impossible, but it will take time.'

Findlay Morrison considered this information from his corporate seat at St James's Park. Floodlights lit up the green rectangle beneath him and the teams were warming up in a steady evening drizzle.

'How much time?'

'I can't really say. I have to go through official channels. If I try to push it, we could get discovered.

'*You* could get discovered, DC Pedersen,' Morrison modified.

'Come on, Fin, I'm doing everything I can,' the voice pleaded. 'Tracking someone who disappeared without a trace over twenty years ago with only a name to go on is…'

'I'm not interested in how difficult it is Pedersen,' Morrison barked down the line. 'It's been four weeks and you're no further forward.'

He dropped the volume of his voice and hissed, 'I pay you good money Pedersen and I expect results. Are police systems *really* that slow or are you just screwing with me?'

There was an audible sigh from Pedersen.

'I hear your daughter attends that expensive private girl's school in Leeds. She'll be fourteen now won't she?' Morrison stated in a deliberately aggressive tone.

'I'll find something on him for you. I'm sure I'll get what you need Fin…' Pedersen replied hurriedly.

Morrison hung up without swapping any pleasantries. He stared thoughtfully through the small rainbows the pre-match sprinklers were now cascading across the football pitch. Usually there was someone identifiable to supply the information he required. Then it was simply a case of extracting it by tempting their greed or through simple intimidation. As he expected, Manton's request was proving to be far more challenging.

He stroked his chin as he considered the options. To fulfill Manton's request he was going to have to draw upon more than police detective work. He needed to come at this problem from a number of angles. Morrison was jolted from his thoughts as a cheer rose around St James' Park and fans around him stood to applaud the teams coming onto the pitch. He rose and joined in the welcome to the home team, wishing everything could be as black and white as Newcastle United.

Twelve

'He's screaming *again,*' Pete Warren pointed out in a telling-tales, childlike tone. He was tiring of Benny Manton's histrionics.

'Oh, for Christ's sake,' lamented Gavin Loretta, tossing a half-eaten paper bag of grapes to one side and getting to his feet. 'He's coming down here again, isn't he…'

Loretta reminded himself of how Manton had described him on the way back from Haydock races: 'Big, strong and *stupid.*' That admonishment was for allowing the police to walk straight into his private box. He'd spent the next few days worrying about what the boss would do with a stupid bodyguard. Pete had told him it was just a throwaway comment, and to ignore it. However, Benny had been angry practically all week since that day at the races.

Manton's voice became louder, reverberating around the high ceilings and open galleries of the large house. A number of his expletives appeared to relate to the fact he couldn't get hold of Charlie Doyle. Warren and Loretta waited, expecting the door to the lounge to burst open any second, allowing a very angry man to enter and begin ranting.

Footsteps crossed the marble atrium and stopped outside the door, but it remained unopened. Warren was pretty sure he knew what was coming and turned his face away from the door, sheltering behind a high-backed chair. Loretta remained standing, but noted his colleague's stance and moved sideways to place a large armchair between him and the door.

Manton kicked his way into the lounge with such force one of the hinges on the ancient wood-paneled oak door sheared off and clunked onto the floor. He was holding one corner of a manila jiffy bag between finger and thumb and panting from the exertion of his entrance.

'Who delivered this?' he demanded. 'Are you two screwing with me?'

Both men peered at the small padded envelope Manton was violently wiggling from one corner.

Warren shook his head. 'Calm down, Benny,' he urged. 'You're not making any sense. What you got there?'

'Never mind what it is, how did it come to be sitting on a table by my doorway? This place is supposed to be impregnable. Do you think someone just wandered up the drive and pushed it under the door?'

Loretta and Warren shrugged in unison.

'Don't know anything about it, boss,' said Loretta quietly.

There was silence in the room. Manton's heavy breathing took centre stage. He stopped shaking the package, throwing it to the floor in frustration.

'Where the hell is Charlie?' he rumbled from the back of his throat.

Loretta piped up. 'He went out at about three-o'clock this afternoon. Didn't say where he was going, boss. Took the Range Rover and headed out the north exit.'

'So you *do* notice some things,' Manton noted with a sneer and took another few seconds to catch his breath.

Noticing Manton's temper appeared to be subsiding somewhat, Warren cut in.

'We'll try him for you, Benny. What do you want him for?'

Manton crossed to the leather sofa Warren was now sprawled upon and flopped into the other end of it, now seemingly a spent force.

'We've got twenty million going through tonight and I've not had confirmation from the Money Tree. I can't get through to them on the private satellite line. Doyle needs to get up there and sort them out.'

'I'm on it,' Warren responded, his mobile phone already to his ear.

'Get you a whisky, boss?' Loretta offered in as placatory a manner as he could muster.

Manton, almost thirty years the boy's senior, smiled to himself, recognizing Loretta's attempt to soothe him. He gave him a nod and then scrubbed a hand across his forehead, smearing the cooling sweat into his hair, causing it to spike slightly.

'Get me that envelope while you're at it,' he commanded.

Loretta scooped up the unaddressed package as he crossed the room to the bar set into the wall of the lounge. Realisation dawned once he looked down at the envelope and the big man felt his heart sink to the pit of his stomach. He poured a large Tallisker whisky from a bottle on one of the mirrored shelves and returned to Manton, handing him his tumbler and the envelope.

'How the hell did this get here?' started Manton. He stopped speaking, noticing Loretta's face.

'Something you want to tell me, Gavin?'

The boy frowned and his hand went to the back of his neck, rubbing at the heat being created by his embarrassment. It was sending hot ripples across his skin at the top of his spine and down his back.

'I know where the packet came from boss. It was left at the gate this morning, hand delivered. I forgot I'd brought it in… ,' Loretta's voice went to nothing once he caught Warren's expression and hand gestures. Suddenly self conscious, he dropped his chin and gazed blankly at the floor.

'Sorry, boss.'

He could feel Manton assessing him. Expecting an explosion of anger once again, he waited, cringing.

Manton looked Loretta up and down and sighed. The tension between the men dissipated. You needed a big, dumb, and dangerous man, ideally one who did as he was told, around you in his line of work. Loretta

66

ticked each of these boxes. Switching his attention away from the huge hunched figure, now standing like a scolded schoolboy, he examined the small oblong of paper and plastic bubbles in his hand.

'Loretta!' barked Manton. When Loretta looked up, Manton threw the package back to the young man, who snapped it out of the air in a movement which belied his size.

'Open it,' Manton instructed.

Uncertain, Loretta pressed his thumbs into the contents. It felt like there was a pack of cards inside, but a shade lighter. Happier now he'd conducted this piece of deeply scientific analysis, he immediately held the bag at arm's length and ripped it open.

A packet of already opened Marlboro cigarettes fell to the floor. Loretta stooped and picked the box up, noticing it was an old version of the cigarettes, with no health warning.

'Want me to open them?' he asked.

'May as well,' Manton replied, taking a satisfied slug of his whisky.

Loretta felt the contents of the box gingerly then teased the top flap open until a line of cigarettes was revealed. Inside, two lines of cigarettes were missing and a folded piece of paper was lodged in the vacant space.

He fished out the paper and passed it to Manton who unfolded the single white sheet and settled into his chair to read. He read the first few lines of the letter and then glanced up at the two men, an incredulous look on his face. He quickly returned to the letter and read the remaining few paragraphs.

'Read it out then,' Warren said casually, redialing Doyle's number for the third time and allowing it to ring out. Once he caught the look of horror on Manton's face he wished he'd never spoken. His boss's eyes were bulging and he was reading the letter with a single forefinger playing with the bottom lip of his open mouth.

Manton was over his initial shock but wasn't aware he was now nervously biting the wick of his finger. His mind was racing, trying to calculate the ramifications of a letter like this even existing. He looked down at the printed name at the bottom of the letter, checking it a second time. In boldly typed capitals was the name Thomas Redblood. He tried to mask an involuntary shudder by shaking himself and grunted at Warren to take the letter.

'Read it,' Manton instructed. 'Out loud for Loretta.'

Warren flattened a few creases, cleared his throat, and started to read. Manton shuffled his backside up to sit on the edge of the sofa, listening intently.

'Dear Benny,

I imagine you'll be full of questions right now Benny. For instance, how could a dead man write a letter after he was left for dead? How could

67

a corpse leaving your Money Tree be walking around a few days later?

You've let things slip Benny, become a bit sloppy and given a man who understands the intricate workings of your criminal empire the opportunity to mess with you. And believe me Benny; I am going to mess with you. I'm going to make you wish you hadn't treated me so badly. All those years in the Money Tree... And when I became unwell, even then, you treated me with contempt. You did nothing for me. And for that, you deserve a punishment which is much more than a mere brush with the authorities.

Of course, I could send some pertinent information to the police. But I'm not stupid; I know your rules of engagement. You'd tie them up in expensive lawyers for years. However, it would be interesting. But you'd get away with it wouldn't you; after all, you never get your own hands dirty. No, the most I can hope for is a little bit of fun with you now I'm dead!

You know something Benny, we were never too dissimilar. We both like to win and I have a challenge for you from beyond the grave! I know you're passionate about your horseracing and I've decided to take you on in that sporting sphere. To make it more exciting, I'm going to use a trainer from our hometown. He's a talented young man by the name of Harry Bolt. But of course, you should know him... after all, you killed his mother.

So, here it is Benny. I'm going to beat you to the Gimcrack. You know, the race you're desperate to win so you can make a big speech at York and fan your ego? Well, I'm going to get there first and steal your thunder.'

Warren stopped reading and aimed a shrug at Manton, as if to indicate winning a horserace was of no consequence. It was difficult to read the boss, he seemed relieved at first, but a frown soon crowded out all other emotions. Warren watched with growing nervousness as Manton's face descended from confused indifference through indignant anger and finally into full-blown rage. Manton raised one side of his upper lip in a snarl and now it was Warren's turn to break eye contact with him, and he forced his eyes down to complete the letter.

'Finally, I've a parting gift for you Benny. You know the millions of pounds of your client's money you've got stashed all over the world, whizzing around from account to account, business to business, busy being washed? Well...it's just disappeared. Poof... gone! Haven't you realised why you can't get hold of anyone at the Money Tree today? It's because they are desperately trying to work out where all your money has gone!

It could be corrected so easily as well. The solution is on a little memory stick that was in my pocket when I 'died' at the Money Tree!

Have fun trying to find it Benny...'
THOMAS REDBLOOD

An uneasy silence descended on the room as soon as Warren completed the letter and noted that it was signed in Redblood's hand. Loretta and Warren didn't move or speak, they waited, eyes on Manton. He still sat on the edge of the sofa, gently rocking back and forth, nibbling at his fingers, and gazing into the distance.

The sound of a door slamming broke the tension in the lounge. Presently Charlie Doyle entered the room, shooting a questioning glance at Warren regarding the kicked in door.

Warren knew full well where Doyle had been for the last few hours. It was always the same in the middle of the week. Out of sheer boredom Warren had once followed Doyle on one of his midweek bunk offs. It had turned out Doyle demanded very specific services when it came to liaisons with the opposite sex.

Warren and Loretta acknowledged Doyle with swift eye contact and both of them immediately returned their attention to Manton, who had ceased rocking on the sofa and was dangerously still. Neither of them moved toward the stricken man and Doyle sensed an atmosphere of fear.

'What?' Doyle enquired.

The question galvanized Manton. He jumped to his feet and stroked his beard a few times, pacing slowly around various pieces of furniture.

'Get the car ready,' Manton barked at Loretta.

'You need to read this, Charlie. But wait until we're on the road.' Manton continued to complete slow circuits of the furniture as he contemplated, eyes to the ground, his beard stroked with growing regularity. Finally he halted and locked eyes with Doyle.

'We're going to the Money Tree.'

Thirteen

Manton's Range Rover flew down the single-track country road, sending the delicate early autumn leaf fall twisting up into the darkness in its wake. Manton and Doyle sat together in the rear seats reading through Redblood's diatribe for the fifth time. Loretta drove, deep in concentration and Warren nodded, chin on chest, half-asleep in the passenger seat. It was a three hour drive north from Manton's house in Lincolnshire to the Money Tree in the East Yorkshire Wolds and dawn couldn't be too far away, the four men having travelled through the night. It was the first time in two years Manton had deemed it necessary to even come close to this part of the country, the region he grew up in and where his rise through the criminal ranks started.

'It's a risk coming here,' Manton told Doyle quietly once he'd read Redblood's letter through again. 'And I'm still not getting an answer from them on the Money Tree phones.'

Doyle ruminated for a short while then answered. 'Playing for time?'

Manton considered, fiddling with his beard. Peering out of his window he told Doyle 'They'll already know we're here. The cameras and monitoring system should have picked us up by now.'

He raised his voice and barked a few directions into the front of the car. Loretta acknowledged them with a flick of his head, his eyes glued to the narrow country road which was ghost-like in the pre-dawn darkness. The satellite navigation showed nothing of interest. They were now up into the Yorkshire Wolds on an arrow straight road which steadily climbed a hill. Empty arable fields with short hawthorn hedges bordered the road on both sides for another mile until the headlights picked out a small wood straddling the crest of the hill.

A few more instructions came from the back seat and the car slowed as it reached the wood before turning off the thin tarmac road onto a shale track. Through the trees the track continued another hundred and fifty yards, leading to a couple of dilapidated farm buildings. One was an abandoned farmhouse; the other was a large shed with half its roof caved in. They toured around the buildings and the track turned sharply right and a large barn painted red, with peeling wooden sides and a corrugated apex roof, loomed up out of the darkness. As instructed, Loretta took a route around a huge oak tree which was standing alone in front of the barn's entrance. The base of the oak was five feet wide and it towered over the barn, its branches filling the sky above them with a dense blanket of leaves.

'And lo, the Money Tree,' Warren announced in a theatrical voice.

'You want me to stop here?' Loretta asked, noting the large double doors to the barn were secured with several cross bolts and large padlocks.

'Straight down,' Manton instructed irritably.

Loretta edged the Range Rover round the corner of the barn and drove down the side of the building. It was much longer than it first appeared. At the back of the barn a small turning circle allowed Loretta to bring the car round to face a huge blank wall of wood with no sign of an entrance. Doyle jumped out and scanned the faded wooden strips on the barn wall. Having located what he was looking for, he fiddled with a small recess cut into the wooden slats. The barn wall made a clanking noise and slowly started to disappear vertically into the ground. Loretta's mouth fell open and he quietly swore to himself, realising the door was metallic and over two feet thick.

Slowly the inside of the barn revealed itself and Loretta gasped as the door finally slipped into the floor and he took the car forward.

'There's a building within the barn, it used to be a grain store,' Warren said, as if these words would explain the enterprise which unfolded as they entered. 'The barn is allowed to age and look uninteresting, and has brick and steel reinforcement inside its wooden exterior walls. You could tear the wood away and still need a tank to get in here. The padlocks on the front door are just for show.'

Loretta placed his chin on the top of the steering wheel and peered up and out, quickly realising they were in a modern, brick and steel built building, about half the size of a football pitch and forty feet high. Large windows interlaced with thick steel bars ran all the way down on one side of the roof, the side facing away from the road, allowing the dawn light to outline a warren of open plan rooms stretching into the back of the barn. However it was the contents of the barn which took Loretta's breath away. A large, modern office building built of brick, steel and glass occupied the entire inside of the barn, complete with its own small car park.

A bulky, pale faced man in jeans and a leather jacket stood on a small gantry to the left of the door. He acknowledged them and once Loretta had inched past, started to fiddle with some controls and the steel door slowly clanked skyward once more. Loretta noticed a small arsenal of weapons hanging from the brick wall behind the man, but thought better of commenting on them.

'Like it?'

Loretta looked over at Warren and shook his head in wonder. 'It's not what I was expecting, Pete.'

Manton snorted in the back seat. His irritation built in strength the closer they pulled into the small parking area which already held a similar darkly tinted Range Rover. When Loretta drew the car to a stop, Manton flew out of his door and strode purposefully to the entrance to the offices. Doyle followed.

Two unsmiling men stood in the entrance to the building, their joint bulk filling the doorframe. Like their colleague, they were dressed in informal attire; however, both sported bulky sidearm sized lumps strapped to their belts. The smaller man nodded to his colleague and they moved back as Manton approached.

'At least something is working correctly around here,' Manton noted brusquely as he disappeared into the building, Doyle remaining silent as he followed, completely ignoring the doormen.

Warren placed a hand on Loretta's arm and gripped it as the big man started to open his car door.

'Best give them a few minutes before we follow,' he advised with a knowing expression. Loretta didn't question the advice. He was quite happy to be nowhere near Manton at the minute and settled back contentedly into his seat.

'Doesn't your mum live near here?' he asked conversationally.

'Pete, somewhat floored by subject change, directed a warm smile at Loretta. He might be a bit dim but Warren couldn't help being amused by the big man; he must have been waiting to ask that question for the last twenty miles of the journey. It had been eighteen months or more since the two of them had dropped in to visit his old mum. They'd been passing Malton, on their way to the coast. Loretta must have remembered.

'Yeah, she's not too far away.'

'We should pop in to make sure she's okay,' Loretta suggested encouragingly.

'She's fine,' Warren replied in a placatory tone. 'I check up on her by phone once a week. I spoke to her last night; she's a tough old bird my mum.'

'You should visit though, Pete. You're lucky you have a mum to visit.'

Warren studied the big man in the driver's seat, then realised where this was coming from. Loretta had been an orphan, a difficult one by all accounts, shifted through the social services system without ever finding a home that could accommodate him for longer than a few months at a time.

'Well, you can visit her whenever you want,' Warren told the big man warmly. 'She'd love to see you, and you'd be doing me a favour.'

Loretta brightened, a childlike glee supplanting the serious grey mask which had been fixed to his face during the journey.

*****

James Deacon had been following Manton's progress to the Money Tree via their surveillance network around the access roads to the farm for the last few minutes. Now he looked nervously toward the door of his data room and swallowed with some difficulty. His throat was dry and yet sweat was flowing freely from his forehead and his armpits. He knew all the risks of working in laundering, however the primary risk to his wellbeing was about to walk through his door. Beside him the only two other employees not part of the security at the Money Tree sat at their workstations. Barely into their twenties, the two coders were blissfully unaware of the one-man tornado which was about to rage into their cosseted existence. They were both surrounded by monitors, busy being entranced by the data which was constantly being spooled onto their screens.

Footsteps on the concrete floor came towards the entrance to the data room and Manton burst in, pushing the double doors apart with a resounding crash against both brick walls. He stood there, glowering across the dimly lit room, scanning along the lines of computer equipment until he found the object of his ire.

'Deacon!' he spat dangerously. 'Where the hell is the money?' He was followed into the room by Doyle who seemed far more relaxed, his skull-like face set with a grimace.

'Good morning, Mr Manton. I wasn't expecting you,' Deacon managed in a squeaky voice. He stood, left his desk, and walked over to greet Manton, trying to smile and look relaxed.

Manton reached him on a stride and threw a fist at the man's face, shattering his nose and sending him to the ground with a hollow thump. Blood cascading down his jaw, Deacon gurgled and held both hands to his nose. Manton raised a booted foot and placed it on the writhing man's chest and started to apply pressure.

'Not answer my calls, eh?'

Deacon immediately started to wheeze and cough in between cries of protest, all of which were unintelligible.

The other two men sat cringing at their workstations as Doyle came at them.

'Tell us where the money is,' Doyle hissed at the two younger men in a low voice. He stood looming over them, flashing expectant skeletal looks at both of them.

'It's still there,' the pasty-faced youth with greasy hair closest to Doyle blurted urgently. He was in his early twenties and wore a stained grey sweatshirt and patched jeans. There was a mountain of empty Red Bull cans on and below his desk. 'Well, it's not lost, we're just having difficulty gaining access,' he added, his nervousness making him bolt through his words.

As these words sank in, Manton stepped off Deacon and joined Doyle. 'So it's not gone?' he asked slowly and clearly.

'No. Your money is…' Manton held up a hand and indicated for the youngster to slow down.

'The balances are still in every system, but an extra level of encryption has been added across the entire network. It's different for every node and we're decoding it to get our access back. It's a complex network of over a thousand servers over forty different countries and hundreds of bank accounts.'

Still on the floor, Deacon had sat up and now he shouted over to his visitors. 'We've broken back into the main hub and recovered access to the primary backbone, but there are over seventy different nodes on the network, they all have to be cleared independently.'

He stopped to spit blood and then tossed his head back. 'But it takes time,' he added, tentatively feeling his nose, pushing it back into some sort of shape.

Manton and Doyle shared a slightly relieved look.

'Okay, so why not call us or answer the phones?'

'They're all out,' said the second seated man, looking up at Manton with a scared look on his face. 'I'm working on it at the moment. We don't have private phones here for obvious reasons; everything gets routed through our internet connection via satellite. The same security encryption hit that system. We haven't been able to make any calls in or out all night.'

He stopped talking and bowed his head to stare at his keyboard.

Manton tapped him lightly on his head with a bloody palm. 'Good. You keep working.'

He turned toward Deacon. 'How long before we're completely back up?

Deacon's face visibly crumpled. 'The primary backbone was easy enough...'

'How long?' Manton repeated, fearing the reply.

'The hub was relatively easy but the further we get the more sophisticated the encryption becomes. Some will take days, others weeks or possibly longer,' he replied weakly. 'We're operating on only twenty percent capacity. But we do know who is responsible.'

Manton started towards the prone man, fists balled, but immediately felt Doyle's bony hand gripping his bicep. He turned to his colleague to berate him, only to find Doyle shaking his head slowly from side to side and warning him with dead sunken eyes.

He addressed Deacon again, this time in a more measured but equally menacing style of delivery. 'Is it by any chance the man I warned you about a week ago?'

Deacon, realizing his error, didn't answer. He held his nose once more and got shakily to his feet.

'Redblood must have left an executable file on the network. When we ran the latest batch of money movements the core security program was over-written and...'

'Okay, we don't need the techno-babble,' Manton interrupted, irritation rising in his voice again. 'So Redblood hacked our security system?'

Deacon thought for a few seconds, answering carefully, 'Sort of, yes,' then added quickly 'But we can sort it. It will take time, possibly a long time in some cases. However there will be a key to unlock it.'

'How can you be so certain?' asked Manton, interest showing in his voice.

'Because we create the key ourselves once a month, each time we renew the security system.'

'And what will that this key look like?'

'It will be another small executable file. There's always a master key which unlocks these sorts of security lockdowns.'

'Security lockdown,' Doyle repeated slowly. 'Redblood's used our own security system to limit our access?' There was a contemptuous fire in his eyes and Deacon was quick to avert his gaze.

Deacon mumbled an agreement and one of the seated youngsters said 'Yeah, pretty cool really,' in a soft voice, before cringing at his faux pas.

Manton scowled. 'So, this *master key*. Could it be held on a memory stick by any chance?'

Deacon blinked, a little shocked. 'Yes, that's how we hold the current security master key. It's too valuable to leave on the network. How did you know…'

Manton grunted loudly and aimed a violent kick at the stack of Red Bull cans on the floor, sending the blue and red tubes in several directions. They bounced harmlessly off the computer equipment and filing cabinets, some of them dribbling lines of bubbly red liquid. Deacon held his hands to his face and let out a quiet whimper, expecting another attack, however Doyle gripped Manton's arm once again.

'Clear the security encryptions and fix your nose,' said Doyle as he guided Manton out of the room. 'In that order.'

Deacon turned and started to walk away. 'Wait!' demanded Doyle. 'Who took Redblood and dumped him at the hospital?'

Thirty minutes later Manton and Doyle were in the back of the Range Rover, once again being driven over the Yorkshire Wolds. Loretta was at the wheel, wishing Warren would offer to do some of the driving and silently cursing the two men in the back who seemed to be quietly plotting something. He'd never even been asked to get out of the car at the Money Tree. That said, given the way Doyle had dealt with the security man responsible for releasing Redblood whilst he was still alive, Loretta had been relieved to be still in the car.

'It's going to cause a severe restriction in our ability to wash the funds,' Manton pointed out for the third time since leaving East Yorkshire.

Doyle nodded sullenly. 'And Redblood must have an accomplice.'

'Who do you think, his brother?' asked Manton.

'He has to be the favourite. Someone is pulling the strings for Redblood now he's dead.'

'What about that bloody trainer in Malton?' Manton spat viciously, scratching his beard. He discovered some dried spots of Deacons blood caught in his whiskers and scowled, disgusted at having to tease them out with his fingertips.

Doyle regarded Manton thoughtfully for a few moments through the reflection in the car window, watching his colleague remove the congealed globules of blood from his beard and drop them carelessly onto the floor of the Range Rover. Then he leaned in and whispered to him for a few minutes.

The car climbed the on-ramp to the A1 and then accelerated onto the carriageway and into the fast lane before Manton spoke again to the three other men.

'Does everyone know what a memory stick looks like?'

Manton paused, waiting for acknowledgement from the front seats. 'Well?' he barked.

Warren grunted and Loretta nodded his head vigorously.

'We need to find the one Redblood stole. We also have Redblood's accomplice on the loose. He needs to be identified and eliminated. It's most probably Billy Redblood, his brother who went into hiding twenty years ago. Deacon will deal with the computer systems; we have to find Redblood's man on the outside if it isn't Billy and then find Redblood's bloody memory stick.'

There was a round of positive noises from the three men.

'Okay,' Manton continued. 'A racehorse trainer in Malton called Harry Bolt needs to be warned off… we need to be direct. Redblood must have contacted him, or have some sort of deal with him. He may be the accomplice we're searching for and might have the memory stick, although I doubt Redblood would serve him up to us so obviously. We need to box clever with Mr Bolt as he's in the public eye and we have history, so Charlie will be dealing with him. In the meantime, Pete, find out how far Fin Morrison has got with finding Billy Redblood and tell him he's done, we'll deal with Billy ourselves from now on.'

'Now there's a job that's well overdue,' Warren retorted appreciatively.

'We also need to have a quiet chat with our tame doctor. He must have colluded in Redblood's recovery from death. Find him, discover whether he has the memory stick and if there was anyone else involved and then make sure he won't go blabbing. Make *dead* sure. I assume the two of you can deal with him?'

'Absolutely,' Warren confirmed.

Fourteen

Harry did his final evening check of his remaining five horses in the yard before returning to the farmhouse. He gave Jill a hug, grabbed his music folder, went back for another hug, and finally shot out of the door, jogging down the single-track road to the main road. He waited on the verge for a few minutes, checking messages, social media updates, and the days' racing results on his phone. When he'd exhausted the interest he could glean from his device he looked around and noticed the discarded police 'do not cross' tape in the bottom of the hedge. It seemed Redblood's demise was already old news after only a handful of weeks.

Presently, an ancient Volvo estate appeared over the crest of the hill from the direction of Beverley and eventually came to an exhaust-rattling halt beside him.

As he put his hand on the rear door handle a short black-haired female head popped out of the passenger window and asked 'So is this where they found that dead bloke?'

Harry climbed into the back seat, sharing it with a double bass and an assortment of drums and microphone stands.

'Hi, Emma. Hello, Pascal! Yes, I guess that's where it happened.'

'Oooh, creepy!' Emma cooed from the passenger seat as Pascal released his hand brake and pulled away.

'You don't know the half of it!' Harry exclaimed, then immediately mentally kicked himself. He couldn't reveal his arrangement to *anyone*; he'd have to get used to that.

Emma was in her early twenties. An intelligent, bonny, and fun-loving postgraduate student at York University, she screwed her head around to meet Harry's gaze. 'So tell all!'

'There's not a lot to tell really,' Harry replied after a pause, purposely attempting to sound bored in order to deflate the excitement. 'He came to see me and then had a heart attack. That's about it.'

'It happens. One minute you're visiting the only black racehorse trainer in Malton and the next you're dying beside the B1428,' Pascal said, heavily lacing his words with sarcasm.

Pascal, a French language teacher at a private girls school in York, lived in Millington, a small village on the edge of the East Yorkshire Wolds. Like Harry he too was of African descent, although he'd been born and grew up in France. He'd come over to study as a teenager, met his wife and stayed in Yorkshire. Harry came across both his musical partners when he and Jill attended a music festival in York. They had jammed for a few minutes, and within a fortnight the three of them were playing small gigs together.

Both sang well and could harmonise, so the combination of Emma's drums and Pascal's double bass, along with Harry on piano gave their trio plenty of scope. They tended to play on a circuit of pubs and clubs a couple of times a week with the addition of a regular fortnightly Wednesday evening slot at the Nags Head in Malton.

'It doesn't happen to *all* my owners,' Harry replied playfully. 'Besides I've got something even more exciting to tell you!'

Emma twisted around in her seat once more, placing strain on her seat belt in order to look at Harry. Her short black bob hairstyle framed her round face and she narrowed her eyes as they met with his. She fizzed with youthful enthusiasm.

'Go on then. What can top someone dying on your front lawn?' she teased.

'Jill and I…'

'Oh my God you're having a baby!' screamed Emma excitedly and immediately thrust both hands out through the gap between the front seats in an attempt to hug Harry.

Pascal, six foot two in his stocking feet and very useful with a rowdy crowd, began laughing in a deep rumble.

'Give the man a chance, he could be trying to tell us they are breaking up!' he managed to choke out between laughs. Even so, his French accent still punctuated his speech.

'No, she's got it right…' Harry started.

Emma screamed her delight once again and stamped her feet on the Volvo's ageing floor panels. She then spent the next few minutes firing a range of baby related questions at Harry, most of which he was unable to answer and some which left him completely bewildered.

As Pascal pulled into the rear car park of the Nags Head, Harry was trying to follow Emma's description of her best friend's experience of an epidural during childbirth. He discovered he was inordinately relieved when the car came to a stop and he was able to escape into the cool evening air once again. Emma jumped out of the car and came rushing round to give Harry a tight hug. Pascal waited and then shook his friend's hand.

'It's about time!' Pascal said with a twinkle in his eye. 'I'm really pleased for you both. Jill must be so happy!'

'She is. But hey, it must be your turn next,' Harry suggested.

Pascal gave a shrug but then broke into a big smile which he flashed at both his fellow musicians.

'Watch this space. Hopefully I won't be too far behind you!' he said conspiratorially.

This latest nugget of information left Emma gasping for air and she started to hug both boys one after another.

'I can't believe it, you are both such dark horses!' she exclaimed. 'Just promise me that if you need any help with anything baby related, I am your girl.'

Both men promised, and then on Emma's insistence, crossed their hearts and hoped to die. Finally following another round of hugs Emma was calm enough to concentrate on unpacking her drum kit from the Volvo and the three of them entered the pub.

The Nag's Head was a free house and as a result was popular with the real ale drinkers. It had a steady trade through the week, but Wednesdays in the back room were always popular. A variety of bands and singers had managed to build up a strong local following and brought the locals out in force for a mid-week drink, dance, or both. 'Nuts and Bolt' were a relatively big draw for the pub, easily filling the one-hundred and fifty person capacity entertainment room to brimming every other week.

The three musicians went straight to the back room and started to get busy setting up on a small raised plinth used as a stage. Emma was still buzzing about the revelations in the car and remained distracted until she noticed Harry setting up one of her cymbals backwards. She relieved him of drum duties, instead dispatching him and Pascal off to wheel the piano over from a small broom cupboard come storeroom at the side of the room.

They were starting to set up their microphones when Bob Leggett, resident manager of the Nag's Head, entered, and shouted a hello across the room. He started making his way through an area of informally arranged tables and chairs before crossing the small, hardwood dance floor.

'Hiya, Bob!' Pascal called back, and stopped twisting the microphone stand into position, extending a hand and offering a big smile in greeting. Bob had a big personality and a friendly disposition and was never at a loss for words. As a result, he was the most successful pub landlord in the town.

'*Good evening,* my favourite set of woodwork fixings!' he bellowed in welcome whilst shaking Pascal's hand effusively. 'Are we fit and well and ready to get my customers boogieing?'

Harry cast an eye over to Emma who was already looking longingly at him, hands clasped together and holding her breath.

'Go on,' he sighed.

Emma exploded with her news for the third time that night, embellishing as she saw fit. Harry reflected he was probably going to witness this performance a few more times before the evening was finished. Having given Emma that initial nod, in her book it would allow her free rein to announce his news to all and sundry. He actually didn't mind, and in fact, found it easier when someone like Emma - who lacked any shred of inhibition - was there to announce things on his behalf. She was fulfilling a role which Jill usually took care of for him.

Bob's ever smiling features offered Harry an even broader grin than usual and he set about pumping his piano player's hand in congratulation. However after the handshakes and exclamations had subsided he took on a more serious air. Scratching the thinning silver hair on the top of his head Bob admitted he had come through to the entertainment room on a less pleasing mission.

'She's waiting in the front bar. It's a policewoman, an inspector I think. She wants to see you,' Bob said apologetically.

'Is she about fifty and a bit…'

'Well built?' Bob offered.

'Yes. And probably wearing a raincoat?'

'That's the one. Said she was from South Wales,' he added with a wink.

'Gwent!' said Harry, groaning at Bob's lame joke. 'Send her through would you Bob?'

'Already done,' replied Bob, tapping the side of his nose with an index finger. 'She's just outside the door.'

He beetled over to the other end of the room and let DI Gwent in, gestured for her to seek out Harry in the corner of the room.

'You're working late aren't you, Inspector?' Harry said, still riding high on a cloud of goodwill. He looked closer at Gwent as she approached and wished he hadn't been so carefree with his greeting, as the woman looked positively done in.

She regarded Harry and his friends, perusing the various pieces of musical apparatus before answering 'Yes. I'm knackered,' she admitted with a downward inflection. 'Can I have a word in private, please?'

Pascal and Emma traded a look, made excuses, and exited quickly.

'I need to ask you to do something for me,' Gwent said in a dispassionate voice. She slumped a shoulder to one side and Harry took pity and asked if they could sit down. Gwent slid tiredly into a hard wooden chair and squirmed a little on it before settling.

'Mr Redblood's case is being wound down. It's been four weeks now and we've got nothing new to go on. He was in the final stages of bone cancer and only had a few weeks to live, if that. It probably contributed to the heart attack, although the insulin was the catalyst,' she explained.

'So there's no link to my Mum's death?'

'I'm not saying there isn't, but without any witnesses, a sick man with no relatives or friends we can locate, there isn't a thread I can pick up to investigate. I admit it's a little strange, but I've another four cases taking up my time at the moment and this one is going nowhere fast.'

Harry remained quiet, however, his mind started to whirr. That did make sense – Redblood *knew* he was dying, so made the video, and set things up in case he went too early to give the instructions himself.

Gwent rolled her eyes. 'I'm afraid we can't find anyone who knew him, or at least, met him in the last few years. So I've an unidentified body in the mortuary which needs a confirming ID. This brings me to the reason for this twilight visit. Would you be able to identify the body tomorrow?'

She tried to stifle a yawn, but it broke free and turned her face into a weird snarl.

Harry thought for a moment. He could put her in touch with Smith, but he immediately thought better of it. There was no way he could explain who Smith was without revealing the deal with Redblood. Besides, Smith had never met Redblood. His first sight of the man had come when he watched the video in the bank with them.

'No problem, Inspector. Let me know where and when and I'll be there,' he replied in as amiable a voice as he could muster. The thought of seeing another dead body didn't exactly thrill him.

Gwent nodded her thanks and struggled to her feet.

'I'd normally push you to stay and listen to us, but I think you need a good night's sleep,' Harry said, helping the Inspector to her feet.

'I would have liked that, Mr Bolt. But I fear you are correct.'

'Perhaps another time, and please, call me Harry,' he offered with a generous smile.

Gwent did try but could only manage a tired grimace in return. She folded her coat over her arm and traipsed toward the exit.

'I'll see you at the Malton station at ten o'clock tomorrow, Harry. Ask for the Welsh region of your choice.'

Fifteen

Harry was led into a pristine room at the mortuary with shiny stainless steel objects lying symmetrically in glass-fronted cabinets. The roof of his mouth tingled with a metallic taste and he found himself running his tongue across it a few times to try and rid himself of the unwanted tang. Gwent stood back as he was led to the side of a trolley and underneath a white plastic zip-up bag he was reintroduced to Thomas Redblood.

As the mortuary assistant held the bag apart, Harry looked down and examined the man's grey face and couldn't help looking along his collarbone. It was where his mother's wound had been. He'd dreamed of it for ten years after her death, even now he could visualize the spot of blood on the neckline of her sweater.

'Could you pull the bag down a bit more?' Harry asked.

The assistant raised an eyebrow at Gwent, who nodded her assent and Redblood was unzipped a little further.

Harry pointed out the small puncture wound within the wrinkles just above Redblood's collarbone to Gwent. It seemed to help, his memory of those few weeks in September 1993 suddenly became clearer.

'Exactly the same as my Mum,' he told Gwent. 'It seemed to take ages for them to find the cause twenty-four years ago. It took the police months before Annie and Willie got a piece of paper with their little report on it and showed it to me.

'I'm sorry about that,' Gwent murmured. 'I guess it was a different time, different people and rules.'

'The one weird thing I do remember is the type of insulin my mum had been injected with,'

The mortuary assistant frowned, asking, 'How do you mean?'

'Well, I was just a kid. I didn't know anything about insulin. But it said on this little report that the insulin was from a pig. I guess I was just curious, but I hadn't realised that's where insulin came from.'

Gwent shared a look with Harry and turned to the assistant who shrugged. She asked Harry to officially confirm that this was indeed the man who had identified himself as Redblood. He dutifully affirmed it was. Gwent thanked him and instructed him to make his own way back to the waiting room.

Raised voices emanated from the mortuary once Harry closed the door behind him and Gwent emerged a few minutes later looking red in the face and a little out of breath.

'Why they didn't specify it was pig insulin on their report beggars belief,' Gwent raged, slamming the mortuary door with a satisfying thunk and rattling of glass. 'Now we have two identical unsolved deaths twenty-four years apart and whoever stuck that needle into Redblood went to a great deal of trouble to produce an absolute carbon copy of your Mother's death!'

Harry's head swam with this news. He began to feel nauseous and before he knew it Gwent was sitting him down and forcing his head between his legs.

'Sorry about that,' Gwent told him a minute later. 'I thought I was going to lose you there. You went a little bit… well, you didn't look right. Better now?'

'I think so.'

'Just stay there for a minute. I shouldn't have hit you with that information about your Mother's case. It wasn't fair of me. I was angry about the cock up with the report.'

Harry, still a little woozy, lifted his head up to meet Gwent's concerned gaze. 'Why is pig insulin important?'

'According to our slipshod mortician, pig insulin was used for all insulin-dependent diabetics until the mid-nineties. It was discontinued once synthetic human insulin provided a viable replacement. You'd need a prescription, but you can still get hold of the old stuff, but it is hardly ever used now.'

'Does this help your investigation at all?'

Gwent scratched the side of her forehead and pursed her lips. 'The circumstances are suspicious; the substance used is very suspicious. But where that insulin takes me next, I'm not too clear yet,' she admitted.

Harry watched as Gwent absent-mindedly tugged at the waistband of her calf-length skirt while her thoughts were elsewhere. He presumed she was trying to sort the facts of the case and come to some sort of resolution. As he watched the detective, he too started to ruminate on the significance of the two deaths being caused by the same substance, but soon lost his thread when thoughts of his mother entered his head. Gwent caught Harry peering at her and audibly twanged her elasticated skirt back into place.

'Come on, Harry, you're good to go now. Let's get out of here. You could probably do with some air.'

*****

Harry had sat in the farmhouse kitchen as if he'd been encased in ice. He was still sat at the kitchen table, his thoughts full of his mother a full two hours after returning from the town. He was cupping a mug in both hands, unaware his coffee had long since gone cold. Jill moved anxiously around the kitchen, wondering if she should call the doctor. She was relieved when there was a knock at the farmhouse door, something to break him from his introspection. Harry heard the rapping on the glass panel and looked up to find Gwent staring through at him.

'Me again!' she announced light-heartedly as soon as Jill opened the door. 'I need your help.'

Harry pushed his mug away and turned slowly to face her. 'What sort of help?'

'I need to know who your Mother was with around the time she died, who her friends were. If she was linked to Redblood…'

Harry looked sheepish for a moment and glanced at Jill. He decided this was too important.

'I think Redblood may have sung, or been on stage with her.'

He tried to remember what Redblood had told him that morning when he visited the yard. It seemed so long ago. 'Yes, I think he played the trumpet,' he added, trying to add a little brightness into his voice.

Gwent regarded Harry with an air of suspicion for an uncomfortable few seconds, which eventually made him shiver.

'How would you know that?' she asked in a low voice.

'He mentioned it in passing when he came to look at the horses, the day he…'

'Died,' finished Gwent.

She nodded, pausing to stand, legs apart in front of Harry with her arms crossed over her ample bosom.

Jill broke in. 'I remember it too. It was definitely the trumpet. He said he played a few times in Laya's band.' She too received a hard stare from the inspector, but then Gwent sniffed and the source of this information seemed to be forgotten.

'Are there any other little nuggets Mr Redblood imparted to the two of you that morning which you'd like to share with me?'

Jill tried to act thoughtful. 'I don't think so,' she replied eventually, in rather a dramatic tone.

'O…kay, so who can I talk to about Laya and Thomas Redblood?' Gwent asked, interested why Jill was acting a little strangely, but also wanting to move things forward.

'I need to find out more about the link between them. Her band is a good starting point, but I need to know more about what was happening in Malton in the late seventies and early eighties. Who would know what was going on in both the world of racehorse training and music venues twenty-four years ago?'

Harry met Gwent's eyes with a crooked grin and a renewed sparkle in his eyes.

'I guess we could ask my other mum.'

Sixteen

Harry and Gwent sat in her ageing Ford outside his adoptive brother's training yard, watching the rain tumble down the windscreen of their stationary vehicle.

'I get the impression you're not in any rush to get into the farmhouse,' Gwent said, slowly undoing her seatbelt and re-arranging her ample figure on the faded leather driver's seat so she could study Harry's face.

'As I said,' he replied, looking vacantly through the windscreen. 'My brother and I don't get along. But I love Annie. Andrew lets me visit once a week as long as I keep out of his way.'

Gwent fell silent for a short while, but her curiosity got the better of her. 'Can I ask why you don't get along?'

Harry grimaced and turned to meet the inspector's expectant gaze.

'He blames me for his father's, my adoptive Dad's death, and my Mum's… issues.'

Gwent looked perplexed, 'I thought there was a car crash?'

'Yes,' said Harry nodding slowly. 'They ran into a tree in their horsebox. The thing is, I was there.'

Harry, realising that he was already too far into the story and would need to tell it from the start, took a breath before continuing. He returned to staring out through the rain-streaked windscreen at the farmhouse, fifty yards in the distance.

'We were racing at Carlisle. I was an apprentice jockey and my adoptive parents had two runners at the meeting, they'd driven over in the morning. They often went to the races together. Annie, my mum, said it was the only way she could get a sensible conversation out of dad. When he was driving their horsebox mum could get him to listen, because he couldn't make an excuse to get away to be with a horse. I'd had a ride in the last race, so I set off in my car later in the day. After I'd ridden I helped them load their two horses and we set off in convoy, but we hadn't gone more than a mile when the accident happened.'

Gwent could see the sadness filling Harry but remained silent and didn't move to reassure him. He was doing fine without any input from her.

Harry continued, 'It all happened in front of me, I was following behind them on the Newbiggin road. That's the dead straight bit of road that leads to the motorway from the racecourse. The lorry was carrying bales of straw. The driver came out of a field onto the road without looking, and my dad tried to swerve. He missed the lorry, but the box was run off the road and hit a tree. It seemed to nosedive and the back wheels left the ground. Then the momentum took the box skidding through a hedge and into a field of oil seed rape.'

'I parked in the middle of the road to stop any more cars coming through and ran over to the cab. As soon as I opened her door I could smell the oil and diesel. My mum was unconscious and she'd banged her head; there was blood over her. My dad looked in a bad way too; his legs were trapped under the dashboard, but he spoke and told me to get mum out. So I pulled her down from the cab and dragged her to the side of the road…'

The base of Harry's throat started to dry up and he swallowed a few times before going on to complete his memory of the day he lost his adoptive father.

'I ran back to the box and could see smoke. The two horses in the back of the box were making such a lot of noise, screaming and kicking the walls of the transport, so I jumped up and released the back bolts and undid the ramp. The smoke billowed out when I opened it. I managed to free the two fillies and they jumped down the ramp and bolted into the field. I remember it being yellow, so the flowers on the rape must have been out. I could hear flames. You know, there was that crackling noise, so I went around the other side of the box to get my Dad.'

Harry turned back to Gwent. 'That's all I remember. The next thing I knew I woke up in Carlisle General. The fuel line had caught and it just went up. I was lucky, just a bit singed and a bad headache. The side of the box had blown off and knocked me out. That side panel shielded me from the worst of the blast. The lorry driver pulled me away, but my dad took the full force and died instantly.'

Gwent allowed Harry to take a deep breath and hold the bridge of his nose for a short while, before asking her next question.

'So you saved your mother and the horses, then you were blown up saving them… why does your brother have a problem?'

'He blames me for dad's death,' said Harry flatly. 'He can't understand why I put the two horses before his dad. If I'd gone straight round to the driver's door and left the horses in the back, he might have survived.'

'I see.'

'But what made it even worse is that dad left me a thirty-thousand pounds trust fund in his will. It stipulated it had to be spent on setting up my own training yard. He knew Andrew would get the family yard. But Andrew… I don't know. He couldn't let go of it. I guess he's angry about losing his dad and wants someone to blame.'

'What does your mum think of this ongoing argument between the two of you?'

'To be honest, I don't think Annie realises. We don't argue in front of her. She took a long time to get over the accident and losing Willie. She has good and bad days. Hopefully today will be a good one and we can see what she remembers about Lay, and, maybe Redblood.'

The rain continued to slosh relentlessly down the windscreen which was now starting to steam up. Having had enough of talking, Harry suggested they make a run for the farmhouse. Gwent reluctantly agreed, spending the next minute awkwardly fastening all the buttons up her raincoat whilst in a sitting position. Just before they were aiming to open the doors and make a run for it, a group of five racehorses and their riders walked past, towering over the car. One of them stopped and the rider shouted down to them. Gwent found her keys, turned on the ignition, and wound the window down, her eyes thin slits against the rain.

Andrew Warcup was sat on an imposing gelding. A fine mist rose from the animal as a result of its workout. Standing perfectly still both horse and rider seemed oblivious to the weather.

'The door's open. But don't you bloody upset her, d'you hear!' Andrew shouted down at the car.

Gwent waved a hand in acceptance and wound the window up. Andrew glared pointedly at Harry before encouraging his gelding to move off. He walked the gelding off into the rain, heading for the heart of the stabling complex.

'He didn't seem *too* bad.'

Harry didn't offer a reply, providing an unimpressed look instead.

They ran the fifty yards to the back door of the Warcup's farmhouse, Harry being nimble and careful to side step the deeper puddles. Meanwhile Gwent reached the safety of the back porch with a trickle of water down one of her ankle high boots, gasping for air and sweating like a racehorse.

Once inside Gwent was impressed with the farmhouse which was spacious, modern, and well maintained. They found Annie Warcup in the second of the two lounges Harry had led Gwent through. She was sitting in an orthopedic chair watching an old episode of Heartbeat on a satellite channel. She didn't stir when they entered the room and Harry had to call his name so they didn't take her by surprise.

'Ahh! Hello Harry!' the weathered old lady exclaimed in a delighted crackle.

'Hello Annie. How've you been the last week?' Harry answered, coming around her chair and planting a kiss on his adoptive mother's forehead.

'Oh I'm fine Harry. Tinker is up to his old tricks again though,' she said, pointing a long thin finger at the huge television in the corner of the room.

Harry frowned, analysing what was happening on the cinema-sized screen. Enlightenment sent a smile across his face when he saw Bill Maynard's character injecting some comic relief into the episode.

'You're getting Lovejoy and Heartbeat mixed up again, mum!' he said with a half laugh.

Gwent hung back, just out of sight, waiting for her introduction.

However, she already had reservations over how useful this interview was going to be.

Harry surreptitiously waved her into the middle of the room which was tastefully decorated and full of high quality, if slightly dated, furniture. The old lady's tartan fabric chair stuck out like a sore thumb though and was clearly well used as there was a crescent of cups, glasses, spectacles and an array of magazines surrounding Annie's throne.

Harry tucked a blanket in around Annie's legs and cleared some of the detritus from the arms of her chair, setting it all down on a sideboard. Then he pulled a chair close up to the old lady and took her hand in his and paused the television.

'This is Mary Gwent,' he told Annie and nodded to Gwent who introduced herself and then sat down in an armchair beside her.

'She's a policewoman and is wondering if you can remember a few things for her?'

'Well, I will try. Is it important?' she asked anxiously, her face suddenly wracked with worry.

'No, no. Nothing that important for you to bother yourself about, Mrs Warcup,' Gwent said in a tone so soothing it took Harry by surprise.

Gwent continued, 'Harry and I were talking yesterday and he told me that you've lived in Malton all your life and you might be able to remember a few people for me. I'd like you to tell me about Harry's mum, Laya, and a man she knew called Thomas Redblood.'

Annie's eyes glittered for a moment. 'There's a name I haven't heard for a long time. It was such a shame, they were nice people, and Bill was ever so good at breaking the yearlings.'

'Really, you remember them, Annie?'

'Yes, of course!' the old lady responded, eyeing Gwent with a touch of rebuke. 'Bill and Betty worked for the Hills for years over at Bestbrook Stables when they were winning everything in the sixties. It was so sad, Betty had a riding accident on the Wold gallop, went to hospital and never woke up. Her husband Bill died of a broken heart a few months later – he just gave up – the poor man.'

Annie dwelt on this, rocking ever so slightly back and forth in her chair.

'And their son, Thomas?' Gwent prompted. 'Do you remember him?'

Annie wrinkled her nose. 'Oh yes, the one who played. Hmm... he was a clever boy, clever and sharp. I can remember him playing in a jazz band, Willie and I went dancing at the town hall. Your mum sang as well. It was a lovely night.'

Gwent was busy scribbling notes but looked up from her pad, giving Annie an encouraging nod to continue.

'Well, he went to University, didn't he. Betty was so proud of him.

She went to his graduation, told me it was one of her happiest days. She died only a few months later though. Such a shame…'

'Can you remember who else played with Laya and Thomas at the dance, Annie?' asked Gwent.

Annie seemed to lose focus and she fell silent, gazing into the middle-distance, recollecting the dance she'd attended over thirty years ago and the news of Betty falling and breaking her neck. Harry gently squeezed her hand.

'Annie, can you remember any more for Mrs Gwent?'

Annie was staring at the television and didn't seem to hear Harry.

'She'll be okay, let's give her a few minutes,' he suggested, indicating the direction of the kitchen.

'I'm going to get you a cup of tea, Annie,' he said, tapping her hand and unpausing the television. It leapt back to life and Claude Greengrass continued his high jinks.

The kitchen was large, modern, and impressive. Gwent entered and had all on not to gasp. 'This is… very nice,' she noted.

'Yeah, it's wasted on Andrew. He could do with a woman to mess it up a bit; he lives off microwave meals from what I can make out.'

'Will she bounce back a bit?' Gwent said, keen to re-engage with Annie. There was something nagging, itching at the back of her mind and she couldn't seem to scratch it at the moment.

'I'm hoping so. Annie comes and goes. But being positive, she tends to remember things that happened twenty or thirty years ago with far more lucidity than what she did twenty minutes ago. I'm convinced she watches the same episodes of Heartbeat over, and over yet still thoroughly enjoys them every single time because she can't remember the plot from the day before.'

'I'm guessing it was the accident that caused the memory problems?'

'No, not at all, she made a full recovery from the crash,' Harry responded. 'No, her issue is dementia; she's got Alzheimer's I'm afraid.'

'I'm… sorry to hear that.'

'Thanks. It's okay, she's happy enough and she's still Annie. It'll slowly get worse of course, so we're making sure she's happy and gets to see her friends when she can.'

The gloomy atmosphere continued when the back kitchen door opened and Andrew walked in, soaking wet, a frown on his face. He pulled off a couple of layers of weatherproof kit, kicked his riding boots off, and glowered at Harry.

'I'm going for a shower. Be gone when I'm finished.'

He passed silently in his stocking feet between the two of them, leaving sweaty footprints on the solid oak floor and a few seconds later could be heard clomping his way upstairs. Harry said nothing and didn't react until Andrew was out of earshot.

'Sorry about that.'

Gwent dismissed the apology with a flick of her wrist. 'So he lives here with Annie. There's no partner?'

Harry caught her eye, indicating he was about to impart a sensitive piece of information.

'He was set to get married when he was twenty, but his fiancé died of a drugs overdose. A spiked drink in the pub and she died of a seizure. He gave her fifteen minutes of CPR himself before the ambulance arrived and watched her die in front of him. He's not been with anyone since.'

Harry's tone was hushed, aware the subject of the conversation could be only a few feet above them.

Gwent nodded thoughtfully. 'You've spoken to him about it, tried to help him perhaps?'

'I've tried a few times…'

'Ah,' Gwent said with a knowing nod.

'That's older brothers for you,' he remarked with a resigned shrug of both shoulders. Harry passed Gwent a mug of coffee feeling a little downcast but noticed the inspector had an unexpectedly bright, enlightened air about her.

'Thanks for that,' she exclaimed, pushing past Harry to be the first to return to the lounge.

Gwent immediately found a place on a sideboard to deposit her coffee beside a number of racing photos and cricketing trophies, and marched straight over to Annie, bobbing down beside the elderly woman's chair. Her itch had just been scratched.

'Annie. It's Mary again,' she murmured. 'I've just one question if that's okay?'

Annie prized her eyes from Heartbeat, looked over at the Inspector, and gave her a wrinkled smile. 'Yes, dear, that's fine.'

'You said Thomas Redblood was the one who played an instrument. Was there one that didn't?'

Annie thought for a moment 'Yes of course. William was four years younger. A nice boy too. But he didn't play any instruments, dear, so I don't know why you would be interested…'

Gwent produced a warm smile for the old lady and thanked her. Then she left Annie to her television programme and returned to her mug of coffee. Harry shook his head in disbelief.

'Well there you go… he had a brother. Did you know that?'

'No. And it's interesting that there is no official record of a brother either,' Gwent pointed out over the brim of her mug. I have to hand it to you, Mr Bolt; this has been… illuminating. It seems we work well together.'

Seventeen

Harry wasn't just tired, he was shattered. Three full days of the Newmarket October Yearling Tattersall's Sales had him aching to be back home and away from the constant monotonous drone of the bidding process. Unless bidding himself - from which he drew a buzz of excitement - the sound of the auctioneer rattling through horse after horse was starting to drive him crazy. You couldn't get away from it, wherever you were; it was piped to virtually every corner of the sales grounds. He was also missing Jill, although he hadn't quite been able to voice this feeling to her in their twice-daily catch-ups on the phone.

Mike had made the trip down to Newmarket with him and was good company, as he wasn't the type to cling to him all day long. He would go off to watch the sales ring action or peruse the yearlings on his own for much of the time. He would also make sure any horse Harry bought was well looked after. On the drop of the hammer, the horse would become the buyer's responsibility, so it had been a relatively busy few days for Mike, as he would take each yearling in hand once Harry bought them. The two of them would meet up a couple of times during each day to discuss the horses over a cup of tea or something stronger and they ate together in the evenings before retiring to their bed and breakfast. As at home, the two of them bumped happily along together.

Harry stretched and leaned back on one of the cushioned, but still only just bearable, benches, and not for the first time wondered why the sales company made them so bum-achingly hard. He considered the possibility of potential buyers falling asleep on nice comfy seats, which seemed as credible a reason as any to keep them on the harder side of utilitarian.

'Keep the buyer's backsides numb and keep 'em awake!' he imagined was the instruction to the supplier of the viewing gantries when these seats had been ordered.

A large ballpoint pen dangled from his neck on a promotional cloth leash and a well-thumbed copy of the Premier Yearling Sale catalogue was open in his lap. The auction pavilion was only half-full at the moment and although it was reaching the end of Book Two the prices were still reaching upwards of seventy-five thousand guineas. He gave a huge yawn and allowed his eyes to close while the auctioneer tried to drum up more business for a grey Clodovil filly currently going through the sales ring. The yearling had been stuck on thirty-eight thousand guineas for two spins of the ring and the auctioneer was on his third turn around, searching for someone to take him to forty thousand guineas.

Harry glanced at the filly's catalogue page and at the breeder's name and muttered, 'Not sold,' under his breath.

Ten seconds later the auctioneer informed the occupants of the sales ring, 'Not today I'm afraid, she's not sold,' in a disappointed voice.

The Clodovil sired filly hadn't reached her reserve and was led out unsold. Harry took up his leashed pen and made a note on the filly's catalogue page. It was a regular enough occurrence; a vendor, usually a breeder, wanted forty thousand for her and had placed a reserve price on the yearling. The auctioneer had run the price up to just under the magic number in the hope that an extra single bid would give him a valid selling value, and pay him a higher percentage commission, as vendor buy backs attracted a lower sales fee. The unsold horse might go back to the stud to be entered in the next sale. More likely, the vendor would sell the yearling privately outside the ring for considerably less than forty thousand, his reserve gamble having failed to pay off.

This was the way Harry had bought a few of his youngsters for Redblood. Even though he had far more money than he'd ever gone to the sales with before, he still couldn't help searching for a bit of value. This philosophy had been drilled into him by Willie Warcup, who had started bringing Harry to the sales when he was ten years old. Willie had been a wily buyer and earned a reputation for being a tough negotiator. Harry's abiding memory of Willie at the sales was when his adoptive father had made an offer outside the ring at Doncaster for a yearling colt that hadn't met its reserve price. The vendor, a breeder with a substantial stud in Ireland had laughed heartily at Willie's suggestion that his yearling was only worth twenty-five thousand guineas and tried to wave him away with a desultory hand.

Willie, straight-faced and steadfast, had informed the seller his offer would drop by a thousand guineas every fifteen minutes and marched away from the stabling block with Harry in tow. The Irishman, having expected a negotiation to ensue, was instead left watching a potential buyer stride away into the distance.

Willie had walked straight to the buying area of the sales ring, instructing Harry to wait at the parading area and run and tell him if he saw the Irishman heading his way. Sure enough, ten minutes later the vendor appeared, clearly trying to find Willie as he hurried toward the auction ring. Harry smiled at the memory; the Irishman's concerned face checking his watch every minute until he'd found Willie and agreed the deal.

There was a big difference now. Harry had the budget to purchase top class horses. He wasn't blasé though, even when bidding in hundreds of thousands of guineas, he'd found himself still searching for that bit of value. He'd been well educated.

As the last day of Book Two wound down Harry had almost completed his team of two year old colts whom he would train to have a tilt at the Gimcrack next season. He had nine youngsters already and the budget would run to another two or three. He was waiting for a run of four potential yearlings, including a couple at the top of his hit list, to come through the ring in the next twenty minutes, lots 1024 through to 1032.

It had been a long and painstaking process to reach the point where he could actually raise his hand in Newmarket and buy his first yearling. It had started well before the catalogue had landed on his kitchen table with a thump at the end of September. With his remit being so tight and centered solely on the Gimcrack Stakes, Harry had spent many hours going through every single winner of the race since the 1980's in order to determine the type of horse he would need to acquire. He had analysed Gimcrack winning sires, mares, damsires as well as entire three generation pedigrees.

Redblood himself had provided a folder on the memory stick with every single race video for the last twenty years. Over the course of two weeks Harry had acquainted himself with each race in minute detail, playing the videos over and over each night. He'd watched how the race was won on soft ground, firm ground, from the front, prominent or by being held up. He'd compared times, pace analysis and weights. Jill eventually called a halt to the evening assault of race replays, banning him from using the lounge television as she had been forced to miss every single episode of Coronation Street for five days straight.

Harry had gone through the sales catalogue many times. It helped that he was only looking at colts, but this still meant analysing the pedigrees of over a thousand horses. He'd visited three of the major studs, pulled in breeding analysis on over a hundred horses and finally arrived at Newmarket armed to the hilt with a hit list of horses. The first job at the sales was to sort out his purchasing rights.

It had been an illuminating conversation with the cashier. The middle-aged woman behind the counter with hair drawn up on her head in a tight bun had sniffed officiously when he told her he would be bidding for The Revenge Partnership. She had tapped a few keys and consulted her computer screen when bringing up Harry's details.

'According to our records, you have a credit limit of ten thousand pounds, Mr Bolt. That was agreed three years ago. I could see whether we can raise that a little for you?' she'd reported in a voice with a nasal ring to it.

When he had asked her to crosscheck The Revenge Partnership with his name, she had returned him a hard-faced stare. Her fingers rattled over the keyboard once again and this time her eyes widened and she swallowed before confirming a slightly different value.

'Your credit limit is now two million pounds,' she'd responded with one eyebrow raised. The cashier had blinked at Harry and given him a forced, plastic smile.

'I trust that limit is going to be enough for you.'

'We'll see. You never know, I might get carried away,' he'd replied with an impish smile.

Harry had walked out of the accounts office grinning from ear to ear. Access to a Weatherby's bank account with a balance of over two million pounds felt good and knowing you could afford practically any of the horses on offer over the five days of the sale had given him a huge confidence boost, despite the money belonging to someone else.

He couldn't guess at the number of yearlings he had looked over. He had run his hands over countless equine legs and backs, inspected mouths, throats, feet, and then watched movement from all manner of angles. He had spoken with vendors, owners, and stable lads and endured all the flannel that went with buying horses.

When the sales had finally got underway, Harry was like a child in a sweet shop. However, he remained choosey and kept reminding himself that he was there to do a job. If one of his target horses became bad value, he would drop out and wait for the next one.

His first purchase of a lovely Showcasing Colt had come in the first hour of trading. He'd spent one-hundred and ten thousand guineas of Redblood's money and it had brought him to the attention of several trainers, agents, and sales watchers. By the time a third lot had been knocked down to him for one-hundred and seventy-five thousand guineas, the Chairman of Tattersalls had made his way over to introduce himself.

Bryan Austin was a bullet-headed Londoner with a sharp eye and a smooth, uncomplicated way of dealing with people. He was far too smooth, bordering on smarmy for some people's liking but Harry found him courteous and engaging. Bryan had eased into the seat beside him and got to know his new big-spending customer with a few tried and tested queries which Harry did his best to accommodate with honest answers. He had to dodge when it came to who was the owner behind the partnership but Austin was used to dealing with clients wishing to remain anonymous and had departed with a warm smile and a promise to catch up with Harry before the end of the sales week.

Andrew had also put in an appearance, approaching Harry from behind when he stood watching a yearling walk in the stabling area. In his usual style, he'd attempted to catch his adoptive brother on the hop. Fortunately, Harry had seen him sidle round behind him and didn't react when he hissed, 'You can't possibly afford that!' in his ear. The subsequent conversation had consisted of derogatory comments from Andrew, met with silent, expressive shrugging from Harry.

Later the same day, Andrew had been aghast at Harry's first six-figure purchase, not knowing how to react. Harry had bumped into him in the entrance to the auction room, their eyes locking long enough for Harry to risk stopping to speak with him. Andrew had opened and closed his mouth a few times, unable to voice an opinion or provide a disparaging remark. Then he'd flared his nostrils and scowled before pushing past, the two of them having failed to trade a single word.

David Smith had also pitched up for an hour or two, clearly

enjoying the buzz of the sales arena but staying at a distance while Harry was working. However, they had a quick chat over a cup of coffee in the corner of one of the bars before David excused himself to head back to London. David clearly wasn't a horseman, and Harry imagined he had attended simply to tick the box on Redblood's instructions to him which stated, 'Trainer is at sales buying horses'.

One of Redblood's more questionable instructions for Harry's activity at the sales was that he should hinder Benedict Manton, should the opportunity arise. Harry had read this instruction and felt uneasy. Knowingly running up another buyer was something he frowned upon. He had no grudge against Manton – he'd never met the man – the ill feeling was all Redblood's.

Both he and Benedict Manton's trainer would naturally be looking for exactly the same sort of horse; the best, sharp, sprint-bred yearling of their generation capable of winning a Group Two contest like the Gimcrack as a two year old in August, only four and a half months into the season, so early promise was essential.

It hadn't taken long for Harry to find himself bidding against Manton's Newmarket based trainer, Eric Goode. Goode was a well-established handler with a string of a hundred horses and Harry ran into him when he was bidding on an Oasis Dream colt. Harry had a bit of a tussle around the hundred-thousand guineas mark, eventually securing the colt for only a little more than he had expected to pay. However, when the next similar sort came along ten lots later and the two of them locked horns again, it was clear that this was going to be a recurring contest whether Harry was looking for it or not.

Harry had never met Manton, but during this battle for a Cape Cross offspring, a bearded man appeared behind Goode in the bidder's area, a standing area with steel bars to lean against and reserved for people who wished to advertise the fact they were actively bidding. The bearded man began giving bid instructions which became increasingly animated as the auction progressed. Eventually the colt was knocked down to Goode for ninety-five thousand, but it was clear from his body language that he had been ready to stop bidding at half that value.

Ten minutes later, a man of about fifty in a tight-fitting suit, slick back hair and sunglasses caught Harry's arm when he was outside the auction ring watching the pre-sale parade. There was a waft of lemons as he bent closer and Harry assumed it must be coming from his hair. The man plastered a wonky smile onto his swarthy, pinched features and without introduction started to ask Harry questions. Which type was he was interested in? What sort of budget did he have? Harry had been amiable enough at first, deflecting the man's queries, but quickly made an excuse to leave, only for the greasy individual to follow him to a new viewing position. The man eventually moved away when Harry brushed him aside to feel a colt's legs in the inspection area, having shrugged diffidently at the man's increasingly pointed questions.

Twenty minutes later, Harry saw the same man speaking with Goode and guessed he was an envoy from the Manton camp. It wasn't unheard of for all sorts of chicanery to be adopted at thoroughbred sales, but this was totally new to Harry and from that moment he kept a close watch on Manton and his cronies. As well as his trainer, two other men drifted in Manton's vicinity; the grease ball and a much larger man, possibly in his mid-twenties, who had the look of a bouncer or personal security guard.

Harry yawned periodically and cast a tired gaze down from his seat in the viewing area, watching the lots tick by in the sales ring below. It was now mid-afternoon on the third day and once lot number 1023 had been led out he extricated his numb backside from his seat and made his way down the steps to stand in the ring entrance. He much preferred bidding from this point, as you could view the entire pavilion and identify who was making bids against you. It also made it easy to catch the eye of the auctioneer and offered an element of anonymity, being out of the direct view of a good proportion of the seated areas if you stepped back into the entrance.

The colt coming up was rated in his top two in the entire sale. The youngster had a wonderful swagger about him and was another by Shamardal, a sire whose offspring had won the Gimcrack twice in the last five years.

It looked like there was plenty of interest in him, as the audience in the entrance started to swell, as the good-looking chesnut with a white flash running the length of his face strode purposefully into the sales ring. There was a slight waft of his tail as he started his circular trip around the ring and his lead-up lass only had to pat the colt's neck once to calm him into an easy rhythmic walk.

The opening bid was twenty-thousand guineas, which marked the youngster out as being above average. The pace of bidding lifted, as the auctioneer recognised the interest around the ring. It stalled a little at one-hundred and eighty thousand and Harry waited for the first call of 'Are you all done?' from the auctioneer before he entered the bidding.

As Harry went to raise his catalogue a pair of hands, no doubt practiced in such maneuvers, gripped Harry's elbow and shoulder and sharply twisted his arm up his back, forcing him to drop his catalogue. Pain shot up into the ball of his shoulder and spread across the top of his back.

'I wouldn't do that if I were you,' said a quiet, insistent male voice into his right ear.

Harry moaned, trying to turn his head and wriggle out of the man's hold, but the grip on his arm tightened, making any rotation impossible.

The voice became a snarl 'Be quiet, stay calm, and look ahead or

I'll break it for you black boy.'

The auctioneer was on his second pass of the ring when another bid was registered of one-hundred and ninety thousand guineas.

'Thank you, Sir. New bidder,' announced the auctioneer, immediately turning his attention to the previous bidder and asking 'Do I hear two-hundred thousand?'

The jangling pain of trapped nerves was ripping through his shoulder and Harry started to form a question about the reason for the man's actions. His query was cut off in a succinct manner within a couple of words with increased pain and a warning.

'Shut up!' the man hissed, increasing the angle of Harry's arm up his back. Harry grimaced with this new agony but for a moment was more anxious about the heat of the man's breath on his neck and the faint aroma of lemons.

Harry flicked his eyes about him, seeking help wherever he could get it. He soon realised the scrum of people packed around him were only looking one way, and that way wasn't towards him. With the noise of the auction, the next waiting lot braying in the background and everyone's attention focused on the ring, even the trainers close to him were totally unaware anything unusual was being played out within a yard of them.

The bidding on the colt continued, the auctioneer taking the price beyond two-hundred and sixty thousand guineas and cleverly slowing his speed as he realised the bidders needed thinking time.

Resigned to remaining stock still, Harry tried to relax his arm, and then his torso, attempting to stem or mitigate the pain. He watched the bid rise to two-hundred and ninety thousand guineas, desperate for the hammer to fall. It was an action he sincerely hoped would signal his release.

The auctioneer's mallet toured the ring once again, searching for a new bidder now the auction had stalled, but he found none.

'Good boy,' whispered the voice again. 'You just stay...'

There was a sharp crack and the man's words contorted into a yelp and Harry's arm was released, providing a moment of blissful relief, before a throbbing ache took over at the top of his shoulder. Massaging his arm he spun around to see a middle-aged, silver haired man bending over a figure whose arm seemed to be at a wholly inappropriate angle.

The silver-haired man looked up and nodded curtly at Harry, then toward the auctioneer.

Sudden understanding rushed at Harry and he turned back and raised his right hand at the same time shouting 'Three hundred, three hundred!' An audible gasp came from a trio of people stood around him and a small gap opened up in front of Harry. The auctioneer's hammer had been raised but now a bid spotter was pointing in his direction, tugging at the auctioneer's jacket.

'New bidder!' announced the auctioneer in welcome.

'A little late to the game Sir, but I'll accept your bid of three-hundred thousand guineas'.

He adjusted his position at the lectern in such a way to place the emphasis back to the previous bidder. 'Do I hear three-hundred and twenty?'

Harry shot a glance backwards and caught sight of the silver haired man bustling an injured figure into the pre-sales parading area. He guessed the injured man had been his assailant. He was hunched over, holding his arm. For a split second the suited, black haired man appeared in profile before disappearing from view. Harry was pretty sure it was Manton's man, the lemon flavoured grease ball from earlier in the day.

However, his attention was drawn back to the sales ring by the auctioneer. Harry was now the centre of attention once again, with the auctioneer's gaze falling solely on him.

'I have three-hundred and twenty thousand guineas.'

Somewhere from within his very core, Harry Bolt felt anger brewing, then bubbling through his veins until he found himself gritting his teeth, his cheeks tensing uncontrollably. His armpits were suddenly wet with perspiration and a surge of powerful focus almost overcame him. He stepped forward towards the auctioneer, though the throng of people around the ring until he was stood right beside the ring in which the lovely Shamardal colt was still circling. He regarded the wonderful animal for a moment then slowly turned and looked up the rows of seats into the bidding area, found who he was looking for and locked eyes with Benedict Manton.

Still looking directly at the bearded entrepreneur Harry stated in a loud voice 'Three hundred and fifty thousand guineas.'

Sensing the theatre of the moment, the auctioneer seized on Harry's dramatic bid. 'The gentleman knows how to play this game! Thank you, Sir.' He twirled his hammer a couple of revolutions and leant forward on his lectern, as if fascinated by what would come next.

'Do I hear three hundred and seventy-five thousand guineas?' he said quietly, reducing the sales ring to an expectant hush.

Manton remained stationary, staring down at Harry, his beard visibly twitching. His eyes were blazing. Beside him Eric Goode was seeking instruction from his owner and apparently bemused by the lack of a reaction.

'Sir, I believe one more bid may be enough...' cajoled the auctioneer. More faces turned to look up to the bidding area where Goode and Manton stood like statues.

Harry renewed his piercing stare, his anger now fizzing in him. He'd never been this... motivated, this... dangerous. Still Manton didn't offer any response, he just stared back. He showed little in the way of physical emotion, however his eyes betrayed him.

'I'll have to push you, sir,' the auctioneer prompted.

'It's with the gentleman on the floor. This lovely son of Shamardal. Out of a winning mare. From the family of Street Cry.'

He paused, and seconds later seemed to lose interest in Goode, who was now facing Manton. He swung his hammer around the room.

'Three-hundred and fifty thousand guineas once. Three-hundred and fifty thousand guineas twice...' he paused for one last sweep of the room, hammer above his shoulder. 'Sol...'

'Four hund...' bellowed Manton.

The auctioneer's hammer cracked like a bullet piercing steel as it struck home on his lectern.

'..red. Four hundred!' screamed Manton. 'I bid four hundred you cretin!'

Goode stood spellbound, looking to his owner and then to the auctioneer with his mouth open. Harry spun around to face the auctioneer, wearing an expectant look. The auctioneer pointedly ignored the insult from the other side of the ring, instead concentrating on Harry.

'Well done, Sir. He's your horse for three hundred and fifty thousand guineas. The gentleman's bid was after the hammer had fallen. Thank you very much and good luck with what, I'm sure, will be a lovely colt.'

Harry nodded his thanks to the auctioneer and turned back to Manton. Immediately sound of gasps, chatter and exclamations were thrown up around the building. Manton, still looking back down at Harry was being pulled away by Goode and another man, tall and thin, who had been in the background throughout the encounter. Within ten seconds he had been guided up the steps and out of an exit onto the back staircase.

The next minute was chaos in the bottom of the ring as eventually the auctioneer had to ask for people to step back to allow the next lot into the ring. Fellow Malton trainers approached him one after another to shake his hand or offer whispered congratulations, several clapping Harry on his back. He was simply shell-shocked, mostly at his own actions.

Harry signed the sale acceptance form, breathed deeply and then sought out some fresh air. Out in the paddock he leant up against the parade ring rail and winced as the pain in his elbow and shoulder returned with a regular pulse. He was instantly joined at his elbow by Mike who immediately ran through the whole scene from his perspective sat up in the viewing seats. It was only after he caught Harry grimacing that he realised he'd missed an important portion of the action.

Assuring Mike that his arm would be fine, Harry realised his catalogue was missing and his mind snapped back to why he was at the sales. He looked up at the current lot number displayed on a gaudy digital counter near the parade ring and sighed with relief; they were only up to 1026. He still had up to two more to buy. Taking Mike with him Harry reentered the sales ring.

******

At five-thirty that evening Harry and Mike emerged from C&C's transport office in the top tier of the Tattersalls sales ring having organised for twelve yearlings to be transported up to Malton the next day. Harry, now dosed up with over the counter painkillers, walked awkwardly down the steps, holding his shoulder.

The sales ring was silent now, with only a smattering of people around, cleaning, tidying, or preparing for Book Three the following day. Harry reflected that the Book Three and Four were the sales he would usually attend, as the lesser lights, and therefore cheaper, affordable yearlings would be on offer tomorrow.

As they made their way down the stairwell, Mike asked, 'So how does it feel to spend just over one and a half million pounds on yearlings?'

'Painful,' Harry responded with a hollow laugh.

They reached the first floor and continued down, Mike preceding Harry.

'Er, Harry?' Mike said, turning with an animated expression on his face and directing his eyes down the stairs.

A silver-haired man was leaning up against the wall at the bottom of the stairs. He looked up and pushed himself off the wall as he heard steps coming down and broke into a smile.

'Mr Bolt and Mr Dunn,' he said in a soft Yorkshire accent. 'I'm pleased to meet you. I'm Cyril Bunt.'

The man held out a manicured hand attached to a muscular arm.

Harry reached the bottom of the stairs and while Mike shook the man's hand, he made no effort to do the same, keeping a grip on his pulsing shoulder. On closer examination the man was stocky, muscular, had a jagged, angular face and azure eyes which exuded a calm intelligence. He was wearing a polo shirt with the logo of a major stud sewn onto its right breast, black jeans and what looked like steel-toed boots. His silver hair was stylishly cut and perfectly parted to one side. A real mixture of refinement and street fighter, thought Harry.

'I think I owe you one... but I'm not sure why,' admitted Harry.

Bunt tensed his bottom lip and rolled his eyes a half revolution, ending in a little nod.

'I can see why you're not so sure. I couldn't explain earlier. There were er... issues which needed my attention.'

Confusion reigned for Mike, as he tried to make sense of the conversation. Harry noticed his friend's furrowed brow and tapped him lightly on the back with the palm of his good hand.

'I think this is Mr Redblood's doing,' Harry explained, raising a

100

questioning eyebrow at Bunt as he spoke.

Bunt pursed his lips and nodded. 'Mr Redblood did want us to take a watching role, with any intervention kept to a minimum. Ideally we were to operate without your knowledge, basically keeping an eye on you and Manton to ensure you are able to buy, train, and race the Redblood horses without hindrance. However, it appears Mr Manton's people are not frightened of conducting their business in clear view. I had to intervene when you were being threatened with physical violence…'

Bunt cut himself short and came closer to Harry concentrating his attention on the injured shoulder.

'Would you let me feel your shoulder?' he asked.

Harry was uncertain for a moment, but then another spasm of jangling nerves shot through his shoulder and he acquiesced. Bunt got him to remove his shirt and ran his hands expertly down Harry's arm, rolling the muscles and ligaments between his warm fingers. He stopped at the top of Harry's shoulder, and applied pressure in a couple of places, giving Harry a jolt of pain.

'Nothing broken, some muscle damage. Warren may have dislocated your shoulder and pulled the ligaments.'

'Warren?' queried Harry.

'Pete Warren is a long-term associate of Manton's. I dislocated his elbow today to allow you to bid for that colt. I can fill you in on the background later, but right now you need some pain relief.'

Bunt produced a wallet from the back pocket of his jeans and popped two pills out from a foil strip, giving them to Harry.

'Opiate based painkillers, take them now. Over the counter stuff isn't going to touch that pain. See your doctor in the morning, but you'll be okay in a week to ten days.'

Bunt turned to Mike. 'You'll be driving him home?'

'Yes.'

'Good. Okay, let's get you two on the road,' Bunt declared, indicating the exit door with an open hand.

'Hold on,' said Harry, his head swimming with the rapidity of Bunt's handling of the situation. 'You're here to look after me… well, us… and paid by Redblood… How long have you…?'

'Snappily put,' Bunt replied with no hint of irony. 'We've been monitoring you and Manton for the last four days and will continue to do so for the next… well, however long it takes for you to win that race at York.'

Mike looked to Harry, confusion once more raging all over his features.

'I'll explain later Mike. It's… complicated,' assured Harry.

'Ah! Apologies, I just assumed you knew…,' Bunt chipped in.

'Never mind,' said Harry waving the apology away. He was tired, in pain and unusually for him, starting to lose his patience. He wanted quick answers and wanted to pick up on something Bunt said.

'You said, 'We've', Mr Bunt. Who else has Redblood got watching us?'

'Ah,' Bunt repeated, raising an index finger. 'Yes, we're good at the protection, not so good at the communication side of things. Covert operations tend to compound that problem. Please...?'

He escorted them to the exit door and pushed it open, holding it open for Mike and Harry and encouraging them to step through. Outside in the cool early evening it was almost dark and a small, wiry oriental man, much younger than Bunt, emerged from the shadows to stand in the lamp light. He wore similar attire to Bunt. Both men would have passed as stud staff and never been given a second look by anyone, but Harry now realised that was the point. He hadn't noticed them, and they'd presumably been following him around all day, every day. He shuddered at the thought.

'This is Wang,' Bunt told them. 'By all means feel free to laugh, but that's his name,'

The Chinaman nodded curtly from the neck but said nothing.

'Right, this is us. I guess you'll have to get used to Wang and I being around from now on. You okay with that?'

Harry was too tired to argue. His shoulder was flowering with pain once more and he was hungry. However, he would be sure to call David Smith to confirm who these men were as soon as he was rid of them.

'Yes, I guess. Whatever,' he managed in reply. 'Nice to meet you, Wang, I suppose we'll see you at the yard sometime next week then?'

'Oh, no,' stated Bunt with some force. 'We'll make sure you get to your car first. Then we'll be staying with your horses here overnight and travelling up with them to Malton – so we'll see you tomorrow.'

Harry stared at Bunt, and the look of measured belligerence he received in return convinced him the man was totally serious. There was no indication that Bunt would entertain any sort of argument so Harry grudgingly nodded his acceptance.

The four men exited the main gates of the sales complex and walked down the hill to the car park which ranged over the rolling grass paddocks at the front of Tattersalls. Bunt led them to Mike's car without needing any instruction and saw them both into their seats. Then he indicated to Mike to roll his window down.

'We've already checked the car over. It's fine. I don't think they planned that far ahead. Today's little fracas was probably spur of the moment. Have a safe journey.'

Mike replied with a quiet, 'Thanks,' and rolled his window back up. With a final acknowledgement from Mike's hand he and Harry set off in silence, touring the car around the narrow tarmac road in the car park. A couple of minutes later they were on the outskirts of Newmarket and without warning Mike indicated, pulled over into a lay by and switched the engine off before turning to face Harry in the passenger seat.

'What the hell is going on!' he gibbered, holding both hands to the sides of his head and rubbing his cheeks. He stared over at Harry, utterly bewildered.

Harry shrugged but immediately wished he hadn't. He cringed with the pain the action had delivered to his neck and shoulder. Fed up, he shoveled the two pills Bunt had given him into his mouth and swallowed with eyes closed.

He opened them again, smiled weakly at Mike and pointed to the road.

'We've a three hour drive ahead of us. Get your foot down and with luck I might finish explaining before we get home.'

Eighteen

Rory Lewis looked around the taproom of the Black Bull in Malton and decided it had gone downhill since he'd been a regular in the late noughties. He hadn't been in here for at least five years, the last time being when he and Harry had been asked to leave following an alcohol-fuelled game of crisp packet tennis in the main bar. A smile curled his mouth up at both ends as the memory freshened in his mind. He'd ridden the winner of the big sales race at York that day, his first really big payday of about fifteen thousand pounds for one win and he'd celebrated in style. That reminded him. He should probably pop in and see Harry and Jill, he'd not seen either of them for a few days.

With curly blonde hair, a slight, but incredibly strong body, and pretty decent looks for a jockey who had weighed around eight stone six since the age of eighteen, Rory had plenty of admirers. With his laid-back attitude, stylish success on the racetrack and notoriety as a fun loving, witty companion, Rory was considered a media darling and had earned himself a reputation as bit of a ladies' man. That said, he failed miserably to keep hold of any of his female friends for more than a few months, as his incredibly high standards, or the female's lack of understanding surrounding his job, always spelled doom to any relationship.

Feeling in a contemplative mood, he swung round on his barstool and did a complete three-sixty of the bar. At a quarter to eight in the evening on a Tuesday it only held three people in its thrall, and that included himself and a barman. The third customer was a portly middle-aged man who had his head stuck in a tabloid newspaper. He was sitting in one of the three horseshoe shaped booths against the back wall and looked like a salesman of some sort, whiling away his evening alone in a pub instead of in front of his hotel room television.

Rory had ridden a trio of horses that afternoon at Redcar, winning in the last on the card. Making a seven thirty appointment in Malton had been a bit of a pain. Irritation was beginning to set in. He'd been sat here for twenty-five minutes now, staring at a drink he didn't want, and waiting for people he didn't know.

He turned back to the bar, and not for the first time in the last few months considered whether Jack Murphy, his agent, was actually doing his job properly. This meeting with a potential new sponsor had been set up at the last minute and Jack had been insistent he made the meeting. He'd sounded excited about the possibilities for a retainer plus kit and transport sponsorship, but at the moment it looked like it was just a wild goose chase. His low calorie lemonade sat almost entirely untouched in front of him and he determined to give Mr Peters, whoever he was, another five minutes before he left for home, a thirty minutes drive away in York.

Rory was composing a rather barbed text message to Jack and

ready to leave when two slickly dressed middle-aged men entered the bar and walked straight up to him. He slipped off his bar stool and nodded, asking 'Mr Peters?'

The first man to offer his hand had slick, greased black hair which didn't sit quite right with his apparent age.

'Yes, I'm Peters, John Peters.' Pete Warren announced. 'This is my business partner Mr Charles.' Charlie Doyle said nothing, providing a nod of confirmation when his pseudonym was mentioned and followed that up by proffering a tight smile. Rory noted how thin this tall man was. His face was drawn, practically sucked clean of muscle and his skin gripped tightly onto his cheekbones. An old joke bubbled up from the past, something along the lines of, 'You must be the picture, so where's Dorian Grey?' but he suppressed the urge to vocalize this. He'd made that mistake with owners without a sense of humour before.

Rory shook hands with both of them, Charles was tall, at least six feet two, so towered over Rory at five-three and as expected, his hand was all bone and no flesh. Both men wore expensive looking suits, although Charles's hung off him.

Warren bought some drinks for the two of them, Rory turning down their offer of something stronger than lemonade, and the three of them chose the unoccupied booth furthest from the salesman.

Rory had an easy charm which he rarely switched off, and so even before he sat down he'd asked the men what it was they were looking for. He'd not made his mind up about these two, and so getting straight down to business looked the best strategy.

'My agent tells me you are looking to sponsor a jockey?'

'That is partially true,' Warren responded once he was seated. He perched on the very edge of the booth and didn't make eye contact with Rory at first, preferring to flick his eyes around the bar for a time before settling on him. Doyle was completely the opposite, locking eyes with Rory immediately, although he continued to remain silent. Rory was penned into the booth by the two of them, one at either side of the crescent shaped table, which was immovably screwed to the floor.

'Okay, so what exactly is it you want from me?'

'The same as everyone else in racing… information,' Warren replied with a wonky grin. 'We are quite happy to pay handsomely for the… *sort* of information we need,' Warren added.

Rory's attitude altered immediately and the mild irritation at their late arrival now switched his dial right around to controlled anger.

'Then our meeting is over,' he said as bluntly as possible and made to leave by shuffling around the table.

'I don't provide betting tips or inside information. Find yourself another jockey.'

Doyle didn't move, effectively blocking Rory's exit.

'Please, Mr Lewis, let us explain,' said Warren in what he probably thought was a soothing tone, but to Rory felt downright creepy.

'We're not interested in betting information. We have a deeply specific interest in one yard.'

Accepting for a few moments that he wasn't going to be released from the booth until these two idiots had said everything they wanted to say, Rory relented, sat back and said 'Go on.'

'We understand you sometimes ride for Mr Harry Bolt?'

Rory produced a sigh and nodded, now somewhat perplexed by the direction this conversation was going. Harry only had a handful of horses, what sort of information was there to discover? Harry and the honest way he campaigned his horses was positively see-through.

'So, we are interested in a relationship he has with a certain *Mr Redblood* – have you heard that name mentioned before?'

Rory shook his head and looked Warren in the eye now. 'Even if I had, I wouldn't tell you. It's privileged information.'

Warren raised an eyebrow, apparently impressed with this answer. Rory immediately felt uncomfortable and strangely cheap.

'Mr Redblood has some sort of deal with Bolt,' Warren continued in a measured tone. 'We simply wish you to keep us abreast of anything you learn about that relationship. Each time you bring us information of value, we will pay you ten thousand pounds. In cash.'

Warren paused, watching Rory carefully. 'That's more than you would earn riding the winner of a quality race isn't it?'

Rory stared blankly at the man. His hair had so much grease on it he was being dazzled by the reflection of the strip-light on the ceiling. He wanted to thump this idiot and scream he couldn't be bought. And the idea that he would sell Harry down the river was an even greater insult. However, these two were looking more dangerous with every minute that ticked by.

He plastered his best poker face on and said, 'Okay, then. Give me your card and when I have anything to tell you I'll call.'

Warren chuckled. 'No need, Mr Lewis. We will be in touch.'

Doyle rose and let Rory exit the booth, nodding his head sagely towards the jockey as he made his escape. 'Thanks for your time Rory, we'll definitely be in touch,' Warren called after him.

The two men remained in the booth and finished their drinks in silence. After he had drained his half-pint glass Warren eyed his gaunt colleague across the table and said in a low voice 'We'll have to use intimidation, y'know, find somebody he cares about. Money won't work.'

Doyle grunted his agreement and without saying another word the two men sidled out of the booth and walked nonchalantly out of the pub.

Nineteen

Her feet ached, her stomach was rumbling and her elderly mother had just sent her third text message of the day. The tone of the text messages had become increasingly pointed, asking the same question: when was her only daughter going to come home tonight? A relatively standard day thought Gwent, as she cast her mobile phone into the depths of her handbag once more and stared out of her office window towards Hull city centre. Drug use, supplying drugs, petty theft, burglary, almost certainly driven by the need for drugs, had characterised her day, as they did most days.

Early evening darkness reigned outside and a brisk wind was rattling the windowpane in its paint-peeled steel frame. At least the rain had stopped. She considered the chances of her getting wet on her way home, looking skyward at low grey clouds which were scudding quickly overhead. She decided it would be a close call.

Car headlights from Ferensway strafed the building every few seconds, sending bright oblongs of light racing across the walls. Gwent preferred this old, decrepit police station in the centre of the city to the brand new places out of town. This building and the people in it seemed to beat to the same drum as the city. She'd walked these streets as a WPC in the late eighties and still liked the feel of the cracked pavements, wobbly curbs, and potholed roads beneath her rubber soled shoes. You were never closer to the heartbeat of Hull than when you walked its streets. She still did it now, only minus the uniform.

Gwent placed her back to the window and looked down at her in-tray, which had grown by two folders since she had been out trying to track down a dealer on the Orchard Park Estate that afternoon. She tugged at the second one down so that the corner of the folder was poking out and the name '… Clarissa Bolt' appeared. Gwent pulled her chair out, switched on her desk light, extracted the file on A'Laya Clarissa Bolt and started to read.

Gwent flicked over the first few pages. She knew what she was looking for; it was the interview statements. In total there were only five, which included Benedict Manton, Peter Warren, and Charles Doyle. Gwent's heart started to thump louder in her breast. She read the names again and realised she may have every reason to go after Manton again. There was definitely something ticking beneath this woman's death twenty-four years ago, she just needed to scratch away at it.

Gwent marveled at the lack of detail in the statements. An elderly dog-walker confirmed he'd seen a young woman on the other side of the road, although it sounded unreliable because he'd stated she was standing at the top of the road, nowhere near where Laya lived. No description of the woman, height or even her shape. The other four statements were from the all-male occupants of the car and read like carbon copies. They had all seen the black girl walking towards Norton and a figure on the opposite side of the road, a white male going the same way. But they couldn't name him or provide any further detail.

The lead inspector on the case had surmised that the unidentified young man would have been the last to see Laya alive, but with no way to determine who he was, and even then, link him to the investigation, the case had run cold very quickly. It had been categorized as suspicious, unsolved and an open verdict provided by the coroner.

Gwent ran down the names of the boys in the car: David Salmon, Peter Warren, Benedict Manton, and Charles Doyle. Her heart lurched and she read the names again. She crossed the room and tapped on the laptop she refused to have on her desk. Following a login and a search, a block of text displayed and she scanned the screen, letting out a whispered 'Yes!' when she found what she was looking for.

Gwent composed a text message to DC Poole: 'Meet me at 7am. We're going Salmon fishing.'

*****

Two hundred miles to the north, Findlay Morrison was laying propped up on his favourite sofa, an open laptop beside him. A muted television tuned to rolling news hung on the wall of his penthouse flat and projected multi-coloured shades into a room otherwise devoid of artificial light. Behind him a floor to ceiling window provided a view of the Newcastle city skyline.

Findlay laid motionless, eyes closed, his chest rising and falling in measured breaths. Within a few seconds of each other the laptop and a mobile phone chimed quietly. Ignoring the laptop he padded barefoot across the oak-floored lounge to a sideboard and searched along the eight mobile phones neatly laid side by side on its walnut veneered surface.

Findlay lived alone. He had reached the conclusion as a young man that his chosen lifestyle would never dovetail with a meaningful personal relationship. He liked people who weren't like him: simple, straightforward, and honest people. He knew they brought out the best in him. However a romantic relationship with Findlay Morrison would end one of two ways; either they would leave once they realised he was a monster, or once exposed to his workplace, colleagues and the realities of organised crime they would become corrupt themselves and his interest in them would quickly wane. He'd based this life choice on two relationships. These two dalliances had been quite enough to convince him that he wasn't cut out for a meaningful relationship. Not that it bothered him. Findlay knew what he was.

He read the text message on the fourth phone, deleted it and returned to the sofa, placing the laptop beside him. He opened an internet email account, one of several dozen already open in separate browser windows, and clicked on an email attachment. The bright white document which filled the screen bathed his face in its glow. He read the title 'A'laya Clarissa Bolt' and started to flick through the pages.

Manton's 'little request' had proved to be an extremely demanding task. Findlay liked that; there was little in his life he couldn't control or manipulate so when his usual lines of enquiry hadn't delivered what Manton needed, he'd been pushed to find a new angle. That was stimulating. He'd recently been dedicating a lot of his time to this investigation and it had been worthwhile, in ways he could not have expected.

It had originally sounded tedious: find this man. He even had a distinctive name, Joseph William Redblood. Tracking people was a daily requirement for Findlay, as there were always debts to collect, information to extract and pressure to apply. This target had lived in his patch from birth to age eighteen so there should have been leads to follow, records to examine. Family to track. But that was just it, at age eighteen JW Redblood, former resident of Malton, East Yorkshire simply disappeared along with any records relating to him. As far as the state was concerned, he had never existed. It was as if his entire eighteen years of living had been expunged from every record and file in every database. Well, almost every record.

Findlay allowed himself a sly smile. The two weeks spent scouring the Malton newspapers on ancient microfiche machines had been a worthwhile expense. Placing children's names in local newspapers helped to sell copies, and luckily the editor of the Malton Times had used this tactic exhaustively during the eighties and nineties. The Redblood brothers had appeared regularly in the local paper right through that period, but of greater interest, so had a certain Benny Manton. That's when Findlay's investigation had become… entertaining.

Findlay examined the five statements and read each through a few times, allowing himself a smile when he came across Manton's name. He discarded the dog-walker's statement and concentrated on the four young men. All of their statements were practically the same: travelling in their car together, they saw the black girl walking away from the town centre with her guitar on her back. They passed her and then noticed a boy of about their age in the shadows across the road. They slowed down to see who it was, but didn't recognise him, it was too dark. They continued into Malton and spent the rest of the night in a town centre pub before driving home.

Findlay read the names of the interviewees and couldn't help smiling. He mouthed words, 'Hello, Mr Manton,' in silent reverence to the art of burying evidence of wrongdoing. Crossing the room to the sideboard, he carefully selected another mobile phone, found a specific contact, and started to compose a text message. He was halfway through his message when another mobile phone started a trill ringtone. He looked down and frowned, pushing the answer icon quickly.

Findlay remained silent. Steadily over the next five minutes a smile crept across his face, building in intensity as the conversation deepened. The caller did most of the speaking and Findlay interjected with only a few words. Finally he answered in the affirmative and finished the call. He carefully replaced the phone back into its appropriate place in the line of devices on his sideboard and with a clenched fist he punctuated the silence of the room with a shriek of 'Yes!'

Twenty

Not for the first time during the last two hours Cyril Bunt looked down the two lines of stables in the top yard at Pickering Farm, shook his head and wondered why he bothered. He'd tried to get a handle on this scene a number of times during the morning of Harry Bolt's stables November Open Day, but he was now resigned to the fact that trying to ensure the security of eighty owners, friends and family of the Bolt's was an impossible task.

Bunt eyed a middle-aged lady with her husband as they peered over the door to an empty stable close to him, both shrugging their shoulders. He and Wang had identified every single car that had driven into the yard, and every occupant. These two had a part share in one of the three-year-old fillies; Mr and Mrs Luscombe. They looked benign enough and before he could stop himself, he felt his feet lift and take him over to them. It was once he'd opened his mouth he realised just how out of character this was for him.

'That colt... er... he's called Five Seven One, well, actually his stable name is Fido. He's is on the walker at the moment,' he offered in explanation to the couple.

'Really? Could I ask why he's named Fido?' queried the well-spoken lady. She wore an encouraging smile, matched, if not exceeded by her husband's who appeared to not only be indulging his partners passion, but positively encouraging it.

Bunt gave the lady a wry smile. It flitted through his mind for a moment whether Harry would want this sort of information passed on. Ignoring the part of his brain which demanded a secure, silent response, he plunged on.

'Sometimes he will sit on his backside with his legs up in front of him. It makes him look just like a big daft Labrador, which is why he got the nickname. He'll pull right up in that position and wiggle across so he's right at your eye level. Harry thinks he likes to eyeball people!'

The lady gave a generous laugh and thanked him. He retreated to his vantage point at the top of the yard, wondering what it was about a racehorse training yard which had brought about his subtle change of personality. He and Wang had been in and around the yard for six weeks now, and both felt the roots of the yard tugging at them.

It had started well, with a complete overhaul of yard security. The place had looked like a building site for two weeks with new gates, railings, security cameras and one of the stables being commandeered as a monitoring office. Then slowly and surely, being around a bunch of young, enthusiastic people with close bonds and doing physical work with mighty, statuesque animals had started to grow on, and into, the two security men. As Bunt and Wang had got to know the horses as individuals - their idiosyncrasies and temperament - so they had been drawn into the ebb and flow of the yard.

Wang had commented on Harry's management style in the first few days. On first look he seemed to leave staff to their own devices, but then slowly over the course of a few weeks you would notice how Harry would engineer short, intimate discussions with each member of staff where he'd be surreptitiously giving tips and suggestions, providing assurances and positivity, or in the case of one or two, eliciting more from them. He always did so in his laid back, but intensely positive manner.

Wang had summed Harry's management style up: 'If you love horses, work hard, and know how to use a brush, you'll love working with Harry.'

Bunt had never been near horses in his life. He was ex-army, ex-police, had an ex-wife, and hadn't even ridden a donkey at the seaside. The nearest he'd come to anything equine was going to a football match as a child and seeing police horses towering above him. Yet he'd become entranced by these young horses Harry had bought at the sales. There was something about being around them day to day that gave him a warm feeling.

He shook himself from his reverie and tried to concentrate on the hubbub that was occurring at the other end of the stables as Harry and Jill paraded their horses. There were only two empty boxes in the yard now, since Billington had brought his half a dozen back. He spied the top-heavy, self-made businessman in the middle of the crowd, his trophy wife, at least a dozen years younger than the balding retiree, stood on her own smoking a cigarette while admiring a view of the paddocks further up the yard.

Bunt had been in the yard when Billington had come back to see Harry. Fair play to the sixty year old, he managed to stump up the courage to admit he'd been wrong about the two year olds, even if it was all couched in the same self-righteous manner that afflicted so many men of a similar background. Nevertheless, Harry had accepted the man's horses after a bit of head scratching and now Billington was enjoying the limelight as Harry introduced one of his older handicappers to the appreciative crowd.

Jill's mother and father were watching proudly on with Millie lying at their feet, flat out on her back and dying for anyone to give her stomach a rub. They stood next to George Plant, a long-standing owner with Harry who owned the horse with arguably the most character in the yard – Paste. A garage owner in Malton, George was a good-looking middle-aged man, thinning slightly, but he struck a commanding pose, almost military in his stiffness. Beside him there was a gaggle of six fifty-something ladies who together formed a syndicate entitled 'The Dangerous Ladies'. They were busy fawning over the unattached vehicle repair entrepreneur, who probably rated a decent catch. Bunt sniffed and moved his gaze elsewhere. To be fair, Mr Plant seemed more than capable of controlling their advances.

News of Harry's purchases at the primary yearling sale of the year had travelled quickly around Malton and beyond. It proved to be revelatory in terms of bringing new interest into the yard. Bunt had walked into a yard with only five horses in late October, but within three weeks a further fourteen had been added to the twelve they saw safely delivered from Newmarket. Twenty-eight horses in total, sixteen of which were two year olds.

Bunt stared through the forest of legs and couldn't help but notice a shapely set belonging to the latest owner to join the yard. Ms Claire Seebar had been something of a talking point among the staff when she had polled up at the yard un-announced in late October, not least due to her elegant good looks. She was also intelligent and engaging, although she seemingly lacked a sense of humour, which Bunt had noticed made her of no interest at all to both Harry and Rory, much to the lady's consternation.

It seemed Ms Seebar had a friend who was happy to indulge her latest fad, whatever it happened to be. She had read about the up and coming young black trainer's two million pounds spending spree in a small article in the local newspaper. On that basis alone, she decided she would place a horse with him. She owned an un-raced three year old filly which had been a relatively cheap buy from the late October in-training sales, being a throw-out from one of the big Newmarket yards.

Bunt had done his homework. Ms Seebar lived in York and did indeed have an association with a fairly rich older man who owned a string of dental surgeries. Whether the man's wife was aware of her husband's indulgent purchases for his 'friend' was unclear. However, it had amused the stable staff immensely when Harry had nicknamed Ms Seebar as the 'Maneater'. Her horse had arrived lame and Harry doubted it would be able to cope with the rigours of training and racing, which he had told her after only three days. However, he was going to try and build the filly up over the winter and hopefully allow the owner to go racing at her home track at some stage.

The explosion in horses at the yard had meant an increase in staff, both stable staff and riders. Five new stable staff plus another three regular work riders had joined the payroll, all of whom had been vetted by Bunt and Wang. Harry had taken their intrusion into the life of the stable with good grace, although a conversation with David Smith had been required to sort out where the ultimate responsibility lay for accepting new horses and staff. Bunt had managed to secure a veto over both, but so far hadn't needed to use it. The new members of staff had joined Mike and Zoe, and all but one of them had worked out. A twenty-year-old, lad who failed to arrive on time on either of his first two days, was asked by Harry not to bother coming back, an action which surprised and impressed Bunt. It transpired Harry had a set of basic expectations from his staff, and reliability was number one. Harry would give one warning and a second infringement would receive a swift, no nonsense response.

Bunt had been a little perturbed when a group of men not on his owners list had pitched up unannounced, but it transpired they had been owners with Harry up until recently, having lost their horse, sort of, in a selling race. He allowed them access on the trainer's say so, ignoring the roll of the eyes he'd noticed Harry deliver as he walked away with his ex-owners. Bunt remained vigilant and aloof from his position at the top of the yard and reflected upon the fact he was starting to get used to the language of racing and the draw it had for many people, from so many different backgrounds.

Harry was enjoying himself, to a point. The sun kept breaking through the grey clouds, warming the yard and making the horses' skins shine, even though some of them had already gone in their summer coats. It felt good to have a yard full of horses and people, although he had been quite nervous beforehand and hadn't slept so well the night before.

The open morning had been Jill's idea, a way of telling everyone that the Pickering Farm Stables was on the up once more and an opportunity to thank the owners who had stuck with them. When prompted by either Jill or Rory, Harry said a few words to the large group gathered around him. He found speaking to a crowd difficult, even when he was discussing his own horses. He always preferred to speak one-on-one with people.

He vividly recalled an instance at junior school where he'd been tasked with reading a poem in the morning assembly. At a small lectern on school stage, and in front of two hundred and fifty cross-legged children staring at him with expectant upturned faces, he had stammered through the first two lines of his heavily practiced ode, before crumpling. He'd been unable to read the blurring words as water streamed from his eyes and his knees turned to jelly. This reaction was in stark contrast to when he played the piano, which he had done many times at school. It seemed it was speaking which created the problem, singing and playing music held no worries for Harry.

So today he contented himself with handling the horses and adding a few comments here and there, relying on Jill and Rory to keep the commentary flowing.

Harry had contacted Rory as soon as the yearlings arrived in the yard, inviting his friend across to the stables to inspect his two million pounds worth of investment. Redblood hadn't specified a jockey for his string of horses, leaving that decision to his trainer, so Harry felt it was well within his remit to appoint a stable jockey for the Redblood horses and offer Rory a small retainer. After inspecting the new inmates, Rory had accepted the offer straight away. He committed to riding out a minimum of twice a week and, in return, he would be the first choice jockey for the Revenge Partnership horses.

It wasn't just friendship that drove Harry's decision. He needed someone he could rely on and Rory was currently riding out of his skin. He had finished the latest season with one-hundred and twenty winners and was at the top of his game. He'd received plenty of similar offers for the next flat season, including an invite to be based in Newmarket, but between Harry's thirty horses and Fred Prosser, another Malton based trainer with a hundred and eighty horses in his yard, Rory was happy to remain in the north for the forthcoming season.

Looking over and past the crowd, Harry noticed Bunt, standing motionless at the top of the yard, staring down towards the stables entrance gate with a finger held to his ear. To all intents and purposes Bunt and Wang had become members of staff. There was always one of them around and although it had been difficult to work around them for the fortnight - that turned into a month - when they were installing all their security equipment and upgrading various elements of the yard, the two of them had now slotted into the stables' routine. Both were showing an interest in the horses as well, which was unexpected and rather sweet, as Jill put it. Whether this was genuine or simply professionalism on the men's behalf in order to ingratiate themselves, Harry remained unsure.

'You would agree wouldn't you Harry... Harry?' asked Jill.

He snapped out of his thoughts 'I'm sorry, I was...'

'Elsewhere?' Jill interrupted, drawing a smattering of laughter from the crowd.

Harry beamed. 'I'm afraid so. Thinking about how we're going to back this one next week,' he added, gesturing to a colt that was stretching his neck over the stable door, in order to land a playful nip.

Harry recognised Jill was in her element, explaining about each racehorse, inviting questions and prompting Harry when she needed to provide detail. With friends and family part of the audience, her own physical condition had come under great scrutiny. Her Mum and Dad were mingling with crowd, along with some of her girlfriends. Pascal and Emma had made a beeline for Jill as soon as they had arrived, wanting to know all the latest news on her pregnancy.

Jill was moving along the boxes, explaining pedigrees and any other interesting points about each of the new yearlings in the yard. Half of the yearlings had already been lunged and three of the more forward types had been backed and ridden away. Jill had explained this process in detail which the audience had found fascinating.

God, she's good thought Harry as he tuned into his wife's description of the next young horse. Meanwhile, Rory was entertaining everyone with racing anecdotes while Mike brought the horses in and out of their boxes to show them off in the open air.

The crowd shuffled down to the next box, and Harry looked over the half-open door to one of the Redblood's Book One yearlings. He immediately knew something was wrong.

Harry's face fell and became ashen as he watched one of his more expensive colts trying to kick its stomach and displaying a lather of sweat. At the same time Bunt looked towards Harry and started a dead run toward him.

'Get the horses out of the boxes!' Bunt screamed, racing past the crowd and up to the top of the yard. He threw the bolt back on the first box and disappeared inside. A second later a horse trotted out, followed by Bunt, still screaming instructions as he moved to the next stable.

Harry took one more look at the distressed colt and immediately understood. He darted into the stable, tethered the horse so he couldn't throw himself around, and as soon as he emerged into the daylight started barking commands to his stable staff and anyone else who knew how to handle a horse. The crowd scattered, many people simply standing with their backs to the stables and watching the melee of stable staff and horses that quickly established themselves in front of them. Within half a minute, there were eighteen horses out of their boxes, some in the hands of stable staff, others being held by novice handlers and a few with no head collars wandering freely around the stabling block.

'Keep them away from the water,' Bunt shouted at the top of his voice as he ran back down the stabling block, heading for the smaller bottom yard.

Harry fired an order at Mike to open the top paddock gate. Mike was already holding a couple of yearlings and he dutifully trotted them to the top of the yard and swung the three-barred gate open. Once he had his two in there, he rushed over to the smaller, side paddock and opened that gate too. A minute later, twelve colts and geldings were roaming the top paddock area, cheek to jowl with each other and the twenty-four cars which had been parked in there by the open day attendees. A further ten fillies were circling the side paddock. Mike jumped into each paddock and cut the water supply to the troughs and stood protecting them until some straw bales could be laid over the top of them to keep the horses away.

More horses came up the yard. Bunt and Wang brought the first two up, with the rest following closely afterwards, handled by Jill, Rory and Zoe. Each animal was directed to the only two paddocks close to the stabling block, split dependent on gender.

Harry glanced at Mike. 'It was quick thinking to divide them up, thanks Mi…'

Harry stood stock still mid sentence, his eyes unfocussed, thinking. He fished out his mobile phone and made a call to his vet in Malton.

'Nigel, its Harry. Can you get all the available vets down to Pickering Farm. Call a couple of other surgeries too and get them down here, we could have multiple colic cases across four yards.'

He cut the call off after waiting for a confirming reply and immediately gave new instructions to several of the younger staff around him to run to the other three yards based around Pickering Farm.

'The horses have to be kept away from any trough with water on demand and humans shouldn't drink the water either. Get them to cut the water off and wait until the vets come. If there's no one around, knock on every door and every window. If you still can't raise anyone, get the horses into a nearby paddock as soon as you can and cover the water troughs.'

Several members of the open day crowd gasped, realisation dawning on them. The words 'contamination' and 'poisoned' started to be spoken in hushed tones. It was Jill who recognised the danger and dealt with it. She disappeared around the corner of the top stable and returned dragging a bale of plastic-wrapped wood chippings. She placed it in the middle of the yard and jumped onto it.

'Everyone! Everyone, please!' she yelled at the top of her voice.

'As you've probably realised it looks like the water supply to this whole area has some sort of contaminant in it. It's probably just an overdose of chlorine, but we have to ensure the horses don't drink any more. Vets are on their way. Can I ask you all to follow me to the schooling and lunging ring until we can rescue your cars.'

This was greeted with a lot of nodding and acceptance, although a couple of grumbles did emanate from the likes of Mrs Billington, which Jill resolutely ignored. Sixty-five people followed Jill down to the entrance to the yard and then over into their schooling paddock.

Heaving a sigh of relief once the crowd has dispersed, Harry sent every remaining member of staff up to the two paddocks to check and monitor whether any of the horses were showing signs of colic. Then he dived back into the darkness of the yearling's box. The colt had lather building under his front legs and was producing regular grunt-like snorts down his nose.

*****

The carriage clock on the mantelpiece was heading towards midnight when the last of the vets finally pulled out of Pickering Farm on the day of Harry Bolt's inaugural open morning. Jill sat in the kitchen, among a mountain of plastic bottles and several huge empty gallon drums of bottled water. She had smears of dirt over her cheeks but these were now being broken up and washed clean by a growing torrent of tears borne out of frustration and anger.

Wang and Bunt stood at the back of the kitchen, gripping mugs of tea and watching grimly as Harry tried to console and calm his wife. They shared a knowing glance and remained silent.

'It's not fair,' Jill insisted angrily. 'We didn't lose anything, but I bet it was us they were after!'

Harry tried to find helpful words but there was little to say and nothing that could come close to mending the situation. The last vet to leave had said it all: 'It could have been much worse. Whoever put the poison into the borehole also managed to bash the cut off taps for the two yards at the bottom of the hill, so they didn't get anything sent through. The water filter your man Bunt had installed a month ago was also a godsend. It reduced the effect of the poison on your horses. The Denmark yard next door wasn't as lucky; they received a more concentrated dose. There are two horses in their paddocks that look like they may not make it through the night. There are still another four horses with colic-like symptoms scattered around and you're lucky no humans drank the water. It wouldn't have killed anyone, but you'd have a pretty bad stomach ache.'

The pesticide poured into the borehole's holding tank had been worst for the two horses closest to the water source, as they got the most undiluted dose. As for the rest of the equine residents in the cluster yards, it was the young and weak horses, or those recovering from surgery or injury that felt the worst effects. Bunt's program of improvements had saved Harry's yards from serious damage; all the yearlings had bounced back quickly once they got fresh clean bottled water into them. Moira Denmark's yard had been hit the hardest.

The trainers in the cluster of small yards were valued friends and the four stables rubbed alongside each other well enough in their own small community. Any equine loss was a major blow, never mind multiple horses losing their ability to race again. While Harry's horses had suffered mild effects, his next-door neighbour, Moira Denmark, had almost lost one of her yearlings and the two older horses closest to the source in the paddock were still suffering from symptoms of colic. Harry and the rest of his staff had spent most of the day going around to Mo's to help where they could, supplying clean water or trying to ease the discomfort of ailing horses.

Mike opened the back door without knocking and came in with a face like thunder, hardly able to contain himself. However, on seeing Jill's ruddy, tear stained face he broke down, his anger dissolving into sobs he desperately tried to hold back. He took a few moments to wipe away the evidence and steadied himself before relaying his news.

'I've just spoken with Mo next door. She's in bits. Her eight-year-old stable star was in the bottom paddock. The gelding was down there recovering from wind surgery and almost died of asphyxiation because the poison attacked his throat and it contracted so much he couldn't breathe properly. He'll need weeks, if not months of rehabilitation.'

Mike was snarling through gritted teeth now. 'A small yard like hers can't cope with this sort of thing. It's plain evil,' he added bitterly.

Harry blinked away the welling tears in his own eyes. The emotion Mike had brought into the room had tipped him over the edge and he took some time to fight back a potent mixture of raw sadness and anger.

'Does she need any more help?' he managed to get out eventually.

Mike sighed and shook his head.

Tired, Harry got to his feet in an ungainly manner and pulled a chair out from the table, indicating for Mike to take a seat and join them; however, Mike waved the offer away.

'I'm too angry. And fed up and…' Mike took a deep intake of breath and shuddered as another wave of emotion engulfed him.

'Need a lift home?' Wang offered, closing the distance between him and the retiree with some speed. 'It's been a very long day.'

Mike cast his eyes to the floor and nodded sadly. He looked up at Harry and Jill and asked 'That okay with you, Guv'nor?' only to find Jill rising from the table and rushing over to hug him tightly.

'That's fine Mike. Come over tomorrow afternoon if you want, you can check over the horses with me,' Harry said quietly.

Once Mike and Wang had left, Jill made her excuses and also headed to bed. Harry waited until she was well out of earshot before turning to Bunt.

'How the hell did *you* know before me?' he demanded.

Bunt sat down at the table opposite the trainer and leant on one elbow, his hand supporting the side of his head. He looked washed-out.

'I just put things together. Wang had seen someone jumping over a fence down the lane thirty minutes previously. We've got it on video, all you can see is a grainy figure run over the field and nip over a three-bar fence and disappear. Nothing too strange about that, it could have been anyone, and it wasn't on your land either.'

Bunt took another sip of his tea and continued, 'I'm sorry Harry, it took me a few minutes to click that the borehole that feeds these buildings is in that paddock. We should have been quicker to realise the danger. When I saw you looking worried, I put two and two together.'

Harry wiped a hand slowly down his face, an action aimed to rid him of a nagging headache and allow him to concentrate. He considered Bunt across the table. His silver hair was matted and there was a mixture of water splashes and dust all over his shoulders as a result of bottle-feeding the horses in their stables. The wrinkles around the middle-aged man's eyes had become grey rings.

'Is this Manton's work?'

'Almost certainly,' confirmed Bunt. 'Who else wants your yearlings dead?'

'He can't be that desperate to win a single race that he has to go to these sorts of lengths…'

'It's not the Gimcrack, Harry!' Bunt broke in, suddenly animated and unable to mask a hint of anger. 'Redblood must have had something on Manton, or possessed something Manton wants, or is just desperate to keep him quiet. Manton's made the connection between the two of you and this is his sick way of letting you know.'

Harry's eyebrows drew together and his bottom lip turned up in determined contemplation as he allowed this statement to swirl around his mind. He looked hard at Bunt and a jolt went through him as he recognised a flicker of conflict in the security man.

'There's more to this revenge than making a speech at York racecourse. More than a suspicious death at the end of our lane… *isn't there?*' Harry asked quietly but insistently.

Bunt pushed his half-finished mug of tea into the centre of the table and sighed. He liked Harry and Jill. The job was engaging and far better than protecting self-absorbed businessmen or shady politicians. Harry deserved to know what he knew, but by sharing it, could he consign the two of them and their unborn baby into even deeper danger? He considered for a few more moments and made his decision.

'You've got to win the Gimcrack, Harry. You've got too much to lose if a rat like Manton decides you're getting in his way. Win the race, or give it up and walk away now. Redblood has placed all of us in danger, something he had no right to do. Whatever his game is, you don't have to play it.'

Bunt paused and studied the young man in front of him, trying to work out if Harry was registering his words and their meaning. It was well known that Harry was a man of few words. However, Bunt had him pegged as a deep thinker too.

'You've probably had your suspicions already but I can tell you now - Manton will not think twice about killing you and your family. If it serves his purposes, and he can get away with it, you will die.'

Harry wore a stunned expression, unable to take his eyes from Bunt's earnest face.

'He's a criminal, Harry, and his associates are extremely dangerous men. I did my research before I took this job, so I knew what I was taking on. It's rumoured Manton has a hand in pretty much all of the organised crime down the east coast of England.'

Bunt fell silent again, watching Harry carefully, looking for telltale signs of emotion in his dark face, hoping he'd made the right decision.

'That's why you're here, isn't it,' Harry stated after a short period where the two men simply examined each other across the table. 'You're not here to protect the horses, you're here to protect us… the staff, Jill… and me.'

'We're here to make sure your family and friends don't come to any harm, but that does include the horses – all the horses,' Bunt corrected.

'But you're right,' he added. 'Redblood's instructions to us were extremely specific. Your protection comes before the horses.'

Again, the two men lost themselves in thought. A floorboard creaked above them, indicating Jill was walking across the bedroom and Harry, breaking eye contact, yawned.

'I'm too tired to think about this,' he admitted. 'I'm going to bed.'

Bunt was thrown for a second, expecting more from the younger man. Nevertheless, he swallowed his disappointment, nodded and got up to leave as well.

'Wang and I will be taking it in turns to monitor the yard. We'll be out in the stables tonight and we've spoken to the other trainers; we'll be making the borehole secure tomorrow to make sure it can't happen again,' he said in parting.

Harry's hand was on the doorknob to the lounge when he stopped and turned to face Bunt, but concentrated his gaze on the kitchen floor as he spoke. 'Thanks for what you did today.'

Bunt acknowledged the compliment with a sad smile and an inclination of his head, expecting this to be Harry's parting words. Instead, he continued.

'I think Redblood chose each person quite carefully before getting them mixed up in his weird plan. Maybe every single one of us is already too deeply invested to turn away.'

Harry lifted his eyes and caught Bunt wearing an uncomfortable expression. It hung there for a moment, to be replaced by his professional deadpan stare, but Harry saw something new and different in Bunt's eyes which the older man couldn't easily shift.

Bunt sucked in a deep breath and slowly exhaled down his nose before he replied.

'If you're right, we're going to have to see it through.'

Bunt started to open the back door, but stopped himself, as if just remembering something.

In a much lighter tone he said 'Oh. Have a word with Rory will you. He rode in a race against one of Manton's horses' yesterday at Ripon. Wang thought one of Manton's men spoke to Rory in the parade ring. It could be worth you checking with him, just in case it's useful. Okay, goodnight.'

Harry's eyelids were already half closed, and so he muttered a stock reply before going through the lounge door and straight up the stairs. He peeled off his clothes with thoughts of jumping into a hot shower when he remembered he couldn't. Cursing Manton once more, he was about to join Jill in bed when a thought struck him. The poison which had been added to the water had been most effective on the youngsters. He'd assumed that meant the yearlings. What if it wasn't the young horses Manton had meant to kill, and instead it was young humans?

He looked toward the slumbering lump under the duvet on the

right-hand side of the bed and bit his lip as he watched the bedclothes rise and fall with Jill's breathing. A surge of panic suddenly jangled through him. His breathing quickened and he could feel his heartbeat banging in his throat. He pulled his clothes back on and ran downstairs.

Harry fell asleep later that night after cuddling up close to Jill, but not before he had padded around every room in the farmhouse, checking every window and locking and re-locking both the front and back doors. He found Millie dozing in her basket and just to be sure, took her upstairs with him.

*****

Harry woke to the sound movement in the bedroom. He immediately wrenched the bedclothes off, jumped up and stumbled to the light switch, flicking it on. Jill sat on the side of the bed, hands clasped to her chest and staring wide-eyed at him. She tried to blink them away but Harry saw tears forming in both her eyes.

Jill wasn't the type to turn on tears for effect, something which Harry had encountered with other girls, and been a sucker for, in his youth. So the fact his wife was crying at all, never mind in the dark, made his natural empathy kick in immediately. Quietly, Harry moved over, sat down beside her, and whispered, 'What is it?' He fought the urge to immediately clasp her to him, she needed to talk, to get this… whatever it was… out.

She rubbed both eyes with her palms and sat, looking small and vulnerable in her nightshirt, her bare feet touching the carpet, twisting on her toes.

'I think it was my fault,' she managed to get out after swallowing hard and calming herself.

'What, the poisoning? No, that's…'

'I got a phone call,' she interrupted. 'Yesterday evening. He called when you were out playing a piano gig. It was a man, an older man I think, judging on his voice, he started speaking really quietly, asking about horses and the yard, then suddenly he said '*Tell me about Redblood.*''

Jill's breath caught in her throat as she filled her lungs and she issued a dry cough.

'Then he started to ask how Redblood was connected to you and the yard, and what did he say when he came over that day, you know, the day he died. When I told him I didn't know what he was talking about he shouted, '*Oh I think you do, Mrs Bolt!*' Now I can't get that out of my head.'

Jill was shaking. Harry had to restrain himself from trying to wrap her immediately in his arms and comfort her.

'Then he started telling me he was going to hurt the horses unless I told him what he wanted to know. He was shouting about someone called

Billy Redblood. He said '*Where is he, you bitch? And where's the memory stick? Tell me or the horses will get it...*' I just slammed the phone down.'

Jill's voice caught, she swallowed and issued a frustrated sigh. Harry noticed her clenched fists on her lap, it seemed in anger rather than fear. She stared fiercely at him.

'I'm not going to let them beat us!'

'*We're* not going to let them beat us,' Harry reiterated.

Jill's features softened and Harry succumbed, wrapping his wife in his arms and hugging her close.

'I've got rid of the memory stick anyway, we didn't need it any longer, besides, I knew the contents by heart,' Harry told her. 'Have you told anyone else about this?'

'No, I was going to say something to you or Bunt this morning, but then we were so busy with the open day, and I forgot about it.'

Harry gave his wife another squeeze, speaking softly. 'Don't worry, even if you'd said something, we couldn't have known what they were planning. Come on, try to get some sleep, things will look better tomorrow.'

He guided Jill back to bed then got in beside her. An hour later he was still wide-awake lying beside her, listening to her breathing, and sporadic twitching as she endured a fitful sleep. Harry stared at the ceiling, his mind swirling with the day's events. Frustrated, he sat up, swung his legs out of bed, and shook his head, desperate to rid himself of another re-run of the poisoning. It seemed to be playing in his brain on a continuous loop. Millie sat up in her makeshift bed on the floor and tilted her head slightly to one side to regard him, her curiosity making her appear a touch comedic. Harry's smiled back at her, and with his mind suddenly flushed of dark thoughts, he determined a course of action.

Padding quietly downstairs he flicked the back room lights on and dragged the small wastepaper basket out from under his work desk. Scrabbling around in the bottom of the basket, his hand closed over the item he was seeking. He took a mallet from his toolbox, unlocked the back door, set Redblood's memory stick on the back step and struck it until the inch-long bit of technology was in several pieces and flattened beyond use. He smashed the plastic and tin stick a few more times for good measure before realising he was being watched. Looking back over his shoulder Millie was stood, that same curious look on her face.

Harry gave the dog his very best naughty schoolboy expression.

'Let them try and use that!' he told Millie triumphantly.

Twenty-One

The East Yorkshire countryside rolled past but Gwent was in no mood to appreciate the splendour of arable fields covered in frost. She'd insisted the car radio was switched off as the morning show DC Poole favoured had given her a headache. The DJ's constantly upbeat and sparky persona didn't agree with her. Poole's driving was also getting on her nerves. He was being so cautious she'd barked at him to get his foot down twice already. It was as if he was transporting his great-grandmother, fearful a single bump could give her palpitations.

Gwent was still in two minds whether dropping into Harry Bolt's yard was sensible, given her history on the case. The roasting she'd endured from her superior over the debacle when tracking Billy Redblood was still fresh in her mind and she winced involuntarily at the memory of the dressing down. Re-visiting the Bolt yard once again, this time on the basis of a bit of ex-employee revenge, would be regarded as a weak reason for wasting more time on the case. Yet here she was, like a moth to the flame.

The thought of that fortnight on the road spent chasing up the leads from the Redblood case made her shudder all over again. She'd scratched her itch, and drawn blood.

David Salmon, the one odd interviewee on Laya Bolt's original investigation hadn't been hard to find, he popped up immediately as a law-abiding citizen, still living in Malton. She and Poole had waltzed into Morrison's supermarket in the centre of town and found him serving behind the butcher's counter, a job he'd held for the past fifteen years. Now a forty-nine year old, in the flesh he could have passed for seventy. A heavy smoker, he'd managed to get through three cigarettes in the ten minutes they'd questioned him under the smoking shelter outside the back of the store. Gwent swallowed hard at the memory; his smokers cough had put Gwent off buying Morrison's tomato sausages for weeks afterwards.

'No idea what y'er talkin about love,' Salmon had related phlegmatically through a cloud of smoke.

'S'nowt to do wi me,' he'd added with a blank look which Gwent had recognised as almost certainly truthful. Mr Salmon may be killing himself slowly with tobacco, but she couldn't believe he'd been involved with the Manton mafia, even at the age of twenty. He didn't fit the profile. However, it emerged he had known the Redblood brothers and Warren, Doyle and Manton; he was the same age and had gone through school from infants to secondary modern with them. But he'd not laid eyes on any of them for almost thirty years.

'Did you know William, er, 'Billy' Redblood,' she'd asked.

'Aye, Tom's brother. He beggared off t'smoke.'

The revelation that the Manton bunch had clearly colluded in a lie to protect a fourth party spurred the investigation on. They'd all claimed to be at The Hornet's Nest pub for the rest of the night, so there was plenty of time to construct the false identity and get their stories straight. Quite why they had needed to construct the lie wasn't clear though. However, it was clear that Salmon was a dead end.

She and Poole had also gone after Billy Redblood, discovering he'd been to London in 1994, working in several pubs under the name Martin Jones. They'd visited his address in Gravesend, a bed and breakfast where the proprietor remembered him clearly as a bit of a 'weird one' who left for Wales with 'some girl'. Next, he'd turned up in Llandudno, working in amusement arcades for a season, under the same name. After that it was up to Newcastle to visit a council flat in Byker. There was no sign of Billy there and a visit to the civic centre and the rent records section had him moving again, along with another change of name, over to the west. He'd ended up in a suburb of Carlisle called Denton Holme which Gwent had hoped would be the final lap of their search. The name he'd given for his rental deposit to be returned was Benjamin W Williams.

They'd travelled to Carlisle from Hull on a Friday, battling through the morning traffic and finally reaching the other side of the country at midday. There was no Ben W Williams recorded on the census in the area or anyone paying council tax or income tax, but perhaps he'd dropped the W, as there were a number of Williams resident in that area of the city. Denton Holme covered a dozen streets; they'd simply have to do the legwork.

Denton Street was surprisingly busy, boasting a thriving community of diverse shops. What had looked like a small area on Google was in fact street after street of back-to-back housing. Poole had slipped the car into the curb of a cobbled side street and turned expectantly to Gwent.

'You take the right-hand side, I'll do the left.' Gwent had instructed. 'Meet you at the top of the street.'

An hour and a half later their search for Redblood or Williams was no further forward. Every shop and business had been systematically visited including launderettes, pubs, estate agents, takeaways, supermarkets, and florists. Poole had run out of options on his side of the road and emerged from a fast food takeaway just in time to see Gwent reach the final shop on her side – a Coral betting shop.

Entering a betting shop was a new experience for Gwent. When he was still alive, her father had been a Saturday punter in the days when the ITV seven was all the rage. She'd never found any joy in gambling; a pound or two in the office Grand National sweepstake was as much as she would indulge. Besides, there were plenty of alternative guilty pleasures Gwent enjoyed, losing money to bookmakers could wait. She was nonetheless fascinated to discover the oblong shaped shop with deep green carpets and an array of flat screen televisions was well populated with locals when she stepped inside. As the steel door clicked shut behind her it seemed the entire clientele and staff behind the counter turned to regard Gwent, as if she was treading on hallowed ground.

Unfazed, she had approached the counter and waited behind a large balding man. He was being served by a sharp-eyed cashier who was ringing through betting slips as the punter laid them on top of the raised green laminate counter. The shop smelled slightly fusty, cut through by the tang of disinfectant and Gwent noticed the carpet was covered in cigarette burns, despite it being illegal to smoke indoors.

'I'd like to speak with you and a few of your customers,' she had told the cashier quietly, flicking her warrant card open.

The cashier had peered over the top of her glasses at Gwent and then inspected her credentials. With a distinctly unimpressed cluck she then spun around on her chair to address an untidy man in his early twenties who was seated behind a built-in desk, also decked out in the corporate green.

Fed up with waiting, Gwent had raised her voice and locking eyes with the young man asked, 'I'm looking for either Ben Williams or Billy Redblood.'

The betting shop had fallen completely silent, save for the burbling commentary from some fictitious computer-generated horse race. The young man got up from his desk and came to the counter. He seemed amiable enough, wore a genuine smile and Gwent realised he was still young enough not to be afflicted with the mistrust of the police the middle-aged cashier had displayed. Despite wearing a shirt and tie his overall profile was one of grubbiness and Gwent was immediately seized with a mothering instinct and the urge to give him some hygiene advice.

She'd pushed these thoughts away and asked again.

'Ben or Benny Williams?'

The shop manager had shrugged and answered, 'Sorry, doesn't ring a bell. What about you Glenys?'

The cashier shook her head and indicated to Gwent to step aside so she could accept a betting slip from an old man with a stick who had shuffled up behind her.

'What about you, John, heard of this bloke?' the young man had asked the octogenarian who was counting out silver coins.

'Jimmy's yer man,' John had replied without looking up from his exercise in addition. However, he did hoist a thumb over his shoulder and Gwent had examined the corner of the shop.

'In the dark coat. Sitting with his back to us,' the betting shop manager had indicated. 'He's the one with the small black dog.'

Five minutes later, with Poole in tow, Gwent had walked, as agreed, three paces behind Jimmy as he made his way through the back streets of Denton Holme. He was a bent over pensioner with a serious back problem and he and his small, yappy black terrier had eventually led the two police officers down a cobbled street with terraced houses running along both sides. Net curtains had twitched as they passed some of the bay windows and Gwent had smiled inwardly as she followed the old man, recognising the same insular nature that typified her own hometown.

Jimmy and his canine companion had reached the middle of the street, slowed and took a few steps toward the kerb. As he stood beside the line of parked cars a single finger from his pocketed left hand had poked out and pointed to a blue door behind him. Without a second look he'd shambled across the road, only pausing to allow his dog to urinate against a car wheel and subsequently disappeared down a thin, arched alleyway cut into the terrace.

Gwent had given the house a cursory inspection before knocking on the door. Her urgent raps had seemed to resonate down the valley of houses and more nets had been swept aside to eyeball them. When after thirty seconds there had been no response, she'd tried again, adopting a greater resonance in her knock. Poole had stepped back to inspect the two windows above: both curtains drawn shut. The curtains at the ground floor bay window had been almost fully drawn across, revealing nothing extraordinary. He'd given Gwent a disappointed shrug. On turning to face the door once again something struck Poole as a little peculiar in the gap between the curtains and he was about to comment on it when Gwent knocked for a third time. There had been a scuffling noise from above, followed by a regular thump as someone bounced down the stairs.

The door had swung open to reveal a man with wet hair standing in nothing, save a yellowing white towel around his waist. He'd been wearing a rather grumpy look on his face. Understanding had rushed at Poole. The handle on the front door had been noticeably low, there were long, thin draw rods on the curtains, and a large flat screen television was hung desperately low on the front room wall. The man in front of them was three feet tall.

'Mr Williams?' Gwent had asked uncertainly.

'Yes?' the diminutive householder had replied in an unexpectedly gravelly voice.

'Mr Benjamin W Williams?' she'd tried again.

'Yes!'

Gwent had flashed her ID and asked if she and Poole could come in. The small man had looked them up and down and then indicated his current state of dress.

'Can't we get this over with on the doorstep?'

'Well, it would be better…' Gwent had started.

'Are you looking for a Mr Blueblood or Green… something or other?'

127

Gwent had pierced the little man with an intense stare. 'Does a Mr Redblood live here?'

'No, there's just me and my wife. Look, I used to be Martin Jones, I changed my name when I started appearing in panto's. Too many Martin Jones' already in the business, eh. But like I told the others, I'm not called Redblood and I've no idea who he is.'

'You've had calls from other people asking for Redblood?' Gwent had asked.

Williams had given an irritated snort. 'Yep, one tall bloke a fortnight ago who went away laughing and then two nasty pieces of work just yesterday who got really angry when this Redblood chap wasn't here. They really upset our Maureen, so I could do with you leaving pronto.'

Gwent sat in the passenger seat of the car half an hour later, picking disinterestedly at her Greggs cheese and onion pasty. The whole trail had been a setup, someone's idea of a joke, most probably Billy Redblood's. At some point he'd managed to swap his details with Martin Jones, knowing the actor's career choice would make him difficult to track down. Jones had worked in an amusement arcade in Llandudno during the summers, but also appeared for two winter seasons in a production of Snow White which had toured Wales.

'At least we've got a decent description of the men also after William Redblood,' Poole had commented between mouthfuls of Cornish pasty.

'So someone else has been trying to find him. It could be the executor of Redblood's will for all we know. Even if it's Manton's men, there's no solid evidence they were here.'

The two police officers had headed back to Hull, Gwent gently snoring for most of the way; Poole driving much quicker when his boss was asleep.

Gwent had been aware that the cost of the investigation into Redblood was starting to look poor value for money, so in desperation she and Poole had sought out Manton at his Lincolnshire house. She'd found it to be on the large side, but certainly not luxurious, which didn't quite fit with her view of the man. They'd quizzed him about his false statement regarding the Laya Bolt death and of course he had shrugged and suggested Salmon was lying or had simply forgotten the facts 'with him being a bit thick' as Manton had eloquently described his ex-schoolmate. With Doyle and Warren there to back him up, Gwent's investigation had hit a dead end. That was until Harry Bolt's stables got hit with pesticide poisoning.

The news of two racehorses almost dying at the hands of person's unknown had hit the local news and inevitably bled into social media. Being a member of stable staff wasn't a role which held much guarantee of long-term employment and the industry was notorious for its turnover of staff. It had been strongly suggested in the media reports that ex-employee revenge was the most likely motive.

Gwent scratched the back of her hand with her fingernails, mulling over the various threads of the Redblood case, as outside her window the Wolds gave way to rolling countryside signalling their entry into the Vale of York.

She considered: I've got Redblood in the mortuary after visiting Bolt, appearing to have died in the same way Harry's mother did twenty-four years previously with no sign of a syringe anywhere near him. Harry leads me to his adoptive mother, who reveals Redblood has a younger brother and then I spend the best part of a month trying to track the brother down. Just as I'm led to a dead end, there's suddenly more trouble at the Bolt stables which requires me to investigate.

'Poole?'

'Yes, Ma'am.'

'What do you think of this Redblood case?'

Poole's astonishment doubled-down and he was lost for words. Gwent watched the face of her DC with unashamed interest. His features travelled through several layers of astonishment, delight, and consternation in quick succession before he blurted out, 'You want my opinion?'

'Yes, I believe that's what I asked for.'

Poole gathered himself, slowing the car as he concentrated. 'Well, I'm confused... er, I don't mean with the case, rather with the fact that every time we get a break, it feels like we're being... misdirected somehow.'

Gwent nodded encouragement. 'Continue.'

'Billy Redblood seems to hold the key, as he could implicate Manton in Laya Bolt's death, but it seems the harder we look, the further away we are from finding him. Then we have Harry Bolt who is plainly involved somehow, but again, it's difficult to pinpoint exactly how he fits into the death. He's at the centre of this, yet he appears to have no motive, quite the opposite in fact.'

Poole fell silent and Gwent stared out over the bonnet of the Ford. He'd got used to these moments with Gwent, and knew better than to interrupt her thoughts, so he waited patiently. He'd come off the A64 and was heading towards Norton when she spoke again, a full five minutes later.

'You know, Poole, being around me might be starting to rub off on you.'

Poole's face started to break into a grin; however, he caught it early and managed to stifle any sign of his pleasure in her response. Instead he gazed at the road ahead and replied, 'Thank you, Ma'am.'

Presently they passed the verge where Redblood had been found and turned off the main Norton-Beverley road into the small, self-contained community of racehorse trainers. Poole stopped the car. In front of them were four single-track roads, each leading to a different training yard. Every stable was indicated on its own signpost. Poole looked over to Gwent and raised a questioning eyebrow.

'Bolt,' she commanded. 'Pickering Farm first.'

Gwent took in the yard as they pulled into a newly painted parking bay on fresh-looking tarmac in front of the farmhouse. There had been some significant changes since she had called in after Redblood's death. Particularly noteworthy were the new security features, including an automated gate and several cameras adorning the top of the stabling blocks. It was noticeably far busier as well. She pushed her passenger door open with a foot and awkwardly clambered out, looking around. Shivering, she scratched the back of her neck, feeling disconcerted by the discovery of an overt change in fortunes at Harry's yard.

A silver-haired man came out to greet them, introduced himself as Mr Bunt and offered to walk them up the yard. He'd plainly been expecting them. Gwent had counted four people working in the bottom yard and the top yard boasted another three staff dodging in and out of stables. There were horses' heads poking out of every stable door as far as she could make out.

They found Harry inside a stable. Gwent, Poole and Bunt stood at the open door and watched as Harry stood crooning into the face of a horse, soothing him while the vet ran his hands under the large horse. The colt was stamping its feet in an agitated manner and snorting.

'Is it just me, or is this chap becoming a bit het up?' Gwent offered in greeting.

Harry twirled round and gave a broad smile. 'Inspector! Good to see you. You're absolutely right about this one; he's just about to be gelded. I think I'd be slightly nervous in the same circumstances!'

Gwent shuddered and looked to Poole who seemed to be fascinated and couldn't take his eyes off Harry.

'They get a better standard of life when they're gelded; it means they don't have all that testosterone running around their bodies and they get more paddock time because you can put them out with the fillies and the mares,' Harry explained.

'I'm not so sure he would agree,' Gwent muttered inclining her head towards the colt.

'So you'll be taking him to a vet for surgery then?' Poole asked.

'Oh no. We're just going to give him a sedative, he'll lock his legs, and John here will do him standing up,' replied Harry matter-of-factly.

Poole scrunched his face up. 'But isn't it an operation?'

'More of a cut, a quick squeeze and out they come.'

'You mean they literally…'

'Pop out? Yes, that's about it,' Harry interjected with the flicker of a cheeky smile.

'Blimey,' cooed Poole, shaking his head.

Gwent cleared her throat as the vet drew a syringe up in his plastic-gloved hand.

'I could do with a word with you, Mr Bolt, when you've er… *finished* in here.'

She stepped back out into the yard and pulled Poole out with her.

'Two minutes,' Harry called from deep inside the stable.

Bunt, satisfied the Inspector and her companion weren't a threat of any kind, voiced the need to get back to the bottom yard and extracted himself from the task of introduction, but not before Gwent tackled him.

'I don't think I've met you before. Are you…'

'Stable Manager,' beamed Bunt standing bolt upright. 'Now that Harry has expanded, I'm here to look after the staff and the horses both here and at the races.'

Gwent took a careful look at Bunt and got the feeling there was depth to this man. He was certainly more than a meet and greet type. Far more. She watched him march back down the two lines of stables and out of sight. Military she thought, or perhaps police? No, it was definitely the forces – there was that touch of ingrained precision about him.

Harry came out of the stable. 'You made any progress on the Redblood case?'

Gwent sighed 'No, I'm afraid not. We're here to discuss the poisoning of the two horses.'

Harry's face fell and he took on a haunted look. 'Yeah, I thought someone would call from the authorities, but thought it would be the racing lot, not you.'

'I'm surprised it's not been reported to your local police,' Gwent said this with genuine interest in her tone and watched Harry's reaction closely.

'Probably someone is trying to get back at one of us. I thought Mo would have reported it – her horses were the worst affected,' he answered carefully.

Gwent winced at Harry's answer. What a hopeless liar she thought, but let it go – for now.

'Is Jill around?'

'Yes, she's in the farmhouse, but she's not too well.'

'Don't worry, I'll be quick.'

Gwent turned on her heel and being careful to avoid a horse being led up the yard, she stumped off, leaving Poole and Harry to share an exasperated glance before breaking into a jog to catch up with her.

'It appears you are on the up,' Gwent remarked to Jill, once the four of them were standing in the kitchen.

Jill looked worse for wear. She sported red rings around her eyes and her skin had a pallid, grey sheen to it. Gwent almost said something, but thought better of it.

'Yes, we've been lucky. We managed to attract a few new owners and rescued a couple of others. It's been hard but we're making it work.'

She smiled weakly and Harry came over to her side.

'I should explain that Jill is eight weeks pregnant and she's finding the morning sickness pretty tough…'

'I'm fine. Really,' she insisted.

Gwent sniffed and congratulated both of them. It made what she was about to say even more difficult.

'Listen you two. I know there's something going on here. I can smell it from Hull,' she fired at them.

'The sudden increase in horses; a military man looking after your security…'

She left this hanging, waiting to see if it elicited any response. All she received was a stony silence and two poker faces.

'… tell me, have you heard of, or met, a William or Billy Redblood?'

Harry produced an angelic look toward his wife and shrugged. Jill looked into Harry's big brown eyes and drew herself up beside him.

'Really Inspector, there's nothing I… *I mean we* can report. We've been sent these horses and asked to train them. One of the requests from the owner was that we increased security and Mr Bunt was recommended. We did meet Thomas Redblood, but no other Redblood.'

'And the poisoning was just ex-stable staff getting revenge?' Gwent asked. She was in a sardonic frame of mind now and allowed her cynicism to bubble up.

'If it wasn't for Mr Bunt, there would have been many more poorly horses,' Harry stated, a little too stridently for Gwent's liking. They were hiding something. She tried a different tack, adopting a softer tone.

'Look, if someone is putting pressure on you, we can help.'

She indicated herself and Poole and immediately wished she hadn't. It looked a weak proposition, Poole stood looking like a goofy young apprentice and she was, well, an overweight and possibly over-the-hill detective who was skating on thin ice even being here.

Jill answered quickly. 'Really, Mrs Gwent…'

'DI,' Gwent interrupted, more from automated reaction than any sort of petulance. However Jill appeared to assume the latter.

'I'm sorry, *DI Gwent*,' she continued in a voice dripping with annoyance. 'Racing is full of characters, little mysteries and, yes, a few stupid people who do really horrid things, and we get affected by our fair share just like everyone else. But really, *there is nothing* we can tell you. If I could get my hands on who poisoned those horses, I would be straight on the phone to the police, but frankly, I think Mo hasn't reported it because it will hurt her business – who wants to have horses with a trainer who has just had two almost die on her land?'

Jill seemed to slump a little into her husband's arms after this diatribe and Harry suddenly looked perturbed. Holding onto her he gestured for Poole to pull out a chair and Jill gratefully slipped into it.

Gwent sucked her teeth and nodded at Poole, indicating their exit was imminent.

'We'll leave you now,' she muttered irritably. 'But when you want to tell me what's going on - *and you will at some point* - call me. Just don't leave it too late. The earlier I know, the more likely I can help.'

She tossed a couple of her business cards over the kitchen table. Finally, with a tinge of regret in her voice she added, 'I hope the morning sickness improves, Mrs Bolt, and Harry, please give Mrs Warcup my regards.'

Once Gwent's old Ford had reversed out of the yard and disappeared down the lane, Jill let out a scream of frustration.

'That woman doesn't give up!'

'Well, you could argue that's her job,' Harry replied in a careful tone.

Jill harrumphed, and looking up at her husband, pursed her lips as she started to deflate. She flashed him a grudgingly accepting look and Harry watched, fascinated, as the anger subsided within her.

Harry found himself pondering the incredibly high number of strong-willed women in his life. He was suddenly struck by the realisation that Gwent and Jill possessed some very similar character traits. Gwent was right, though, he might need her assistance at some point. Jill may be strong enough to dismiss intimidating phone calls and stride onward, but she might not be as undaunted once she had their baby in her arms. Harry returned to the kitchen table and picked up one of Gwent's business cards, tucking the small, rectangular piece of shiny card into his wallet.

Twenty-Two

'You did *what*?' screamed Manton at Loretta and Warren. The two men stood in front of Manton's expansive, leather topped desk with heads bowed slightly, Warren with his hands behind his back; two schoolboys being scolded by the headmaster.

Manton picked up a brass bust of a racehorse's head from a display cabinet and made his way around his desk to stand in front of the two men. He hefted the trophy from one hand to the other, its weight making a slapping sound as he transferred it from palm to palm. Warren tried to resist the urge to take a backward step; there was a malicious gleam in Manton's eye he knew only too well.

He'd briefed Loretta before they got back from their fortnight-long flit around Britain in search of Redblood's brother and his medical accomplice, Gupta. Cringing subservience was the order of the day when reporting bad news to Manton. No eye contact and above all, stay silent. He'd drilled this into the young giant and sincerely hoped he'd gotten through to the lad. Manton was in explosive mode by the look and sound of him, easily his most dangerous mood.

'The Doc is gone and is nowhere to be found, you find Billy Redblood but he's turned into a *bloody dwarf,* and then you think that killing a couple of horses and shouting Billy Redblood's name down a phone at Bolt's wife is going to solve everything?' Manton roared.

Doyle sat in the background, leaning back on a reclining chair, his hands entwined delicately on his chest. He was watching Manton carefully.

Manton held the trophy by its base in one hand and stroked it with the other, staring at Warren and Loretta standing forlornly in front of him. He made a show of flipping it over and gripping the horse's mane, holding the square green baize base up to the men's eye level and shaking it.

'I ought to kill both of you,' Manton spat, fizzing with rage and waggling the trophy in their faces. 'You're *stupid…*' he barked into Loretta's chest before moving to Warren '…and you're just bloody useless,' he added with similar menace, sending several blobs of spittle flying onto the man's perfectly ironed suit.

'But we…' started Loretta.

'Don't you *dare* speak to me!' Manton hollered, shaking the statue's stand in Loretta's face. The big man pushed his chin into his collar and leant back, clearly wounded by Manton's words and agitated by his aggression.

Doyle started to get up, seeing the danger signs, but he was too slow. By the time he rolled off the recliner Loretta had already started to speak once more.

'I'm not stup…' uttered the big man, his words being cut short by the base of the trophy being smashed into the side of his head. He crashed

134

to the floor, unconscious before his body came to rest. Loretta lay in an unnatural jumble of limbs, a spatter of blood on the polished parquet floor.

Manton didn't stop, he bent over and went to follow up, but his arm was caught by Doyle before he could strike again and the horse's head was shaken from his hand.

'No!' Doyle hissed. 'This isn't the w-w-way,' he stammered.

Manton rocked back, his eyes still blazing. Warren, who had remained standing stock still, slowly lifted his eyes and studied Manton's face and recognised the malevolent streak which lived just beneath the man's eyes.

'What you looking at?' Manton demanded, steadying himself against his desk. He almost felt drunk; the sudden rush of endorphins his violent outburst had created was still coursing through him. An idea flitted through his mind: perhaps he could do with a better fitness regime. However this thought whisked away when he caught sight of Warren's features, which were screwed up in shock.

'I'm looking at someone I've known for forty years, Benny,' Warren stated deliberately slowly. 'A man I've grown up with, served, and defended. But you don't kill one of your own, at least, not for something... like this!'

'He's not d-dead,' called Doyle from Loretta's side.

Manton ignored Doyle and started forward toward Warren, his jaw slack, eyes fixed on him, only to halt again when Doyle yelled, 'Benny, S-s-stop!'.

'Take a b-breath, Benny,' Doyle instructed, leaving Loretta's unmoving shape. He walked purposefully over to Manton, took his arm and started rubbing the man's back. 'Take another. And another,' Doyle insisted.

Manton did as he was told and within a minute he was sitting in his office chair looking harmless and spent. Doyle stood over him like a mother calming her unruly child, making him sip water, dabbing his forehead and face with a wet handkerchief. He spoke quietly to Manton, utterly absorbed with him.

From the floor Loretta twitched and moaned. Warren had pushed him onto his side and as he regained consciousness, the big man croaked, coughed, and struggled to push himself up from the floor. As soon as his head left the herringbone parquet the room whooshed away in a spiral of pain and nonsensical colours. He collapsed into blackness once more.

'Get him into one of the ground floor bedrooms,' Doyle called to Warren, gesturing to the door with a sharp flick of his nose. 'I'll get hold of someone to see to him. Go on!'

Warren looked to Doyle and Manton and not for the first time he wondered why he'd spent so much of his life with these two men. He was fifty-one and it had always been Manton, Doyle and Warren, in that order, inseparable since they were eight years old. He was always the last of the three, Benny and Charlie enjoyed a special relationship, far deeper than he could ever manage with either of them. Sure, they were murderous, evil bastards – anyone could see that – but they had something else between them. They were like brothers. Warren corrected himself, no; they were practically a single entity. The two of them possessed an unhealthy bond that went well beyond family.

Warren looked around for something to wrap Loretta in. He managed a wry smile as he recognised his own professionalism; how many people would have experience of moving inert seventeen stone bodies from one place to another? He liberated a throw from a sofa at the back of the room and returned to Loretta.

The kid on the floor was just transient muscle, he wouldn't last; they never did. But he couldn't help feeling bad about the stupid lump, he should have protected him a bit more.

Warren felt self-conscious all of a sudden and looked up to find Manton watching him tend to Loretta. Doyle had backed off and was stood a few yards away now, staring out of a window.

'How is he?' Manton called over.

'It's a bad cut, plenty of blood and bruising, but I don't think you broke any bones.'

'Tell me when he's up and around. I'll come and see him. You like this one don't you Pete?'

Warren looked for a hint of sarcasm in Manton's words but found none. It seemed to be genuine concern, although it couldn't be classed as regret. He started to lay the throw out on the floor.

'He's young Benny. He hasn't learned the ropes yet.'

Manton returned to his desk, sat and leaned back in his chair, then shuffled forward in order to prop himself up on his elbows.

'You know he'll end up dead,' he stated baldly.

'Yes.'

'So why bother?'

Warren gritted his teeth and gave a small grunt as he rolled Loretta's body over onto the throw. He was relieved to see the boy's chest was still heaving in and out.

'Like I said, he's still young. He's not so stupid, he might learn.'

'No he won't,' Manton scoffed. 'It's not like when we were young and could afford to make mistakes and learn on the job. He won't have time and he's not got the intelligence, which is why I brought him in. If I don't kill him, the job will.'

Warren didn't answer; instead he walked to the door, opened it and returned to expertly wrap up Loretta. Gripping the end of the throw with both hands he pulled him across the floor and out of the room, careful not to strain his shoulder, which still stung from his altercation at Tattersalls.

Doyle waited until he heard another door open, then made a short call.

'The boy could still be useful, B-Benny. But you're right, he'll have to be d-dispensed with at some p-point.'

Manton looked up at Doyle. 'Are you okay? Y'know you're stuttering?'

Doyle nodded, trying in vain to hide his self-loathing. He managed a tight smile, which was lost on Manton as he quickly looked away, apparently no longer interested.

Instead, Manton got up and started to pace around the room.

'Redblood's security lockdown is still strangling us. We can't get enough money through the accounts and can't set up new laundering avenues. Warren and the boy visited the Money Tree when they were in Yorkshire to put more pressure on Deacon and his kids but they've only managed to resurrect half the network so far. Our suppliers will start to get edgy soon, if they don't see the cash flowing back into their businesses.'

Doyle remained silent, but prompted Manton to continue with a twirl of two fingers.

'Are more coders needed at The Money Tree?' Manton asked.

Doyle considered, quickly rejecting the option. 'Too dangerous.'

'But we're going to run out of clean cash soon. The clean businesses in Britain aren't doing enough revenue to satisfy the clients are they?' Manton asked, continuing to pace.

Doyle didn't answer; instead he gazed out of the huge eighteenth century bay window that dominated Manton's office. The manicured front lawn ended with a line of fir trees which marked the edge of the property. The small mansion they had bought and converted twelve years ago echoed the way they ran the business. It was not expansive; the grounds didn't run to many acres. It was comfortable, yet conservative. It reflected the income they could expect from their legitimate business investments. Anything bigger would draw attention from the authorities.

However Doyle wasn't concentrating on the view; it was the Halo business that occupied all his thoughts. The business was under huge strain. He was under strain too. He'd not stammered for years; he was sure it was a symptom of the pressure. A combination of the problems at the Money Tree and poor trading in some of Halo's straight, clean British businesses meant they were paying out more money to the crime rings than the legitimate businesses were earning in revenue. Halo had plenty of cash, in fact huge reserves sat in bank accounts around the world, but it was dirty, traceable cash which needed to be laundered. It would be dangerous if it was used to get them out of their current predicament.

Doyle screwed his face up in frustration; their problems could be easily solved if they could locate that missing memory stick. The business would return to normal and Manton would calm down. He could concentrate on winning his precious horse race he kept banging on about. If they could find Billy or whoever else his brother had been working with, returning their network to full operation would simply be a matter of extracting the information. He found himself smirking at the prospect of a spot of torture, it had been a long time…

Fed up with waiting for Doyle to answer, Manton stopped pacing and examined the blood on his office floor whilst stroking his perfectly trimmed inch-long beard. He glanced at Doyle's back; the way his shoulders were hunched, how most of his weight was on one foot. A pang of doubt washed over him.

'Charlie?' he started in a low voice. 'You're the money man. Can we make the client payments this month… I mean, we only just managed it last month?'

Doyle wiped the smirk from his face and straightened. He spun round to meet Manton's uncertain gaze and answered with an emphatic 'No.'

Manton felt anger starting to rise in him once more, but Doyle was at his side in three strides, and he felt the man's bony hand grip his shoulder.

'We'll just have to release some dirty funds,' Doyle said simply.

Manton, still examining the blood on his floor was about to reply, but instead straightened and looked up as Warren re-entered the room. Doyle left his side and sat on a sofa which faced a gaudy modern fireplace.

'He's comfortable. I'll let you know when he's fit to be spoken to about his… er, actions.' Warren reported, keeping his head bowed, eyes firmly on the floor.

Manton said nothing. He hadn't heard Warren. His mind was elsewhere. 'Did you follow up on how Redblood's packet of cigarettes got into the house?' he asked Doyle.

'Yes. Tell him Warren,' Doyle ordered.

Warren swallowed down the disenchantment that was growing within him for these two men and provided his report.

'A man tipped a local newspaper delivery boy to post the data stick through the front gates. The security guard picked it up and gave it to Loretta. The boy could only say it was a middle-aged man in a coat and hat who gave him his instructions.'

Manton considered for a moment, absent-mindedly smearing Loretta's blood over the floor in small arcs using the toe of his boot.

'Our only remaining link to Redblood and his brother is Harry Bolt. He's been involved ever since Redblood died.'

He paused again, feeling his blood pressure start to increase once again as he thought through the situation.

'We should have killed Billy twenty years ago, as soon as the Money Tree was operational,' he said through gritted teeth. 'Now we're going to have to squeeze the information we need from Bolt or his family and friends. But there's too much interest in him and his yard at the moment. He's got protection too.'

Manton extended his index finger toward Warren and prodded him twice in his chest. Warren chanced looking up. Manton appeared to be holding his breath, trying to contain his anger. Beneath his beard Warren could spot Manton's red raw flesh glowing with heat. He knew it was the reason he grew hair all over his face: it masked the fact that Manton could not control the burst of raging scarlet which coloured his face each time his temper got the better of him.

'Your schoolboy chemical experiment and ill-judged intimidation haven't helped us, Pete, the police will be circling. You should know better...'

Warren didn't reply to deny the accusations, knowing any reaction, verbal or physical, could result in retribution. He'd only ever seen Benny this agitated once before: the evening Doyle killed A'laya Bolt.

Manton gave up waiting for Warren to reply.

'Blood on the floor,' he barked at the slickly dressed man and pointed a thumb downward while maintaining an eye on Warren's reaction. Once he received an accepting nod Manton turned on his heel and sat beside Doyle on the sofa. Warren disappeared wordlessly from the room.

'We still have options...' Manton ruminated. 'We need to be far more direct with Bolt. If we can squeeze the whereabouts of Billy from him or even better, locate the lost memory stick, so much the better. I can keep our clients at bay for a few months if I need to. We'll just have to soak up the pressure until Deacon can fix the mess Redblood left behind.'

Doyle nodded his approval.

'If a direct approach doesn't work with Bolt, we'll be playing a long g-game. We'll need a failsafe b-backup,' replied Doyle, subsequently biting his fist in frustration at having mangled his words once again.

'It's been a while since you've stammered so much,' Manton pointed out, his face expressing surprise at Doyle's reaction. 'Do you need to see a doctor too? We can take a look at you...'

For a moment Doyle's skull-like face twisted into a sneer and betrayed a flash of contempt for Manton, but as quickly as it appeared, it winked out. He closed his eyes, took a deep breath, and tried to imagine the tension draining from his body. He wouldn't let another speech therapist anywhere near him. Finally, thirty seconds later he opened his eyes to find Manton peering steadily at him. At first the look appeared solely inquisitive, but perhaps there was also a slightly concerned edge. He locked eyes with his colleague.

'No, Benny...' he answered with purpose. 'I'm golden.'

Twenty-Three

Harry was relieved he hadn't sold his fifteen-year-old two-berth horsebox when the new horses arrived in the yard back in October. He'd considered it, as the training fees were rolling in and Redblood had made arrangements in his plan to lease a new horsebox if required, but he'd resisted the temptation.

'Betsy,' – as named by Jill - rattled, complained when she was going up anything more than a minor incline and drank diesel like an insatiable alcoholic, but she was comfortable, homely and well… reassuring. What's more, Betsy did the job and always got you home, albeit a little later than you hoped. Betsy's reliability and steadfastness was highly valued by Harry at a time when change was all around him.

He was currently slumped in a delicious doze in Betsy's over-sized passenger seat. It was late on Saturday afternoon in February and with the light already fading fast, Harry had taken the chance for a well-earned snooze as Mike drove Betsy to Wolverhampton races. The transport had her nose pointed south, munching steadily through the miles in the inside lane of the M6, heading for an All-Weather night meeting under the Wolverhampton floodlights. She had a full complement, namely Paste and Smasher loaded into her. Outside there was a light dusting of snow on the ground and the external temperature gauge showed minus two degrees, falling gradually with the light; it was one of the few gauges that still worked.

The one area of expertise Betsy's burbling engine wasn't lacking was as a provider of warmth. Smelling faintly of diesel, an intense heat wafted up from the floor of the cab, making Harry's shoe leather feel like it was curling. The aroma from the horses, people, and tack combined with the heat to provide a wonderfully soporific affect.

In a warm, woozy state, Harry reflected on life at Pickering Farm Stables since Redblood's visit. It had become hectic from late November through to January as he and his staff broke all fifteen of the yearlings: twelve for Redblood and three others for smaller owners. As they became backed and ridden away, he'd followed the tried and tested techniques he'd learned from Willie Warcup. Once broken, he would back off the youngsters and allow a fortnight to three weeks for them to relax and find their feet. This 'breather', as Willie had called it, gave the yearlings time to recover from the sudden change to their lifestyle.

A couple of the colts had been difficult to handle and needed a few more weeks in the lunging pen than was ideal, but overall Harry was pleased with his new recruits. To be busy and training high quality horses had made a big difference to his yard. The place had a buzz around it seven days a week, and he loved it.

Harry had a particular liking for two of the Redblood yearlings, a

Shamardal offspring nicknamed 'Fletch' and a lovely intelligent colt by Showcasing known as 'Jelly' because he'd wobbled all over when they'd been backing him. In contrast, Fletch was always in a bad mood and looked like he was in prison when he poked his head over the stable door. This chap was only happy when he was out in the paddocks. The name Fletch came from the 1970's prison sit-com 'Porridge', a favourite show of his stable lass, Zoe.

Both horses were compact, powerful sorts and had been very forward in the way they dealt with being backed. He had great hopes for them. But then everyone in the yard had their favourites. Zoe was keen on a large, beefy yearling given the stable name 'Samson', Jill liked an unassuming colt who was always the first with his head over the stable door in the mornings who she'd named 'Mr Greedy'. Meanwhile Rory, who was a regular around the yard now, was already calling the other Shamardal colt Harry had beaten Manton to at the sales a sure-fire winner. They'd nicknamed that one, 'Luckyman', simply because he'd come home with Harry and not Manton.

Of course none of these young horses had been ridden in any sort of serious work yet. At the moment it was swinging half canters for some and simple trotting for the others, so it was pure guesswork which youngster would eventually rise to the top, if indeed any of them did. Harry had experienced a few moments of toe-curling self-doubt over his choice of horses – what if he'd blown two million on a bunch of selling platers? However, he'd managed to quash these thoughts with one look over the more forward of his youngsters; they moved well and generally had the right temperament.

All twelve of the Redblood horses had grown since joining the yard and Harry had recorded with increasing delight the changing size, weight, and shape of each colt. Everything could, and would change in the next four months as they entered full time training, now that the worst of the winter weather was hopefully behind them. This latest snowfall had hit most of the country, but with racing still available on artificial sand-based surfaces, it meant Harry could get his older horses out racing before the turf season got going properly in April, even though the ground was freezing and jumps meetings were getting abandoned every day.

Harry opened his eyes, jolted out of his hazy thoughts by a sudden sideways movement. He rubbed his eyes and grunted a 'Wha..' at Mike who simply pointed through the windscreen at a set of rear lights disappearing into the darkness. Understanding came seconds later; a car had passed them at high speed in the middle lane of the motorway and the wind resistance had caused the box to quiver as it whooshed past. It was an unwelcome, yet regular motorway occurrence for any horsebox driver.

Bunt and Wang were still around, firmly entrenched as part of the team now. They had added a third member to their team, a younger man around Harry's age called Moore. He tended to look after Bunt and Wang's duties at the yard when they were out supporting Harry with runners. He was a part-timer, but like his colleagues, Harry had found the Geordie extremely capable. He was tall, muscular, and completely lacking in hair anywhere. As a result he had a striking profile.

Harry squinted into the nearside mirror. Moving his head slightly he spied the familiar red BMW following them – the Bunt and Wang mobile - which tracked the horsebox, protecting and securing them everywhere they went. Tonight it was just Bunt following, as Wang and Moore were sharing the night shift back at the Malton yard.

Thankfully there hadn't been any further incidents since the open morning. It had taken a couple of weeks for their next door neighbour Mo to put that episode behind her, but her two worst affected horses had thankfully pulled through. The yard security had been strengthened even further. Straight after the incident Bunt had insisted on frisking every member of staff entering the yard. Harry had eventually pointed out that it wasn't helping employee morale, and even more pertinent was the fact that if any of the staff wanted to harm a horse they didn't need to carry a weapon, poison or acid. One well-aimed kick would be enough. Bunt had flipped at this revelation and subsequently installed camera feeds in every single stable. The frisking was quietly dropped the following day.

As a result of the new security restrictions from Bunt and Wang, Harry had overheard Zoe and Rory referring to the yard as 'Stalag Pickering' during a snatch of banter on the walk home after working the horses on the Wold gallops. He'd initially disregarded the comment as idle stable gossip, but it had gnawed at him for several days. Finally, he had a quiet word with Zoe who eventually admitted she and some other members of staff were a little concerned by the constant surveillance. Harry had organised for Bunt to show all six of the stable staff how the system worked, and to re-assure them it was to secure the staff's safety as well as the horses. This seemed to work, as the atmosphere in the yard immediately returned to its previously relaxed state.

The equine residents at Pickering Farm Stables weren't Harry's only issue at present. The impending arrival of Harry Bolt junior in three months time had become a source of unrelenting activity and associated stress. The selection of cots, clothes, changing mats, buggies, car seats and the redecoration and remodeling of rooms had become Harry's new afternoon jobs, once the work was completed in the yard.

Leaning on one elbow, his cheek touching Betsy's cold glass window, a smile creased his face when Jill entered his thoughts. He'd never felt closer to Jill. He wouldn't have believed the bond they enjoyed could strengthen any further, yet just being around the farmhouse with his pregnant wife filled him with a sense of wonder he hadn't experienced since his infant school days.

Jill was positively blooming now she was over the morning sickness. Her pregnancy was progressing smoothly and the two of them were thoroughly enjoying the build up to the baby's birth. Harry, in his early pregnancy zeal had come across a website which would email regularly, telling them how the baby was developing as the days ticked by. They'd both found these missives on the development of their infant fascinating, often sharing them with the staff.

'It's the size of an orange now!' Harry had called over to Rory one morning as they led two of the young colts down to the walker, to which he'd received the tongue in cheek reply 'Don't worry Guv'nor, I'm sure it will go down if you don't keep scratching it!' That quip had travelled around the local yards for several days afterwards.

Harry had attended parenting and birthing classes with Jill, which had run smoothly enough, apart from one truly horrific session describing everything that could possibly go wrong during the birth itself. They'd been subjected to a particularly gruesome video which had left the class of eight first-time mothers and partners stunned. Jill had shrugged the experience off quickly, but Harry had wandered back to the car park with knees of jelly, hitting the whisky once he was home in an attempt to wash the horrible images from his mind. It hadn't worked. He still winced whenever he recalled that night.

The other constant in Harry's life was his music. At present he still managed to fit in one or two gigs a week with Pascal and Emma. But it couldn't last. Once spring came along, the pressure of work in the yard and runners at racetracks all over the country would impact on his ability to perform. He hadn't mentioned this to his fellow musicians yet, perhaps in the hope that he could still fit everything in, but he knew once night racing started in May, the chances of him stealing away twice a week to play were negligible.

Mike pushed the indicator stalk down and squinted through the slightly misted windscreen as he turned off the motorway. Betsy changed her engine note as Mike rattled through the gears and Harry heard Paste snort behind him as they turned right onto the roundabout. Harry was convinced the gelding could sense when they were getting close to a racecourse. Paste had run at Wolverhampton a dozen times in his career and it was always when they reached the A5 turning where he would start to snort. The left turn onto the Stafford Road would be the prompt for the six-year-old to stamp his feet and when finally they edged over the speed bumps on the entry road to the racecourse itself, Paste would aim a few hearty kicks to the sidewalls of the box in anticipatory excitement. The clincher was that Paste would provide the same auditory markers when he was travelling to Beverley, Thirsk and Ripon too, always ending in wall bashing prior to reaching their destination.

Paste announced their arrival at Dunstall Park with a third and final shuddering slap of hoof on the aluminum walls of the box just before Mike switched the ignition off. Bunt had peeled off to park in the public car park.

Located between two large housing estates, the track didn't have the individuality of a country racecourse or the prestige of a city venue, added to which it tended to host fairly low-grade flat racing during the winter. However, its night meetings attracted a hardy group of enthusiasts through the colder months and the racing offered horses like Paste and Smasher, rated around the mid sixties, handicap opportunities on a surface which was kind to their aging joints.

'Hold up,' Harry warned as Betsy shuddered into silence. 'Has Andrew got a runner tonight?' He peered down the poorly lit stables car park, trying to confirm the transport he'd spotted further down was indeed Andrew's.

Mike fiddled with his phone for a few seconds. 'Yes, he's got a three-year-old called Millers Print in the eight forty-five.'

As if to order, Andrew's head suddenly popped up at the passenger side window. Harry hadn't seen him approach and he jumped a little in his seat. This reaction seemed to please his adoptive brother as one side of his mouth rose in a wonky smile. Andrew stood still, his chin pointed downward, both eyes staring slightly upward at Harry; a ghoulish pose in the winter twilight.

Harry wound the window down energetically and faced Andrew nose to nose. 'Can I help you, Andrew?'

Andrew was about to reply, but instead something drew his attention to his left and he screwed his neck round. Harry stuck his head out of the window and saw Bunt standing two yards away, providing his brother with a steely look.

'You've even got a bouncer now?' Andrew stated, turning to face Bunt down.

Harry filled his cheeks with air and blew it out dramatically. He signaled with a wave of his hand for Bunt to back off.

'Come on Andrew, what do you want?' he asked resignedly.

'It's Mum,' Andrew answered, turning back to Harry.

Harry examined his brother's face, and saw worry lines across his forehead where previously there'd been none.

'What's wrong?' he replied, his tone altering to one of concern.

'You need to come and see her, she's… worse.'

Harry got down from the cab and the two men shared the most civil conversation they'd had for a number of years.

Mike stayed in the cab, watching Harry rub his chin whilst nodding as Andrew stoically explained. He couldn't hear the entire conversation but odd words and phrases carried through the open window. They were sober and serious. A few minutes passed, by which time Harry was rubbing the back of his neck and blowing more air into his cheeks, unconsciously this time. Andrew nodded curtly and Harry slowly held a hand out and gently took his brother's shoulder and said something, upon which they parted.

When Harry climbed back into the horsebox his eyes were glistening with sadness. He stuck a hand into his black jeans, produced a cloth handkerchief, and used it to dab his eyes and compose himself. Behind them the horses were becoming restless, Paste snorting short bursts down his nose in a bid to attract attention. Harry produced a joyless smile. Mike remained silent.

'It's my Mum… well, my adoptive Mum – Annie. She had her regular monthly doctor's appointment today. Andrew got a call on his way here… the doctor thinks it's bad... her heart.'

Mike nodded solemnly and the two of them stared wistfully through the windscreen. Bunt appeared at the open window. He glanced at them before speaking.

'I'm guessing it's not good,' he stated, wearing a sombre expression. 'Mike and I will get the horses stabled for you.'

Mike smiled a sad agreement in response.

The next hour was filled with phone calls and the booking in procedure for the horses. Harry would be calling to see Annie tomorrow, but for now he had to place thoughts of her to one side and concentrate on his two runners, their owners, and riders. The latter was easy enough, as Rory had been booked for both rides. Smasher, or 'Smashing Lass' as she was named in the racecard, was due to run first in the eight fifteen and then Paste – Magic Jewel – was in the seventh and final race on the card.

At seven-o'clock Harry was sitting with Mike and Bunt at a table in the owners and trainers room. He was absent-mindedly pushing a few carrots around his plate. For a small course, the facilities were decent, with a large room being dedicated to those with racehorse connections. Bunt had insisted on a table against the wall, and he sat hawk-like on the corner of the four-seater, eyeing the human traffic.

'Well, well,' Bunt suddenly declared with surprise.

Before Harry or Mike could query the comment a chair was drawn out and both of them looked up and into the face of David Smith.

'Good evening, Harry!' Smith exclaimed, planting himself opposite the trainer. 'Mike, Mr Bunt, good to see you again,' he added in greeting, meeting the gaze of each man in turn and offering a quick handshake.

'I thought I'd drop by to get a quick update on how Mr Red…' Bunt cleared his throat and gave Smith a warning stare. 'Er, yes, of course – I wondered how our young horses are getting along?'

Harry clamped a smile on his face and went into trainer mode. After a few minutes of general conversation, Smith made it obvious he wanted to speak with Harry alone and Mike made an excuse about leading up while Bunt took the opportunity to move, proceeding to station himself at a table at the back of the room. Harry ran through a potted synopsis of each Redblood colt, doing so in few words. However, he spoke concisely and with confidence.

'So do you have one or two mapped out for the Gimcrack?'

Harry sighed and flicked a look at Smith that dripped with suppressed irritation.

'You have to understand we're dealing with very young horses which at this stage of their development, alter every single week.'

'But you must have some sort of idea…?' Smith pushed back.

Harry paused, considering what would placate the man.

'At the moment I'd say every single one of them can't be ruled out.'

Smith smiled knowingly, accepting the news with a business-like nonchalance. He made a few short notes on his racecard and Harry got the impression the man was satisfied and the interview was over.

Whether it was Andrew's news on Annie which prompted Harry to pursue Smith, or the fact that the man seemed to be in a convivial mood, he felt compelled to ask questions this evening. With the ex-bank manager's queries having dried up, Harry waded in.

'I wonder if you could answer a few questions for me?'

Smith nodded, inviting Harry to continue.

'Do you know a William or Billy Redblood?'

Smith studied the trainer across the table, his face a grey slab of stone, although his eyes still danced with what Harry read as boyish excitement.

'Yes, he was my client's brother,' he replied in a measured tone.

'Was?'

'He disappeared from Malton when he was eighteen. Why do you want to know?'

'So… he could still be alive?' Harry queried, ignoring the question.

Smith shrugged. 'I'm afraid I don't know. Mr R… sorry, *Thomas* never shared anything at all about his family. I only know about William because Thomas asked us to close his brother's account a few years after he disappeared.'

Harry considered this and decided to keep pushing.

'When we got access to our security box, did you get one from, er, Thomas, as well?'

Smith quashed a faint smile. 'Certainly. It held all the instructions for me to conduct on his behalf. But Harry, there was nothing in that box which would affect you in any way. I received a copy of what you were given and a short brief on the security people. I also received details of how everyone involved must be paid. That was it.'

Smith paused, studying the young trainer. 'I'm not hiding anything Harry, really, I'm not. Thomas was quite clear in his instructions; I must give you every possible support.'

In the background, the third race of the evening went off, and a small knot of owners and trainers congregated in front of a television mounted on a nearby wall. They were standing a good five yards away from Harry's table; nonetheless, he waited until the noise of encouragement from both inside and outside the stands ebbed away and the group of race watchers had dispersed.

Harry regarded David Smith once more. Sitting in his grey suit and red tie he looked every bit a retired bank manager and he had no reason to suspect he knew any more than he was letting on.

'Did you know that my wife is due to have our baby in early May?'

Smith smiled generously. 'I did. Mr Bunt provides me with a monthly report and he mentioned it because…' Smith looked furtive for a moment. 'Oh gosh, I'm sorry Harry. I'm really not cut out for this cloak and dagger stuff. I was going to say… when Jill became pregnant Bunt felt she and the baby could be more of a target to anyone wishing to er… blackmail you.' Smith watched Harry carefully for any signs of distress or anger. To his relief nothing more than a slightly raised eyebrow developed on the trainers face.

'Yes, he told me the same thing,' Harry admitted. 'Jill and I both get the feeling we're only playing with half a deck of cards at the moment. We're not quite sure what we've got ourselves into and very soon there's going to be another, far more important person involved.'

Smith appeared to tense for a moment as he considered this. When the realisation that Harry was referring to his wife's pregnancy hit home, he resumed his relaxed posture and leaned back, crossing his legs.

'Thomas was very secretive when he was alive, but I always found him to be a man of his word. Like you, I'm sure there is far more to his relationship with Mr…' he slanted a look around him, then whispered 'Manton. However, I would be astonished if he hadn't put in place all the necessary safeguards to ensure your family and his horses are fully protected.'

Smith leaned forward conspiratorially. 'Thomas was very intelligent and quite fastidious. He could read markets and even countries' actions incredibly well, which is why he made such a substantial fortune in stocks, shares, and commodities. He certainly never gave me any reason to mistrust him or his intentions.'

He leaned even closer now, his stomach touching the edge of the table. Harry realised he too was leaning toward Smith in response.

'I believe I'm as much a target as you are, but I keep telling myself

Thomas will have thought of this. To be honest it's scary, but also terribly exciting!' Smith exclaimed, his eyes alive and his cheeks suddenly flushed, their usual greyness replaced with a rouge tint.

Harry felt a wave of guilt wash over him. He'd treated this man as the enemy, but everything about Smith felt genuine and it seemed this mild mannered office worker was just as much caught up in Redblood's plans as he was. He also hadn't even considered Smith's own position and the fact he could have a family to protect.'

'I'm sorry Mr…' Harry began.

'Please call me David,' Smith pleaded. 'I'm retired now, it all seems far too formal for surnames, and especially given we're at a racecourse.'

Harry grinned at the ex-bank manager and Smith beamed back. They spend another minute wrapping up the conversation and then he shook Harry's hand again, promising to visit the yard soon.

Once smith had departed Bunt rejoined Harry almost immediately.

'Watch the man in the flat cap over my left shoulder. At the coffee counter,' he hissed as soon as he was seated.

As inconspicuously as possible, but feeling exceptionally self conscious, Harry glanced over and watched as a muscular man in his late twenties wearing a dark jacket, gloves, corduroy trousers and a flat cap took a sip from his coffee cup. He looked over the polystyrene rim at Harry's table and almost immediately turned away, well before he met Harry's gaze. The man deposited the half-drunk cup on a nearby table and made his way out of the Owners and Trainers room. Harry thought something was odd about him, but couldn't quite work out why.

'He's following Smith,' Bunt warned.

'How do you know?' Harry queried, heart suddenly thumping against his ribs.

'All the right… signs,' Bunt replied distractedly, his concentration clearly elsewhere. 'Stay inside the racecourse. Don't call anyone or follow, leave it to me.'

Bunt crossed the room, sidestepping the mess of tables and chairs and followed the flat-capped man into the central corridor which ran the length of the stands.

Harry, his pulse now racing, was wondering whether he should call Smith to warn him, but rejected this; he had been told to call no one. He nervously checked his phone, cursing the fact he'd been left with nothing to do when a familiar voice called his name and four fiftyish 'Dangerous' ladies surrounded his table wearing huge grins.

Then it struck Harry. His cloth cap and up-market country clothes all looked new. He wasn't a Wolverhampton race-goer. The man had dressed like someone who *wanted* to look like a racehorse owner, but hadn't been racing before. He may have got away with his 'look' at

Goodwood or Ascot, but at Wolverhampton on a Saturday evening in the middle of winter his appearance had jarred with his surroundings.

Harry greeted his dangerous ladies and went into trainer mode once more.

Bunt followed the tall figure halfway along the corridor and saw him descend the two flights of steps which led to the ground floor. Instead of following down the stairs he continued into the premier suite and positioned himself at one of the viewing windows overlooking the parade ring. He spotted Smith opening one of the large swing doors to the Holiday Inn to his left and then watched the cloth-capped man set off after him.

The hotel was an integral part of the racecourse, providing the entrance and exit for premier suite customers. It looked like Smith was on his way home.

Bunt scanned the scene below him and spotted a couple of horses being led from the pre-parade ring up the parade ring chute. Officials were already closing the walkway. Hopefully they would slow down the stalker long enough. He hurried to the other end of the premier suite and gave himself mental tick for his prep work on the course layout, as he opened an inconspicuous swing door which led into the side of the hotel, cutting out the need to cross the parade ring chute. He ran down the corridor and then tumbled down two flights of stairs, slowing once to avoid a chambermaid climbing the stairs with her arms full of towels.

He slipped smoothly through a side door and into the hotel foyer, which doubled as the entrance to the racecourse. Taking in sharp breaths to fill his lungs, he turned his face away from the swing door when a gloved hand started to push it open. Smith would be walking to his car now. The cloth-capped man strolled purposefully past without giving Bunt a look and the automatic doors to the car park exit swished open for him, sending a blast of cold air into the foyer. Bunt followed moments later, busy calculating what options he had open to him.

Once outside Bunt breathed out deeply, the lack of any breeze producing white clouds that hung around before melting into the crisp evening air. He darted across the yellow hatched area outside the hotel entrance, placing his feet carefully onto the frosty surface and put a line of parked cars between him and the stalker. The car park was full of vehicles and empty of people, all sensible race-goers making the most of the heat in the belly of the grandstand. A few horses snorted and the chatter of stable lads lifted over the wall behind Bunt, being quickly drowned out when the public address announced the runners in the seven-thirty.

The cloth-capped man reached the end of the hotel grounds and halted, peering across the top of hundreds of cars neatly lined up in rows. He hesitated for only a second or two before kicking off at a jog into the sea of vehicles.

Bunt skipped to the end of the row of cars outside the Holiday Inn and looked around him for a suitable car. His decision made, he headed for a SUV at the end of the line and holding its roof rack he pulled himself up onto the back wheel and then onto the roof, using the door handle as a foothold. Standing upright on the roof Bunt scanned for Smith and then his stalker, making a mental note of their directions of travel. He carefully picked his way down and after rifling through a nearby bin, he set off at a dead run toward the stables entrance before turning right and continuing the two hundred yards up the entry road.

Bunt was fit for a man in his early fifties, but he cursed internally as his breath started to shorten and his throat and lungs began to burn. As he ran from the racecourse entrance, the number of cars started to thin out and he looked to his right for any car movement. As he reached the entrance to the car park, out of breath and with sweat cooling immediately on his forehead, David Smith approached in a new VW and Bunt waved him down.

At the driver's window Bunt spoke quickly and they exchanged a few words. Smith gunned the engine and shot through the housing estate, indicating right once he reached the 'T' Junction, as if heading into the centre of the city. His VW sat at the junction, waiting for the traffic to clear.

Bunt prepared himself, gulping icy cold air into his lungs. He rubbed his cheeks and ran a hand backwards over his nose to entice it to redden. He undid his jacket, pulled the hood over his head to hide his silver hair, and ripped open his shirt. Then he poured the last dregs of cider into his hand from the bottle he'd liberated from the bin and rubbed the old, foul smelling alcohol into his neck and chin.

A sports coupe turned onto the exit road and accelerated toward him, headlights blazing. Bunt staggered into the middle of the road, waving the cider bottle wildly and faced the oncoming vehicle. For a horrible moment he thought the driver wasn't going to stop but to his relief the low-slung car squirreled under braking and then wandered left and then right, in an attempt to find a way past him. Bunt staggered right and wavered, hands cartwheeling theatrically. The driver, still wearing his cloth cap, now started to blast his horn. When the coupe was a couple of yards in front of him, Bunt screwed his eyes up, started to sing 'A Hard Day's Night' badly, edged backwards toward the car and splayed himself onto the bonnet. The bottle made a tinny clunk as it connected with the shiny blue paintwork and he was careful to scrape the bottle right to left a few times for effect.

Bunt stole a look up the exit road and watched Smith's car finally find a gap in the traffic and disappear from view to the right. He continued his drunken singing until he heard a door open and the click of steel as the man's heel touched the tarmac.

Smith's stalker was younger than he'd looked in the Owners and Trainers lounge. He was in his mid-twenties, tall and stiff. A long face gained character from a bulbous nose and close-cut black hair. His small mouth provided a wiry, lipless grimace. Enraged, he was hurling expletives in a Scottish accent before he reached Bunt who was now busying himself by scraping the bottle down the driver's side wing, head on the bonnet, listening to ensure the engine was still running.

As soon as a long-fingered hand landed roughly on his shoulder Bunt spun and launched himself up at the man's chin like a human bolt from a crossbow. Such was the intensity of Bunt's upward assault; his head bounced off the man's jaw and continued its trajectory into his nose, splitting it open with a sickening sound of tearing cartilage.

Even before the Scotsman barrelled over and his backside hit the tarmac, Bunt was slipping in the coupe's driver's seat, whipping the keys from the ignition. The man sat on the road dumbfounded, a fountain of blood streaming from the centre of his face.

Bunt returned with the keys in his fist, stood in front of his seated foe, and pulled his hood back. The man glanced up and recognition registered in his eyes. He growled more expletives whilst holding his nose between thumb and forefinger.

'Who you working for?' Bunt demanded.

The man looked up at Bunt, ran his tongue around his mouth, and spat a gobbet of blood onto the road before hurling another string of bad, and mostly incomprehensible language at his aggressor.

'Well you are 'Cam' apparently,' Bunt continued, his words saturated with sarcasm. 'One second Cam – ah, here we are, Cameron Greene…'

He produced a mobile phone he'd palmed from the central console of the car and dangled it in front of the man, who took note and suddenly looked ready to spring, a hand on the road and leg bent, ready to push up.

'I'm ex-military. Try to come at me and you'll lose the use of your throat, an arm or a leg – your choice,' Bunt said quietly and with as much malice as he could squeeze into his words.

The man looked weary once again, fell back, and resumed fingering his nose to stem the free flow of blood down his chin.

'Your boss or client's name and you'll get your phone and keys back,' Bunt offered, swinging the car keys from a finger. 'Your boss doesn't need to know anything about this incident; you simply lost your mark in the city traffic.'

*****

'Are you okay, Harry? Rory asked quietly. 'That's the third time you've checked your mobile in as many minutes.'

The two friends stood in the parade ring ahead of the eight fifteen race, Rory hopping from foot to foot in an attempt to remain warm in his dreadfully thin but colourful silks. They were surrounded by 'The Dangerous Ladies' who were proving once again to be relentlessly enthusiastic about the chances of their racehorse. Smashing Lass was on her toes, as she always was before a race, Mike having to keep a short rein on her through the preliminaries. The filly was jig jogging around the almost circular parade ring, throwing her head around and constantly barging into Mike, wanting to get on with things.

'I'm fine, I'm expecting a call to confirm… something,' Harry replied distractedly.

As he spoke, a text message alert sounded and he read the two lines. Relief expanded across his features.

'I'm guessing good news?' Rory offered with a raised eyebrow.

'Yep, all's well,' Harry confirmed, slipping his phone into his back pocket and heaving a satisfied sigh.

'Good, so come on, how do you want this one ridden? Rory demanded loudly. 'I've only been on her back once before at home.'

Having missed the start of the conversation between the two men the four ladies now leaned a little closer to catch Harry's reply. The owners had clearly visited the bar prior to the race as Harry and Rory received a blast of alcohol breath as the ladies came into range. Harry studiously ignored this, but Rory sensed the fun in them and grinned mischievously at the two ladies closest to him.

'By gum ladies, I'd better win this race tonight!' he exclaimed. 'I get the impression you girls are looking to celebrate!'

Clearly delighted with their jockey's cheekiness the four ladies cackled and snorted their pleasure back at Rory and the five of them continued to share jokes for the next minute. Harry smiled wanly and watched on without really getting too involved. Rory was good with people. He had a knack of connecting with anyone, from the most serious city gent, through millionaire footballers to gruff northern pub landlords. The social niceties came easily to him, although he could take things a smidgen too far on occasions, which is where Harry would swoop in and rescue him. As Harry surveyed the four ladies taking selfie's with Rory he reflected there was little chance of Rory pushing these particular ladies too far, it seemed they were up for just about anything.

With the ladies attention firmly on Rory, Harry fished for his phone again and re-read the text message from Bunt. It read *Man with cap sorted. Smith safe. Back soon to update.*

The bell rang and the call for jockey's to mount was made. Harry provided a few more words of encouragement to the ladies, indicating he was hopeful of getting placed, and he and Rory approached the filly.

Mike was relieved when Harry took pity on the older man and offered to lead Smasher out onto the track. The filly was almost bunny hopping by the time they reached the end of the chute.

'She certainly loves her racing,' Mike noted as the filly kicked off down the home straight. He carefully rubbed his right arm and his ribcage, shaking his head 'She better blummin' win now. I want these bruises to be worthwhile!'

Ten minutes later the 'Dangerous Ladies' were back in the Owners and Trainers lounge celebrating. Not a win, but a second placing – the filly's best result to date.

Harry spoke with the group once more as he dissected the race for them and the forward plans for Smasher, respectfully declined a glass of something that smelled very alcoholic and left the four delighted females to enjoy the rest of their evening. The sound of their raucous laughter bounced around the room as he crossed to the door to the Owners and Trainers lounge.

He had intended to head to the stables in order to help Mike saddle and prepare Paste for the last race on the card, but as Harry pulled the door to the lounge back, he bumped into George Plant, the gelding's owner. George wore a good quality, yet slightly tired looking, grey-flecked lounge suit but it seemed to match his character; a well-worn, unflappable, intelligent single man who took time to get to know, but once you did, was full of rich, engaging conversation. Harry enjoyed George's company and he would always offer him a coffee and a seat in the farmhouse kitchen on his weekly visits to the yard. Their conversation could be anything from football to politics, buying antiques to dog breeding; George had an entertaining view on virtually any subject you cared to discuss.

George also had a healthy view of horseracing, being in the sport for the joy of the race and the breed. He enjoyed a bet by all accounts, but rarely referenced his gambling. He was far more interested in the welfare of his horse, which he considered to be entirely his responsibility, regardless of the fact Paste lived with Harry and Jill. George had joined the yard on day one at Pickering Farm Stables and always had a horse in training with Harry, earning himself a special place in his and Jill's affections.

'I believe we may have a chance tonight Harry. Your thoughts?' George began in his usual open manner.

'I agree,' Harry answered, smiling brightly.

George's eyes narrowed, sensing this was a ploy. He waited for his trainer to expand his comment and when nothing was forthcoming he examined Harry with his sparkling blue eyes, allowing his face to betray mild amusement.

'Ah hah! I see,' George cajoled. 'You're hoping to hear my analysis *before* you commit to revealing your own. Very sensible… you're toying with me, Harry.'

Already I'm being drawn into a sparring discussion which could last all night thought Harry. He considered, and went for flattery next.

153

'Come on, you analyse... no you *dissect* races far deeper than I do, George. So tell me… where will Paste finish tonight?'

'Fourth,' George replied immediately. He was smiling with his eyes whilst his symmetrical, learned face remained unmoving and waxy.

'Playing my game, eh?' Harry managed to get out between a few chortles, followed by a laugh as George's face broke into a grin.

'I think it's a weak race and if Rory can get him up there early on and keep him interested I think he might just trick Paste into winning.'

'Draw? Pace?' George quizzed.

'Seven furlongs, so stall five should do us – wouldn't want to be drawn too wide in a field of thirteen here - but we need to get away sharply; the pace will probably come from outside us, there's a couple drawn in double figures who may duel. If they do, those horses probably won't get home, but we'll still need to be holding a position just off the front rank down the back straight, so we don't get caught if they slow it down in front and kick for home off the bend. How am I doing by the way?'

'Not too shabby,' replied George while stroking his chin in contemplation. 'I'd like to see Rory take a length from the field over a furlong and a half out and try to hold that position to the line.'

'No, no,' Harry responded, shaking his head slowly. 'He'll slow and wait for them to catch up.'

'If he gets a length he won't stop before the line.'

'Okay we'll hit the front early then.'

George guffawed in a deep, caramel tone and placed a warm, soft hand on Harry's bicep. 'If only it was this easy Harry, he'd have won twenty races by now instead of being placed second every time!'

Forty minutes later, Rory threw his reins over Magic Jewel's head and slipped off the gelding's back as they came to a stop in front of the second placing pole inside the tight, oblong winners' enclosure in front of the stands.

'Sorry guys, I went too early,' he said by way of an apology which was immediately waved away by both Harry and George.

'Caught on the line *again* waiting for the pack to catch you up, you old rogue,' George whispered into Paste's pricked ear. He gave the six-year-old a satisfied pat on his neck and looked around for a bucket in order to give his favourite chum a drink of water.

*****

'Two more seconds isn't going to help my win ratio become attractive,' moaned Harry, as he crossed the M54 roundabout on the edge of Wolverhampton and pointed Betsy's nose to the North and into the countryside.

Mike looked across at the trainer from the passenger seat and realised Harry was still buzzing from the evening's exploits on the track. He gave a short reply in agreement but his eyelids were becoming heavy, probably due to Betsy pumping out some serious heat as her engine reached its optimum running temperature. Mike tried to maintain the conversation but when Harry asked him another question a few minutes later, he was already out for the count, snoring quietly in his seat.

Harry blinked a few times, concentrated on the road ahead, and tried not to dwell on Annie's condition; he would see her tomorrow. So he considered what Bunt had told him before they set off back to Malton. Thinking about Bunt forced Harry to check his mirror. The red BMW driven by the middle-aged man with a shock of grey hair filled his view and he enjoyed a combined feeling of relief and security.

Harry glanced over at Mike, who was snoring quietly. He didn't need to know about Smith's stalker, it would only spook him. Only the three of them knew anything and it would stay that way; there was nothing to be gained by worrying Mike, or any of the staff back at the yard, come to that, including Jill. *Especially Jill*, Harry determined.

Trouble was, it *was* worrying... and terribly confusing.

Bunt had given him a potted version of how he managed to delay and then discover who sent Smith's stalker. The details of how he'd extracted the information were scant, but up popped this name and it meant... nothing.

Fin Morrison.

Harry tried again to search his memory, hoping for a spark of understanding but nothing fizzled; he was in darkness. Bunt had been similarly perplexed, but convinced it was the correct name – he'd checked the man's mobile phone for the entry.

Bunt had apparently been unimpressed with the cloth-capped man's professionalism. He'd fallen for a simple ruse and folded far quicker than he expected from a Manton employee. He'd explained in racing terms: Manton was a Group performer, rated over a hundred but the guy tonight was only capable of being competitive in run-of-the-mill Class Five handicaps.

After somehow debilitating the man and leaving him sat on the frosty entry road, Bunt had driven the man's car into the local housing estate before walking back with the keys and instructions where to pick it up. His phone had also been returned, minus its battery. Smith was long gone.

Harry wracked his brains again in a final attempt to place Morrison, but to no avail. It would have to wait until Bunt could investigate further. He became aware his palms were sweating, making Betsy's steering wheel greasy as he turned onto the M6 slip road. Tonight had been a good night, despite being winless. Yet he was driving home fearful of... what? Manton, or was he just one in a long line of people seeking the truth about Redblood?

This association with Redblood is drawing these people to us, the yard and the horses thought Harry. How many more would there be, and if more came what were the chances they would only be operating in Class Five company?

Despite the overpowering heat in Betsy's cab, Harry fought off the effects of an involuntary shiver.

Twenty-Four

Harry loved the May Dante meeting at York. As far as he was concerned this was the start of the flat season in the North. Usually he and Jill would take the afternoon off on the Wednesday and enjoy an afternoon of top class Listed and Group races as race-goers. They would mingle with the public, looking over top class, expensive animals, and dream; during his three years as a trainer Harry had never had a horse good enough to run at this meeting. Now, thanks to a radically changed situation, the Dante meeting would not only offer him the chance to field runners, it was where he would be introducing the best of his Revenge Partnership two-year-olds. He now had runners with a serious competitive chance in classy looking juvenile maiden races.

Through February and March the serious preparatory work had started. Three of the twelve colts had been ruled out even before they had completed any fast work on the Malton gallops. They would appear much later in the season, having grown hugely over winter and now being backward and big framed. All three would need more time and the Gimcrack in August would come far too quickly for them.

The remaining nine colts had all been x-rayed to ensure their knees would stand the rigours of early training and racing. This was a staging point Harry had picked up from Willie Warcup, it ensured the youngsters weren't pushed on too early. As Harry had explained to his new stable staff at the time, like humans, a young horse's knee joints are open when born and don't mesh until into their second year of life. The x-ray would determine whether Harry could kick on with their preparation or he would need to give the colt more time to develop, which generated a nail-biting morning with the vet in the first week of April.

Two of his nine remaining colts had needed more time, making it touch and go whether they would see a racecourse before July, but it meant Harry had seven classy Redblood colts to go to war with. He stepped up their home work and the yard held its collective breath.

It was the third week in April when Harry had sat down at the kitchen table following a morning of fast work with the youngsters on the gallops and revealed to a heavily pregnant Jill the outcome of his sales preparation and what the previous five months of hard work had delivered: three of the colts were showing little speed and appeared to be moderate, another couple were of better quality and had some promise and the remaining two were quick, precocious and classy.

'Better than one, or none being classy!' Jill had announced brightly.

'I don't know if we have the strength in depth to win the Gimcrack,' Harry had lamented. 'I'm just not sure they are good enough. Yes, we've a handful of nice horses, the best I've ever trained, but Group class as two-year-olds? It doesn't feel like it.'

'Oh stop being so gloomy! Where's *my* Harry gone to? So much can change in three months.'

'It was easier being optimistic when we only had moderate horses,' Harry pointed out. 'Any win was a big win for us. But I've spent two million pounds... If I can't get it right with horses from Book One... I'm not a racehorse trainer.'

Jill had looked hard at her husband, watching him mope around the kitchen as she creaked to and fro in her newly acquired antique rocking chair – the only comfortable seat she'd found after visiting what felt like every single furniture shop in York.

'Go play piano until you're optimistic again!' she'd finally ordered. He had slunk off to the lounge and started playing. She knew him far too well he thought, better than he knew himself. By evening stables he'd been smiling again.

As Jill had predicted, there had been some changes too. In the next four weeks one of the more moderate performers had started to improve. By early May Harry was down to eight possible contenders for the big race in August: Fletch, Jelly, Samson, Mr Greedy, Luckyman, Fido, Po and Headcase. Of these, he felt Jelly and Fletch were leading his charge for the Gimcrack.

Now the flat season was underway, he'd started to give his string of two year olds some much needed race education. Racing them at York was tantamount to throwing his youngsters in at the deep end, but he reasoned that giving them a glimpse of what they would face three months later in the Gimcrack wasn't such a bad thing, besides, he thought they were ready. Today he would be running three of his leading lights against each other in the same Maiden race.

In fact, his runners at the Dante meeting weren't Harry's first two year olds to race. He'd already sent Mr Greedy and Fido out to contest a lesser Maiden race at Haydock a week previously. Mr Greedy had performed the better of the two, finishing second in workmanlike fashion to a southern-trained horse called Erudition. Fido had been terribly green, travelling in rear before he picked up late on to finish mid-division in a field of twelve. However, the Haydock form had worked out well, rating the race as an above-average Maiden and so both horses appeared to have outside chances of being good enough to go to York in August. Nonetheless, Harry was in no doubt that substantial improvement would be required from both of them over the next few months.

Harry had left the York racecourse stables and was now standing with his two year old colt at his side, waiting to lead him across the racetrack's back straight. He paused and sucked in a chest-expanding breath, taking the opportunity to appreciate the view; the cluster of huge stands with the old chocolate factory tower behind, the expansive green blanket of the Knavesmire laid perfectly flat and miles of interlocked white race-rails denoting the extent of the challenge ahead of the equine athletes.

It was four o'clock; an hour before the race was due to run and the low hum of the race-day crowd was drifting across the Knavesmire as thirty thousand people made their way through the various rings, stands, bars and expansive lawns at the opening meeting of York's season. Best of all, Harry could taste the distinctly sweet tang of chocolate hanging in the air. The Terry's factory located next to the racecourse may have closed for good, but the influence of Henry and Joseph Rowntree meant the aroma of melting chocolate wasn't lost to the city just yet.

Behind him, Mike walked up with his second two year old runner, quickly followed by Zoe with another. Harry glanced back at his trio of runners, all of which had already been saddled, and lifted an arm as if directing a convoy. They set off in Indian file, walking along the railed walkway that snaked its way over the Knavesmire to the pre-parade ring. The ever-present Wang and Bunt trotted into their positions on either side of the equine train, scanning the vast expanse of dead flat grassland for threats. Harry shook his head, a smirk developing; there was no one within two-hundred yards of them as they walked across the Knavesmire. He caught himself and wiped the cockiness from his face, begrudgingly admitting to himself that he admired the consistent professionalism the two security men maintained. He and his staff could probably learn a thing or two from their unfaltering approach to their job.

The winter had proved to be hard in some respects and rewarding in others. Watching their child grow within Jill had been fascinating, awe inspiring and scary in equal measures. However, while one life got closer to beginning, another was ebbing away. Annie had remained at home, but she now needed full-time supervision as her condition was inoperable and she was struggling to cope. It was only a matter of time, so Harry visited most days, squeezing out as many precious minutes as he could with the lady who had brought him up from the age of eight. He and Andrew would probably never see eye to eye. However, a mutual respect had sprung up, powered by their love for Annie. It kept their relationship cordial and on some occasions, bordering on friendly.

Given the importance of the race today, Harry had agreed to phone both Annie and Jill afterwards to give them the un-expatiated version of what happened, even though both of them would be watching live on television. Neither of them could stand up for more than a few minutes - for very different reasons – and there had been no argument from either when it had been strongly suggested they stay at home in Malton.

Before the three horses and five handlers reached the security entrance to the racecourse, Wang ran up and ducked under the railings to take the lead rein of the colt Harry was handling. Both he and Bunt were now trained, signed-off race-day handlers and Wang in particular had impressed in this role. Besides, it gave both men access to virtually every area of the racecourse, something they had insisted was essential once the Revenge Partnership horses started racing. Harry handed over the colt, gave some stern instructions to all three lead-up's - information he'd already given them twice before - and he and Bunt saw each horse booked into the stabling area and then safely installed into a saddling box.

Harry systematically went through each racehorse, checking their tack, teeth, washing their mouths and extending their front legs. Luckyman, Headcase and Po were taking the preliminaries well. Headcase, as his stable name indicated, had been a challenge to break and the colt had very distinct ideas on what he would and would not do. He was by the sire Showcasing, and was sweating up ever so slightly. Luckyman was taking everything in, but on his toes. Meanwhile Po, a name provided by his stable lad Rob, seemed totally nonplussed by the entire experience. It had been suggested the colt was 'like the short, daft one in the Teletubbies'. It emerged Rob's young daughter loved the children's show and little else was allowed to grace his television when she was around.

Po was indeed on the small side and had always been overshadowed by other colts in the yard, but Harry felt he needed to get a run into the young horse to bring him on. He was always completely switched off and seemed to be in a world of his own most of the time on the gallops, happy to follow rather than lead. He'd shown some ability, but nothing like Luckyman or Headcase. Harry had been hopeful a trip to the races would teach Po there was a job to do and give him some purpose, and perhaps even get him revved up. However, so far it seemed the colt was his usual laid-back self.

The Revenge Partnership colt's racing names had been a source of much frustration in the yard, which is why each horse had a distinct stable name, their race names hardly ever mentioned. Redblood had been very specific when it came to the race name given to his horses: there was a list of names which had been reserved with the British Horseracing Authority, the first eight of his horses to gain race entries took a name from his list. Redblood hadn't seemed too bothered about the horses which came later; he'd only provided names for the first eight of his runners. The complication was down to the names Redblood had chosen; they were all a mixture of numbers.

Luckyman's racing name was 'Fifteen Four'. Headcase had been named 'Five Four' and Po 'Nine Two'. Harry did wonder what the racecourse commentator's reaction had been when he'd read down the list of fourteen runners at the declaration stage. Race calling was difficult enough without three of the runner's names being a jumble of numbers. However, Redblood's instructions had been specific in this regard, and as Jill had pointed out, they were only names in a racecard.

Bunt and Harry stood in the middle of the pre-parade ring, Harry taking in the horseflesh, Bunt surveying the humans. The four-thirty race had just finished, so a few members of the public were already massing on the other side of the rails. Only a smattering of owners and trainers were within the ring.

'Over there,' Bunt whispered under his breath. He lifted his eyes over his shoulder, indicating the corner of the stables.

Harry had never mastered nonchalance, and immediately transferred his weight to one leg, peering over Bunt's shoulder. Bunt watched the whites of Harry's eyes widened when he recognised an immaculately suited Manton speaking with his trainer, Eric Goode. Like Harry, Goode had targeted this race, fielding two Manton owned two year olds.

Harry noted Manton seemed to be bigger around the waist since their last meeting at the sales in October; also, his hair certainly had a good deal more silver in it.

'Harry!' Bunt hissed. 'Don't make eye contact. Look at me.'

Harry refocused his gaze onto Bunt and shrugged. 'Too late, his good-looking mate has already clocked me I think.'

Bunt, still with his back to the trio rolled his eyes at Harry's attempt at sarcastic humour.

'That's Doyle,' he scolded gently. 'Just ignore them and do your job. Remember, they are mine and Wang's problem, not yours. We need to avoid them…'

Bunt watched as Harry's eyes narrowed. He turned in time to halt Doyle's approach no more than a yard from Harry.

'Mr Bolt,' Doyle said through his teeth.

Harry was fascinated by the man's face. It seemed his skin was stretched over chin and cheekbones, his muscular system somehow missing. He wondered whether this was the reason he hardly moved his lips when he spoke – would he split the wafer thin skin? Harry was boggled for a few seconds and didn't reply. This seemed to trouble the man, whose eyes were rapidly becoming black slits.

'Mr Bolt,' he repeated in the same level tone. 'One query, Mr Bolt.'

Now Harry purposefully said nothing, instead trading a set of narrowing eyes with Doyle.

Doyle licked his lips. 'Where is B-Billy Redb-blood?' he blurted through his stammer, his voice carrying across the ring. He faltered for a split second, rumpling his bony nose with self-loathing at his incoherent words. However he recovered quickly enough to gauge Harry's reaction. Doyle must have been satisfied with what he saw, as a contemptuous grin creased his mouth while his eyes remained unreadable black lines.

Behind him, Manton had heard the question and started to cross the lawn at a belly-wobbling trot.

'Well? Where is he?' Doyle demanded, cold and assured.

When no reply was offered, Doyle sneered at both men, leaning forward to examine Harry's features.

'You can't win, Mr Bolt,' Doyle crackled from the back of his throat.

Harry suddenly became aware of his heart. Quick, strong beats were sending pulses through his neck. He wondered if they were visible to this skeleton of a man in his ill-fitting suit, standing bony chin out, in his face.

Quite unexpectedly the absurdity of the situation crashed into his consciousness and he couldn't help it, he laughed. Harry clamped his hands to his hips and laughed so whole-heartedly and infectiously from the base of his stomach a slew of faces from right around the pre-parade ring looked over with querying smiles.

Doyle straightened, confusion written on his skull-like features and Manton arrived, taking his colleague's arm to pull him away. Doyle shook himself free. Harry's chest juddered as he attempted to stem another peel of laughter. Then he caught Bunt's look. It was as if the security man couldn't decide whether what he was witnessing was hilarious or horrific. Harry bit his lip and contented himself with watching Doyle's anger bubble inside the man.

Bunt seized Harry's arm and strode off in the direction of the parade ring, manhandling the trainer along for the first few yards until Harry fell in step with him.

'I don't know whether that was incredibly stupid or totally inspired,' Bunt admitted as they navigated around a few other groups of owners in the parade ring. He parked Harry as far away from Manton as was possible, in the opposite corner of the forty-yard wide expanse of manicured grass.

'Just do your job now and ignore them. I'll keep them at bay if they approach us again,' Bunt instructed, stealing a glance up to the other end of the ring to where Manton, Doyle and Goode were standing. Manton was in deep discussion with his colleague while his trainer was stood head down, studiously inspecting a racecard and if Bunt wasn't mistaken, he was edging slightly away from his owners. All the signals were that Goode wasn't too delighted to be associated with them.

'He's got two runners in the race,' Harry pointed out. 'I was expecting a few evil looks, not such a brazen approach... were you?'

'No, not at all, I'd assumed they'd keep their distance... especially in public. It's a strange move. I can't believe it wasn't planned,' Bunt murmured thoughtfully as once more, he eyed Manton at the other end of the parade ring.

Harry bowed his head slightly. 'Sorry about the laugh. But he was being so... well, like a Bond villain. And that skull face. I couldn't help

162

myself; it was partly adrenalin I think.'

'Forget it. It actually unsettled him. No sense of humour these career criminals. He was trying to get a reaction, so I suppose he achieved that, although laughing in his face wasn't what he was expecting.'

Harry considered Bunt's reply and tried for a few moments to understand what might have provoked Doyle. He ignored the half a dozen horses that were now circling the parade ring and instead fixed Bunt with a serious looking gaze.

'Do *you* know anyone called Billy Redblood?'

Distracted, Bunt replied 'No, not a clue who he is, or his relevance to Manton. He's certainly not mentioned in our instructions from Redblood.'

He was glancing around the ring at trainers and owners as well as scanning the crowd surrounding the ring, unaware of Harry's unease.

Harry knew Redblood had an issue with Manton, he'd said as much in his video, and Manton had confirmed this at the Tattersalls yearling sales, but why should Manton expect him to know where this 'Billy' was? After all, he only trained horses for Redblood; Harry hadn't the first clue about his sponsor's private life. He shook himself from his introspection enough to realise his three horses were now being led around the parade ring, along with the majority of the runners. Harry soon became consumed by the job at hand, his attention drawn to the bloodstock on show. He pushed Manton and Doyle to the back of his mind and examined the opposition.

A loose gaggle of colourful silks entering the bottom of the parade ring, signalled it was time for Harry to greet his jockeys. Rory led the trio over, with his fellow pro riders Shane Brown and Madeline Cook. Each wore the Redblood colours, two of them with an alternatively coloured cap. Shane was in his mid-twenties, a seasoned pro who had visited the yard a couple of times to sit on the Redblood horses, while Maddy was only eighteen and had just ridden out her claim. She was riding out of her skin at present and Harry was hoping Headcase would appreciate a lass with soft hands and great balance in the saddle. He'd already spoken to each of them regarding their riding instructions, so there was only a little small talk before all three were legged-up and safely out into the parade chute. The three youngsters behaved well, and although Headcase needed some persuading to kick off down the narrow chute, once he got going he behaved kindly for his young pilot.

Their job done for the moment, Harry and his staff left the confines of the parade ring to take up a viewing position on the rails. They positioned themselves just after the finishing pole in order to watch the race, being close enough to quickly recapture their horses once the race had finished.

Harry was glued to the large television screen in the centre of the course as the youngsters started to load into their allotted starting stalls. Nerves started to jangle in the bottom of his ribcage; there was nothing left to do but watch the race unfold. Eight months work would be judged on the next seventy-five seconds. The stalls opened and the racecourse commentator announced the race was off.

Luckyman's race finished at the start. As the stalls flew back Rory seemed to be jolted sideways and when the colt jumped Rory was unbalanced. The partnership remained intact, but the first four to five strides of his race consisted of Rory finding his stirrups and trying to get Luckyman straight and then into a gallop. He'd lost ten lengths on the field, was well in rear, and without a chance before the first furlong was completed.

Harry let out a growl of despair, with similar grunts and sighs voiced by his staff. However, Headcase had jumped from the stalls well and was travelling on the far side about two lengths off the leader and Po, as ever, was in behind a wall of horses in the rear of the field, but at least within striking distance. Harry scanned back to where Luckyman was in splendid isolation, detached from the main race, and he realised Rory had made the decision to treat the race as a schooling run, guiding the colt tenderly at a gallop, but no attempt being made to catch the other thirteen horses. Sensible, Harry thought, and switched his attention to the front of the race where a Manton owned colt with the apt name of 'My Way Or No Way' had just moved to the front at the two pole.

Several riders in rear started to get animated, pushing fiercely up the necks of their charges. Headcase was still travelling well within himself on that far side as the leader was asked to lengthen. Harry tried to spot where Po was, but he was lost in a sea of bobbing jockeys, a length or two behind a breakaway group of three which included Headcase.

As the field approached the furlong pole, the bookies' favourite, a horse from a renowned southern yard and boasting fancy breeding, poked its nose in front of the Manton runner. The race caller's rendition of this change in fortunes was greeted with a huge, surging roar from the stands. However, two strides later Headcase was alongside the favourite to create a line of three, which was when Harry's staff, including Wang, started to jump around in front of him.

Subsequently, Harry couldn't understand why at that particular moment he took the decision to look away from the television screen in favour of peering straight down the track. It provided a head-on view of the action, which from his view point behind the winning line, gave him no real indication of the relative positions of his horses. However, what it did allow him to witness was Po being pulled out from behind a wall of horses to switch onto the nearside running rail and under a hands and heels ride, charge up the home straight right in front of the crowd. They were bellowing as the Manton horse, the favourite, and Headcase fought out their finish in the centre of the course while Po shot up the stands rail.

Shane Brown, pumped Po along and still hadn't raised his whip. He simply crouched low and pushed in synchronicity with his mount. Po's response was to lengthen his stride and cut the distance with the leading three as if biting out huge chunks of the turf between them. As if sensing the split second timing required of him, Po dipped his head and struck the winning line at full stretch in synchronicity with the three colts away in the centre of the track.

Po immediately flashed past Harry and his gaggle of terribly excited members of staff, retaining his position on the stands rail, Shane high in the saddle as he slowed and directed the colt around the bend at the end of the straight. Wang, usually silent and watchful, waved a head collar around in great loops above his head and was whooping in delight. In contrast, Bunt watched his colleague's celebration, slowly shaking his own head, but with a silly grin plastered on his face.

As the commentator completed his post race analysis the racecourse announcer declared a photograph between Headcase, Po and Manton's colt, who had fought back well in the last few strides to go past the fading favourite.

'Did we win?' Mike shouted excitedly over to Harry as all five of team Bolt jogged down the rails toward the chute into the parade ring.

'No idea,' returned Harry in a bit of a daze, with half an ear listening for the result to be announced. He only then became aware he was wearing a smile so broad it was forcing his face to ache with its breadth.

Zoe, Wang and Mike ran to the top of the chute, bobbed under the rails and onto the track, walking a dozen yards up the inside rails, looking toward the centre of the Knavesmire for their returning charges. Luckyman was the first to appear, having crossed the line in last position at a pedestrian swinging gallop. Rory's approach telegraphed his disappointment via his body language well before he'd dropped off the colt. He produced a sullen look while quietly retrieving his tack and waved Harry away to deal with his other runners, promising to speak with him later.

'This is taking forever,' complained Zoe as she led Po into the parade ring once more. 'What numbers are we waiting for?'

'Seven and four,' Harry replied quickly, before slapping a hand on Shane's boot to congratulate him on a great ride.

She was followed by Wang with Headcase while Mike had disappeared in the opposite direction back to the racecourse stables across the Knavesmire with Luckyman and the other unplaced horses.

'Look at him,' Harry remarked to Zoe, gesturing toward Po in amazement. 'He's... strutting!' he exclaimed.

The colt was animated, holding his head high and positively statuesque as he swaggered over the parade ring grass toward the winning positions for the first three home. By far the smallest of the first three finishers, it was almost comical and yet Harry immediately felt warmth spread in his breast for the little show-off.

Zoe laughed, her pigtail flipping from one shoulder to another as she glanced back at the diminutive colt.

'I'll stay with these two and...' Bunt started but cut himself off when the public address system crackled.

'Here is the result of the photograph for first place,' stated the racecourse announcer in a steady, measured tone. 'First number four...' The result was greeted with a cheer which rang through the stands and Zoe emitted a 'Yes!' which made Po shake his head from side to side for a second or two.

Harry was immediately surrounded by a number of well-wishers, several of which were his own owners who had popped up from nowhere to help celebrate the win.

Bunt was patiently trying to cope with the influx of people approaching the winners enclosure. He caught the trainers' eye and in a raised voice said, 'Heaven help us if you actually win the Gimcrack Harry, this is only a maiden. Is it always like this?'

'No, not at all,' Harry snorted happily. 'It's because they know they've seen a classy, Yorkshire trained horse,' he managed before the paddock announcer welcomed Nine Two into the number one spot, adding that this was Yorkshire born Harry Bolt's first ever winner at York.

Shane jumped off Po and was bursting to tell Harry about the ride.

'He was just padding along following the midfield group along and I thought he was just going to go past a couple when I pulled him out,' said the rider breathlessly, more from the excitement than any physical exertion. 'Then he cocked an ear at the crowd at the furlong pole and he exploded. I've never felt a horse change the way he did. There's not much of him, but what there is caught fire!'

Shane's rosy cheeks were matched with the excited flame in his eyes and he clearly wanted to continue but Harry pointed to the weighing room and told him, 'That's great, Shane. Go weigh in. I need to see to my other two, I'll speak with you later... and great ride by the way.'

Shane was immediately swamped by reporters and a television crew and Harry made sure Zoe got the colt some water before looking around to try and spot Wang and Headcase. Instead of the small, neat, Japanese man, it was Benedict Manton's frame that filled his line of sight, Doyle lurking ghost-like in his shadow. Harry was caught in the man's lurid gaze and unlike Doyle's earlier approach, he couldn't find any room for levity now. Manton exuded an aura of managed aggression, glowering over the five yards between them. Harry got the sense the man was sucking the joy from him.

Bunt was quickly at his elbow, escorting Harry further down the line of winners into the third placed horse spot where Headcase had been dismounted. A trio of racing reporters followed Harry down and started to quiz him about his three runners. They were scribbling copious notes once he revealed the Gimcrack would be the target.

The course reporter from *The Racing Post*, a squirrely young chap wearing a fedora over a prematurely balding pate furrowed his brow before asking, 'The winner of this Maiden has won the Gimcrack twice in the last four years. The...' he checked the name of the owner in his racecard '...Revenge Partnership must be keen to win the race, having fielded three today?'

Harry regarded him with interest, it being rare for a racing hack to be quite so insightful. 'Certainly,' he answered carefully. 'I'm keen to win any Group race.'

'And your owner?' pushed the young man.

'Mind your backs!' broke in Wang, effectively killing the conversation as Headcase was led straight through the group surrounding Harry, scattering the reporters in several directions.

Harry looked over at Bunt, who had been at his side, but now stood on the other side of Headcase holding one arm at his elbow while his right hand rested on his chin. One eyebrow was raised in mock astonishment.

'Incredible timing, Mr Bunt,' Harry observed with a wink.

'Yes,' said a tinny voice. 'Very... clever.'

Doyle had somehow sidled up behind Harry. He spun round and the odious man was so close he breathed in a waft of pungent, stale cigarettes.

Doyle remained rigid and silent, examining Harry's face from close quarters. Bunt was on the move now, Doyle noticed and held up a palm.

'One th-thing. One,' Doyle insisted.

'You won,' he quirked his lip, the hint of a sneer quashed. 'But what... have you lost?' He paused enigmatically before whipping round and stalking off, leaving Harry and Bunt staring after him.

****

The two horseboxes pulled into Pickering Farm stables at eight-fifteen in the evening and Harry was immediately convinced something wasn't right.

His pulse had been racing for the last thirty minutes and all his thoughts were of Jill. She hadn't been reachable on the house phone or her mobile since the race. The longer it had gone on, the more nervous he had become. Both her mobile and the landline had been unobtainable, immediately going to voicemail. His concern had started as soon as he had jumped into the horsebox to set-off for home. Jill didn't pickup or reply to his text messages and as they had drew closer to Malton he was redialling her number once every thirty seconds, desperate to hear her voice. The last two miles on the local roads around Norton had been pure torture.

The farmhouse was dark as the horseboxes stopped at the yard gates. All the lights were out. Questions, fears, and possible reasons for the yard to appear so quiet rushed at Harry. He slammed his eyes tight shut for a short time, trying to clear his head. The gate creaked open and the horsebox trundled forward, Harry willing the vehicle to come to a halt. Was the farmhouse ever in complete darkness at this time? It was twilight and while the side of the farmhouse was still being struck with some semblance of sunlight, long shadows were cast everywhere else. Up in the top yard to the right of the farmhouse, Harry could hear horses whinnying for their feed and there was a faint smell of smoke hanging in the air.

He sent Mike and Wang straight up to see to the horses while he and Bunt set off round to the back of the farmhouse to check on Jill and Moore. Zoe had been instructed by Bunt to stay in the box or be sacked. She shot him a frustrated glance, shrugged belligerently, got down from the box and ran up the yard after Mike.

Bunt had done his best to keep Harry on an even keel, but even he had privately started to have qualms. Should he and Wang have left the yard to Moore and civilians alone? There were security gates, closed circuit television in every stable and around the house... but was it enough? He had secretly been attempting to contact Moore for the last forty-five minutes.

Cries of Jill's name went up from Harry as he got to the back door and similar shouts came over the tiles of the farmhouse from the top yard. Before Harry could enter the farmhouse, he heard his own name being called from the top yard. He left Bunt checking the kitchen and his heart soared when he rounded the farmhouse and spotted the figure of a very pregnant woman calling his name again. She was standing at the top on the yard, hugging herself, the setting sun bathing her outline in a faint glow. As Harry ran toward her he called to her again and looking up she gave a tired, relieved smile. Zoe appeared from further up the yard, hot tears streaming down her face, Mike with his arm around the girl. Harry's run slowed and now he could see Jill's face. She was covered in a film of dirt, the thin watery lines carving pale white rivulets down her cheeks; her dress was similarly stained and smudged.

'What is it? Are you okay' Harry asked as he took her carefully up in his arms, delighting in her smell and her warmth.

'They killed Jelly,' Jill wailed, before burying her face in her husband's chest.

Twenty-Five

That night Harry experienced anger so strong he found it hard to calm himself. He'd met with anguish and grief at a young age and allowed these to fill him until he felt he would burst, but eventually he'd pushed them back into the recesses of his mind, to the margins where they couldn't damage him any further. This evening he discovered proper, adult anger was far more powerful. He and Bunt sat Jill down in what was left of the kitchen and by candle light she related the last few hours at the farmhouse.

The visitors had been thorough. Three had arrived, two men and a woman, just after the stable staff left for the day at half-past four, the exact time Manton and Doyle had been very vocal in the stabling area at York. They came with the tools of their trade; hammers, axes and picks.

Moore was caught by surprise, probably by someone climbing over the neighbouring buildings at the back of the yard. He'd known nothing of his assailant, having been rendered unconscious in the stable yard with a single blunt strike. They'd dragged him into a stable and locked him in with a less than impressed filly. She had given the inert young man a few initial nips for invading her space. Once Moore had come round the filly had bullied him around her box for a couple hours while he dealt with a banging headache. Bunt had released him and admitted to being extremely relieved when the man in his twenties bounced to his feet, angry as hell and ashamed at having failed to contain the unwanted visitors. His first action was to run up the yard in order to apologise to Jill.

The woman, tall, shapely, wearing a wide brimmed hat and almost black sunglasses which she never removed, had walked to the farmhouse door, smiled sweetly, and then forced her way in as soon as Jill had answered the door. The two men followed moments later. They had been dressed in grey with masks over their faces, which they never removed. The woman proceeded to pepper Jill with questions about Billy Redblood, demanding to know where he was, what she knew about Thomas Redblood. There were questions fired at her regarding someone called Doctor Gupta and finally, and with the threat level at its highest, they wanted to know where they could find the 'memory stick'.

'I didn't know what you'd done with Redblood's memory stick, but they never found it. The woman checked the computer and said it wasn't there either. She said something about it not having the right file on it.'

Jill took a breath before continuing. 'They never touched me though,' she explained in bewilderment. 'One of them, the small thin man started poking my stomach and the woman got really angry with him. She was, well… strange. I think her accent was from the North East and I never got to see all her face, but she was quite elegant really, a bit out of place compared with the other two thugs. This big one said almost nothing and caused most of the damage around the house.'

Jill had recounted this, before going on to describe how Millie had largely ignored the woman and larger man, instead persistently yapping and snarling at the wiry man to whom the Westie took a sharp dislike.

'He eventually got sick of her and tried to land a kick. The big chap picked Millie up by the scruff of her neck and I thought he was going to hurt her, but instead he gave her a pat, took her outside, and left her in an empty stable. Strange that, he was really quite soft with her,' Jill related thoughtfully.

The two men had taken their ancient computer and then torn the farmhouse apart looking for the information Jill had insisted didn't exist. Then she had screamed it, and then pleaded with them. Harry had felt physically ill at this point in her story, before vowing to expel every Redblood horse from his yard immediately, only for Jill, who remained calm, collected, and incredibly centred, to take her husband aside, and bring him back down to earth.

'I'm okay, the baby is okay, Moore is okay and Millie is okay,' she told Harry quietly while staring deep into his dark brown eyes, her own soft, pale blue eyes forcing his anger to crumble away. 'As long as you're okay too, that's as much as we will ever need.'

'The baby?' he'd asked worriedly.

'He's kicking away.'

Harry had looked quizzically at his wife. 'He?'

'Or she,' Jill had replied with a grin.

The security system had been the first item to be rendered inoperative, along with every recording of the intruders' presence at the yard. Then they had moved on to telephones and any mobile, old or new, had been smashed to bits. Every room in the farmhouse was systematically turned over while Jill had been kept hostage in the kitchen, listening to her home being ransacked.

The devastation had been completed with professionalism. Harry's piano was now in hundreds of splinters across the lounge floor having been maniacally hacked to pieces with an axe. Photos and pictures had been ripped from walls, cabinets raided, floorboards lifted, furniture smashed, and paper… paper in every room, strewn over the floors. Their computer had been smashed open and the hard drive ripped out, a brand new tablet now had its workings hanging from a light fitting. Each of their two bedrooms could no longer boast a working bed, having been shredded with knives or some other bladed instrument. The axe had also been applied vigorously to several walls in an ad-hoc fashion.

Finally, they had taken Jill outside and threatened to kill the horses one by one until she gave them answers to their questions. To Jill's horror the thinner man had produced a handgun, waved it around, and asked where he could find the Redblood horses. When Jill had refused to provide an answer he had entered a stable in the top yard at random and shot the horse inside. It had taken six shots; Jill had known this because the man had to reload his gun afterwards. Amid the sound of the bullets was the man's hysterical screaming and swearing at Jelly, who refused to simply keel over and die immediately. The man had eventually emerged, covered in horse blood and complaining at the way the horse had thrashed about until he'd finally got it right.

When Jill had pleaded with him that she didn't know the answer to any of the woman's questions, he'd gone into the next stable.

'It was Paste,' Jill told the small group which were now gathered around her, only the slightest tremor evident in her voice. 'He... Paste I mean, was already pretty upset at all the gunshots and I could tell he was up a height even without seeing him, he was kicking the box wall before the thin man opened the stable door. I told him not to go in, but he laughed... unbolted the door and threw it open. I still only saw a fraction of what went on, but I know Paste went for him even before he managed to raise his gun.'

Jill paused, wanting to get her story right. Hugging her stomach with both arms, tears came to her eyes once more but she fought them back.

'He was leaning up against the stable wall and screaming at me to give answers. When I couldn't he started to raise his gun arm, I think he was getting ready to shoot, and Paste rushed into him, shouldering him to the ground and aimed a couple of kicks with his front legs to his head and neck. I could see the man on the floor, writhing around and Paste moved forward and stamped on him a few times with his back legs. His partner, the big man, started towards the stable, but it was too late. The man got to his knees and started to crawl toward the stable door and that's when Paste turned around and aimed a kick with his back legs.'

Jill's voice cracked and she swallowed, but waved away an offer of a glass of water.

'The hooves hit his head so hard, he tumbled back in the yard, just an unmoving, blood spattered black lump. He looked so... unnatural,' she said whilst wiping her eyes. 'I don't know if he was okay, I never saw him say anything or do anything after that.'

She took a breath and it caught a couple of times as she attempted to stave off a sob. Around her were serious, shocked faces. Jill placed a hand over her mouth for a few seconds then rubbed the rest of her face. When her hand finally fell away she told the surrounding group; 'I think Paste might have killed him.'

Her audience, consisting of Bunt, Wang, Mike, and Harry made placating, positive noises while sharing troubled looks between them. Paste's reputation was well established and if he wanted to kill something, unlike the thin man, the gelding could be trusted to get it right.

'The big man was straight over to his partner,' Jill added. 'He started calling him 'Pat' or 'Pete' I think, which got the woman really angry, she started screaming at him, calling him stupid. She disappeared with her phone to her ear and when she came back I was pushed into an empty stable and they bolted it. I was there for about an hour before Mike found me.'

Jill tried hard to answer Bunt and Wang's many questions. They also apologised. In fact they apologised so profusely, Jill had a quiet, but stern word with them, convincing them she was not in need of any mollycoddling. Eventually fatigue set in and she started to fade.

Bunt insisted Jill should be taken to her parents' house at the other side of Malton for the night. Harry drove her there and explained to her parents that they'd lost all power to the farmhouse due to an electrical problem and it was safer to have her with them, given her condition. This much was true; their visitors had taken their axe to the electricity control panel. Jill's parents agreed without hesitation and happily waved him off, unaware of the depth of the issues at Pickering Farm.

Bunt sat Harry down at the kitchen table as soon as he stepped back through the kitchen door and placed a coffee in front of him. It was only then that Harry realised the electrics had been fixed, or at least fudged enough to provide some light. Harry thanked him and flopped into one of the two kitchen chairs which remained usable, although the other was now totally backless. Bunt straddled the newly formed stool, placed his elbows on the table, propped his face up in his hands, and waited for Harry to take a few sips of the strong black liquid from an old cracked mug which had missed the devastation.

'I know it's been a long, stressful day...' started Bunt before pausing, apparently stuck for his next few words. '... and you'll want to straighten everything up as soon as possible...'

'We need to move the dead horse,' Harry broke in.

'That's being taken care of now.'

Harry sent a questioning frown across the table.

'Yes, Moore and Wang,' Bunt said, a hand moving around the back of his neck, massaging the top of his spine. Harry thought the silver-haired security man looked unusually jaded and a little uncomfortable.

'Things have... developed since you left an hour ago. We have a couple of people in the farmhouse I need you to meet. Come on...'

Bunt got up and led Harry into the lounge. Two tall men in similar attire stood amongst the broken furniture and other assorted household jumble strewn over the floor. They both looked up when Harry entered the room and he immediately recognised the closest figure as George Plant.

'Hello, George!' Harry exclaimed in surprise. 'What brings you here so late?'

He went forward and shook George's extended hand, partly out of habit, but it seemed to be the right thing to do to avoid commenting on the mess the house was in.

'It's good to see you, Harry,' said George. He smiled but the usual glint in his eyes was missing. 'I need to introduce you to someone...'

Harry shuffled round a little, transferring his outstretched hand to the stranger.

'This is my brother... Thomas Redblood.'

Twenty-Six

'You can't leave him here you stupid big ape!' wailed Deacon at the sight of Pete Warren's crumpled body lying across the boot of Loretta's Range Rover.

Loretta placed his hands on his hips, sucked in a lungful of the air from the inside of the Money Tree, and decided it tasted of diesel fumes, presumably from the generators. He sighed, turned, and strode up to the still gibbering Deacon wearing a blank expression, all business. He thrust out a single, large hand. Gripping the man's throat just below his Adam's apple he started to squeeze. He watched carefully as Deacon's eyes bulged. He listened intently as gagging noises started to issue from the man's constricted airways. Loretta went about his task with a patient, almost bored look on his face.

Deacon pounded weak fists onto Loretta's arms and chest and he even tried a willowy kick to his attacker's groin, with no effect. Deacon's two security men looked on from their sentry positions, poised, but unmoving, Loretta's eyes daring them to challenge him. He waited until Deacon's eyes started to dilate and then released him by throwing the object of his discontent to the floor.

Squinting over the mess of brick built rooms that made up the living and working quarters for the five residents of the Money Tree, Loretta considered his options.

'Thomas Redblood had a room here, didn't he?'

Deacon was coughing between muttered profanities and didn't reply. Loretta poked him with a steel toecap.

'Redblood, he must have had living quarters here?'

'Yes, *of course*!' Deacon replied in a hoarse voice but still managed to lace his speech with a touch of sarcasm.

Loretta tutted and then calmly kicked the man hard in the stomach. Deacon immediately ejected the noodles he had eaten for his supper and proceeded to roll in his own vomit, grasping at the floor to steady himself as pain flowered through his body.

'You're not listening to me,' Loretta admonished. 'I'm taking Pete into Redblood's old room and your guards are going to show me, so I can make my friend comfortable.'

Deacon appeared to have learned from Loretta's most recent act of violence. Kneeling on all fours, he nodded his head and waved a few fingers at the nearest guard who immediately trotted over to the car.

Loretta joined him and together they rummaged around in the back of the car, emerging with a ghostlike Pete Warren, wrapped in a blanket. Loretta cradled his friend and carried him into the main entrance to the buildings.

The guard hung back, helping Deacon to his feet, bending down to retrieve a few pens and a small wallet Deacon had left on the floor. He popped them in Deacon's jacket pocket, whispering into his superior's ear.

'I don't know if you want to tell him just yet Mr Deacon, but Mr Loretta's partner is dead. I'd say he's been that way for quite a while, Sir.'

Deacon let out a series of expletives under his breath and hobbled into the building after Loretta.

Loretta kicked open the steel door to Redblood's vacant sleeping quarters and placed Pete Warren's limp body gently onto a single bed covered with recently laundered sheets. He reverently laid his friend out and cradling his greasy black hair in one hand, he slipped a thin pillow beneath his head. Footsteps approached and Deacon's face appeared around the open door. Loretta, kneeling at the bedside, turned to glower at Deacon, daring the man to come any further into the room. Deacon snapped his eyes away and backed out, closing the door behind him with a positive click.

Loretta returned his gaze to his dead friend. He pulled the bedclothes closer to the man's chin and palm down, smoothed down several clumps of Pete's jet-black hair which had fallen forward over his pale face. His hand returned to his side, sticky with a thin layer of waxy gel combined with dried blood. Loretta peered closer at the back of Pete's head. It looked wrong. He realised a small crescent of Pete's scull was pushed in, ringed with matted, almost black blood. It didn't worry him, he'd seen it before. He arranged the greasy black hair so it covered the offending area and allowed himself a faint smile when the smell of lemons reached him.

Loretta noticed one of Pete's eyes was still slightly open, which he corrected. He looks right now, Loretta thought. He's asleep. He stood up, looking down at Pete's angelic pose, wishing the white sheet over him was indeed white and not a faded grey.

'You'll do, Pete,' he told the corpse.

Scanning the room he located a small wooden chair, no more than a child's desk chair. Various books and magazines stacked on top of the chair were dumped in the corner of the room and Loretta placed the chair in front of the bed before carefully easing his backside onto it.

He needed time. Time to think. Pete had been the only person he'd met who hadn't called him stupid, who had treated him as an equal, who had cared, even a bit. Sure, there were people who were afraid of him, but Pete had been an equal and might have even *liked* him. Pete had looked after him that time Manton smashed that trophy in his face…

Loretta stared at Pete's body, but wasn't focusing. Manton came into his thoughts, Manton and Doyle. He'd phoned them as soon as he and the Geordie woman, Lisa, left the trainer's yard in Malton. As usual, they'd been angry. Angry because he'd called them, angry because he hadn't found Billy or the memory stick thing, and *very* angry Pete was hurt.

They weren't *concerned* though, Loretta decided bitterly.

He was given screamed instructions. Drop the girl off now. No hospitals. No treatment for Pete. *Dispose* of him.

Loretta winced, but there were no tears. He'd stopped crying when he was eight, when he'd fought back and floored his father. He cast the memory away, consigning his broken childhood to the recesses of his mind where it usually lay festering.

He'd decided. Pete wasn't a bit of rubbish to be disposed of, he'd take him to the only place he could, the Money Tree; to get help. But it had been too late for Pete; he'd died during the car journey. A grim smile tightened Loretta's mouth when he remembered Pete's words. He'd warned him about Manton.

'He'll only look after himself and Doyle. We don't count,' Pete had told him. 'Have a backup. Either fix things or have somewhere and someone to run to,' he'd warned.

But Loretta didn't have anywhere or anyone to run to.

He let out a quiet groan, rubbing his face vigorously, eventually running his fingers through his hair, and holding his entwined hands at the back of his head. He opened his eyes and stared at his friend Pete, wishing for inspiration. He remained static for so long his fingers started to tingle with numbness. Suddenly realisation sank into Loretta's tired mind; Pete had a backup.

Loretta made his decision. He almost felt elated. He carefully covered Pete up, said a few words over his body he'd learnt during a very short spell at Sunday school, and taking one of the Range Rovers, left the Money Tree before dawn.

****

The oak tree was impressive, although gnarled at its base with roots striving for moisture. In places they crested the chalky soil and curled over each other in their attempt to drive outwards in search of growth giving nutrients. Late May saw the tree full of life as young, light green leaves filled its branches. Despite being impressive, it was rare for anyone to spend any time examining it at length.

On a ridge on the opposite side of the valley the oak tree was currently of huge interest. A pair of binoculars with night sights scanned up the hillside, alighted on the tree and hovered there. Every few minutes they repeated the same manoeuvre, waiting for movement.

An hour passed. There was movement. A set of headlights, a car emerged nose first from the end of the red building. It disappeared behind the barn, reappeared again seconds later before melting into the darkness.

The sound of digital dialing. A click at the other end of the line.

'Your information was correct. It's here,' reported a man's voice.

Twenty-Seven

Harry retracted his proffered hand and stared at George Plant, seeking confirmation he'd not been mistaken. A grim, stony-faced response from his longstanding owner established the introduction was indeed genuine. Harry's throat suddenly felt dry and he swallowed twice before returning his gaze to the man at George's side who had been introduced as Thomas Redblood. A shot of anger climbed his spine, a sensation which was becoming all too familiar.

The man was standing at a slight angle, leaning gently on an elegant wooden and silver cane to support his right leg. That's where the similarities with his original namesake concluded. This Redblood was a lithe, lean, younger looking man with a full head of neatly cut dark brown hair. He managed to pull off the prosperous older country gent look with aplomb. Under his long leather and cloth coat was a chunky green jumper. A pair of fashionably worn jeans and expensive boots completed his outfit. Harry eyed him with suspicion and he found himself wishing he had Jill by his side. She could have guided him through what was surely going to be a confusing and stressful conversation.

'This is Thomas, Harry. My brother.'

'He is the *real* Thomas Redblood,' George repeated when Harry didn't acknowledge his statement. Unaware that his continued lack of movement or speech had started to become awkward, Harry remained rooted to the spot, regarding Thomas Redblood with fierce intensity.

George tried to place a hand on Harry's shoulder.

'Will you allow us to explain?' he asked reaching forward, only to see the trainer flinch and step away before he could touch him. Harry had a hunted expression and he backed away a few steps, flashing an incredulous look at Bunt. Bunt responded by tucking the corner of his mouth into his cheek and shaking his head.

'They arrived just after you left. I'm just as confused as you are. They checked out though. These guys pay our wages; I've checked the bank accounts.'

A wave of tiredness swamped Harry for a few moments and he wiped a palm across his face. His mind was racing. Worry over Jill and his unborn child, mingled with anger at his dead horse and the carnage left by Manton's men, well, he assumed they were Manton's men... So many problems, so much to sort out.

'Harry...' Redblood rumbled in a deep, crackling voice. It was nothing like the original Redblood's voice. Harry thought it lacked warmth. '...Mr Bunt. I owe everyone at Pickering Farm an apology. I learned of this awful event this evening. Mr Bunt reported to Mr Smith, who in turn informed my brother and I decided I needed to see you both.'

Redblood flicked his eyes toward an overturned armchair and

asked, 'May I…?'

Bunt and George flipped the chair over between them and Redblood folded his tall frame into the broken seat which was devoid of a cushion and had one arm half wrenched off.

'Perhaps, if we could dispense with the awkward introductions, and instead I answer some of the many questions I'm sure you have?'

In making this statement Redblood's heavy East Yorkshire accent burst forth. He rested his cane between his legs and gripped both arms of the chair as best he could, although it was more likely he was holding the broken arm together.

'Please, sit down gentlemen. This may take some time,' Redblood added.

Bunt resurrected the sofa which was now missing one armrest but he located the cushions; ripped but usable. He and Harry sat, Bunt languid at the back of the sofa, Harry perched on its leading edge. Incredibly, the piano seat had survived being thrown across the room and George cleared some carpet space and sat down opposite Harry and Bunt. The two of them squinted at Redblood under the glare of an unshielded electric light which had been rigged up from a bare wire protruding from the ceiling. The rose and plaster which had until recently surrounded an ornate four-armed ceiling light were now lying on the carpet in a pile of twisted steel, glass, plaster and dust.

Redblood waited patiently until all three members of his audience were settled before he spoke again.

'I'm aware all of this is my fault, and I want you to know it will be corrected,' Redblood informed them, his azure blue eyes meeting Harry, Bunt, and George in turn. Harry noticed for the first time how similar Redblood was to George. They shared many of the same facial features, although Redblood was thinner in most respects and he lacked the laugher lines which peppered the corners of his brother's eyes and mouth.

'Billy, or rather 'George' and I grew up here in Malton,' Redblood began. 'Our mother and father both worked as work riders and stable staff all their lives. In fact they worked out of this farmhouse for many years when it was a single yard with over a hundred horses.'

'That's what your dead stooge told me before I got my family into all of this,' Harry interrupted testily, crossing his arms.

Redblood regarded the younger man carefully, his face a blank mask, making Harry set his jaw and narrow his eyes in response. Finally, Redblood twitched his nose and sucked air noisily up his nostrils, his expression altering to one of benign understanding.

'You are angry and resentful,' he said softly. 'I would have similar feelings if I were in your shoes. All I ask is for you to listen to what I have to say. Whatever your reaction when I've finished… I will accept.'

Harry shivered, partly because of the chill in the room, but also because he felt uncomfortably chagrined after his petulant outburst had received such a measured response. He closed his eyes and rubbed the bridge of his nose while nodding his ascent in Redblood's direction.

Redblood blinked rapidly a few times and returned a weak smile Harry's way, being extremely careful not to appear patronising.

He continued, 'I grew up with Benny Manton, Charlie Doyle, and Pete Warren. They were my classmates, but never my friends. George is two years younger than me and in his youthful ignorance became ensnared in their drugs business at the age of eighteen.'

George grimaced at the mention of his name and shifted uncomfortably on his stool.

'In 1993 Manton managed to force George and I into a corner so tight it was essential George left Malton quickly and got as far away from Manton, Doyle and Warren as possible. Meanwhile, I was forced into working for Manton and his cronies.'

Redblood almost snarled at the memory. 'Manton and Doyle knew exactly what they were doing. They needed someone with my skills and so they ingratiated themselves with George. When the opportunity arose they placed him at the scene of a crime in order to blackmail both of us. I'd just spent three years at Newcastle University studying financial systems and computer engineering, so I was exactly what they wanted. Fair dues to Manton, he recognised the potential the internet and online banking could offer to organised crime well before many others. But, he didn't have the technical skills needed to set up an electronic laundering process. Manton threatened to track George down and either kill him or implicate him in a serious crime, or alternatively I could work for him. I was naïve and stupidly agreed. Once I started working for their organisation I had no way out. Either I continued to work for Manton or he would track George down. At least my brother was able to enjoy some sort of freedom, albeit he would always be looking over his shoulder.'

He paused, astute eyes scanning the sofa. 'They put me together with a hideous creature called James Deacon. He became my boss and I became his prisoner. Together we built a state of the art electronic cash laundering process.'

A duo of blank stares returned to Redblood from the sofa.

'Okay,' Redblood said with a barely disguised sigh. 'More explanation needed.'

This reaction prompted a warning glare from George and a mumble of self-admonishment from Redblood before he continued.

'You take drugs, protection and prostitution revenue and turn it into usable, legitimate income. You feed the process with the illegally generated revenue and get clean, usable cash in return. It starts by being paid into bank accounts of individuals and companies and the software does the rest, passing the dirty money through endless bank accounts, company business accounts and deposit accounts via bogus goods and invoices all over the world until it returns into the country as clean, untraceable revenue.'

'I get that,' Harry cut in impatiently, 'But what has Manton's gang got to do with a dead man at the end of our lane pretending to be you?'

Redblood nodded and leaned back, the leather in his coat squeaking against the nylon base of his wrecked chair.

'Manton created a remote workplace out in the sparsely populated East Yorkshire Wolds. They installed generators, living and sleeping quarters and made it very secure. To run their business they used a state of the art computer system with satellite communication. Finally they named their secret location the 'Money Tree' because a large oak tree dominates its entrance. There is only one way in and out, security being of paramount importance.

The Money Tree literally sprouted electronic money from day one. Manton moved me there in the mid-nineties and even now I have no idea exactly where it's located. He's obsessive when it comes to maintaining security. They gave me the use of a small cottage on the east coast for a couple of days every few months, but even there Manton's security staff would be with me. Any behaviour outside their strict rules and I would be forcibly returned to the Money Tree. All five staff were driven there blindfolded, and only one member of the security staff knew its true location.

Over the years, Deacon and I built a system so sophisticated it was almost impossible to determine where the drugs money originated. We must have laundering billions of pounds garnered from illicit activities from dozens of crime gangs. Manton built a small empire from his percentage on every pound that dropped through the system.'

Harry leaned forward again and Redblood looked up, raising his bushy eyebrows to encourage the question which was quite obviously on the trainer's mind.

'So Manton had a hold over you. But he's involved in organised crime! Why couldn't you just pick up a phone and call the police? You had *twenty-four years* to do it!'

Redblood's mouth cracked a sad smile. 'Once you are involved in a crime syndicate, death tends to be the only way out. Even if the police did believe me, found the Money Tree and understood I was working against my will, I'd be forced into hiding for the rest of my life.'

He showed a glazed expression for a few seconds, focusing on the far wall of the living room. When Redblood started speaking again he had a resigned, frustrated quality in his voice.

'Besides, Manton has people everywhere. I would have been dead long before I could ever testify against him. And what would I show the police to prove my story? Manton has police on his payroll. He'd have made it his business to track myself and George down and kill us before we could testify against him.'

Redblood paused, took a breath, and continued with a renewed vigour. 'I spent hours every single day for years trying to perfect a means of escape. The one thing in my favour was George. He knew the situation I was in, he was the only one. But we had to be careful. Then a few months ago I saw a route out: I had to die.'

'You've got to hand it to the Scandinavians,' George interjected. 'It was Bluetooth which gave us a lifeline.'

George's words seemed to give Redblood further impetus and he gave his brother a tight smile. 'Yes, a simple text message app... Deacon will be kicking himself. That's if he's found the way we did it yet!'

He switched his attention back to Bunt and Harry, far more animated now. 'I didn't have internet access and, of course, I wasn't allowed a phone, so there was no way I could interact with websites, send email, or written messages. However, Deacon carried his phone everywhere. His big mistake was leaving his Bluetooth activated.'

A mischievous smile played on the fringes of Redblood's mouth and his eyes twinkled.

'When the first phones with Bluetooth came out, we were investigating the criminal applications. I immediately saw the possibilities and quietly loaded a small messaging app onto Deacon's phone when he was distracted and then found a way of depositing text messages onto his phone via Bluetooth from my workstation computer. As soon as a message was sent the app immediately deleted the history.'

George broke in again. 'When Tom helped me leave Malton he told me to keep the same mobile number just in case. Three years after he'd got me out, there he was! It was only one way of course, I could never reply, but it was so good to know he was okay, and I could manage his portfolio and build a fighting fund.'

'His portfolio...' Bunt said knowingly. 'You siphoned money from the laundering process...'

'Absolutely not!' Redblood blurted, gripping the arms of his chair so hard they creaked. 'I'd given George everything I had to go on the run with. He was working and added his own money and we started to trade shares like anyone else. I had little to occupy me, so I analysed stocks and shares in my spare time. It was what I was trained to do. I would tell George volumes and share codes and he would complete the investments. I analysed technology stocks in particular and over the next twenty years we were lucky and amassed a small fortune, money I would put to good use once I could extract myself from Manton's grip.'

'The Malton branch of The Bank of Yorkshire really looked after us once our deposits got beyond a couple of million,' George chipped in.

Redblood relaxed and leaned back. 'There was no illegality. I had my fill of that every single day. Billy... sorry, George and I, played the markets and we did well. Our portfolio is substantial and it's all in my brother's name. It's what's paying for your security services and Harry's horses and training costs.'

Bunt sniffed and scrutinised Redblood once more. 'We only have your word on that.'

Redblood gave a chuckle. 'My dear Mr Bunt, that attitude is exactly why I chose you to look after Mr Bolt here! You are fiercely loyal to those you believe in and have a superbly unfaltering distrust of everyone else. You are incredibly well matched to your chosen line of work.'

'It didn't stop... *this* happening,' Bunt replied bitterly, gesturing to the desolation around the room.

'Indeed,' Redblood agreed. 'And this is the only reason I'm here tonight. I had no intention of revealing myself at all, until this happened. However, I'm here now to make you both a guarantee that all this,' he opened his arms, palms up, indicating the farmhouse. 'All this will be put right and you will be able to continue with my plan to win the Gimcrack.'

He paused, apparently in thought, before continuing. 'George can confirm all our cash is in his name and we can prove where every penny of our capital came from and *believe me*, the two of you need our help now more than ever.'

Bunt inspected Redblood closely before turning to Harry, who shrugged. 'I guess it sort of makes sense,' Harry admitted. 'It's a weird story, but sort of believable.'

'Believe me, it's about to get weirder!' said Redblood darkly. 'You need to know about the poor man who died for me.'

Twenty-Eight

Redblood paused, surveying the mess on the floor, or rather, glazing over as if contemplating the next slice of story. He clicked back into the present, shivered, and asked, 'Is anyone cold?'

Ten minutes later the four men were back in the living room having scoured the farmhouse for blankets. Harry had located an old two bar stainless steel electric heater from the loft and they had prepared hot drinks. At least the destructive thoroughness of the visitors hadn't extended to items such as the steel pans, which had allowed them to boil up some water on top of the stove.

Nursing a mug of instant coffee, Redblood noted the time on his wristwatch. 'It's late, so I'll hurry along and try and get this situation in some sort of order,' he told the others.

A check of his own watch informed Bunt it was 1-35am. He grunted his ascent toward Redblood, aware he was due to start his morning security detail in less than five hours time. It had been a long, arduous day which was about to get extended even further. He didn't feel Redblood or his brother were currently a threat, however having been lied to for the best part of five months he was loath to take everything the men said as gospel. In his experience a liar tended to remain a liar, and a serial liar couldn't help himself - it was ingrained into their psyche. That said, Redblood was more believable than most.

Bunt caught his thoughts mid-flow and smiled inwardly. He was reminded that Redblood being wholly believable was almost certainly the most dangerous ability the man could possess. He was intelligent, resourceful, had access to sizeable funds, and was, well… alive! Even the authorities believed he was dead. He could feel the tiredness beginning to seep into him, the extra warmth from the blankets and electric fire causing his eyelids to become heavy. Determined to stay lucid and concentrate throughout Redblood's next set of explanations, he removed the blanket from his upper body and left it over his legs only. He swallowed a deep draft of coffee and took time to examine the two brothers' faces in detail once more, searching for signs of duplicity. His conclusion was that George was an intellectual whilst his brother Thomas Redblood was astute and street-wise. Neither exhibited signs of being pathological liars.

'About two years ago, I became depressed and ended up refusing to work for Deacon,' Redblood began. 'Call it cabin fever or simply caprice, I downed tools. Manton turned up the next day and took a baseball bat to my right leg, breaking it in two places to teach me a lesson.'

'He was the consummate professional though,' Redblood noted wryly. 'He was careful to ensure I could still sit at a computer and type programming code even though my splintered leg bones had broken through the skin.'

Redblood added a hint of irony to the way he delivered his final few words, although he quickly made a decision to tone down further mentions of violence. He'd noticed Harry shiver, colour draining from the trainer's dark face until it took on a grey hue, dark rings appeared around his eyes. Living in a violent, destructive environment for the last twenty-odd years had hardened him, he had to remember that.

He stole a quick glance at Bunt who had increasingly sagging bags under wide eyes. Redblood determined there was no need to inflict that harsh world onto innocents like Harry unnecessarily. He picked up his story with a lighter, more positive lilt to his voice.

'It was that injury which provided the germ of a plan to break free from Deacon, the Money Tree, and Manton. They brought in a doctor from York. His name was Ferdinand Gupta, a medical student in his mid-twenties who had made the mistake of losing more than he could afford on a roulette table in a Leeds casino owned by one of Manton's clients. Manton bought his debt and the normal pattern of friendly requests to patch up a knife wound here, or a gunshot there quickly became a threat to expose this nefarious work to his employers and be struck off. Within a few months they owned the poor man.'

Redblood shook his head before adding, 'If Manton gets his hooks into you, you're as good as dead.' This comment received another warning stare from George to move on.

'Gupta was picked up in York each time he came to treat me. He would be blindfolded and driven to the Money Tree. Gupta told me he was studying bone cancer, it was initially just idle chatter as he worked. He treated terminally ill patients, people in huge pain and with little time left. Gupta was a good man. He compared his own self-inflicted problems with the lives of his patients and counted himself lucky, despite being on Manton's leash. He also told me of a patient, a man similar to myself in his late fifties who only had two or three months to live. He was Syrian by birth and his name was Sali Malik. He came to Britain with his young daughter fifteen years ago and was wracked with guilt because he would be leaving her with nothing but debt. The strain of watching his health slowly fade was already placing a great strain on her. That's when it came to me. On the third occasion Gupta came back to reset my misaligned leg, I managed to pass him a note. It outlined a plan to release both of us from Manton's grip and also provide Sali Malik with a way to look after his daughter when he was gone.

When Gupta returned a week later to complete his work with me, he indicated he and Sali were in agreement and left a note in my plaster cast with details of what was required of me. This time Gupta demanded to see Deacon before he left and announced I had bone cancer with only a few weeks to live.'

Redblood paused, glancing round the men in turn to ensure he still had their attention.

'Deacon reacted as you would expect, he was straight in touch with Manton. He didn't even speak to me. In fact, I was worried for a few days they might kill me to save themselves unnecessary strain. That was before I made it clear they needed to understand how to operate some of the processes only I knew about,' explained Redblood, momentarily allowing his mischievous smile to return.

'Deacon was furious I'd kept some things about the system to myself,' he added with a smirk.

'Gupta returned a few days later and managed to convince Deacon my health had declined and I was about to die. He showed Deacon some faked test results and meanwhile I had conveniently started to display as many symptoms as possible to make the illness realistic. Gupta was brilliant. He examined me again and played his role perfectly, that was... until I had to die.'

Harry and Bunt were staring open-mouthed at Redblood. As fantastical as his story was, the man was carrying his audience with him.

'The plan required I would die while Gupta was with me. He would give me an injection which would render me unconscious... well, comatose actually... dead enough to fool Deacon and his security men with an almost impossible to find pulse. He would pronounce me dead and offer to take me back to York Teaching Hospital with him. He arrived a week later to deliver my treatment as normal, and we put the plan in action.'

'One of the security guards was always with us, but he wasn't monitoring what went into me. The injection went smoothly and we waited for it to take effect. It should have taken hold immediately. Ten minutes later I was still awake, with Gupta becoming agitated and running out of excuses to stay, so he injected me again. It was five minutes later that he realised he had brought the slow acting version of the drug, and I had now been given an almost fatal dose.'

Redblood grinned. 'As you can see gentlemen, I survived. In the end I feigned a death mask and by the time Deacon had been informed and organised to get rid of me, I'd succumbed to the drug. Gupta did redeem himself though. The guard blindfolded Gupta as usual and tossed me in the back of the car. He drove us to Scarborough General car park, shoved my body out the back of the car, and left Gupta to carry me the rest of the way. He managed to get some adrenaline into me and luckily I came round a few hours later. I contacted George, got access to our bank account, and went into hiding.'

'Which still left you with a problem. A dead person without a dead body,' Bunt observed.

'Precisely.'

'I still don't understand!' Harry moaned. He had the impression

Bunt was ahead of him somehow. 'Why did you involve us in all of this, why not go straight to the police once you were free?'

Redblood flashed a toothy smile at Harry and gleefully clasped his hands together. 'Look around you, Harry. This is the type of destruction Manton brings down upon the people his life touches. He's been getting away with it for *decades*. He deserves to be brought to heel but no one has been able to do it. If I walked into a police station now I could no doubt demand some attention, but what evidence can I use? I don't know where the Money Tree is located and if I mention the laundering process the police would demand evidence. That's information I simply haven't got.'

'Like I've said before, Manton is always two steps away from any wrongdoing,' Bunt remarked ruefully. 'That big show of threatening us and creating a scene at York races today was simply Manton ensuring he had a perfect alibi for what happened here.'

Harry looked back on his day at York races. It all seemed such a long time ago, the joy of his first winner at the track had long since evaporated. His anger started to rise in him once more. This time it was specific to Manton.

Redblood watched various emotions flash across Harry's face and a minor wave of guilt washed over him when the boy's features settled into a glum, unfocussed stare. The effect the visitors to Pickering Farm had wrought on Harry's wife and wider family around the yard were not lost on him. For a moment he wondered whether the cost of seeing this through could be too high… he quickly dismissed such nonsense. He'd waited over twenty years for this opportunity and made plenty of sacrifices, he wasn't about to exit the plan now.

He cleared his throat and sat up as best he could in his cushion-less armchair. 'Let me continue my story, Harry. I promise you'll see how things can fit together. I needed to flush Manton out… to apply pressure... get *him* to be the one to wield the axe, the one to pull the trigger.'

Harry's squinted under the raw glare of the light bulb, his anger quickly transferring to Redblood. He raised his voice a notch.

'Are you for real? You actually *want* Manton to attack us… I can't believe…'

Redblood's hands were quickly spread, fingers splayed out in a calming motion, at the same time he shook his head in an animated display to try and placate Harry.

'I'm not speaking literally, Harry,' Redblood insisted. 'The reason I'm here tonight is because I want to *protect* your family. I want the violence to stop, which is why I want to see Manton behind bars. I have to give the authorities hard evidence of his involvement in criminality. In short, I need to force Manton to make a mistake.'

Harry shook his head and rubbed a bloodshot eye which was starting to tingle with tiredness.

'I can't take much more of this,' he admitted, his anger dissipating as exhaustion took hold. 'Just tell us, what happened to Sali?'

Redblood shuffled back in his seat, elbows on the armrests and interlocked his fingers, resting his chin on his self-made steeple.

'He made a supreme sacrifice,' he intoned darkly. 'I dropped him off at the top of the lane here and he came to see you. I'd been coaching him for two days and then we filmed your video in the bank's unused rooms. It didn't matter he looked nothing like me, he was the right age. After all, no one knew what I looked like apart from Manton and his gang. I have to admit, he was very convincing, despite the pain he must have been experiencing. Sali became me, both in the video and visiting your yard, and by the way, I saw and heard everything when he was here.'

He paused, plainly expecting a query. With no reaction from his audience he cleared his throat and continued.

'Sali had an earpiece so I could advise him what to say and do when he was here. I could see and hear your reactions from a video device he was wearing.'

'So you fed him everything he needed to fool Harry?' Bunt asked coolly.

'Not everything,' Redblood sniffed. 'Besides, it was essential Harry believed Sali was indeed me. I knew it wouldn't be too long before Manton found out I wasn't handed over dead at Scarborough hospital. Harry had to identify Sali's body as Thomas Redblood in order to give me the freedom to initiate the next part of my plan.'

Redblood crackled with a short laugh. 'It worked as well. I've managed to disable about sixty percent of Manton's laundering network.'

Harry was staring at the bits of plaster and the layer of white dust covering his carpet, slowly shaking his head, lips pursed. 'So Sali left here and you killed him?' he asked, his eyes still concentrated on the devastation around the room.

'No. Absolutely not,' Redblood said firmly in rebuke. 'We had to get the police to take an interest. I'm *sorry*, but I needed to bring you into the plan. It was essential.'

He was staring fiercely at Harry now, his bushy eyebrows fixed in an exasperated downward angle. 'Sali was in great pain and about to die. I provided him with peace of mind. He was given the syringe holding the insulin and he injected himself.'

Harry looked up at George who was biting his lip nervously, flicking worried glances between himself and Redblood. Harry and he locked eyes for a moment and the hurt swamped his features.

'I can't say it was a glorious, triumphant moment. It wasn't,' Redblood stated sadly. 'Sali was brave though, he injected himself, got out of the car, sat cross-legged on the verge and simply... waited.'

George's lip started to quiver. 'He...' Unable to continue his sentence he took a long breath before starting to speak once more. 'Tom told me afterwards Sali smiled, closed his eyes, and waited. He lost consciousness quickly...'

Redblood took up the story, speaking quietly. 'I took the syringe with me and drove straight to Leeds and told Sali's daughter everything. George also deposited a substantial sum into her bank account. She was extremely upset of course, but also relieved. However, the lack of a body did distress her. Sali had written a letter to his daughter which explained everything. He was a very sick man who wanted to leave a better future for his daughter. We helped him do that. I think she understood and thought no less of him for making his decision. I also arranged for Gupta to skip the country, he's now in Canada with plenty of money behind him and well away from Manton's influence.'

The four men sat in silence, each fighting emotion, and tiredness in equal measure. Finally, Redblood sucked air in through his nose and his eyes skipped around the other three.

'It had to ring true you see, Harry. You, the police and Manton; everyone had to believe I had died. It allowed me to start the process of pressurising every area of Manton's life; his business, his personal life and using his passion for horseracing to bring him down.'

'You used us!' protested a female voice from beyond the open door to the lounge.

Harry and Bunt jumped off the sofa like scalded cats. They immediately sprang to their feet and backed away from the source of the unexpected participant in their conversation.

'Bloody hell, Jill!' Harry cried as his wife entered the room, stomach first. She was cradling the base of her tummy with intertwined fingers and wore a look of fierce injustice on her face which forced all four men to root themselves to the spot.

'You've been playing us from the very moment Sali walked in the yard,' Jill declared, her gaze set on Redblood. She crossed the room awkwardly, picking her way through the debris, her intentions and direction of travel was clear. She reached her mark and stood firmly, legs apart, commanding the attention of the room. Jill planted herself directly in front of Redblood, who was seated on the edge in his dilapidated armchair, staring up goggle-eyed at her.

Harry gawped at his wife, feeling a smirk start to develop from the corner of his mouth, driven by pride and admiration for her. However, it never reached its full potential. Instead his mouth dropped open and he watched in fascination as a terrified and unbalanced Redblood scrabbled to get to his feet.

'My dear lady...'

'Don't you dear lady me, you stinking liar!'

'Oh no, really...I,' Redblood spluttered, managing to stand up. He

188

stood a good foot above Jill, but adopting the higher ground did him no good whatsoever.

'You may have these idiots wrapped up in your story,' Jill ranted, 'But you don't fool me. You need to take Manton down *for yourself* don't you! Bunt, Harry and I, in fact everyone here are just pawns in your game of revenge.'

Redblood, whose cane had dropped to the carpet, was holding his elbows close to his chest and waggling his hands in a placatory shushing motion. He had virtually no experience of women, and especially angry, pregnant ones. He found himself completely bewildered and yet hugely impressed by the force of nature in front of him. These feelings didn't express themselves well though, his eyes were popping, and he blinked hard several times before mustering a reply.

'Mrs Bolt…,' he paused for a heartbeat, considering. Then he dropped his hands to his sides, his head drooped and said disconcertedly, 'Yes, you are completely correct.'

Jill took a step back and regarded the man calling himself Redblood with suspicion, the gale force wind in her sails having been reduced to a light breeze with this admission. She had her hands on her hips now, her eyes burning, assessing.

'Could I get you anything, Jill?' asked George in an attempt to foster a lighter atmosphere.

'Not just now George, and don't worry, I'll come to you in a minute.'

George winced, searching for something else to say, finally coming up with, 'How long have you been listening to us?'

'Long enough to recognise what this man was up to.'

'Please Mrs Bolt…' Redblood said, raising his head to meet her intense stare. There was sadness in his rumbling voice now. 'I did purposefully bring you and Harry into this plot of mine. I brought in Mr Bunt and his colleagues in order to protect you, but I'm afraid it has proved to be inadequate. Manton is brutal and his people are arrogant enough to believe they are untouchable.'

Bunt looked on uncomfortably as Redblood sank back into his armchair. George immediately jumped up and offered Jill his piano stool. She refused and remained standing in front of Redblood.

'My plan has yet to play out, but it must be allowed to,' Redblood pleaded. 'Manton cannot be allowed to continue ruining people's lives. These criminal gangs, he calls them *his clients*, are responsible for misery, hardship and death on the streets of Yorkshire, Lincolnshire… in fact, most of the country every day. The fact I aided him for so long sickens me. He has to be stopped.'

'So, it's okay to kill us in the process of reaching your goal?' Jill challenged.

'Absolutely not!' Redblood countered. 'You're safety is of the utmost importance to me.'

Jill crossed her arms over the top of her stomach and allowed her gaze to drop to the floor. 'I know why it's us,' she said quietly.

'What do you mean?'

'I've worked it out Mr Redblood. I know why Harry is so key to your plan.'

Redblood glanced at Harry and at that moment Jill knew for sure. She wrestled with the knowledge for a few moments before turning to Harry. Her eyes softened and she bit her lip.

'I'm sorry Harry, but I think Manton may have been involved in Laya's murder.'

Harry didn't respond. He inverted his eyebrows and angled his head to the side, trying to make her words make sense in his sleep-deprived brain.

Jill continued, 'That's why this worm needed Sali to die after seeing you, to expose a link between you and Manton.'

Harry's eyes became watery bloodshot pools of profound confusion, his face a slab of rippling anger.

'My plan will make the violence stop, Harry,' Redblood cut in, an air of grasping hope in his words.

After a few seconds scrutiny of Redblood's face Harry asked, '*Did* Manton kill my Mother?'

Redblood licked his lips. 'Well...,'

'No!' George said, getting to his feet. 'It was Doyle. Doyle killed Laya.'

Every head in the room turned toward George, the only sound was a resonant high-pitched singing from the light bulb above his head. He stood straight, defiantly holding his head up. He took a few moments to meet the incredulous stare of each person, one by one.

Harry held George's gaze for as long as he could but seconds later turned his back, holding the bridge of his nose between finger and thumb. He shook his head slowly and his shoulders jumped involuntarily as he tried to control heaving sobs.

'I was there,' continued George, his speech cloaked with sadness. 'It was my car that stopped that night. I was driving.'

Bunt's eyes hardened. He checked Harry, who looked emotionally wrecked. Redblood stared despairingly at his brother, slowly shaking his head. George's outburst was clearly not part of his plan. Bunt jumped to his feet.

'Sit down George,' Bunt commanded. 'You owe these people an explanation.'

'Now!' he barked when the man didn't respond.

George seemed to regain his composure, gave Bunt a curt nod and replaced him on the sofa.

Redblood cleared his throat in order to speak but was flashed an intense stare by Bunt.

'Don't you dare,' Bunt warned him. He spun back to George. 'Your brother obviously knows already, so go on. Whatever it is, tell them.'

George smiled weakly and steeled himself, taking a few deep breaths.

'I was seventeen. Manton, Warren, and Doyle came into the pub, flashing money around and buying drinks. Manton got talking to me, in retrospect he must have known who I was. They suggested we go for a drive and I thought it was a bit of fun, you know, hanging out with the 'bad boys' for an evening.'

Harry was watching George now, with Jill gripping his hand tight, her knuckles white. George took another steadying breath and continued.

'We toured around Malton for about an hour, Warren and Doyle dodging into a few houses every now and again, I guess they were supplying their pushers with drugs and collecting cash. Doyle came out of the last house and showed Manton something he'd picked up; a small glass bottle and a syringe. They laughed in the back seat about taking it from a girl who was off her head on their drugs. I started to get uneasy and said I had to go home. Then we turned onto Commercial Road and there she was, your mother, walking home with her guitar on her back.'

George clasped his fingers together around one knee and started to rock on the sofa as he spoke.

'They told me they were going to scare her. That's all,' he added, shooting a look around the listeners, seeking understanding but received no solace in return.

'I brought the car to a stop on the pavement as they instructed. Warren stayed in the front seat to make sure I didn't drive off. They spoke to her for a bit and when Manton and Doyle got out I saw the syringe in Doyle's hand...' His voice trailed off and he blinked rapidly a few times then swallowed hard.

'She looked okay. I thought they'd just threatened her. She ran off, I slowed down to check in my mirrors. Later that night when I found out what had happened to Laya I was... If I'd known I would have protected her...'

Again George was unable to continue. Tears welled up in the corners of both his eyes and he dabbed them away with his thumb. He tried to form new words, but his voice cracked. Bunt stepped in once more.

'Okay. That's enough. I think we get it,' he said in a softer tone, looking to Harry and Jill and receiving nods in return, although Harry wore a glazed expression.

Redblood caught Bunt's eye, seeking permission to speak. Bunt lifted one side of his top lip in begrudging acceptance.

'None of this should stop what we've already put in place!' Redblood exclaimed.

Harry snorted and moved even closer to Jill, unable to maintain his silence. 'For Christ's sake Redblood, a horse was killed today, and my wife – who is heavily pregnant if you haven't noticed – was going to be next by all accounts. It's only by sheer fluke that Paste managed to do your job for you and saved her life!'

'You will also gain your own revenge on Manton and Doyle for your mother's death,' Redblood pointed out hopefully.

'Really? Harry screamed. 'You think *I'm* as twisted and eaten up with revenge as you are?'

Harry felt his anger venting during this outburst. He hadn't realised how loud he'd become and was surprised to find himself out of his seat, towering over Redblood's armchair, bellowing his words at the cowering man. Evidence of his tirade dotted the leather on Redblood's coat as numerous tiny flecks of his spittle sparkled in the stark light thrown from the naked bulb above. A hand landed on his shoulder and he reacted immediately, spinning round to find George displaying a pained expression.

'We know it's really, really hard, Harry,' he said smoothly. 'That's why we're here... and *we will* put this right.'

'Really?' Harry retorted sarcastically. 'And how will you do that then?'

'*You* win the Gimcrack and *we* will put it right,' Redblood stated boldly.

He's bloody incorrigible thought Harry. The scared middle-aged man from a few moments earlier was now sat upright, his eyes twinkling once more and flashing a boyish grin at Harry.

He clapped his hands together.

'Let me explain.'

****

Redblood and his brother left the farmhouse at four o'clock in the morning. Harry and Jill spent the last half an hour alone with George, who explained how he'd wanted to tell Harry his true identity from the start; however, his brother had convinced him to remain incognito.

'We feared reprisals from Manton if I was discovered. I love racing and wanted to support the yard because of... well, you know my reasons. I went along with Tom's way of handling things. I used a little of the money we earned from playing the markets and bought Paste,' George explained.

'Why on earth are you living in Malton, surely this is the first place Manton would look?' Harry asked.

'My brother gave me instructions on how to create a false trail around the country. I changed my name a few times and even altered it to the same name as a travelling actor with whom I shared a flat for a short time, just to throw anyone tracking me off the scent. I needed a new name. and became George Plant. Then I went to college and learned the motor trade. When Tom eventually got in touch again he told me the last place Manton would look would be Malton, as he hated the place. So, I came here and started a small garage doing van and truck repairs five years ago and kept my head down.'

'But surely people would have recognised you? Jill had asked. 'After all, it's where you grew up.'

'You'd be amazed,' George replied. 'I've not had one person realise who I am. Even the few school friends I've bumped into from fifteen years previously haven't recognised me. I got older, changed my appearance, and people forget I guess.'

George had asked to be forgiven, and both Harry and surprisingly, Jill, grudgingly accepted his apology and agreed to continue calling him George, rather than William or Billy.

'I'll be watching you carefully mind!' Jill had cautioned him as he got up to leave. That wiped the smile from Georges face and he'd left with his tail firmly between his legs.

Harry watched the two Redblood brothers reverse out of the dark yard in George's small Honda and continued to keep an eye on the car until its lights disappeared out of sight down the lane. George had admitted that this night was the first time he'd met his brother since he'd gone on the run, twenty years previously, so they had some catching up to do. Even so, Redblood had apparently insisted he should not stay with his brother for reasons of security. He had told everyone there would be no further face-to-face communication with him unless it was essential.

'It's time for bed, I'm shattered,' Jill muttered from beside her husband.

'You might be struggling with that. The bed has been slashed to within an inch of its life.'

'I don't care. I'm too tired,' Jill said, stifling a yawn.

'And… there are no blankets.'

She eyed Harry wearily. 'No blankets?'

'It was cold in the lounge,' he replied with a shrug.

'So Bunt has gone to sleep in the lounge on the sofa with our blankets?'

'That's about the top and bottom of it.'

'Well you'll have to come and keep me warm then, Tiger,' called Jill over her shoulder as she headed to the foot of the stairs.

Harry double-checked the back door was locked and followed Jill upstairs. He found her pulling down a bunch of blankets from a cupboard drawer he'd missed on his forage for warmth earlier that night.

'I'm glad you came back home.'

'So am I,' she winked. 'I almost missed all the fun.'

'So why *did* you come back?' asked Harry.

'I woke up after an hour and couldn't sleep. I just wasn't comfortable. I wanted to be back here with you. I persuaded my Dad to drop me back off. I could tell by the way the conversation was going it was serious, so I hung back a little. It was a bit of a shock when I realised who George's brother was.'

They carefully laid a white sheet over the mattress, which was ripped in places and shredded in others. A couple of springs were poking through the cloth covering and from virtually every rip the mattress innards were spewing onto the floor. Jill threw a few blankets on top of the lumpy bottom sheet and they climbed into their makeshift bed.

'Are you okay?' Jill asked, encouraging Harry to come closer to warm her up.

'Yeah... fine,' he replied sleepily.

'About your Mum, Laya I mean,' Jill persisted. 'Well... and the rest of Redblood's plan?'

Harry adjusted his position to allow him to sit up and lean on an elbow. With eyelids half closed he tried hard to conjure up a meaningful answer. The last hour with Redblood had been exhausting, but he'd come round to thinking the plan was partly doable, possibly the only option and partly crazily dangerous. He looked down at Jill and opened his mouth to provide his wife with his considered opinion only to discover she was fast asleep.

'It'll keep,' he whispered to himself. He snuggled down against Jill's back and was asleep as soon as his eyes closed.

Twenty-Nine

William David Bolt was born a week after the raid on Pickering Farm. The baby was the proud owner of a brand new cot, in a newly created and redecorated nursery in what was turning out to be one of the most heavily guarded farmhouses in the country.

His dark brown skin and laser-like blue eyes gave him a striking appearance which everyone, including the delivery nurses at the hospital, had commented upon. Jill was radiant, having taken the birth in her stride, the horror she had witnessed in the yard the week before already a fading memory. In fact, Harry had been astonished at how effectively Jill had pushed that visit from Manton's men into the background. During the last few days of her pregnancy his concern had manifested itself with a constant need to know his wife hadn't been mentally scarred by Manton's men. He had peppered her with queries about her health and wellbeing. Eventually Jill sat him down, and as if speaking to an insistent four-year old, patiently explained how she viewed the experience.

She asked Harry how many horses he had lost on the gallops or from illness, or on a racecourse.

'Not a huge number. A few and luckily only once on a racecourse,' he had admitted.

'You know we work in an industry where death is a constant; wherever there is livestock, there is dead stock,' Jill had explained slowly.

'Yes, but…'

'We lost *one* horse. Of course it's sad. It's awful for the people who were there and for the staff who cared for Jelly. It's horrible how it happened, but you and I have lived with the death of horses all our lives.'

Harry had been reminded of his first equine loss, when a beautiful chesnut mare had to be put down at Willie Warcup's yard after snapping a cannon bone out in the paddocks. He had been nine years old and had cried for hours afterwards. The image of the vet removing the dead horse from where it lay in its field had haunted him for years afterwards.

'But you don't seem afraid of these… people either,' Harry had insisted.

She had become steely in response to this, proving once again, as if he needed further proof, he had married an incredibly strong and resolute woman.

'We both knew the risks when we took these horses on. Besides, I'm not going to allow some lowlife criminals to make me a victim. I've got *two* boys to look after now, and no one is going to get in the way of that!'

She had shot Harry a stern look and picked William - or 'Will' as he'd quickly become known - out of his sleep chair and hugged him protectively to her bosom.

'Besides' she had added, casting her eyes out of the bedroom window and down the yard. 'We've more protection around here than we can wave a stick at!'

That much was true. Redblood had been true to his word. The farmhouse and the yard had been put right and improved upon. The yard had received a major overhaul since the raid, starting the day after. Of course there had been no police involvement and as the colt had been one of the Redblood draft, Harry had thankfully been saved the torture of explaining the death to an owner.

The farmhouse had been totally gutted then redecorated with emphasis on secure doors and windows. Redblood had delivered on that promise within hours of leaving. A seemingly never-ending line of workmen, delivery vans and trucks lay siege to the yard for the five days following the 'the visit' as Jill referred to Manton's destruction of the house. Within a week the wrecked farmhouse became a home once more and as if to order, Jill went into labour the day after the renovations were completed.

Bunt had overseen the upgrade and extension to the security features around the yard. He had taken on the project with a maniacal eye for detail and overflowing zeal which could be put down to his profound regret over his past failure. No matter how many times Harry or Jill reminded him all was well, Bunt sought his own professional redemption by dedicating himself utterly to the project the second time around.

An eight foot high wire fence now encompassed the paddocks, the roofs of the bottom yard, where the first of Manton's men had dropped in and caught Moore out, now boasted razor wire around the entire perimeter, bent back and out to save any equine injuries. Bunt and Wang's control centre no longer looked like a stable; it had been decked out with what Bunt had assured Harry was the very latest in surveillance monitoring equipment.

Jill had been particularly pleased with the nursery, something she had wished for, but never expected from Harry. Previously dank, unappealing and small, their spare room had become a bright, happy and surprising spacious without all their discarded junk clogging up the room.

There had also been a shock for Harry. He'd returned home after a day at the races to discover a top quality Schiller upright piano was being manhandled into his lounge. Compared to his ancient, well loved, but now defunct upright this all white instrument played like a dream and Jill had found him sneaking in during the day to play his new toy while she walked Will in his pram.

There had been no news on the man Paste had clobbered. Jill had scoured the local newspapers and looked online but there was no mention of anyone suffering a kick from a horse. Bunt was convinced it must have been a man called Pete Warren in the yard, just from the description of the wiry man and his antics. He had rung a few hospitals within a short drive from Malton but hadn't found any evidence of a man with a head injury being booked in that evening. He feared the worst, but didn't voice this conclusion to anyone in the yard; they had enough to worry about with the rebuilding of the farmhouse and the arrival of Will.

Harry's gigging with Emma and Pascal was something he insisted would continue, much to Bunt's displeasure. Either he or Wang now acted as a roadie for his twice-weekly shows. Harry had pointed out that Redblood's plan was being enacted with these gigs, as they demonstrated it was business as usual at the yard, which to some extent helped to douse the security man's fiery discontent.

Two days into the work on the farmhouse, David Smith had knocked on the kitchen door with a new set of lease papers in his briefcase. Redblood had not only bought Pickering Farm, he'd secured all four of the yards which clustered around it. The new terms were at a twenty-five percent reduced rate for all of the tenants, which came as a welcome surprise, especially for Mo next door.

'The reduction in monthly rent is a way of compensating for any repercussions felt by the trainers as a result of the poisoning episode,' Smith had explained after being quizzed by Jill.

He'd been unaccountably joyous in his manner to this point in his visit, apparently unable to keep a Cheshire cat grin from lighting up his face. It did him a lot of good, flushing some colour into his stone-like features. Harry hadn't been sure whether Smith was aware of the rebirth of Redblood, but kept quiet just in case.

The reason for Smith's pleasing demeanor had been teased out of him by Jill as he was leaving with the newly signed leases tucked under his arm.

'Oh, has George Plant been in touch?' Jill had enquired lightly as the ex-bank manager headed through the back door.

'Yes, I met…' he started.

Smith's reply had tailed off and he'd stopped, reentered the kitchen, closed the door soundlessly, and turned to Jill with a meek expression.

'You've caught me out.'

'Mmm. Sorry about that Mr Smith. Was it a good meeting?'

'Yes. Very… productive, shall we say.'

'Perhaps in a financial way?'

Smith's eyes had become sharp. However they read the amusement in Jill's face and relaxed.

'Among the many people and businesses Mr Redblood has been supporting recently,' his eyes flitted around, indicating the farmhouse. 'I became one of the lucky recipients of his generosity.'

'That's great news.'

'I trust this can be kept between the three of us?' he'd asked with wide eyes.

'Of course, Mr Smith. We're getting good at keeping Mr Redblood's secrets,' Harry had answered with a touch of irony.

Will's arrival had brought a different type of joy. Annie had been granted her final wish. She got to hold her grandson before she died. Harry had driven Jill and Will straight to the Warcup's yard from York hospital, once they were released two days after the birth. They were lucky and hit a good day, Annie was lucid, and the newly created family enjoyed a happy hour with her before she faded back into speaking gibberish through tiredness. She died that same night in her sleep.

Harry hoped she died contented. Jill affirmed this to a degree, having overheard Andrew telling a concerned stable lass that in his opinion the only reason the old lady had lasted this long was to clap eyes on her first grandson. She'd been quick to point out that Andrew's words had been spoken not only in admiration for Annie, but also a grudging acceptance that Harry had brought joy to the old lady.

Andrew stayed in Annie's room during their visit, without delivering any snide comments. He and Harry were still careful, dancing around each other, side stepping any dangerous topics and limiting their dialogue to small talk. The two of them concentrated their attention on the old lady and Will. This thawing in their relationship wasn't missed by Annie. She had tightened the wrinkles around her mouth into a warm smile, peered down into the little boy's face and told him several times that he had a mother, a father and an uncle to look after him, so he'd be just fine. Jill had realised the wily old woman was making a point, for the benefit of her sons.

Harry's thoughts brought him back to the present. He stood at the top of his yard and looked down the two lines of horseboxes, waiting for the second lot of the day to leave. Melancholia swept over him when he envisioned Will with Annie once again; the look of happiness on Annie's face. She'd been ready to go, she'd said as much. Snapping back, he dried the corners of both eyes with index finger and thumb and tried to concentrate on the horses once again. It was late July, the sun was beating down, the yard was full, and so much had changed in the eight weeks since the real Redblood had entered the yard.

Halfway down the line of stables a box door clanked open and Rory emerged with Headcase tacked up and ready for second lot. The colt gave Harry a lethargic impression in his first few steps, not extending his legs or pushing off his feet. However, the colt pulled back at his reins, stood still and shook himself before pricking his ears and squinting at the bright sky. After an appraising snort he deigned to walk forward for Rory. Harry curled his mouth into an amused grin; Headcase must have been sleeping and had just woken up, he really was a lazy so-and-so. Rory glanced up the yard and paused to aim a nod Harry's way.

'Ready for next lot in two,' he called.

Harry raised his hand in reply, but said nothing.

Rory was having a solid season and had ridden a few winners for Harry among his successes. Given the backdrop to the season, the yard had been going well with regular runners and winners. The attendant security measures that had to go with any trip to the races, vets or even to the gallops were starting to wear thin with the staff, but a quick reminder of what happened to Jelly was enough for them all to continue with the draconian rules imposed by Bunt. The increasing number of security staff was met with incredulity by other trainers and stable staff, especially at the races. Harry continued to warn every member of his stabling team to feign ignorance if questioned. In the racing world an expressive shrug of the shoulders followed by silence was a universally accepted signal that further investigation was pointless. The majority of nosey outsiders would then back off.

Bunt had taken the Redblood night in his stride while Zoe, Wang, and Mike had needed a week to come to terms with the sight which greeted them in Jelly's stable. Harry was relieved all three of them seemed to have pulled through and remained loyal to the yard. He hated looking around him and not trusting people; it went against his nature, so having two long-term stable staff and a security man around who knew the score, and in whom he could rely upon, was hugely reassuring. In truth, he couldn't wait for the Gimcrack to be run, so things could return to some sort of normality.

Harry sniffed, rubbed his newly wrinkled eyes, and set off down the yard. Will's sleeping patterns hadn't settled down just yet, so battling with sleep loss was another issue. He didn't mind that task though, even if it did find him resting his son on his knees at four in the morning while the infant gobbled down yet another bottle of milk. Looking down on Will each night as he slept, hands above his head, completely floppy and at rest, a rosy tint to both chubby cheeks, Harry's goals; to protect his family, win the Gimcrack, and build a yard full of premier horses had actually intensified since his son's arrival.

This line of thought reminded him there were only four weeks to go to the Gimcrack at York. 'Bring it on,' he told himself, clenching both firsts as he walked toward the waiting horsebox.

Fifteen minutes later Harry stood at the top of the Wold gallop, a set of binoculars around his neck. He appraised the first two horses in his second lot of the morning, working up the All-Weather track. Behind him, Wang scanned the fields, looking for threats. He hardly noticed the security any more. It had become a constant in the life of the stables, like jockeys and horses.

This lot was an all-Redblood group of six horses, coming up two by two. The initial nine potential candidates for the Gimcrack were now down to eight, with the loss of Jelly. Harry felt downcast every time he thought of the colt's demise. He'd been a quality horse with an excellent, trusting temperament and hadn't deserved to die the way he did.

Harry shook the loss from his mind and refocused on the first two horses working over five furlongs uphill. Po and Mr Greedy came up, Mr Greedy working hard in his straightforward, unimpressive manner, Po, as usual, dossing in behind and messing around as if training work wasn't worth the effort. His rider rowed along to get him upsides Mr Greedy and gave Po a flick of the whip, he quickened for a few strides to draw level with his workmate before easing off as they reached the last couple of hundred yards.

'Too bloody intelligent and a blummin' show boater,' Harry mumbled to himself. However, he was happy enough. He aimed to give both a run prior to going for the Gimcrack in order to give them the extra experience they would need to be at their best in a high-class field at York.

The next two up were Headcase and Luckyman. Headcase hadn't come on as much as Harry had hoped, following his debut at York. Both horses had been sent to Nottingham for a second six furlong maiden race outing and run respectably without showing the sort of ability that would see either of them winning a group race. At least this time Luckyman had got out of the stalls, but ridden by Rory again, he'd not picked up over two out and was proving to be something of a conundrum. A Manton runner called 'Mr Thirty Percent' had won the race on debut and looked a decent prospect. Harry had no doubt that colt would be aimed at the Gimcrack, so that was at least two Manton owned horses he would have to contend with at York in mid August.

The two horses scooted past Harry's position, Luckyman quickly asserting by a couple of lengths against a weakening Headcase as the ground started to rise up the hill. Harry made a mental note to check Headcase's bloods when he got back to the yard, the way the colt was shaping, a run in the Gimcrack would be pointless.

Thirty seconds later Fletch and Fido straightened up for the last few furlongs up the hill and Harry clicked a stopwatch when they reached a marker indicating four furlongs out. He'd given strict instructions to the riders to give these two a piece of fast work.

Zoe led on Fido by no more than half a length at a good clip and with three furlongs still to run she crouched lower and went a further length up, extending to put daylight between her and Fletch, ridden by Shane Brown, who had come in to ride a couple of lots.

'Come on, Fletch,' Harry said quietly, binoculars stuck to his face.

Fletch seemed to hit a flat patch with two furlongs to run, but as the two horses met the rising ground his stride lengthened again and he pulled back one of the lost lengths. Harry clicked his stopwatch as they reached the furlong marker, the two horses flashing past together. As they continued up the hill, Fletch joined Fido and the two of them battled for a few strides before their riders eased off.

Harry maintained a steady gaze on the horses as they slowed and trotted off the end of the gallop, making sure both of them looked limber after their workout. Tucking his binoculars into the inside pocket of his jacket, he checked the time which told him the two horses had covered the middle three furlongs of their run up the hill in thirty-four seconds. A warm, fuzzy feeling shot up his spine. Fido and Fletch had covered the half mile in less than twelve seconds per furlong.

Instead of heading straight for the top gate and the walk home, Shane and Zoe were walking on the grass beside the makeshift road toward Harry, as instructed.

Shane, usually a thoughtful rider with soft hands and a measured approach to his craft, started to call to Harry from a full thirty yards away. Harry had been giving him progressively more rides as the season had developed.

'That felt fast, Guv'nor. There was plenty more left in him...'

Harry jogged to the two horses, his index finger held to his lips.

'Keep it down,' he warned the two of them, flashing an excited smile. 'It *was* fast.'

Harry looked up expectantly at Zoe on Fido,

'I'm thinking five furlongs for this lad?'

She was beaming. 'Definitely,' she replied breathlessly. 'He's so quick. That's as fast as I've ever gone up there. He gives you everything, and when he's done, he keeps on trying! I guess he might get an easy six?'

Harry didn't reply at first. With his head down, he circled the grey searching for any nicks or cuts on his legs. With his inspection complete he nodded his agreement to Zoe and gave the colt a slap on his neck.

'I doubt he's going to win a Gimcrack over six furlongs, but he's good enough for a crack at one of the sprint races at Ascot.'

Shane dropped off Fletch, allowing the colt to take a mouthful of grass and waited for Harry to come around to him.

'He wanted a pick,' he offered in explanation.

'Probably deserves it too,' Harry said with a warm smile. 'Come on, tell me what you think.'

Shane's face lit up. 'He's your Gimcrack horse, Harry.'

Harry gave the two riders more instructions and after they departed with Wang following, he made two phone calls. The first was to Jill, the second to DI Gwent.

Thirty

Harry's computer screen shone weakly in his newly built study alcove in the centre of the farmhouse, tucked under the stairs. He'd been refreshing the same page of the Weatherby's website containing the Gimcrack declarations for the last ten minutes. He clicked the refresh button once more.

'They're in!' he called excitedly to Jill, busy feeding Will in the lounge. She placed the baby carefully into his sleep chair and came though to peer over Harry's shoulder at the list of final, declared runners.

'It's like a Redblood Manton face-off!' she exclaimed. 'Look at that. Twelve runners and eight are in the ownership of only two people.'

Harry remained silent, examining the list of names in detail, analysing the declarations one by one. The final four horses he was sending to York for the Gimcrack in two days time were Po, Luckyman, Fletch and Fido. He didn't rate Fido as serious challenger for the win, however with three potential hold-up or 'stretch' horses in Po, Luckyman and Fletch, Harry wanted to field Fido for his speed. The chance of the colt getting the sixth furlong in this company was questionable, but Fido would inject pace into the first five furlongs to the benefit of the other Redblood runners. Headcase wasn't in the race. Harry had been called to the colt's stable two days earlier and found the colt lame. He'd developed an abscess in his front right foot and after treatment the colt was on box rest for a week. Ten months work ruined by a minor ailment three days before the race, who'd be a racehorse trainer…

Jill was right, the race had a strange look to it, with either Harry's or Eric Goode's name set against two-thirds of the runners. With each of the horses carrying the same weight the list was headed by two of Manton's entries simply because the runners were listed and allocated race number alphabetically. Manton horses topped and tailed the racecard with 'Ambitious Manton' and 'Mr Thirty Percent'.

Harry grimaced when he came to the name 'My Way Or No Way'. As well as running Po and Headcase to a short head Manton's colt had followed up with a winning run in a quality maiden at Newmarket and Harry believed this two year old was the primary threat to his own chances. He'd half hoped the colt wouldn't be declared. He also noted Erudition, the colt which had already beaten Mr Greedy and Fido, was declared to run.

He and Jill pulled the form of the race apart for another half an hour, re-reading the form for the eight opponents, checking going reports and draw biases before Harry pushed his chair away from the computer. He felt he had chances, real chances. Jill looked at him, the excitement already flowing through her and from the look on Harry's face, he felt it too.

They shared a few minutes of animated discussion about a multitude of angles on the race and ended up dancing around the hall in order to release some of the electricity they had managed to work up in each other.

After a calming cup of tea, Harry settled back into the office chair.

'The weather report says there is rain expected on Thursday evening, so we could be racing on Good to Soft by Friday afternoon,' he told Jill

'What's the going today?'

'Good. Hopefully it will stay that way, although Fletch might like a bit of cut and I suppose Fido would go through it as well.'

Jill came up and stood behind Harry's chair, her tea in her left hand. She draped the other hand over his head, stroking his short hair a few times before continuing down the back of his neck. She felt him shiver and started unconsciously rubbing his shoulder blade and nape of his neck.

What do you want?' he asked playfully.

'Oh, nothing really.'

Harry remained silent a short while, allowing the unsaid question to hang in the air.

'Nothing?'

'Doh! Stop teasing me!' she blurted.

'Teasing? This is from the girl with a hand down the neck of my t-shirt?'

Jill quickly withdrew her hand from Harry's neck and lightly slapped the top of his arm.

'I want to come to York for the race on Friday,' she admitted with a theatrical sigh. 'I know I'm not supposed to, but…'

Harry spun round and gazed levelly at his wife, pursing his lips and wearing a pained expression.

'You know you have to stay here with Will. We agreed.'

'Redblood, Bunt, and you agreed!' she countered. 'I can't remember Will and I casting a vote.'

'Bunt has arranged for extra security both here and at the racecourse to make sure nothing happens. Besides, Will is still too young to go to the races for the day.'

Jill tilted her head back.

'Oh… ok!' she said in exasperated defeat. 'I guess Will and I are watching on TV. Just don't expect me to stay home all the time once this Redblood thing is over. You know I'm riding out again starting next Monday!'

'Yes, you've told me once or twice,' Harry confirmed with a roll of his eyes.

Right on cue, Will gave a little cry from the lounge and Harry looked to Jill, creasing his forehead in expectation. She found a spot to deposit her teacup, crossed her arms, narrowed her eyes, and gave Harry an amused smirk before setting off for the lounge.

'Don't worry, Mummy's coming,' she told Harry before leaving the room. He grinned and picked up his phone.

'I need to speak with George about jockey bookings,' he called after her and started tapping the phone's small screen.

****

Manton decided the Lincolnshire house felt much bigger without Loretta and Warren around the place. Loretta was no great loss, but he had felt a tinge of regret after instructing Deacon to dispose of Pete's body in the field at the back of the Money Tree. He'd known Pete a long time...

Manton looked into the huge mirror which was showing his naked torso and realised he'd been holding the beard clippers to his face for some time. Mentally chastising himself for daydreaming, he resumed his daily routine. He finished clipping his beard, located a bottle of moisturiser and squirted its contents onto his hands before applying the white cream all over his beard and face. He wondered whether Pete's mother in Malton knew her son was dead, but soon discarded all thoughts of Pete Warren in favour of taking up a pair of small, hooked clippers and surveying his nose hairs in the mirror.

Pushing his nostrils back he'd managed to snip off the first of the wispy black hairs when a chord sounded on his phone. He dropped the clippers and scooped the phone up, tapping the face of the device with hands still greasy from the moisturiser. He sat on the side of the bath and scrolled down the list of runners for the Gimcrack. His eyes hardened when he reached the first of Harry Bolt's runners, his anger increasing with each new Bolt runner he came across. A couple of expletives rolled easily off his tongue.

A few minutes later Manton was screaming Doyle's name down the stairs. When no acknowledgement was returned, he thumped angrily downstairs and found the object of his ire in the open plan kitchen stood with a coffee in his hand, looking out onto the acre of grass behind the house.

'Doyle! Remember we're at York races on Friday,' Manton barked without any preamble. Doyle took a long sip of his coffee and watched Manton approach from over the rim of his cup. Manton had a bath towel wrapped around his waist but was otherwise naked. When the half dressed, hairy and significantly overweight fifty year old reached him, he raised a questioning eyebrow.

'Are we?'

'Yes, of course. We're going to win the Gimcrack,' Manton stated gruffly.

'I though the dinner was the big day?' Doyle queried lightly, his mouth set in a straight line.

Manton waved the question away. 'Yes, the dinner comes later.'

Doyle spun lightly on the tiled floor to face Manton. He tried to keep his frustration from showing, but couldn't help narrowing his eyes when he caught Manton's belligerent expression.

'It's d-dangerous,' he stammered, scowling inwardly, partly at his own inability to vocalize his words but also at his own growing discontent with Manton. The man's lust for self-promotion, his expanding waistline, and his violent mood swings were becoming increasingly tiring. Pete used to deal with Manton's hissy fits, that's why he'd kept him around for so long. His mild manner with Manton was sorely missed.

Manton continued, 'Listen Doyle, Redblood's threats have come to nothing. The police have stopped sniffing around and we're slowly getting the Money Tree back to full capacity. Getting nationwide coverage of our success will be good for business and speaking to an audience is what I'm good at.'

Doyle nodded thoughtfully. Manton was right in a sense. It would certainly show their laundering clients they were back in control after a few rocky months. He reminded himself that the Money Tree was still only back to seventy percent operation. Redblood's little security lockdown had applied pressure to the business but not quite enough to lose them clients. That said, the business was admittedly creaking a bit. The quicker they could get back to full capacity, the better.

He looked back at Manton, assessing the man he'd guided through the criminal fraternity for the last twenty-five years. Was he on the downgrade? Manton crossed the kitchen in search of coffee and croissants, his belly wobbling with each step. Look at him, Doyle thought, he's poncing around with his disgusting chest puffed out, he just doesn't see it, he never has. It had been the perfect match Doyle reflected, Manton speaking his words for him, appearing to be running the business, when all the time he was feeding the plans into Manton's mind. That threatening, malicious bent combined with a flair for self-promotion which characterised Manton as a young man now seemed jaded. Doyle idly wondered whether the man's mind was becoming as bloated as his belly. However at present, Manton was the man with power and *he, Doyle,* had created him. Now he needed to wrestle back the power.

Doyle snapped back from his ruminations as Manton began speaking once more, turning to face Doyle with an overfilled coffee cup. He was even slopping the brown liquid onto his stomach and the floor, however Manton hadn't noticed, and Doyle did his best to hide his disgust. It was becoming more and more difficult. Perhaps when the laundering system was back to full capacity...

'Win this race and we've got the perfect platform to get the Halo name out there Doyle!' Manton proclaimed enthusiastically before slurping coffee noisily. 'We've got to be there when we win.'

Doyle forced a smile, his skin pulling tight from his nose to his ears.

'Okay, we'll go.'

Manton returned the smile and headed for the open plan lounge area where a muted flat screen TV was tuned to a live morning show.

Doyle took another sip of his coffee. It had cooled and tasted far too bitter. He cringed as the hairy, barebacked Manton fell into the large L shaped leather sofa and stretched over his stomach to grab the remote control. Doyle tried in vain not to imagine how much of the man's sweat and hair would be deposited on the furniture. Presently, loud and wholly banal banter from the TV started to pollute the ambiance of the morning. Doyle left, saving his grimace until he'd closed the kitchen door behind him.

Thirty-One

York racecourse was uncharacteristically empty. Ebor Friday usually sees tens of thousands of enthusiastic Yorkshire race-goers converge on the course, but not this year. The wettest few August days on record meant the going was heavy and getting worse as the afternoon wore on. Huge pools of dull, windswept standing water had started to appear on the Knavesmire overnight and there had been talk of a possible abandonment. However, the drainage system combined with some adjustments to the course's rails meant that after a morning inspection by the stewards, racing went ahead, much to Harry's relief. He'd been up at five o'clock, checking the forecast and the Weatherby's website, waiting nervously for the meeting to be given the green light.

Harry and Wang stood with Fido and Po waiting patiently to be checked into the racecourse pre-parade area by race day attendants. The rain pounded down relentlessly and every member of Harry's stabling staff was struggling to cope in the conditions.

'This is a bloody nightmare,' Harry called to Zoe, having watched the young stable lass wring water from her ponytail. He shook his own head and even his short, black fuzz produced an arc of droplets.

'Yeah, I'm so chuffed I took the time to have a shower this morning!' Zoe called back and rolled her eyes.

Wang grinned appreciatively toward her. They both stood with shoulders hunched against the onslaught pouring from the sky.

Mike joined the queue behind Zoe to complete the group of four horses. Bunt watched grimly from a few yards to the side of the chute but there wasn't anyone within a hundred yards of them. All of the Pickering Farm team wore thin plastic raincoats emblazoned with Harry's name. There was no surreptitious surveillance today, it was brazenly obvious.

The horses were behaving well in the circumstances although this extended wait in stair rod rain made Po and Luckyman start to snort with impatience. Po stamped his front foot and Harry shot a pleading look at the two men checking the horses in.

The attendant finally got his plastic bag covered clipboard sorted and the four horses and their sodden stable staff moved into the racecourse pre-parade area.

Harry had watched the first race on the card, the attritional going having reduced an otherwise quality race into a farce. Four of the ten runners had declared as non-runners due to the radical ground change and three of the remaining six had failed to go on the ground, their jockey's having eased off their mounts from over three furlongs out. In the end, the Group Three Strensall Stakes was fought out by two mud-loving geldings with the third placed horse over eighteen lengths behind. The race time had been ridiculously slow, over twenty seconds slower than standard for the nine furlong trip.

Harry had struggled with his choice of horses for the Gimcrack and now he was considering whether allowing Luckyman and Fletch to run was sensible. Both colts' possessed an action which wasn't suited to deep ground. Finally, Harry decided to let them take their chance. He'd spoken with George and pointed out that none of the two year olds in the race would be sure to cope with the going, as they'd never encountered such conditions. Together they had decided all four would race, with the added proviso that the jockeys should ease off their mounts if they weren't handling the conditions.

As the horses were pulling up in the second race Harry checked for non-runners. He was pleased to find there were three out in the Gimcrack, including one of Manton's, reducing him to three representatives in the race. My Way Or No Way and Mr Thirty Percent were still in the list though, making Harry quietly curse in mild disappointment when he brought up the latest runners list on his phone. Manton's colt would be made favourite for the Gimcrack, and a short one at that. His latest win had been impressive.

Harry wiped the screen of his phone clear of rain droplets and set his jaw against the breeze; it was time for his final checks. Entering the four stables separately, Harry set about preparing each of the colts. The rain continued to pour unrelentingly from a grey sky which was thick with clouds. They seemed to be scudding so closely overhead you could almost reach up and touch them.

Mike poked his nose over the door to Luckyman's stable and called out to Harry. 'Have you seen the state of the first three home in that last race?' he queried, hoisting a thumb toward the returning horses. 'It's like they've been in a mud wrestling contest!'

Harry walked out into the growing maelstrom once more and dutifully inspected the winner and three placed horses as they returned through the chute entrance. Their flanks were dark and greasy and when each of the victorious horses turned toward Harry a gooey layer of mud became visible on their heads and chests. A stream of dirty water dripped from the base of their stomachs. Every jockey's face was peppered with a combination of grass and mud spots. Three of them sported large white rings around their eyes, the result of pushing their racing goggles up onto their helmets.

This race is going to be a bloody lottery, Harry decided. Anything could win it in these conditions. He felt a wave of indignation crash over him. All those months of hard work with the horses and the upset in the yard, everything had been timed to work toward today's race. He had planned meticulously to ensure these top quality horses would peak at this very moment and all his preparation looked set to be undone, not by Manton or the quality of his horses, but by the weather conditions on the day.

The common land surrounding the racecourse was named The Knavesmire for good reason. The city mire where 'the knaves' were hung had seen people like Dick Turpin meet their end in the eighteenth century, dangling from a hangman's noose. In that moment as backsplash bounced even higher on the pre-parade walkway, Harry wondered whether the track was set on returning to its roots. The mire was there for all to see in the middle of the racecourse, rainwater pools were becoming small lakes as the afternoon wore on. Harry grimaced, idly wondering whether he would be the knave following the result of the Gimcrack.

A sharp breeze whipped up and whistled around the pre-parade area and Harry shivered as his sodden clothes suddenly felt cold against his skin. He shook the remaining thoughts of failure from his head, and checked the large clock on the oldest stand. They could probably keep the horses boxed up out of the rain for a few more minutes. A solitary runner was already touring the parade ring, but otherwise all the other Gimcrack runners were being kept out of the monsoon as long as possible.

Harry remained standing in the middle of the pre-parade ring, the rain provided a constant pattering soundtrack on his hood. He shivered once more, this time because Eric Goode had appeared, backing out of one of the stables. Goode swung round and looked up. His gaze settled on Harry, an almost comical lone figure standing, hands in pockets, out in the deluge. Their eyes locked for an uncomfortable second or two. Unexpectedly, and to Harry's amazement, Goode directed his eyes upward indicating the rain and the trainer's face broke into a broad smile. Harry found himself half raising a hand and giving an embarrassed wave in response. Still providing a generous smile, Goode nodded once more before loping down the line of boxes and opening another stable, closing the door behind him.

Rubbing his chin, Harry realised he had a silly grin on his face. He let it stay there, enjoying the feeling of lightness. Goode was just going about his work and had recognised another trainer experiencing the same difficult conditions. Harry wondered if Goode realised the lengths Manton had gone to in order to secure a victory today.

This line of thought reminded him: he was under strict instructions from Redblood not to engage in any sort of communication with Manton. Harry was relieved upon scanning the area that there was no sign of either Manton or Doyle. Fair weather owners he thought to himself, but scowled when he realised his heart had quickened its beat at the merest suggestion they could be close to him.

A shout of; 'Horses please!' went up from the stabling attendants, interrupting Harry's train of thought. One by one the stable doors opened and lads and lasses with faces crumpled up against the rain, led their horses out and into the parade ring. Bunt and Moore followed, scanning the area around them and seemingly oblivious to the rain.

Harry's four runners walked into a virtually empty parade ring. He made his way across a soggy few yards of short, perfectly cut grass and stood, arms crossed and rigid, eyeing each of his runners in turn, seeking anything which looked out of the ordinary. It struck him that all of this was extraordinary. This was a Group Two contest and there were barely twenty people surrounding the paddock. He and five other people were in the parade ring itself, which included his two security guards. Two of the remaining three were sheltering under a small pergola beside the winners rostrum.

As if to reaffirm its intentions, the rain burst forth with renewed vigour, thumping onto Harry's hood in sharp, rapid shots. After a minute of listening to this wet cacophony he could stand it no longer and whipped the hood down, accepting he was going to be drenched whatever he did. Bunt's extra security people were easily picked out in the public area, wearing Harry's yard jackets, one on each side of the ring. Both were young men who under the guidance of Wang were ready to vault into the parade ring at any given moment to protect people or horses.

With most of the connections deciding to remain in the warmth of the stands and no audience to speak of, the atmosphere was extremely subdued. Even the media people had decamped, delivering their race assessments from under an awning attached to a deserted champagne bar.

'Depressing, isn't it,' said a rich, clipped voice behind Harry. He turned to find Matthew Nottingham, the Clerk of the course standing a yard away from him under a huge golfing umbrella.

'Care to join me, Harry?' he asked with an encouraging shake of the umbrella's handle.

Tall, with an almond shaped face, and a winning smile, Matthew had always struck Harry as a perfect man for the Clerk at York. He exuded all the trappings of a publically educated blue blood, but unlike many in his position, was a breeze to deal with and didn't patronise those around him.

Harry noticed Matthew's hair was dry and still boasted its perfect right to left parting. He took a quick glance around the ring; they were now the only two people out there.

'Perhaps just for a minute,' he replied appreciatively, slipping under the other half of the canvas umbrella. The two men crouched slightly and watched a procession of wet, disgruntled horses and stable staff file past.

'I wanted to thank you for your support today. Four runners in the Gimcrack, that's quite an achievement,' Matthew stated in an upbeat tone.

Harry wondered for a moment whether the Clerk was fishing for information, but decided he simply sounded interested. Still, he was careful with his response.

'Thanks. We're really glad to be here.'

'Good, good,' Matthew said slowly. 'These are your first runners in Group company aren't they?'

'Yep, so no pressure!' Harry replied with a short laugh.

He stole a quick glance at Matthew who was still watching the parade. A broad, genuine smile hung on his face.

'This must be a nightmare situation for you,' Harry observed, pointing an array of fingers to the sky.

'To be honest I've come out here to escape. The board is whining, the stewards are complaining and I've got sponsors spitting venom. Frankly, being stood in a downpour with you is a welcome relief.'

Harry forgot his own stresses and strains for a few wonderful moments and laughed again, only this time it was whole hearted. His shoulders sagged a little as the stress was dissipated by the laughter. Matthew comically raised one of his long thin eyebrows before issuing an overly dramatic sigh.

'Thanks for that,' Harry responded. 'I thought it was just me having a stressful day.'

'No problem, Harry. Listen, best of luck with yours,' he nodded to Harry's runners. 'I'd love to see you winning.'

The public address system crackled into life, sounding a little ropey. The runners and riders were announced for the Gimcrack, sounding like a Norman Collier routine, prompting Harry to consider whether the rain was affecting that too.

Matthew groaned. 'Oh, dear God. That's all I need. Best get the electricians onto that.'

With that, Matthew strode off toward the exit to the parade ring, grasping his umbrella with both hands so it wasn't wrested from his grip by the breeze.

Decked out in his tailored suit, the Clerk's gangly frame leapt with surprising grace up the parade ring steps. Harry watched as Matthew headed off, his umbrella bobbing. Then he turned his attention to the large clock on the stands wall. It showed there were still fifteen minutes to the off time.

'This is killing me,' Harry muttered under his breath, and once again, scanned the parade ring.

Even less people were now watching at the rails, half their initial number giving in to common sense. Even the stewards seemed to have conceded defeat to the elements, their gazebo standing empty. Harry could identify a trio of trainers or travelling head lads spotted around the ring now, hunched over, rubbing their hands together. The one change to the scene was the addition of two figures at the other end of the parade ring. He wandered over to the side of the ring for a clearer view.

The two outlines coalesced, and then parted. It was Manton… and Doyle. An adrenaline surge fizzed through Harry's body once the identification became positive. He'd never thought he could experience loathing, but there it was, strong, bold, and dangerous. He remembered the warnings from Redblood and Bunt, and blew out a few short breaths. He checked the extra security people; they were still outside the parade ring, close to the rails. Bunt met with Harry's glance and nodded back slowly, flicking his gaze to the two men at the bottom of the ring before returning to Harry and nodding his assurance.

A flurry of activity at the top of the ring signalled the arrival of the jockeys and Harry easily spotted his four riders wearing the Revenge Partnership silks, each with a different coloured cap. He waited for them, noting as they approached that each of them was already dripping wet. All four jockeys examined the security around Harry wearing bemused expressions.

'Ahem!' he barked authoritatively.

Four sets of eyes snapped back and swivelled to Harry. All at once the splash of rainfall was the only sound.

Harry took a steadying breath and focused on what could be the most important few minutes of his training career. Rory, Shane, Madeline and Seamus looked to him expectantly.

'I've already discussed this race with all of you separately. You each have your own plan.' Each jockey confirmed their understanding to Harry as he paused to glance at them individually.

'But, the conditions out there will almost certainly mean you have to disregard the plan and ride for luck,' he added. 'I'm giving you all plenty of latitude to ignore them if you see fit. I can't tell you if your mount will handle the conditions, you'll have to get a feel from them and decide for yourself and ride your race accordingly. If you have a chance of winning, you go for it. All of these horses have been prepared to win this.'

'Blimey, Harry, you been taking English lessons?' Shane said with a grin. It was met with a chuckle from Maddy and Seamus. Rory remained tight-lipped and serious.

Harry opened his mouth, but didn't have time to reply, as the 'Jockeys mount,' announcement came swirling through the air and he and his riders went to work. Each was given a final few words and their leg up into the saddle. Two minutes later, each of the two year olds were safely cantering down the chute to the six furlong start and there was nothing else Harry could do. Ten months of work, sent on their way. They were on their own now.

Thirty-Two

Matthew Nottingham was braced with legs apart and arms outstretched, hands upturned and fingers splayed as he attempted to calm the situation. Breathing heavily, he glanced quickly left to right in an attempt to read the intentions of the two sets of connections. Confident there was at the very least a breath-restoring pause in the confrontation; he took in the condition of the primary protagonists.

Benedict Manton had come off worse. His cheeks blazed red and the fire of anger continued under his beard, radiating a glowing heat through the bristles. He was covered in mud. It was matted into his hair, smeared on one cheek and dirty water droplets hung in his beard.

Matthew looked the man up and down. His expansive chest filled his dirty shirt in a regular rhythm as he gasped for air. He held one hand to his back and was producing phlegm crackling coughing between expletive filled rants. Matthew had started to filter out his outbursts minutes ago. The man's suit was sodden in places, covered in a mixture of grass and mud. Both knees were large dark patches. For the time being Mr Manton looked unlikely to attack once more.

His heart rate still elevated, Matthew took a couple of steadying breaths and blew the air out through his nose. He'd thought he was in decent physical shape; God, he'd been wrong. He inadvertently ran his tongue across the side of his cheek and winced when he found a slit which shot pain racing through his jaw. Of course, the punch. The strange, almost sweet tang of blood burst across his taste buds.

Manton was stretching his back and muttering further swear words and Matthew thought it was worth gambling a transfer of his attention to the other individual involved in this unseemly skirmish in the winner's enclosure.

Harry Bolt was wet and dishevelled in appearance, yet his expression, stance and silence gave him a gladiatorial aura. His fists were by his side, still balled Matthew noted, and he was scrutinising the complaining Mr Manton with wide, piercing brown eyes. He oozed an aggression which was barely contained.

Matthew shivered; the back of his suit was wringing wet where he'd ended up on the floor. His trousers were sticking to his calves and he got the feeling his suit jacket wasn't sitting right. A quick glance down confirmed a large rip where his pocket had once been. He cleared his throat purposefully and loudly.

'Gentlemen!'

Manton rattled out another set of expletive laden bile, only to have Matthew's hushing hand waggled in his face.

'May I remind you both that we still do not have the result of the photo for second or the steward's enquiry. I insist that you remain in this room and stay apart. Once the final result is decided you will both leave separately and I strongly suggest vacating the racecourse immediately to avoid any further confrontation.'

Harry watched as Manton leaned on the semi circular table and with a complaining groan, pulled a chair out, carefully placing it opposite Harry to allow Manton to pin him with an evil glare.

They were in the wood built pentagonal winning connections room at the corner of the parade ring. Outside, a line of three racecourse security people stood with their backs to the room, watching the small huddle of defiant, mud splattered staff members from the Bolt yard. Several yards behind them stood the stick thin figure of Doyle.

Harry relaxed his stance a little, sniffed, and unclenched his fingers. Manton continued to glare glassy eyed at Harry and he took a few seconds to stare back, but recognizing the absurdity of the situation he broke eye contact and instead turned his head to nod at his people outside. The heat in his chest started to drain and he gave Matthew a meaningful look which resulted in him dropping his outstretched hand. Harry backed away and leant up against the side of the room, starting to reflect on what had brought him to be attempting to pound the life out of another human being.

Ah, yes, Harry recalled. *Po had won the Gimcrack.*

Run into what the participating jockeys had described as a continuous sheet of descending water, the field had kicked away from the starting stalls and huge clods of the Knavesmire turf immediately started to be lifted into the air behind the nine horses. From the stands, the first two furlongs of the race was a whiteout to any watcher, the race caller's commentary consisting of nothing more than an extended apology. With grey and grainy television pictures Harry had only just been able to pick out Fido who had managed to bag the lead and was whipping over the boggy ground quite effectively, using his speed to get a few of his rivals off the bridle already. One of the early strugglers was Luckyman, who was labouring from the first furlong and by halfway Seamus had sat up on him and allowed him to come home in his own time.

At this stage Po was in behind horses, he and Rory almost obscured by the amount of large, black balls of earth which were being tossed into the air. The closely packed field of runners had resembled an earth moving machine, eating its way up the straight, leaving a tattered, pock marked trench up the inside rail. The jockeys, as one, had angled over to the far side rails, searching for ground which might tease an extra length from their mounts.

Fletch, with Shane on board, wasn't visible in the early stages, completely hidden at the rear of the main body of the field. When, after three furlongs, the commentator could start to call the race, Fletch was at the back of the main group, but making progress.

Out in front, Fido had still been thoroughly enjoying himself over two furlongs out. The colt picked his way over the treacherous terrain, ears back, and going well within himself a couple of widths off the rails. As he'd scooted past the two marker, a length and a half up on his pursuers, Harry had experienced that twist of emotion, when flickering hope wondrously alters to become belief; Fido could win this.

When the runners hit the furlong marker Fido had been in unknown territory. Still a length up, he suddenly began to look vulnerable, his stride starting to shorten. Only three runners in behind him could have possibly reached him now, and all of them were struggling in the ground, wandering off a true course. Fletch had moved into second place, being challenged by Manton's My Way Or No Way who looked the stronger of the chasing trio. Po in fourth, a further length and a half away, in behind horses, his tail was swishing around, was clearly hating having mud kicked into his face.

Fido had got into trouble just over half a furlong out. The three chasing colts had started drawing him ever closer to them with every stride. Yet he still maintained his lead with head down, ears back, straining to give Maddy every last ounce of stamina he could muster. She never picked up her whip, maintaining her riding style throughout, cajoling and urging Fido whilst keeping him balanced, and he kept finding that little bit extra for her. In stark contrast My Way Or No Way's pilot had shown his colt the whip and had been throwing everything at the two year old since two furlongs out, but he'd responded, moving into second place with a hundred yards to run.

The last five strides of the finish to this Gimcrack would be replayed for days afterwards on Racing TV. It became the primary talking point of the Ebor meeting, every racing column in every newspaper printed a report, and the race trended across every social media platform for the next forty-eight hours. It was reported upon across the world and the last fifteen seconds were watched by five million people on YouTube.

All four horses had been slowing as they attempted to cope with the barbaric conditions. The cold breeze had become a stiff headwind which increased in intensity in the last furlong; the grandstands and rolling banks of the course enclosure funnelling the swirling wind. It had smashed the rain into the faces of jockeys and horses alike, each drop stinging as it thrashed against them.

Fido had weakened terribly forty yards out, his lead being eaten into with every passing moment. My Way Or No Way made relentless inroads, closely followed by Fletch. Po, still a length down had no huge surge of crowd noise to urge him forward this time. The stands, viewing galleries and rails had been almost devoid of race watchers. But it seemed the colt didn't need a crowd today, when Rory pulled him out and asked him for his effort, the maelstrom all around him gave Po every scream of encouragement he'd needed. Four strides from the finish he was on the outside of the group, a length down. Three strides away he went level with Fletch and My Way Or No Way, Fido still a neck away in front.

All four horses had been all out. The turf on the track had deteriorated to the point where their hooves were penetrating the surface and disappearing several inches. With two strides to the winning post Fido was caught and Po's momentum took him up to create a line of four horses abreast, jockey's pumping, urging their mounts for that last effort. Then… chaos had reigned.

Rory had given Po a back hander, one final request for everything… and the colt faltered. His head came up and he veered violently left, crashing into the Manton horse beside him. This caused a ripple effect, squeezing Fletch and Fido up against the inside rail. My Way Or No Way's jockey had been hard at work, but now found his whip hand thumping into Shane's chest, in turn he reacted, pulling the reins on Fletch, trying to take them out of trouble. This reaction was the catalyst for Fletch to jink further left and make a solid connection with the retreating Fido, propelling the tired colt sideways. Fido crashed into the plastic rails, bounced back and catapulted Maddy upward and created a concertina effect with the other three horses. Maddy had bounced onto Fido's neck and fallen to her right, across onto Shane and Fletch.

The four colts passed the finishing post as one; a mass of horseflesh, with reins and limbs at awkward angles. Po continued to go left through the line and the bumping had continued for a few more strides.

With ninety percent of the race-goers staying indoors, the sound around the racecourse was muted, although gasps had gone up from the knot of stable staff waiting in the deluge at the paddock gate to retrieve their runners.

The television coverage caught Maddy crossing the finishing line lying half across Fido and Fletch, almost in Shane's lap. He had grabbed Maddy's britches and dragged her, face down, across Fletch's neck as he pulled his horse up and Fido finally parted company with his pilot. Maddy had been bumped along with Shane for thirty yards, before being allowed to slither down Fletch's neck and land in an ungainly manner onto the sopping wet turf.

In the immediate aftermath of the race, the result was initially of no consequence to Harry and his staff. They had one focus; to ensure the safety of both horses and riders. It wasn't until Fido had been caught and reunited with a shaken, but physically fine Maddy, save for a couple of bruises, that Harry had become aware of the result.

Po had been called the winner and there was a photo for second place, but that announcement was closely followed by another; the three chimes over the public address system which signalled there was a steward's enquiry. It was for interference in the final stages of the race.

Harry had told Rory on his return that it didn't take a mind reader to work out which horse's actions the stewards would be assessing.

Manton produced a hollow cough, snapping Harry's focus back into the winning connections room. He glowered over at the man who was sitting with his legs wide apart, flabby gut flopping over his trousers. The object of Harry's distaste was too busy puffing on and inspecting the end of his cigar to notice. A plume of foul smelling smoke reached Harry and he snorted, crossed his arms, and looked though a rain splashed window onto the parade ring outside. The only sound now was the continued pummeling of the rain onto the roof of the wooden pentagon.

The silence was cracked open by Matthew Nottingham's phone buzzing. He retrieved it from his suit pocket, but not before it sent out a jangling digital ringtone which made both Manton and Harry regard the clerk of the course intently.

Matthew listened, gave a couple of short responses, and cut the call. Harry felt a rush of sympathy for the clerk. He'd been pulled into an argument which wasn't his. He doubted Matthew would have expected to be at the centre of a brawl when he set off for work this morning.

'The stewards enquiry...'

Three chimes rang out around the racecourse, breaking into Matthew's news. He paused, ensuring both men heard the announcement.

'Following the Stewards enquiry there is an amended result,' boomed the public address system.

Manton let out a roar and started a gleeful laugh. Harry winced and looked away.

The announcement continued, 'The stewards found that the winning horse, Nine Two..'

'Bloody stupid name for a horse,' Manton muttered.

'... interfered with the placed horses. Nine Two has been disqualified and placed fourth.'

Manton jeered at Harry, pushing himself to his feet and pumping both his fists in the air, still puffing on his cigar. Harry wanted to push the long fat thing right down the man's throat.

The announcement continued, 'The amended result for the Gimcrack Stakes is; A dead heat for first place between Fifteen One and My Way Or No Way, third Nineteen...'

Manton's celebrations halted and he tore his cigar from his mouth and threw it across the room.

'What the...?' he screamed, sending spittle flying in Matthew's direction.

Credit to the clerk, he faced Manton down, instructing the angry owner to, 'Sit down now, Mr Manton!' in a surprisingly stern voice.

Harry stared incredulously at the clerk. 'Fido... I mean Fifteen One finished in a dead heat for second?'

Matthew nodded and Harry mumbled to himself, 'The tough little sod kept on!'

'It was announced while you and him, and it seems, half the people in the parade ring where busy kicking seven shades out of each other... and me.' Matthew confirmed bitterly, glancing down at his muddied and ripped attire.

Manton looked ready to explode; his face had suddenly turned scarlet. Harry watched in morbid fascination as the man's eyes flitted around the room as he digested the new reality: Manton and Redblood had *both* won the Gimcrack.

'Who gets to give the speech?' Manton demanded.

Matthew looked thrown by this, giving Manton a confused shake of his head.

'The Gimcrack speech you...' Manton blurted, searching for an expletive strong enough to offend.

Matthew's eyes narrowed and he tilted his head toward his questioner, daring Manton to complete his query. The tactic worked; Manton blew nothing but air from his lungs.

With eyes still on Manton, Matthew said, 'In the event of a dead heat the owner whose horse has been allotted the lowest race number gets the honour of delivering the Gimcrack dinner speech, however, the owner of...'

Matthew continued but Manton was already scrabbling in his suit pockets, swearing when he couldn't find his racecard. His patting of pockets eventually produced a rumpled, mud-stained booklet which he feverishly leafed through. But Harry already knew.

He nodded to Matthew, extended a hand and apologised once more for his part in the skirmish, opened the door to the winning connections room and stepped into the rain once more.

'I'm sure the BHA will be in touch regarding your fisticuffs in the winner's enclosure,' Matthew called after him. 'And please leave the racecourse immediately,' he added grimly.

As Harry closed the door to the winning connections room the rain started soaking his hair once more and behind him a roar of animal intensity issued from Manton. Harry walked down the steps towards his waiting stable staff, who shared bewildered looks. He decided there was no joy in Manton's bellow of success; it was filled with malice and laced with the intent to subjugate.

Thirty-Three

'I've had enough,' Harry told Jill in exasperation for the third time in a matter of minutes. He was pacing around the kitchen table, head down, biting the inside of his mouth.

Jill was seated, nursing Will, and had been trying to calm her husband down since they'd got out of bed six hours earlier. She'd reached the point where she was starting to repeat herself, her increasingly stern suggestions being cast aside by Harry as he fought an inner turmoil.

It was the day after the Gimcrack and he'd been in the same self-admonishing spiral since his return from York. She watched him do another circuit of the table; he was muttering about Manton, Doyle, Laya, George, Redblood, the horses, the jockeys, the British Horseracing Board and all the calls, texts and emails which were still arriving by the minute. Jill knew this introspection was Harry's way of working things through, but it didn't make being a spectator any less painful. She'd seen him as distracted as this only a few times before, usually when it concerned difficult life decisions. This set of issues was much bigger, more complex and Jill wasn't too sure whether her usual method of shaking him out of his funk was working.

Harry circled again, eyes to the floor, his chin almost touching his chest. Jill pushed a kitchen chair out to block his path.

'Sit down!' she commanded, allowing her frustration to seep into her voice just enough to warn him that ignoring her would be a bad idea. He looked up and caught her no nonsense stare and returned a baleful look, sighed and flopped into the seat, holding his head in one hand. He sat uneasily on the hard wooden chair, jiggling one leg.

It was almost noon on Saturday and, apart from Bunt doing his security rounds, the yard was now empty of staff. They had no runners today and all the stable work had been completed. Jill adjusted her baby's position, placing Will in the crook of her arm so she could touch Harry's trembling knee. He felt the warmth of her hand melt through the material of his jeans and noticed for the first time the movement of his leg, and ceased its jiggling. He instinctively reached down and encased her hand in his own.

'The hardest part is over,' she declared in a level, positive tone. 'You won the Gimcrack for heaven's sake!' she added lightly.

'Then lost it in the Stewards room…'

'Then won it again,' Jill insisted. 'You've delivered what Redblood wanted.'

'Yeah,' Harry agreed. 'I can't quite understand why he's so happy though. Manton gets to speak at his precious Gimcrack dinner.'

'It doesn't matter, he's sorted now.'

'Hmm… Not quite.'

'You spoke with him this morning didn't you? We've already been promised the money for winning the Gimcrack. He's got his winner, so that's it. Job done, isn't it?'

Harry sighed. 'If there's a dead heat *both* owners get to speak, one does the main address, the other responds with the toast. Redblood wants me to attend the dinner and do the blasted toast! In fact, he's insisting it was part of the agreement. We get paid the bonus after the dinner in early December. He's already been in touch with York racecourse, reserved some tables, and wants me to invite some people, I've no idea why.'

His leg started its involuntary jiggle again, but Jill held his knee and brought the movement to a stop. He looked into his wife's blue eyes, suddenly aware he was placing his own burdens onto her.

'I'm sorry, but I don't know if I can bear to be in the same room as Manton and that reptile Doyle.'

Jill could feel Harry's pulse gain strength through his hand, and the familiar haunted look he'd worn since the Gimcrack returned to his face.

'I could have killed him,' he said quietly, flicking his gaze nervously away into the corner of the kitchen. 'In those few seconds I could have... I was so angry.'

Jill recalled Harry's version of events. He'd managed to tell the story once he'd calmed down on the evening of the race. Manton, initially being restrained to some extent by Doyle, had come straight over after the race to where Harry was unsaddling Po in the winner's enclosure. He had started by loudly accusing Rory of cheating because of the manoeuvre Po made in the last few strides. Rory had studiously ignored him until Manton in a fit of frustration had grabbed the jockey's shoulders from behind and shaken him. The response from Rory was immediate; he'd spun round and landed a punch to the man's stomach. Manton had doubled over and looked to be backing off but then stepped forward and threw a punch at Harry, which he returned.

In the ensuing melee, Harry, Bunt, Manton, and Doyle all ended up in a tangled mess in front of the winner's podium. Mud, grass, and fists were flying. The Clerk of the course had waded in to pull people apart, only to be drawn into the fracas. Once they were back on their feet, the two opposing sides had parted, which prompted Manton to start screaming abuse at Harry. Matthew had finally enlisted his security staff to escort the two of them to the winning connections room.

'You had every right to be angry,' Jill conceded. 'But surely it was just handbags in a mud bath rather than anything more serious?'

'It seemed serious at the time,' Harry moaned, but he did appear to Jill to be a little brighter. She seized upon this chink of sunlight on a grey day and tried to build on the moment.

'Bunt said it was such bad weather there wasn't anyone there to video and share it on social media. It's a shame really; I'd have liked to see you and Rory rolling around in the mud. It would be just like old times!' she joked, flashing Harry a cheeky little smile for good measure.

Harry returned a subdued grin. Rory and he had got into plenty of scrapes as young men including one or two bust ups with other jockeys which had resulted in a few punches being thrown. He supposed in a roundabout way, he'd been sticking up for Rory again at York. For some reason, it seemed less embarrassing to consider the skirmish in this way.

He cast his mind to his other problems. The BHA was sure to charge him with bringing the sport into disrepute. He'd not heard anything yet, but knowing them, an official letter would be winging its way to the yard on Monday. These sorts of official rebukes could take months to resolve and it wasn't a great advert for the yard.

The media interest in the race hadn't dissipated one bit overnight, if anything, it had increased as the insatiable appetite for intrigue in the racing industry was propelled by the reports of a punch up. Both the Racing TV and Sky Racing channels were agreed that Po didn't deserve to keep the race, which Harry tended to agree with. However, the way Fido crossed the line, without Maddy being in full control of him, had become contentious, especially when he was promoted to be joint winner.

There was suggestion from various online racing sources that Manton was about to lodge an appeal against Fido, citing jockey contact had been lost with the horse and therefore disqualification should be considered. Harry thought it would be unlikely to succeed as Maddy hadn't really left her saddle until she was over the line.

He had dipped in and out of social media all morning, feeling sick to his stomach when reading some of the comments which promoted Manton as the severely wronged party of the piece. Harry would have loved to have waded into the debate but again, Redblood's contract forbade any discussion of his horses with any representatives of the media.

'You know what causes me the most heartache?'

'I can guess,' Jill replied. 'How about... you're pretty sure you know who killed your mother but you're not able to do anything about it until Redblood has had his Gimcrack dinner.'

Harry stared at his wife with his mouth open and after a short pause, swallowed hard.

'No, well, there is that of course... but I'd put it to the back of my mind. What Redblood has planned should sort that out... hopefully.'

'So, what then?'

'It's the fact that we got three horses home in the first four at York in a Group Two race and no one is talking about what a great performance either Po or Fido put in.'

'Really? *That's* what's bothering you?' Jill said in amazement.

A smile washed across Harry's face.

'No, as if! Well, maybe a little bit...' However, his smile faded as quickly as it had appeared.

'Apart from you, I don't know who to trust,' he blurted. Harry took a few quick intakes of breath and gazed into the middle distance.

Jill looked into her husband's deep brown eyes and saw a sadness which hadn't been there a few months earlier. She squeezed his hand but remained silent.

'We've faced so much in this year,' he continued. 'Stupidly, I thought winning the Gimcrack would see it all end, so we could get back to normal. Yet we're still lost in this... no man's land full of dead people coming back to life, murderers, poisoning... so many secrets and lies.'

He was becoming emotional, his eyes sparkling with a dewy mist. Jill let this last comment settle on them both for some time before offering a response.

'We said we'd take a chance on Redblood. We took that decision together. Somehow we've got there, Lord knows how, but the finishing line is in sight. The Gimcrack dinner will see things come together. We've almost done it.'

She unlinked her hand from his, reached up, and turned his dark face toward hers. 'Don't you forget your friends, Harry. You can still trust them.'

Harry closed his eyes and sucked in a big breath, held it, and then blew the air out slowly through rounded lips.

'Thanks for reminding me,' he confirmed, forcing a sad smile. 'I guess you're right.'

He kissed Jill tenderly on her forehead as he got up from his seat.

'I'm going to go and see Rory, you know, make sure he's okay. But first I think I'll play for a while.'

Jill nodded, pleased with him, 'Play something happy, Tiger.'

Harry disappeared into the lounge, his piano struck up and presently the first few bars of a boogie woogie version of Oh bla di oh bla da filled the farmhouse.

Thirty-Four

Jill was starting to lose her temper.

'*Harry!* Will you for the love of god, stand still!'

'I'm trying my best!' he gurgled as Jill tried once more to fasten his bow tie into place.

He screwed his neck to one side as Jill tried again, unsuccessfully, to make his bow tie look anything like the Googled photo on their iPad.

'There you go!' she sang out in triumph two minutes later. She backed away, tilting her head from side to side to admire her handiwork. On the bedroom floor Will lay on his play mat, holding one foot and babbling happily to himself.

'Thanks,' said Harry uncertainly as he reviewed Jill's attempt in the mirror. He examined the fancy white shirt and dinner suit trousers he'd hired, and wasn't best pleased. He looked stupid and they felt like cardboard against his skin. He pulled the jacket on and wondered how anyone could enjoy dressing like this.

'Daddy looks like a dog's dinner,' he told Will. His son responded by blowing bubbles and babbling some more.

Harry got down on his knees and blew a raspberry on the boy's tummy, eliciting a deep-throated giggling noise from Will. Harry had been completely smitten with this reaction from the first time he'd tried it and grinned manically while teasing his son.

Eventually, Jill could stand no more and she pulled Harry up.

'Come on, Tiger, time to go and finish Manton off,' she told him as she picked a few stray dog hairs off his jacket. 'Bunt will be waiting for you. Nervous?'

Harry caught Jill's gaze and was reminded how adept she was at reading him.

'Yes,' he replied baldly. 'I can't believe Redblood has talked me into doing the piece after Manton's speech.'

'Ah! The toast.' Jill said with a smirk. 'Have you got your lines?'

Harry produced a blank postcard from his inside pocket upon which three handwritten lines were printed in blue biro. He waggled it around for a few seconds.

'If the dinner is a bit dry and uninteresting up to that stage, your speech should get things going.'

'That's what I'm worried about.'

There was a shout of 'Harry?' from downstairs. Bunt's voice carried right up to the top of the house and Harry moved to the landing to shout, 'Two minutes!' downward in reply.

Jill had Will on her hip when he returned to the bedroom. She came up and gave Harry a peck on his cheek, stood back to evaluate his overall look and gave him an appreciative nod.

'You'll do. Go on, get going. Oh, and come back in one piece this time please.'

Bunt was checking his watch when Harry walked out the back door of the farmhouse. It was bitingly cold. A heavy frost had meant the gallops were closed and the stable staff had been reduced to placing the All-Weather horses on the walker rather than riding them out. Bunt was also decked out in a dinner suit which, Harry noticed on second look, was refined and tailored to the man's physique, which could not be said of his own.

'Nice threads!' Harry exclaimed, clapping the silver haired man on his shoulder as they walked to the car.

Bunt glanced over at Harry. 'You're nervous aren't you? You always become jovial when you're nervous. I've seen you do it at the races.'

Harry wrinkled his nose. 'Yeah, I do that. Sorry, I'll stop.'

With a final pat of his jacket to make sure he had his wallet and his phone, Harry jumped into the passenger seat. Bunt gunned the engine and they set off for York Racecourse and what Harry sincerely hoped would be the final day he'd have to worry about Thomas Redblood and Benedict Manton.

****

'Time?' Manton demanded of Doyle.

Doyle sighed in exasperation, reached out, and tapped the transparent face of the clock set into the centre of the car's dashboard.

'Ten thirty-five,' he said quietly.

Benny Manton, Doyle had decided, was now no better than a child when he was nervous. In the several months since the York debacle he'd become worse. Their joint trips around the country to pacify clients becoming frustrated with the logjam caused by the Money Tree had placed their relationship under serious strain and at times Doyle had wondered whether Manton was going to cope. He had cursed his speech impediment and his inability to contribute during those interminable meetings. Still, they'd got through it and today's speech would hopefully be well reported and give their clients a good feeling that Halo was back on track. But Doyle wasn't under any illusions: Manton was here today to claim his victory, bathe in the accolade, and inflate his ego.

'Everything is in place, as we've rehearsed?' Manton asked in a tone which sought reassurance.

'Yes, Benny,' Doyle replied calmly. 'I checked the presentation out myself twice yesterday and the screen we installed worked perfectly.'

He examined the man sitting in the back seat, a position Manton insisted upon when travelling by car, although Doyle believed it was more about the prestige rather than travel sickness. Manton was very clearly overweight and his skin had an unhealthy grey sheen. Doyle took in his flabby, bearded colleague and reckoned Benny was half the man he'd been a few years before in terms of his mental prowess, and twice the man in terms of his weight. Even his speech, which had been his forte, had started to deteriorate. He slurred the odd word, was slower on the uptake, and was prone to nodding off at all times of the day. He's getting old, Doyle decided. He was becoming fragile and, possibly, vulnerable.

'We'll go in at ten forty,' Manton instructed, riffling through a bunch of papers.

Doyle nodded his acceptance into the rear view mirror. Manton was set for his big moment in the limelight; meanwhile he would case the room. He'd already spent time walking the room the day before, today he needed to spot where people were sitting, where the threats may lie. All the usual contingencies they used for public appearances had been put in place. Doyle shuddered; these dips into the media limelight weren't to his liking. He'd never quite understood why Benny got such a kick from them. The man changed in front of a crowd, it seemed to fuel him.

He'd managed to talk Manton out of further retribution against Bolt, and there hadn't been any more messages resulting from Redblood's week of freedom before he died. That said, the Money Tree was still under immense pressure, the missing memory stick still hadn't been found and Deacon's progress in reinstating the laundering system was frustratingly slow. However, the Redblood and Bolt threat had receded during the last few months. Even so, there could be no repeat of Gimcrack day, Benny flying off the handle and causing more issues. It had to go smoothly today.

'You ready?'

Manton shuffled his papers, looked into Doyle's eyes via the rear view mirror, and bared his teeth.

'Let me at 'em Charlie. Today's my big day.'

****

Gwent was uncomfortable. For a start, the chair she was sitting on wasn't big enough for her backside, but that wasn't her prime concern, these sorts of events always gave her an over arching feeling of discomfort. Her unease wasn't going to be mitigated by eating with strangers and listening to interminable self-congratulatory speeches. If the lunch and early afternoon progressed as she anticipated, dinner would be topped off by a round of corporate backslapping and small talk, two more of her pet hates. The only reason she was here was because Harry Bolt had asked her... and it was free.

She slanted a glance at Poole beside her. Her constable was conversing with a large, expressive, and annoyingly happy man sitting beside him. Poole's astonished features were busy being more astonished by the raconteur's tale. She surveyed the joyful man again, and felt she recognised his face, but couldn't place him. She determined to find out from Poole when he'd finished gassing with the man.

They were seated at the back of the room, at one of three large circular tables furthest from a stubby stage with a lectern placed at its centre. The backdrop to the stage was a tall, wide white projection screen. The entire stage set up had a temporary, modular feel to it but still impressed. A little way behind her a wall of ceiling to floor glass windows with glass revolving doors at their centre, provided a view of the empty stand steps and a frost covered racetrack beyond. Weak winter sunshine shone through the windows in short bursts, sporadically being extinguished by the cloud cover. Gwent had tried the revolving doors when she first came in; they had been disabled, so there was no way to step outside onto the terrace or the stands. So much for grabbing a quick breath of fresh air she had thought; the room smelled of carpet cleaning fluid, which was getting up her nose.

For a room built within a large grandstand, it was capacious and airy. The tall walls were draped with the colours of a corporate betting sponsor and a few adverts for the bookmaker were dotted around. There were only two entry points; one of them was for staff only to the left, with the entry for guests to the right. That was manned by the clerk of the course, Matthew Nottingham, who was greeting everyone with a glass of champagne on arrival. She imagined on race days this area would be crammed with race-goers enjoying a silver service meal and afternoon tea between the races. Waiting staff would be buzzing around guests, who were content to pay exorbitant sums for their premium day at the races. She counted the tables; there were fourteen, with seating for eight people at each.

The tables themselves were lavishly presented with thick white tablecloths holding a myriad of sparkling glassware and shiny cutlery. The ostentatious centrepiece of flowers wasn't to her liking, but Gwent reflected that she was well out of her comfort zone anyway. It was unlikely any aspect of the dinner would receive praise from her today. It was actually a bit of a shame; there were three chilled bottles of free champagne on each table. It might have got interesting if she wasn't here in a working capacity.

The tables were slowly filling with what Gwent assumed were the great and good of the racing industry. There was a table for media types which contained one or two faces she half recognised, but virtually every other table filled with dinner-suited men and immaculately dressed women meant nothing to her. In contrast, Poole pointed out a range of people from the BHA, Weatherby's, studs, horse sales companies as well as trainers, jockeys and prominent racehorse owners.

Gwent watched Harry Bolt and his security chum arrive. She noted they refused the free champagne and Harry appeared a shade nervous. Not surprising really, from the order of events card provided to every guest, he was about to produce a response to Benedict Manton's speech. From what she knew of Harry, he would probably be happier with a piano in front of him and a song to sing, rather than some dry words recited from a script. She caught his eye as he picked his way through the tables, and he waved a hello and flashed a quick smile before sitting down at a table in the middle of the room.

Poole nudged her. 'He's had a cracking season,' he told her. 'Bagged a group race at Royal Ascot with one of his 'Revenge' horses, won a couple of big two year old handicaps and a sales race. Even his lesser lights have been winning. He's really made an impact from out of nowhere.'

Gwent acknowledged the comment with her eyes but remained silent. Benedict Manton had just entered the room.

****

Matthew Nottingham greeted Manton with carefully managed stoicism. As a result of a complaint he had lodged with the BHA, both Manton and Harry had received severe warnings and fines of three thousand pounds each for their actions at the Ebor meeting. However, he had been mildly surprised when Manton had submitted his speech for vetting to find it to be a relatively short and succinct celebration of the racing industry, with no contentious issues broached.

Matthew extended his hand. 'Thank you for submitting your speech, Mr Manton. It will make a fine contribution to the dinner. Your words will be broadcast far and wide!'

He indicated the television camera and boom operator making final checks at the corner of the stage. Manton surveyed the media people for a moment, smiled and shook Matthew's hand enthusiastically. His face registered further delight upon being offered a glass of champagne. He then took Matthew's arm, launching into a teeth-gritting account of his trials and tribulations whilst writing the speech. Matthew noted Manton was speaking in a voice designed to carry well beyond him and into the room.

He's trying too hard, Matthew decided a minute later as Manton's self-congratulatory vignette drew to a close. He retrieved the fluted glass from Manton, the champagne had been drained in one swallow at the end of the man's diatribe, and tried to move the conversation in another direction. Without asking, Manton grabbed another glass of champagne from the small table beside Matthew and bolted half the drink down in a single gulp.

'In days gone by, the winning owner of the Gimcrack was expected to supply six dozen bottles of champagne for this dinner, as you may already know,' Matthew ventured. 'It's a tradition which has been lost for the last couple of decades.'

Manton returned a blank look to the clerk, betraying his lack of understanding. Matthew disregarded Manton's glazed expression, determined to reach a conclusion to his story.

'We were delighted when The Revenge Syndicate, your co-winning owner, decided to resurrect this ancient custom! You have just partaken in a complimentary glass and you'll see there are several free bottles on each table!'

Manton baulked a little and his first reaction was to examine the fluted glass he was holding. He scanned the tables the clerk was indicating. On each perfectly presented table numerous bottles of Moet were sitting in chilled silver buckets.

'I.. I'm pleased *you* appreciate their gesture,' he finally responded, thrusting his almost empty glass back at the clerk of the course. There was an awkward pause while Matthew simply regarded the glass and during which Manton's cheeks pinked slightly. He shot a troubled look at Doyle and received a shrug in return.

'Well, enjoy your moment in the spotlight, Mr Manton,' Matthew said with a forced smile, 'I'm sure your speech will be well received. Your table is at the front of the room,' he added, pointing an outstretched palm to the table placed directly in front of the stage.

'That little bugger Bolt did that just to embarrass me,' an indignant Manton complained to Doyle once they had been seated.

'Forget it,' hissed Doyle. 'You're on s-soon.'

Manton gave his colleague a contemptuous snort. 'I'll be fine!' he retorted. '*You're* obviously not.'

Doyle stared at Manton, his eyes filled with a dull contempt. He didn't reply. Instead he leaned over the table, plucked a bottle from its ice bucket, and refilled his champagne flute.

****

Harry was busy being introduced, shaking hands, and trading smiles with a managing director and financial controller of a high street bookmaker, the head of the Horseman's group and his wife, and the publisher of Owner Breeder Magazine, when he spotted Andrew entering the room. Bunt, also aware of Harry's brother's entrance checked for a reaction. He was pleased when Harry turned to him, none the worse for spying Andrew speaking with the clerk of the course.

'Andrew's here. Wasn't expecting that,' Harry whispered.

'He's probably here hoping to get a laugh when you cock up your speech!'

'Oh yes, *that's* why he's here!'

Harry watched Andrew wander around the outside of the room with a glass of champagne in his hand. He sidled around two tables, looking at the card nameplates and finally, with a look of relief, pulled a chair out beside Mary Gwent.

The occupants of those three tables at the back of the room played on Harry's mind, and a few seconds later he turned back to examine the faces in more detail. There was something about these people which resonated somewhere deep in his subconscious. A couple of the men wore dinner jackets, but most, like Andrew, were in lounge suits. The ladies were well dressed, but none were in the couture fashions prevalent at the tables closest to the stage.

It wasn't until Bob Leggett turned around that the penny dropped. The publican was there with his wife, beside him were Poole, Gwent and Andrew. To his right was another face he recognised... he wracked his memory and eventually came up with the notion that the chap worked behind the deli counter at Morrisons supermarket in Malton. He checked all three tables at the back of the room and the result was the same. Although he couldn't place a few faces, out of the twenty-four people now sat in their three groups of eight, everyone he recognised was from Malton.

Yet again, the feeling that there was a deeper subterfuge being played out by Redblood washed over Harry. Aware the first speech was about to be introduced, he quickly shared his observations with Bunt who took a long look over his shoulder.

'Strange bunch,' Bunt admitted. 'I can see the chap who runs the fish and chip shop in Norton over there.'

'I know, what do you suppose he's here for...'

Up on the stage, Matthew Nottingham checked his watch one final time. His second hand ticked through eleven o'clock at which point he nodded at an assistant standing beside a panel of switches. The lights went down slightly and the tables started to hush. He stepped up to centre stage, tapped the cordless microphone clipped into the lectern and peered out over fourteen tables and one hundred and twelve of the most prominent people in horse racing, plus some extras from Malton.

'A warm welcome to the annual Gimcrack dinner once again held at York Racecourse,' Matthew announced in clipped public school tones. 'Today, I'm delighted to present not one, but *two* winning owners of the Gimcrack stakes. This season's race produced plenty of controversy, but I was delighted when the BHA upheld the result our own stewards decided upon on the day. As a result, we have Mr Benedict Manton providing our state of the racing industry speech and Mr Harry Bolt will provide the following toast.'

Harry zoned out of the rest of Matthew's preamble, concentrating instead on Manton seated with his back to him, two tables in front. The man was definitely bigger… no, Harry corrected himself, *fatter* than he had been on Gimcrack day. He could pick out a dribble of sweat rolling down the man's bald patch at the back of his head.

A polite round of applause saw Manton jump to his feet, stride to the steps at the right-hand side of the stage and approach the microphone. Matthew allowed the large man to pass before he skipped down the three small steps to join his clipboard-wielding assistant, standing against the wall.

Manton grasped the lectern with both hands and expertly reduced its height so his face could be clearly seen. He placed a sheaf of papers down, looked to his right to check the television camera was rolling, and then peered slowly around the room at the gathered luminaries of the British racing industry. One or two quiet conversations were summarily hushed once Manton produced an expectant but meaningful glare in their direction. The free champagne was already having an effect on some sections of the audience.

Harry watched Manton go through this pre-speech routine and couldn't help but be impressed with his professionalism. He certainly commanded his stage.

'My Lord President, My Lords, Ladies and Gentlemen,' Manton started, pronouncing each word clearly, precisely and with reverence.

'I am deeply humbled to be delivering a speech as the winning owner of the Gimcrack. It's a race which bestows upon the winning horse's connections an opportunity which is rare in any sphere of sport or business. Furthermore, I am honoured to have been afforded this prestigious platform, allowing me to not only address the British racing industry, but also the rest of the world.'

Harry leaned back in his seat. It seemed Manton was going to try and ingratiate himself with every part of the racing community. He slanted a frustrated look over to Bunt who rolled his eyes to the ceiling in silent reply.

The speech continued with Manton thanking his jockey, trainer, and stable staff and once again Harry zoned out, his attention caught by Matthew, who was following every word Manton uttered. However Harry realised Matthew wasn't just listening, he was reading the speech from a clipboard and glancing up at Manton from time to time. Harry wondered what Matthew's reaction would be when *he* got up on stage. His speech certainly wasn't going to follow the version Matthew had in front of him.

Harry switched his attention back to Manton. He'd apparently reached a new section of his speech and was turning over a page of his notes on the lectern. Harry's forehead wrinkled as he realised Manton had just turned over the last page of his speech.

Manton, his chest expanding as he drew in breath, seized the microphone from its clip and picked up the lectern, depositing it at the side of the stage. As he returned, he began speaking once more, his voice lively, entertaining.

Doyle's lips tightened as he produced a thin smile. He looked around his table and saw six people transfixed by the man on the stage. He'd chosen the right boy to befriend at school. Manton may not be too intelligent but he could hold an audience. And what he lacked in intelligence he made up for with sheer bloody mindedness.

'It has been a dream of mine for a number of years to win the Gimcrack and take the opportunity to address the industry,' Manton told the audience as he moved his bulk around the stage.

'This year was the most important, because I have a rather special announcement to make,' he continued. Over on the far wall, Matthew was scrabbling through the papers on his clipboard, his countenance developing into a frown.

'Most of you will know me from my television appearances as a high profile owner. However, I also run a significant number of businesses and this is the perfect place to announce a seismic shift in the way the racing industry is operated worldwide.'

Manton was smiling gleefully, clearly energized by having the freedom of the stage and speaking words which were gripping his audience. He slowed his perambulations, moving to the front of the stage.

'Stallions and broodmares are the literal lifeblood of racing. However, at present there are deep-rooted issues in the bloodstock industry. These issues could bring the thoroughbred breeding business *to its knees.*'

Manton paused, his audience hanging on his next words. He plastered a grave expression on his face now, extremely effective when paired with his own grey skin colour.

'Congenital physical problems are rife in our pool of stallions and mares. Dyspnea, or wind problems to you and I, are the primary concern, accounting for sixty percent of racehorse retirements. But there are more; lung capacity deficiency, hip dysplasia, and susceptibility to colic… I could go on.'

Manton was standing in the centre of the stage. He looked out to his audience and then turned to face the television camera and spoke directly to the green light which blinked above its lens.

'So how can we rid the world's population of thoroughbred racehorses of these debilitating diseases?' he asked quietly with a shrug of his shoulders.

Suddenly the white screen behind Manton sprang to life, illuminated from behind with colour and movement. A video projection of racehorses running at full tilt toward the camera danced in front of the audience. The sound of hooves thumping onto turf and the crack of encouraging whips accompanied the huge visual which stretched right across the backdrop to the stage. There was an intake of breath and shocked gasps from the audience, quickly followed by a ripple of embarrassed laughter, from those onlookers amused at their own reaction.

Manton smiled benevolently and allowed his audience to settle once more. He walked purposefully back to the centre of the stage and the racing horses faded and a map of the world appeared with the word 'Halo' overprinted hundreds of times and scrolling slowly from bottom left to top right of the huge screen.

Harry was aware of movement to his right and glanced sideways to catch Matthew silently waving his hands at Manton. He had his hand to his throat and moved it a few times in a cutting motion, a gesture clearly intended to instruct Manton to cease his speech. A tall, wiry man got up from Manton's table and sidled over to Matthew. Harry recognised Doyle's drawn features as he passed and watched as Manton's henchman had a short exchange with Matthew before taking him by his arm and out of the room.

Ignoring this minor distraction Manton continued.

'Mr President, my Lords, Ladies and Gentlemen, may I present Halo Bloodstock,' he declared, holding an arm up to the video wall which immediately exploded into spinning graphics and huge images of horses flashing across the length of the video wall accompanied by dramatic music. They faded away and the wall return to the map of the world.

'Halo Bloodstock intends to operate across the world. We aim to own fifteen percent of the world's top stallions within the next five years. Together with partners in Britain, Ireland, America, Canada, Brazil, Germany, France, Saudi Arabia and Australia, that percentage should climb to twenty five percent. That's enough to make a big difference!' Manton bellowed as the video wall highlighted places around the world, the countries being enlarged via slick animation.

'We have analysed the pedigrees and genetic markers of all the major stallions throughout the world and I can announce today that our work will see the eventual eradication of congenital equine defects in every single yearling which is bred from Halo Bloodstock.'

The video wall altered again and displayed veterinary laboratories and a montage of reports and statistics which appeared and vanished so quickly they couldn't actually be read.

'We will only breed from sires without defects. We will only breed to broodmares without defects,' Manton's mantra continued. 'This will change the face of thoroughbred management around the world,' he added theatrically with a spin of his wrist. The video wall changed once more, displaying the flags of twenty countries, all flapping wildly to the sound of wind whistling.

Harry sensed movement on the right-hand wall once more and

standing red faced was Matthew, clutching his clipboard. Harry looked closer and right behind Matthew, almost obscured because of his thin stature, was a straight-lipped Doyle.

Manton beamed out over his audience and felt his heart swell. This felt so good. For one moment he actually found himself believing he could deliver this brave plan, but caught himself and hardness entered his eyes as he laughed inwardly at how easy it was to sell snake oil to stupid people. This business was make believe and would never come to fruition, however it would elevate his status for years to come and signal to his *real* clients he was in control and untouchable.

Manton took a breath and started wrapping things up, speaking with gusto about the opportunities his new business would bring, but Harry maintained his scrutiny of Matthew. He tilted slightly in his seat, intending to nudge Bunt, but a quick glance over at his security man confirmed Bunt was already aware of the situation. He flashed a set of warning eyes at Harry and signalled him to remain seated.

Manton was confident his message had got across to the audience in the room. On the table dedicated to the media several of the reporters were scribbling furiously in notebooks, while a couple more were staring up at him dumbstruck. Now he would speak to his *real* partners and clients. He turned his attention to the television camera which was tracking him as he moved across the stage, smiling as he raised the microphone for his big finish. He looked deep into the lens and dropped his voice slightly. He needed to project ambiance, but with a serious edge.

'The Halo project will start operating this month,' Manton stated, hoping the malicious twinkle in his eye would be picked up by the camera. 'All the systems, companies, and contracts are in place. If you wish to join this opportunity and share in our success, you know how to reach us.'

He walked backwards a few paces and lifted an arm to indicate the centre of the video wall. In perfect synchronicity the flags faded to a dull grey and the Halo logo, consisting of a single ring hovering over an idealised representation of the earth, shone brightly in white before being replaced by corporate contact details.

Manton held his pose for about ten seconds and was eventually provided with a smattering of applause by a largely boggled audience. Harry watched him give a slight inclination of his head in Doyle's direction. Doyle waited until Manton had descended the steps before saying something into Matthew's ear and escorting Manton back to his table.

Aware that he needed to regain control of the event, Matthew waited until Manton had settled and then made his way onto the stage. He carried the lectern back to its original position and replaced the microphone. Normally he would thank the previous speaker for his illuminating speech, but given Manton had delivered an entirely different speech to the one he'd scripted, he was in no mood to commend him. Manton's colleague had made it quite clear that any attempt to halt his boss's speech would result in a bodily assault. He purposefully looked beyond Manton's table, tapped the microphone twice and decided alacrity would be the best policy.

'Now, Mr Harry Bolt, a local Malton trainer and joint winner of the Gimcrack, will provide the toast.'

Harry rose from his seat. On hearing his name prickles of perspiration broke on his forehead. He passed Matthew, showing him a half smile and reached the centre of the stage in silence, the smattering of applause having petered out. He stopped at the lectern and turned toward the audience and was shocked by the number of upturned faces. A lump developed in his throat and he found himself staring out into the room somewhat bewildered.

Manton stood out, right in front of him, his big, unappetising grin shining through his beard. It took a short while until Harry realised it wasn't a smile, Manton was baring his teeth in a snarl. Beside him, Doyle stared up at the stage, his angular head slightly dipped, his crooked lips producing a sneer. He looked like a praying mantis which was determining when to strike and kill its prey. Harry shuddered, feeling the ripples pass down the right side of his body, terminating just below his hip. His mother's killers were sitting in front of him, baying for blood.

Harry took hold of himself, trying to shake the image of Laya's dead body from his mind, finally placing his speech card onto the lectern. Beyond the edge of the lectern Manton's face caught in his line of vision once more. He was urging Harry to fail, he was sure of it. It was a smug, pitying look that the victor gives their crushed opponent after a battle.

Manton started to mouth something. Harry was drawn to the vile man's silent words. Manton repeated them and then drew a line under his neck and the meaning hit home. Manton was mouthing, 'You're going to die.'

Harry froze. The sea of faces seemed to be washing in and out of focus and he took hold of the wooden lectern with both hands to steady himself. He wasn't aware at the time, but he'd been standing at the lectern for thirty seconds, the room in total silence, people rolling their eyes and shrugging at each other, when Andrew stood up at the back of the room and started to clap loudly and strongly. Gwent jumped up and immediately joined him and Poole followed suit. Suddenly all three tables at the back of the room were applauding loudly.

Like a drunk suddenly finding a moment of lucidity, the noise woke Harry from his stupor, and he chanced looking up again and cast his gaze to the where the noise was loudest. He saw his brother and Gwent, not just applauding, cheering too, and encouraging others to do the same. The sound of clapping increased, spreading through the room, table by table, some people getting to their feet. The louder it became, the stronger Harry gripped the lectern, the brighter his eyes became, the taller he grew.

The front tables were applauding now. And there, still seated directly in front of him were Manton and Doyle, shifting uncomfortably in their seats, looking up in distain at the smiling dinner guests around them. Manton's face was turning red. A smile crept across Harry's face.

'Mr President…,' Harry started, and the applause raised to a final crescendo before is slowly died away and people started to return to their seats. '…My Lords, Ladies and Gentlemen.'

Harry looked down at his spidery writing on the two cards in front of him. He probably wouldn't get this chance again. He made a decision.

'Winning the Gimcrack was the greatest achievement of my career,' he said shakily. He swallowed, dryness having invaded his mouth to the extent that he had to run his tongue across its roof to continue.

'Losing the race in a Stewards' enquiry was the worst moment. It's just as well I had the second home as well,' he added with a self-deprecating smile. The audience provided his comment with a smattering of laughter, but it was enough to fill Harry with more confidence.

Harry heard the turning of papers and shot a glance over to the left hand wall where the Clerk of the course was once again flicking the pages on his clipboard and shaking his head. It was Bunt's turn to have a few words with Matthew, having crossed to the wall when Harry left his seat. He nodded an assurance to Harry. Clearly frustrated, Matthew crossed his arms, hugged the clipboard to his chest, and glowered up at Harry.

He took a calming breath and continued.

'I am blessed with a great training yard in Malton…'

Harry paused when a small cheer went up from the back of the room.

'…and I have a brilliant, loyal, and dedicated team who have really stepped up to the challenges we've faced this season. You'll know from the media coverage from our friends down here,' he indicated the table of journalists, '…the Gimcrack was the primary target for us, so to win the race, even in a dead heat and in such strange circumstances, was the highlight of the year.'

Harry's expression hardened. He glanced down and took a prompt from a few words on the cards. As if a switch had been flicked, Bunt looked out over the audience from his position beside Matthew at the door. He located the face he was searching for and locked eyes with Wang, who nodded in response, slid from his chair and quietly took up a position against the opposite wall, beside the staff door.

'I now wish to toast our first speaker,' announced Harry. 'However, before I do, I'd like to make a few comments on Halo's excellent plan for the bloodstock industry,' Harry remarked without any hint of sarcasm.

Manton had been lounging in his seat, studiously examining the social media updates from his speech. Once Harry mentioned Halo he sat upright, eyed the speaker appraisingly, and traded an inscrutable look with Doyle.

'In fact, I'd like to introduce you to someone who has firsthand experience of Mr Manton's method of operation... Mr Thomas Redblood, could you please stand up?'

Harry watched in delight as Manton's cheeks drained of their colour. Then he began whipping his head around the room in a state of panic. At a table behind and to the right of Manton a slumped figure jumped smartly to his feet, tore off a false beard, and removed his wig. Redblood turned his face up toward the stage and stated, 'I'm right here Harry!' in a positive voice. This was met with a shuffling of bottoms on seats and craning of necks as the audience dealt with another twist to what was turning out to be the most eventful, and certainly the strangest, Gimcrack dinner in recent history.

'Mr Redblood,' continued Harry. 'Perhaps you could explain your relationship with Mr Manton?'

'Certainly Harry! Until recently I was an employee of Mr Manton, providing computer related services.'

'And what *exactly* were these services, Mr Redblood?' said Harry, almost starting to enjoy himself.

Redblood edged out from his table and cane in hand, he got up and stood on his chair. Doyle was tapping something into his phone and whispering something angrily to Manton, who was too busy staring at Redblood to provide any reply.

'I used to help manage Mr Manton's international money laundering operations,' Redblood announced slowly and deliberately.

The room fell deadly silent. Heads turned toward Manton and Doyle. Some of the guests stood to peer over to Manton's table. There was the clicking of a camera from the table of journalists and the video camera operator swung round to capture Manton's response. Doyle remained preoccupied with his phone, while Manton stared open-mouthed at Redblood, apparently unable to comprehend the situation.

'But you...,' started Manton, but was interrupted by the louder, steadier and altogether more commanding voice of Redblood.

'In short, Mr Benedict Manton and his associate Mr Charlie Doyle are involved in organised crime,' Redblood told his audience. His eyes were sparkling as he watched Manton squirm in his seat.

He continued. 'Let me give you an example. At the back of the room we have three tables of hard working, honest people from the great town of Malton.'

Mutterings of agreement sprang up from the back of the room.

'Before Mr Manton became a money launderer, he ran all the

drugs, extortion, and protection rackets in his home town,' Redblood said matter of factly. 'Could Mrs Grant stand up please?' he asked.

A small, demure lady of about sixty pushed her chair back, stood up, and gave a small, embarrassed wave.

'Ah, thank you my good lady,' responded Redblood. 'Mrs Pam Grant and her husband Horace were forced out of their profitable shoe repair business in Malton by their landlord in 1995. Their lease wasn't due to expire for another ten years and they lived above the shop. Mr Manton's company bulldozed the business to build a cash only hand car wash. Horace threatened to report this crime and in return he has now spent more than twenty years in a wheelchair, unable to walk.'

Manton jumped up and shouted 'This is rubbish; I've never met the woman!' Redblood waved his protest away and Doyle pulled Manton back down and started to whisper something. The two of them stood up, but were soon back in their seats.

'You will notice there are security men on both exits, Mr Manton. I suggest you stay for a few minutes, this won't take long,' beamed Redblood.

'Please remain standing, Pam. Mr Swanson, Mr Nigel Swanson, could you stand also please?' requested Redblood, peering once again toward the back of the room.

The owner of the Norton fish and chip shop, a robust gentleman of about fifty-five stood up, a concerned and slightly embarrassed look on his face.

'Thanks, Mr Swanson. For those of you who haven't tried Nigel's fish and chips, they are among the best in East Yorkshire. You'll find him on Norton High Street,' Redblood explained. 'Even though he sells a wonderful product, a look at his accounts will reveal he hardly makes any profit. The reason for this is that he has paid Mr Manton hundreds of thousands of pounds in protection money over the last fifteen years. You see, Nigel has an exceptionally talented daughter. She plays the violin. I can tell you, Nigel, that this is the man who controls the people who regularly threaten to smash your daughter's hands to pieces.'

Swanson's eyes narrowed to black slits. 'Is this true?'

'Certainly,' Redblood replied. 'But Benny here doesn't like to do the dirty work himself, you see; he makes sure there are at least two people between him and any threatening behaviour. But believe me, it's Benny who collects your profit every month!'

'Mr Leggett, could you stand please?' said Redblood, keen to maintain momentum.

The Landlord of the Nag's Head got to his feet and shrugged. 'I don't know why I'm here,' he told the people around his table.

'Your daughter, Mr Leggett. I believe she died at the age of seventeen.'

'Yes, that's correct,' Bob Leggett replied uncertainly, suspicion starting to tell on his face.

'She died from a drugs overdose whilst attending a private party for one of her schoolmates. A party which had been infiltrated by a local pusher who was run by... I think you can guess where I'm going with this,' said Redblood, allowing a tinge of sadness enter his voice.

'Mr Smith, Mrs Harriot, Mr Kite, in fact the rest of the people sitting on the three tables at the back may as well stand,' said Redblood, increasing the volume of his statement. 'Every single one of you had your lives affected in some detrimental way by organised crime. Crimes which have been organised by... Mr Benedict Manton.'

A number of discussions broke out at this news and Gwent started to deliver instructions to Poole over the general discontent, which was now becoming quite vocal at the back of the room.

Harry, who had been standing silently on the stage, was watching Manton. The man had pulled his bow tie off, was sweating profusely, and wore a hunted expression. Doyle was fending off questions from a ring of people around them. It didn't feel like there could be violence, but it was definitely leaning that way. He decided to take control.

'As Mr Redblood has stated, Mr Manton here likes to stay away from the sharp end of his wrongdoing,' Harry said into the microphone. He waited for this to sink in, and slowly the level of sound in the room ebbed away.

'However, there is a reason I am still standing in front of you.'

The room became completely still. Manton and Doyle stared up at Harry with thunderous malcontent in their eyes.

'William, could you stand up please?'

From one of the Malton tables at the back of the room, George Plant got to his feet. Redblood, starting to get down from his chair, watched his brother acknowledge Harry's request and take a deep breath. George spoke in his deep, oaky tone, his words heavy with sadness, remorse, and relief.

'I am William Redblood. I grew up in Malton. I am able to provide eyewitness evidence that Harry's mother, A'Laya Bolt, was murdered by Benedict Manton and Charlie Doyle in Malton in 1993. I watched as Benedict held her and Charlie injected A'Laya with a fatal dose of insulin.'

George crumpled slightly once he'd completed his statement. Head drooping, his chin coming to rest on his collarbone. He maintained the pose during the silence that greeted his statement. Then George lifted his head and locked eyes with Harry at the other end of the room, tears already staining both sides of his face.

There was a pause of about two seconds, followed by increasingly loud discussions regarding George's words. Some guests started to make for the exit and others descended toward Manton and Doyle. Several official shouts demanding calm came from Gwent, Poole, Matthew, and his team of organisers.

A powerful, ear-splitting crack ripped through the room, sending people cowering to the floor or freezing them like statues. Having initially recoiled from the piercing noise, Harry pulled himself back up to the lectern and looked out into the room. The shock of the gunshot subsided, and a combination of screams and concerned gasps rose up. A curious circular space, devoid of guests, started to grow around Doyle and Manton's table which drew Harry's attention.

Doyle was on his feet, one arm in the air, the other held out palm first, as a warning not to approach. A burnt, metallic taste reached Harry as curiously, he watched Doyle's thin frame revolved to face him. A jolt of panic whipped through his spine when he realised a stubby black handgun barrel was protruding from Doyle's right hand. A few puffs of white plaster descended slowly from the ceiling. The man sneered angrily and started to extend his arm toward the stage.

Harry's eyes widened as Doyle took aim. Until now the lectern had been a crutch, something to grip, to help maintain his self-control; now it offered scant protection. He tensed, caught in a moment of inevitability.

A flash of silvery green arced through the air, having started its trajectory from just out of Harry's field of vision and simultaneously a gunshot rang in his ears. He threw himself to the stage floor, expecting pain, but instead experienced bemused relief when he couldn't find any. He lifted his head.

Doyle was clutching his gun arm and inspecting a champagne bottle at his feet. He rolled his shoulders and shot a disgusted look toward the back of the room. Harry followed his gaze and spotted Andrew. He was in his cricketers post-bowling stance, his arm still pointing in Doyle's direction. From the floor Manton hissed something and Doyle turned back to scowl indignantly at the stage. He grabbed Manton's arm with his left hand and displaying strength his physique belied, hauled the larger man to his feet.

'G-get out of the w-way!' Doyle screamed through his stammer, waving the gun at people around him who cowered in their seats or under tables. Manton added his voice to the demands, venting his fury on people, furniture, and the contents of tables. He aimed a vicious kick at several people as he and Doyle made their way toward the rear of the room.

Wang held his hands high as Doyle and Manton raced past. Once their backs were to him he set about conducting guests into the kitchen exit, trying to manage the flow. Harry saw the diminutive young man pull a woman twice his size out from under the feet of suited gents clamouring to escape. The cameraman and soundman had disappeared and the room was descending into chaos.

Bunt stalked down the left hand side of the room doing a similar job to Wang, one by one, pulling people from the crush as they attempted to clamber over each other and out through the only exit on the right-hand side of the room.

Gwent and Poole were shouting at the two Halo men, trying to get them to see the folly of their actions. There was no way out of the room. Doyle ignored the protests and continued to wave the gun around, threatening, kicking, and punching anyone who came close.

It was when the two men reached the back of the room and the wall of glass, that their intentions became painfully obvious. Manton tried to push the revolving door in order to exit onto the stands steps, but it stayed rigidly in place. He slammed a hand into one of the revolving panes of glass and tried kicking at it, but the mechanism was securely locked and didn't budge. Doyle turned, his sharp features alert and pulled tighter than ever over his bony face. His appearance was becoming more alien by the minute. He took in the chaos and saw both exits rammed full of panicking dinner guests trying get out. Some people were on the stage, trying to stay as far away from the two men as possible. There was no exit behind it unless they were prepared to go over the balcony and drop fifty feet to the concourse below. The rest of the guests tried to make themselves appear small, hiding under upturned tables, heads down, so as not to catch the gunman's inhuman gaze.

Pulling the panting Manton away from his attack on the revolving door, Doyle raised his right hand, aimed, and fired two shots in quick succession into the glass wall, eliciting more crazed screams and frenzied pushing toward the exits further down the room. No one fell injured; the shots were directed into one of the thick glass panes that allowed race-goers to view races from inside the stand. From the floor of the stage Harry watched a huge chunk from one of the yard wide panes of glass splinter, then crack before peeling away from its steel frame in the ceiling. The glass sheet crashed to the floor in front of Doyle, leaving a jagged four foot long piece of fractured glass still projecting upwards from the floor.

Gwent, with Poole at her side, continued to shout warnings at the two men but received no acknowledgement or reply. Doyle picked up a chair and in a single lithe movement lifted it above his head. For one awful moment Harry thought he was going to step forward and bring it down on Gwent's head, but instead, he spun and launched the chair at the base of the remaining glass which rose from the floor in dangerously sharp shards. The chair did its work, removing most of the glass and Doyle kicked at the remaining few fragments before stepping through the gaping hole left by the missing pane, into the freezing December air.

Harry realised no one was in pursuit. Bunt and Wang were engaged elsewhere and Gwent and Poole were warning guests away from the back of the room with no intention of following.

His reaction was instinctive. Before any sense of danger or risk reached his limbs, Harry felt a wave of righteous indignation surge through him. He gulped in a lungful of air, pushed himself to his feet, jumped from the stage, and made a charge for the end of the room and the gaping hole the missing pane of glass had created. Manton stepped carefully through the hole in the glass wall and Harry felt a frosty breeze sweep into the room. He gave an involuntary shiver as he watched his mother's killer disappear in ungainly fashion down the stands steps and out of sight.

It started as a squealing drone but within seconds a mechanical noise filled the room and Harry's eyes bulged as he realised something unnatural was forcing frosty air into the Gimcrack room. A high-pitched whine and the whipping of rotor blades soon answered his query. As Harry covered the ground to the glass wall, the racetrack rose up with each step, eventually filling his view. He could see a black suited pilot in a small, micro light helicopter about to land on the frosty white racetrack. Clouds of ice particles were being thrown into the air by the down draught and Harry caught the hint of an orangey chocolate smell hanging in the air. Doyle's sticklike figure scampered across the viewing lawn and was about to negotiate the two sets of wire and plastic rails which maintained the public's distance from the canter chute and the racetrack itself. Manton was at the bottom of the stand steps, forty yards behind Doyle, holding his back with one hand. He was struggling to keep up.

Andrew, Gwent, and Poole, with arms raised, were shepherding people away from the glass which littered the carpet. The two police officers were simultaneously barking information into their mobile phones. Harry looked again at the distances between the two men below, and allowing his muscles to make his decision, he made to surge forward.

Sensing movement, Andrew raised his head and locked eyes with his brother, who flicked his eyes down to the racetrack and back. Andrew allowed a mixture of concern and comprehension to wash across his face before he dropped one arm to his side. Harry acknowledged Andrew's action with a tight smile and sprang forward.

Ducking through the hole in the glass wall he paused briefly at the top of the stand steps, spotted his quarry, and began leaping down the giant stands steps two at a time, dropping downward in pursuit. He was dimly aware of shouting from the room behind and above him, but plunged on without looking back.

He flinched as the cold air sparked pain in his lungs and prickled against his cheeks, while trying to judge leap after leap onto polished concrete steps which sparkled with a frosty sheen. Doyle, waving his gun and shouting encouragement to Manton, was now on the track, only a few yards from the helicopter. Manton had reached the racing rails and was standing with hands on hips, exhaling freezing white clouds as he attempted to get his breath back before scaling the two wire and plastic obstacles that were between him and the helicopter.

Harry reached the bottom of the stands steps and skidded on the tarmac, his dress shoes providing virtually no grip. He hit a patch of ice and lost his balance, landing on his hands and knees. The stinging pain was worse in his hands, but he didn't stop to inspect them, getting up and starting a dead run for Manton who was thirty yards away, midway through heaving his gut over the first set of rails.

Up in the Gimcrack room, Gwent looked down at the chase she had tried to prevent. Harry, though closing in fast wasn't going to get there in time. Manton was already over the first rail and was climbing the second, with Doyle ready to pull his boss over. She shouted again for Harry to halt and get out of range of Doyle, but the young man was sprinting toward the fat fifty year old like his life depended on it.

Harry had made the same calculation. He wasn't going to get there in time. To scale both rails would see him get there far too late. He made his final on the hoof decision of the day.

With her hand held to her mouth Gwent watched in morbid fascination as Harry angled his run away from Manton for three to four strides, now running at a more acute angle. He looked up, as if lining up a long jump and then came belting in toward one of the wooden picnic tables which were scattered around the grass. The one Harry was heading for was close to the rails, but still a good eight feet away. As Manton reached the top of his final horizontal white running rail, Harry's first leap landed him on the top of the picnic table. He skipped a step, used his momentum, and launched himself toward the first set of rails. Sheer impetus carried him to the top of the rail, where he slammed his hands down, and using a leapfrog action, both legs at ludicrously wide angles, landed in a rolling ball on the chute's All-Weather surface.

Manton was in the process of being man handled over the top of the racetrack rail by Doyle. A few more seconds and the two of them would be crossing the racetrack. Harry wrenched himself up, leaving bloody handprints, his feet slipping on the waxy sand. He took three steps across the chute and flung himself upwards at Manton's back, bloodied hands scrabbling for any grip he could get on the man.

Manton shrieked in terror as someone landed a heavy hand on his shoulder and pulled him backwards. For a second or two Doyle and Harry were in a human tug of war, Harry pawing desperately at Manton's bulk, ripping his dinner jacket from his shoulder to his elbow. He brought his other arm up and hugged Manton's waist, digging his fingers into his fat. Gravity was on Harry's side, and he felt the large man slip toward him. Suddenly Doyle shrugged Manton's grasping hands off him and watched as Harry and his boss crumpled on the other side of the rails.

Doyle shouted something to Manton, but it was impossible for Harry to make it out. He and Manton were both scrabbling to get to their feet. Manton went to start climbing the rails again and Harry tightened his grip on his waist once more, the man's wispy hair whipping at his face. The blades of the micro helicopter swirled around with a chopping noise and the high-pitched squeal of the engine cancelled out all other sound. Doyle took out the gun from the holster tucked under his left armpit, braced himself against the downdraft and, legs apart, lifted his arm up and pointed the pistol at Harry.

'Kill him, Charlie. For Christ's sake, kill him!' shrieked Manton. Doyle stood motionless, his jacket and trousers flapping wildly in the downdraught, his gun raised. Doyle contemplated the situation. He flicked his eyes up to the stands, judging the time it would take to get Manton over the rails, factoring in the two-person microlight and the fact he only had two bullets left in his clip.

'Screw this,' Doyle said quietly and he pulled the trigger. He remained stock-still, concentrated once more, and repeated the action. The first shot found its way through flesh and organs before settling, the second sent a spurt of hot, dark, treacle like blood into the air which splattered into Harry's face. Manton, staring vacantly at Doyle, went limp and collapsed backwards, taking Harry down with him.

Doyle turned, strode to the helicopter and after another cloud of icy frost particles had been sent spiralling into the air, the racetrack returned to being a silent winter idyll.

Thirty-Five

Findlay Morrison pressed the end call symbol on his mobile phone and slipped it into the inside pocket of his jacket, immediately pulling his glove back on. The hillside was empty of life and bitterly cold, its usual woolly inhabitants having been brought in for winter or sent to Malton market many weeks before. Findlay could understand why this desolate place had been chosen as a base for managing the laundering business. Apart from the odd farm vehicle and stray walkers following The Wolds Way, there was no good reason to be sniffing around the top of this bleak, uninspiring hill, unless you were a sheep. Despite the winter shutdown of growth and colour the glacially carved valley and its chalky outcrops held beauty for Findlay, although in his present company the landscape's stark appearance wasn't something he was willing to table for discussion.

He inspected the hill on the opposite side of the valley where a huge oak tree dwarfed the red barn at its side and ran through the planned manoeuvres one more time in his head. Satisfied, he turned to address the five men and one woman behind him. Dressed in army fatigues and hunkered down beyond the crest of the hill he gave them some short, direct orders. Each of them pulled a plastic mask down over their face. They all immediately took on the features of the president of the United States.

Fifteen minutes later they were at the steel door of the Money Tree having faced nothing during their approach, bar some faint shouted threats of resistance. Findlay consulted his mobile phone and started to run his hand over the wooden slats of the barn wall. A smirk creased his lips when he located the keypad and intercom hidden behind a false wooden panel. He pressed the speak button and provided a stark warning to the men inside.

Two minutes later the thick steel door slammed into its foundation following a ground-shaking explosion which cut the winding mechanism. From inside the Money Tree, three bulky men in black leather jackets emerged into the cold sunlight with hands raised. They peered through the foul smelling smoke, offering placatory noises of surrender. Behind them Deacon and his two young coders wore astonished looks as six people, holding what appeared to be automatic rifles and wearing Donald Trump masks, surrounded them.

'Deacon?' one of the masked men barked.

Shivering from the cold draft, Deacon stepped forward, produced a little wave, and blinked nervously. The Trump lookalike led Deacon a little way into the Money Tree, and with his back to the door, flipped up his mask and delivered his ultimatum.

Thirty-Six

Bunt carried Will out to Jill's car, careful to keep the boy's head covered and out of the light rain. Jill followed, skipping around some of the bigger puddles the incessant rainfall had created around the yard during the night. Bunt rounded the brand new Golf, opened the rear door, and strapped the giggling infant into his car seat.

'I'll miss this,' he called over to Jill.

'You're always welcome to visit. You know… babysitting duties are very similar to looking after Harry!'

Bunt looked sheepish for a moment. 'I didn't manage so well last time,' he moaned, closing Will's door carefully but firmly.

Jill shook her head at him dismissively, tossed an unopened umbrella onto the passenger seat, and climbed in behind the wheel. As Bunt toured around the front of the car, she zipped her window down and stuck her head out.

'I'd better get going, I want to call at the supermarket before I go to the Children's Centre. I got a funny look from the instructor last time I was late for his baby massage class! I'll see you before you go tonight won't I?'

'Yes, I'll be here until evening stables,' Bunt assured her.

He watched the car trundle down the yard, turn right into the lane, and disappear. He remained standing in the rain for a half a minute, contemplating the fact his work at the Pickering farmhouse stables was now reaching its conclusion.

It had only been a week since the Gimcrack dinner, but the effect on the stables had been seismic. His service finished today, after more than a year of twenty-four hour surveillance on behalf of the Bolt family. The Manton threat had evaporated with his death at the racecourse. He'd died instantly from the second of Doyle's shots, the one to his head. Doyle himself had managed to skip the country, probably destined for South America, if Gwent's information from the customs people was correct. Harry… well, Harry was a hero… although not in Bunt's view, or come to that, Gwent's either. They had both agreed he'd been downright reckless.

A clicking set of easily recognisable footsteps made Bunt turn his head to the corner of the farmhouse and the object of his thoughts came striding into view, a set of tack in his hand, hair ruffled and muttering some tune or other under his breath. He looked into the familiar, smiling face of Harry Bolt.

'Has Jill gone then?' Harry asked.

'Just now.'

'You'll be staying around to see *our visitor* then?' Harry asked mysteriously. He added an abrupt laugh and a knowing stare as he passed Bunt on his way to the tack room.

245

Bunt tracked Harry into the tack room and the trainer started to rummage through a cardboard box full of clasps, buckles, and odd bits of leather leads.

'Has Gwent worked out what happened to Redblood yet?'

'Don't think so,' Harry replied distractedly.

'The fact he disappeared and couldn't be found after he'd delivered his little speech?' Bunt pressed.

Harry stopped clanking around in the box, turned and leaned against the wall of the stone built tack room.

'Gwent wasn't happy. Let's be honest, she wasn't best pleased with anything that went on that day. She was screaming blue murder at me once they'd hauled me out from under Manton and discovered I hadn't been hit.'

'I think that first bullet was meant for you,' Bunt pointed out. 'You were just bloody lucky with Manton being so… large.'

'I'm not so sure,' Harry cut in, shaking his head. 'Gwent wasn't convinced either. She thinks Warren saw an opportunity and took it. Manton wasn't going to make it out with him, and maybe Warren wanted to make sure he didn't talk, as well as running with the money.'

Bunt nodded. 'Yeah, but I still think that first shot was for you and Manton just got in the way.'

Harry shrugged. 'I'm hoping Gwent will finish up soon. As well as us, she's had George in and out of the police station all week. I'm hoping he'll end up being released without any charges. I feel a bit sorry for him.'

The sound of an unfamiliar car pulling into the yard and parking beside the farmhouse cut their conversation short. Bunt peered out of the tack room.

'It's George,' he confirmed. 'And he's in a new car by the look of it.'

George leapt out of the newish looking large SUV with a wide smile on his face. He clapped Harry on his shoulder whilst shaking the trainer's hand. It was the first time Harry had seen him since the day of the Gimcrack dinner.

'Sorry, I haven't been over before now. Gwent has been keeping me busy for the last few days,' George said in apology. Then he grimaced. 'Mainly questions regarding my brother and his inability to stick around long enough for Gwent to ask him any pertinent questions.'

'Still no word from him?' Harry asked.

George shook his head and appeared to be a little cut up that he hadn't been contacted by his brother, so Harry suggested the three of them move to the upper yard and out of immediate sight of prying eyes. The three men walked up to the stable door where Paste lived, and George looked in and produced a carrot from the pocket of his well-worn jacket.

'Was there a reason for your brother to leave without speaking to anyone?' Bunt queried airily. He was keen to keep the conversation friendly, but still get as many answers as possible from Redblood's brother.

George looked uncomfortable for a moment, as if he was struggling internally with a decision. He fiddled with the last portion of carrot before answering.

'Well, he did leave a note. I found it on my front door mat when I eventually got home. It said he was absolutely fine and basically apologised, said he was going abroad and wanted to put the whole thing behind him. I took it straight to Gwent.

'What reaction did you get when she realised Redblood was already out of the country?'

George winced. 'Not good. I think she got a bit of a roasting from her superior.'

'Redblood must have headed straight for the door when it all kicked off,' Bunt suggested.

'And there was me thinking he'd stick around for the meal once the bullets started flying!' Harry said with a laugh which ended abruptly when Bunt shot him a withering look.

George continued. 'I think Tom was keen not to get caught up in a dialogue with the police. He said he was sorry for leaving that to the three of us, but he finished by saying you will find that he is extremely grateful for your understanding. Speaking of which, Mr Bunt, Harry, here are your balancing payments for your hard work and understanding over the last year.'

George produced two long thin envelopes, each with handwritten names, which he passed to Bunt and Harry.

You'll find a short non-disclosure agreement which requires a signature, and a cheque. Please take a look,' prompted George.

He studied the faces of the two men as they scanned the documents. A whistle from Harry followed by a gasp from Bunt denoted they had scanned the document and reached the figure on their cheques.

George grinned. 'As you will see gentlemen, you have been compensated quite generously for the results you have generated. Each cheque is drawn on the account in my name, from funds earned through share dealing, so is perfectly legitimate. It's Tom's and my way of saying thank you.'

'The horses!' Harry exclaimed, the short disclosure agreement open in his hand. 'You're signing all your horses over to me?'

George beamed. 'Tom's interest in racehorses was primarily to expose Manton. So, he no longer has a reason to keep them.'

'You must be aware there are two group winners and another two which I think will be similarly capable among them as three year olds?' asked Harry incredulously.

'I did explain that to Tom before the dinner,' said George with a shrug. 'We spoke by phone the night before and he was crystal clear he didn't want any ties in England, whatever happened after the dinner.'

Bunt looked confused. 'So regardless of how things worked out, he was leaving?'

'He was a bit coy about a number of things to be fair. He told me he had nothing else apart from quiet retirement in mind. I was hoping I'd get to see more of him when things settled down, given I've had my life placed on hold for the last twenty years, but it seems he's gone for good.'

Harry examined George carefully and it struck him that his longest standing owner was perhaps one of the biggest losers from this whole affair. He'd initially had to go on the run, lived out of sight, and for all Harry knew, didn't marry, or have a family because he knew he would be placing them in potential danger. The more he thought about it, Manton had consigned both Redblood brothers to a pretty miserable existence.

'Have you been catered for, you know, from a money perspective?' Harry asked.

'Oh yes!' George exclaimed, brightening in his face, but his eyes betrayed evidence of sadness. 'I've a sizeable lump of money to enjoy.'

Harry suddenly felt awkward looking at George and he decided to steer the discussion away from his situation 'Tell me George,' he queried 'Why did Redblood insist on naming your horses with such...'

Harry was interrupted by a peel of laughter from George.

'That's something else I must apologise for,' he said between chortles of laughter. 'I can imagine it made your identification of the horses a little challenging.'

Harry considered informing George that each horse had a stable name and their racing names were rarely mentioned apart from on the racecourse or in conversation with their owners, but thought better of it and simply smiled benignly back at him.

'The first eight horses were all a combination of numbers, a little joke Thomas was playing on Manton, I guess. If you map the numbers to the alphabet and rearrange them, they spell out 'Redblood is alive'!'

Harry saw George's enthusiasm for his subject fade from his face and his line of sight altered to hover over Harry's shoulder.

'You have another visitor,' he said indicating the bottom of the yard with a flick of his eyes.

Harry swung round and instantly recognised Rory walking toward them.

'Hiya, Rory,' he called, removing a hand from his jacket and raising it in greeting. There was no response from the jockey. As he drew closer Harry sensed something was very wrong. Rory was dressed for riding out; he still had a line of dirty sand ingrained into his forehead, indicating where his helmet had sat. He must have come straight from the

All-Weather track on the Wold gallop. It was the middle of the morning; he shouldn't be walking into the yard at this time. He should be riding. It was all... wrong.

Harry caught a movement behind him in the corner of his eye. Bunt was quietly sidling around, his steady gaze not leaving Rory. Harry assumed the security man's own internal alarm had also started to ring. As Rory approached, Harry's heart jumped into his throat. Every fibre in Harry's body told him his best friend was exhibiting signs of extreme stress.

'What is it, Rory?' Harry demanded, narrowing his eyes, fearing the answer. George slowly backed away to the stable wall and Bunt moved even wider, his body tensed.

Rory's eyes started to water and he shook involuntarily for a couple of seconds. Curious, Harry took a step forward. A tinny voice barked something from within Rory's chest and he withdrew a mobile phone from the top pocket of his riding jacket.

Rory tapped the phone's screen twice, held the phone out at arm's length, and swept it around in a half circle. When Rory's movement came to a stop, a man's voice became audible to all four men in the yard. The voice on the phone was squealing in delight.

'Tell... them,' the voice commanded after the laughter had subsided.

Rory tried to lock eyes with Harry but his best friend was too busy glancing down at the phone, trying to identify the face on the screen. Rory waited until he knew he had Harry's undivided attention. He rubbed his eyes and taking his right earlobe, caressed it nervously between his thumb and forefinger. Then he began to speak.

'The voice on my phone is Charlie Doyle,' Rory said carefully. 'He is sitting in Jill's car in the Morrison's supermarket car park with Jill and Will.'

Harry's mouth went dry and his nervous system jolted. He took a stride toward Rory. Bunt did the same and George followed behind.

'No, stop there!' Rory pleaded, holding out his free hand, palm first. 'He'll kill them if he doesn't get what he wants. He's got a knife and unless I...'

'Hold on,' interrupted the stammering Doyle from the phone. 'B-billy Red... blood?'

The laughing from the phone started up again, but this time it quickly broke into a cruel cackle before being abruptly quashed.

'This is priceless. Let me see him,' Doyle said, suddenly sounding serene and in control.

'He told me to say...' Rory concentrated, making sure he had it right, 'Run, shout or cut him off and Jill dies.

Spying George a little behind, Rory blurted 'He knows there are three of you, I had to tell him before I walked up. Do something wrong and hes said he will kill Jill, then Will.'

'How do we know he's got her?' George asked, ensuring he was revealed wholly to the phone's camera.

'Take a look,' returned Doyle.

Rory moved closer to the three men, who were now close together, watching a jerky picture on the small phone screen he held up to them. The image revolved around the inside of a car, came to a stop, blurred a little, then Jill's panic stricken face came into focus. She was in the driver's seat and was bound to the steering wheel by her hands, thick, wide tape wrapped around her head and mouth. She turned her head to face Doyle and the men could see the anger burning in her eyes.

There was a blur of images again and when the phone screen settled it showed Will. He was fast asleep in his car seat, exactly where Bunt had placed him twenty-five minutes ago.

Finally, the images rushed around once more and this time they resolved themselves into the head of a man with slits for eyes and skin drawn over his face so tight you could trace the outline of every bone.

Doyle leered into the phone's camera, his crooked smile extending, whip like, to link the two depressions where his cheeks should have been.

'A life for a life. Tell them, jockey boy,' Doyle ordered, maintaining his camera on himself.

Rory's phone started to shake in his hand.

'I have to kill Harry...' he said in a jerky, frustrated outburst.

'What?' cried an incensed Bunt.

'...with this insulin,' Rory finished. His free hand went back into his top pocket and he slid out a hypodermic needle already loaded with a clear fluid.

Harry inspected the needle and then flicked his eyes back to Rory and nodded an assurance.

'What guarantee do I have you will leave my wife and child alone if I allow him to inject me?' Harry asked, barely controlling the anger which was bubbling under his words.

'None!' Doyle answered lazily, showing a long, thin bladed knife to the phone's camera. 'If I'm not satisfied, one cut into the right artery and she'll b-bleed out in thirty seconds. Less for your son.'

Doyle took a few breaths during which he played with the knife, turning it between his bony fingers. Its blade made the picture on the phone turn white when the sunlight flashed off its surface.

'If you d-die, I will walk away. You have taken my life from me. I will take one from you, one way or another,' he added levelly.

'Bunt, do something!' pleaded George in a quiet, desperate voice.

Bunt opened his mouth to answer but nothing came out.

'Oh, don't worry B-billy,' the tinny voice on the phone chimed in.

'I will be coming for all of you *and your b-brother*. One at a time.'

Doyle allowed this statement to settle on his audience, toying with his knife once more.

'What do you want? Money?' George barked angrily.

'Ah, it's the invisible man,' Doyle answered sarcastically. 'Did you really think you and your brother would get away with stealing my business?' spat Doyle angrily. 'I will slowly rip you all apart, just for fun.'

Shuddering, Bunt looked up at Rory and tapped the side of his head; indicating Doyle was not in his right mind. George became very still and stared long and hard in the one direction, straight into Doyle's pixilated face. He started to ask a question, but was cut short by Doyle's voice ringing out again, barking commands at Rory. Something had spurred him on. It seemed the talking was over.

'He wants you two in the stable, or she dies,' Rory said sharply, indicating Bunt and George. 'Harry stays outside,' he added wearily.

There was another shout on the phone as Doyle demanded the camera be fixed onto Bunt and Doyle and their phones to be collected. Rory corrected the angle, apologised, and received a string of expletives from Doyle in return.

Bunt and George each handed over a mobile phone and filed into Fido's stable, closing the bottom half door behind them. Fido stared balefully at the two men and stamped a foot, which made a slightly fearful George back away. Bunt approached the colt, rubbed Fido's nose and gave his long, muscular neck a scratch. The horse nuzzled into his shoulder and with hands on his neck and shoulder Bunt gently pushed the horse onto the far wall where he settled but continued to inspect the men.

'Don't worry, he's as quiet as a lamb this one,' said Bunt as he returned to the stable door to join George who was peering over the bottom of the half-door at the two men outside. George shivered in the semi-darkness and swallowed hard when the top half of the stable door was slammed shut, plunging the sixteen foot square stable into darkness.

In the Morrison's car park, Doyle sat in the passenger seat of Jill's Golf and watched on his mobile as Harry backed up to stand up against a stable door. He regarded Jill, tears of frustration mixing with her sweat as she struggled with the industrial wrapping tape around her hands, pulling at the steering wheel. Muffled grunts came from her mouth and she was blowing and sucking air through her nose.

'Settle down Mrs B-bolt or you'll miss your husband's death.' Doyle told her awkwardly. 'But let's make sure he knows I mean b-business,' he added with a sneer.

Doyle sucked in a couple of deep breaths before screaming 'Bolt!' into his phone. Harry walked forward until his head and shoulders filled the small screen. Doyle altered the view so Jill's legs were visible to Harry. 'Watch,' Doyle demanded.

Doyle shifted position on the seat and in a single fluid movement plunged the knife vertically into the flesh just above Jill's knee, puncturing the skin. He held the knife there for a second then drew it slowly out.

It was so unexpected. Jill didn't feel anything at first. She peered down and saw the small, penny piece rip in her jeans and a few frayed cotton edges. The sliced material soon turned red as blood started to bubble and then gush from the small incision. An agonising pulse raced to the injury and remained there, throbbing with an all-consuming insistence and behind the mass of tape around her mouth, Jill started screaming.

'See that?' asked an excited Doyle.

Harry was shouting into the phone and Doyle allowed him to do so, while he filmed the injury, poking at it with his bony index finger.

'Shut up! If jockey b-boy doesn't go through with his little task,' threatened Doyle. 'I'll fill your wife's b-body with a hundred more holes. Then I'll d-do the same to your son...'

'Jockey man!' Doyle hollered. 'Do it, and be sure to film, or she dies.'

Doyle shifted once more in his seat to allow Jill a view of the phones' screen and licked his lips. 'See, he's going to die just like his mother did.'

Jill made to reply, but couldn't get anything coherent to emerge. The tape was tight to her mouth, impossible to shift. Her wrists had been cut into and she thought they were bleeding as something warm was travelling up her arm, but still she tugged at her bonds. Her captor produced an ugly smile and pushed the small screen closer to her face. She spotted a syringe and Harry's face getting larger. She looked away.

'No, no Mrs Bolt. You must watch!' Doyle commanded, placing his knife carefully on his lap and grabbing her head roughly and turning it.

'Or would you prefer I kill your son instead?'

Jill swivelled her head around immediately, her eyes bulging, filled with fear and disgust. She stopped struggling and squinted at the coloured screen through watery eyes.

Doyle bent his head close to his phone, surveying Jill's reaction as he spoke. 'Do it Jockey b-boy. Or his wife dies. Do it now, you know where!' he insisted.

Holding his phone out in his left hand and the syringe in his right, his thumb on the top of the plunger, Rory took a deep breath, looked Harry in the eye and asked him to hold his jacket open.

Slowly, Harry undid his jacket and the shirt below. He knew where Doyle wanted the injection to be made. Baring his chest, he looked up at his childhood friend, offering him a weak smile and then yelled at the phone 'I love you, Jill.'

Harry winced as the needle entered the skin just above his collarbone. He could feel the insulin being pumped into his body. Rory was groaning, but managed to complete the operation within a few seconds. As soon as he had whipped the syringe out of Harry he turned the phone round and demanded Doyle leave the car, as promised.

'I need to see him die,' Doyle insisted in a singsong voice, as if he was addressing a child. 'Show me,' he barked.

Rory filmed for the next two minutes, until Harry lay slumped against the stable door, his body inert and unmoving.

Finally, Rory turned the phone around.

'Okay, it's done. Now leave the car!' he screamed.

There was no answer. The screen was dead. Doyle had gone.

Thirty-Seven

Doyle found himself in a fit of giggles. This feeling of power was so... exhilarating. Strangely, he found himself analysing his response to the death of Harry Bolt. He was watching the man's wife, Jane, Jill or June... something like that... stare wretchedly at the image on his phone and marvelling at how alive it made him feel. Harry Bolt's knees had just crumpled under him and real tears had started to form in the girl's eyes. Oh, how he had missed this; he'd almost forgotten the rush he received from wielding power first hand! Always being a couple of steps away from the actual act made the infliction of pain and suffering distant and fuzzy, just names, faces and scores settled. He'd been disengaged from real life for too long.

Doyle smiled inwardly; he could feel the blood coursing around his body, pumping life around him, raw and powerful. He would enjoy picking off the other three... in his own time, savouring each death. Killing this girl and her boy would be sweet too.

Jill blinked her tears away and regrouped, swallowing hard and sucking air in through her nose. Doyle had lost interest in her reactions for now and was hunched over his phone, his shoulders bucking sporadically, indicating another wave of sick mirth. Her heart was thumping, waiting for the moment the man would lose interest in Harry, pick his knife up from his lap and use it on her again... or Will.

She looked wildly around, hoping someone might be walking past the line of parked cars outside in the Morrison's car park, but even if there was someone, she'd parked nose in against the wall, they wouldn't see her or hear her. She looked into the rear view mirror. Will slept on, one chubby cheek pushed up against the side of the car seat, totally unaware of the danger he was facing.

A glance in her wing mirror provided no avenue of escape. Unless a shopper returned to the car right beside her, she could be sat here for hours. Even then, they would need to look right into her car, recognise there was a problem, and be courageous enough to act. She threw her head back onto her seat in frustration, the tape cutting into her wrists as she bounced back off the back of the seat. Her movement fleetingly caught Doyle's attention but he soon returned his gaze back to his phone and ignored her, too busy with Harry's final moments.

A shadow fell over the passenger door and a dark shape suddenly filled the window. Screwing her head down and to the left Jill watched as a large gloved hand was placed on the doorframe. Doyle, still engrossed in his phone, didn't see the large, red object being swung back. The brick smashed through the window with such force it continued into the side of Doyle's face. Splinters of glass flew around the cabin and the car rocked, waking Will, who let out a cry. Jill shook tiny shards of glass from her hair and squinted back up. The hand gripping the brick pounded twice more into Doyle, a blow to the top of his head, another to the base of his neck as he was forced forwards and downwards in his seat.

Another hand now reached in, flipped the locking mechanism and the passenger door was wrenched open. There was a dull metallic thump as the door pinged into the car parked alongside. Head down, arms limp, Doyle groaned quietly. A steady ribbon of blood was dribbling from his chin, the top of his scull a gooey deep red mess mixing brick fragments and dust. The aggressor's hands dived into the cabin, grabbed Doyle's phone and then hauled him from the car, dragging the lightweight man out by his shoulders.

It was as if Doyle had been sucked from the passenger seat. Jill screwed her head around and checked each of her mirrors. There was no sign of Doyle or the brick wielding mystery man. She surveyed the empty seat; Doyle's long, thin knife with its razor sharp blade lay among the glass and blood.

****

Loretta dragged the semi-conscious Doyle out of the boot of his Range Rover and expertly broke his leg, just to make sure he couldn't run, before tying him to the tree. Doyle didn't react to the break; pain wasn't registering for him anymore. Loretta crouched down in front of the ghostly white face and whispered to him.

'I only came out for a box of teabags. Imagine how excited I was finding *you* sitting in the supermarket car park. It was your car that gave you away, Charlie. If Manton hadn't been so obsessed with black Range Rover's, I might have walked past. But there you were, a few cars down from where you'd parked, being nasty to a lady. And a baby in the back seat too! Pete would never have allowed that. Do you remember what happened to Pete, Charlie?'

Doyle desperately tried to raise his chin, but failed as his neck muscles wouldn't respond properly and his head lolled. He attempted speech and produced an unintelligible guttural noise. His head swam and his vision was dancing crazily.

'You wouldn't let me take him to a hospital. So he died,' Loretta continued sadly. He was so close to Doyle's ear he could feel the man's hair brush against his lips.

'You're a wanted man, Charlie. So by your reckoning, I can't take you to a hospital,' said Loretta, his voice now laced with sarcasm.

'You gave me my instructions. So, I'm leaving you here. The same place you told me to leave Pete.'

Loretta straightened and took one last look down at Doyle's wrecked body.

'Best of luck with that, Charlie.'

Loretta strode away from the huge tree and over to Doyle's car. After carefully wiping it clean of any prints, he drove the Range Rover into the town of Pocklington, made a short call using Doyles phone and then dropped it into the beck. Then he headed back to Malton, observing speed limits and taking circuitous country roads.

Back in Malton, he grabbed his Morrison's bag for life from the passenger seat, wiped the car down again, and left it on a side road on the outskirts of the town, well away from any cameras. Tossing the keys into a municipal rubbish bin, Loretta whistled quietly as he walked the last few hundred yards before arriving at his home. He regarded the stone built semi-detached Georgian house for a few seconds and smiled before striding up the drive. He let himself in with his key and immediately removed his shoes, tucking them away neatly into the shoe cupboard. The sound of a television came drifting into the hall from the lounge. He sucked in a deep breath; it smelled of home. It made him smile.

'I'm back, Mrs Warren,' he called. 'I've got the tea bags, do you fancy a brew?'

'That would be lovely, Gavin,' an elderly female voice replied. 'I was starting to worry, you've been longer than I was expecting.'

'Oh, I'm sorry Mrs Warren, but you wouldn't believe my luck today! I bumped into someone I knew and had a nice chat with him. The time just flew,' Loretta replied, hanging his coat on a tall wooden stand by the door.

A thin, silver haired lady appeared in the frame of the door to the lounge. She was slightly bent over at the shoulders but her eyes were sharp and lively. Loretta bustled down the hall with his bag of groceries, scolding her gently for walking without her stick, and guided her back into the warmth of the lounge, helping her into an orthopedic armchair.

'I'm sorry, Gavin, I don't mean to be a burden, I was just getting a bit worried,' she told him as he plumped up a cushion and tucked it behind her.

'I should be the one saying sorry, Mrs Warren. If I'm going to be late again in the future, I'll be sure to call you,' he said gently.

Mrs Warren's eyes twinkled with pleasure. 'That would be lovely, Gavin, you know I've come to rely on you since Pete went away.'

'Well, I like being around here Mrs Warren, and I'm here to stay. Besides, I promised Pete I'd look after you,' Loretta said with a genuine, broad smile.

'So, let's get that cuppa sorted out, I don't know about you, Mrs Warren, but I'm parched!'

Thirty-Eight

They had been in the stable for about three minutes. The darkness was almost complete apart from the odd chink of light where the walls met the roof. Bunt and George listened, bowed heads at the door, desperately trying to hear what was happening outside.

They had heard the soft thump against the stable door, and shouted, knocked and kicked as the sound of synthetic material scratched and caught against the slats on the other side of the stable door. The noise had travelled down the door to the yard floor. Gurgling, cries of pain and sharp, quick breath became slower and then faded. Eventually, only the tinny treble voice from a distant mobile phone could be heard through the stable door. The monotonous, unintelligible diatribe had continued for at least half a minute. Finally, Rory's voice had drowned out the noises from the phone. His was a strident, demanding tone which was suddenly, unceremoniously cut off. Then silence.

Bunt's eyes had just become accustomed to the dark when the sound of bolts being drawn back and several unrecognizable voices from the stable reached him. Independently, both men surreptitiously wiped their faces. Listening to the sounds coming from the other side of the stable door and imagining what Harry was experiencing had been intolerable. Even Bunt, who had never knowingly wept since his early twenties, blinked away moisture.

Bunt and George, shaded their eyes, blinking at the square of light which quickly doubled in size as the bottom door was pulled open. Two fuzzy figures were standing in the light. They slowly coalesced into the recognizable features of Poole and Gwent. The latter was staring up at George, amusement playing on her lips. Bunt arched his eyebrows at the policewoman, stared down, but the expected corpse wasn't slumped on the floor of the yard. He could hear several conversations being held beyond her. Among them, one recognisable voice.

Bunt and George pushed through into the sunlight. The two policemen moved aside to allow the two men out; three more policemen, another one in plain clothes, waited behind Gwent.

On the other side of the yard the figures of Rory Lewis and Harry Bolt were standing, Rory gazing intently into his friend's face. Harry had his mobile phone clamped to his ear. He held his free hand to his forehead, rubbing his temple, his gaze fixed to the ground and he spoke in short, relief filled bursts of words, aimed to convey safety, security, and love. He sporadically looked up into Rory's face and produced half smiles and nods.

Dishevelled and close to tears, Rory had an arm hooked around Harry's shoulder. Together, Bunt and George strode over to the two men, their relief mixed with bewilderment. Bursting with questions they added their own arms as support to Harry and Rory.

Thirty-Nine

The song ended and was received with generous applause and even a few whoops from the audience in the back room of the Nag's Head.

'Thank you! We're going to take a fifteen minute break so you can visit the bar and wet your whistle before we boogie woogie you right into Christmas Day.'

Harry pushed his microphone away and grinned. The dance floor started to clear and he fired a broad smile over the top of his piano at Emma and Pascal.

'They love us!'

'No, they don't!' Emma replied sarcastically. She rolled her eyes dramatically as she stepped out from behind her drum kit and up to Harry's piano.

'They love our Malton hero,' she teased, tousling Harry's hair as she passed behind him.

He sat in silence, his cheeks turning crimson, unable to think of a suitably witty reply. Emma walked round, leant her chin on the top of the standup piano, and smiled sweetly, victory written all over her face.

'My work here is done. One ego well and truly deflated,' she told Harry, before heading to the bar with Pascal in tow. He smiled after her. It was true; the local press had been full of his exploits at the Gimcrack dinner, and Jill's close call in the local Morrison's. Malton hadn't had this sort of intrigue to discuss for some time and he'd just have to accept that he could expect the public's attention for a few more weeks at least.

Harry crossed the dance floor, stopping momentarily to reply graciously to the compliments he received as he passed tables full of tinsel, party poppers, balloons, and loud, happy people. The audience was a real mixture, from the young stable workers through to elderly couples enjoying the dancing. A silver haired lady who looked to be in her seventies and a tall man, who was probably her son, left their table as he approached and assured him they were having a wonderful time, both of them shaking his hand vigorously before the son guided the elderly woman away again, thanking Harry profusely.

He reached a table filled with his stable staff and after reacting to several catcalls and comments about his playing, he fell into an empty seat beside Jill. She was wearing her party dress, which just about covered the thick bandage which protected her leg wound. It would mend, he thought, and she was tough, much tougher than him. Her only thought when the police had arrived in the car park was to get Will into her arms and demand they got a squad car up to the yard. In fact, one had already been on the way.

'Everyone seems to be having a good time,' he told Jill, casting his gaze right around the eight friends at the table.

'Oh yes! That's what happens when you offer a works outing where you're paying for all the drink and its Christmas Eve!' she replied, finishing her response with a pretend drunken hic-cough and a glazed smile.

'Ah! I see you have made the most of it too!'

'Never look a gift horse...' she laughed before giving him a peck on his cheek.

Harry scanned the table again and realised there were indeed a number of glassy eyes among his guests. Bunt was sharing a joke with George while Wang spoke quietly with Zoe. Jeff and a couple of the other lads were toasting something or other and Mike was telling one of his tall stories to two of the stable lasses. Finally his gaze fell on Andrew, who was in conversation with Rory. Andrew happened to look up and the two of them shared a short, warm moment before an icy cold pair of hands landed on Harry's shoulders.

'Mr Bolt!' Gwent announced in an officious tone.

Jill turned and looked up at the Inspector. She was wearing her ever-present neck to calf length overcoat, but there was something a little different about her tonight. Gwent casually removed her coat and Jill couldn't help but start to gush with praise for the woman's outfit.

Harry twisted round to find the ample policewoman bearing down on him. He looked her up and down while she returned a quizzical look, daring him to make the wrong comment. She was wearing make-up, her normally straggly hair was rolled in curls down to her shoulders, and she was wearing a navy blue three quarter sleeve chiffon lace dress which seemed to have several layers, finishing just below her knees. A pair of high heels completed the ensemble and she looked... transformed.

His appraisal complete, he left his chair to greet her.

'You've a fair pair of pins there, Inspector!' he exclaimed, planting a kiss on Gwent's cheek and then taking her by the hand and holding her out as if showing her off to the rest of the table. She recognised the compliment and went with it, striking a pose.

'Where have you been hiding those for the past year?' he added cheekily.

'You said to dress appropriately, so here I am. Make the most of it, I don't get dressed up to the nines often. Oh, and Poole's here too. I've brought him along for the education,' Gwent added, winking conspiratorially.

On cue, her constable popped up behind her and once he'd taken in the full effect of Gwent's outfit his standard astonished look bent so out of shape, Harry feared the young man might faint.

'Well, you look fabulous too, Poole,' Harry joked. 'But I have to say, you're not a patch on your boss! I hope the two of you will have a drink on me and enjoy the second half of our show?'

'I can't wait,' said Gwent. 'But could we have a quiet word first?'

Harry nodded, thought for a moment, and then led Gwent and Poole to the back of the room and out into the cold night air. They walked across a decked area where a couple of industrial sized heaters glowed and under which three scantily clad young female smokers stood shivering. In the zero degree cold, they nodded a hello and sucked gratefully on their cigarettes, although Harry noticed their trembling hands made locating their lips a hit and miss affair.

Harry and the two police officers took up a position beside the second heater, Gwent keeping her arms close to her sides and welcoming the warmth with upturned palms. Her outfit may well have caused something of a sensation, but it wasn't built for keeping her toasty warm. The inspector looked up into the clear night sky. Even with the light pollution from the streetlights, the stars were out in force.

'You've had an eventful fourteen months, Harry,' she started, bringing her gaze back down to rest on what now rated as a beatific face, being backlit with a golden glow from the heater.

'I wanted to let you in on a couple of developments and perhaps clear up a few loose ends. Poole wasn't aware of the details of our little arrangement, so he's here to catch up.'

Harry slanted a sympathetic look Poole's way and twitched his eyebrows. 'No problem. Fire away.'

'Well, you know following a tip off, Doyle was found tied to a tree on a hill up in the Wolds, about fifteen miles from here?'

Harry nodded.

'Well, he died this morning. He never regained consciousness, so we didn't get to question him. I just thought your wife would like to know.'

Harry pursed his lips in thoughtful contemplation and nodded his thanks.

'However, we did discover something rather special beside the tree. We believe it was the control centre for Manton's money laundering operation. Unfortunately, it had been vacated, in a hurry by the look of the place. Still, it's a bit of a find for the organised crime department. They've been crawling all over it for the last few days.'

'Do you know who saved Jill yet?' Harry asked, a little too much eagerness in his voice than he had intended.

'My apologies once again for not getting our people to Morrison's car park any sooner,' Gwent said, sucking air in over her teeth.

'I immediately organised two cars to head for Morrison's as soon as you mentioned where Jill and Will were, and I dread to think what would have happened if our mystery man hadn't turned up. But to answer your question, no, we don't have any leads. He appears on the CCTV once with the brick in his hand and then disappears. It was a clever attack. He covered his face, hunched up to mask his height, and planned his exit route carefully so he could drag Doyle off without us catching another sight of him.

'Whoever he was, he saved their lives,' Harry stated pointedly.

'I'm certain he was a professional. The fact he also led us to Manton's control centre tends to back up that theory. Maybe he was from a rival laundering gang. To be honest, after the Gimcrack stuff hit the local paper, I would reckon on there being a few hundred people in Malton who would happily smash a brick in Doyle's face!'

'I'd still like to shake his hand,' Harry admitted.

'Well if you do, stick some handcuffs on him afterwards. I'd like to charge him with murder,' Gwent stated baldly.

'How's it going with Redblood and David Smith?' Harry asked brightly, keen not to dwell too long on his lenient views on a murderer. Gwent and Poole traded a disgruntled look before Gwent answered.

'Mr Redblood and Mr Smith are still evading us, but our investigations are continuing,' the policewoman said though gritted teeth.

'Your recording did help us to get most of the facts of the case sorted out though,' Poole chipped in.

Gwent let out a gasp of irritation. 'Poole, you do remember me informing you that Harry and I had a plan since June, put in place at the time we were told to leave the case alone?'

Slightly abashed, Poole confirmed with some rapid nodding that indeed he did. 'Yeah, but Harry still needed to make it happen,' he said defensively. 'And he and Rory Lewis managed to catch and record everything that Doyle talked about.'

Harry grinned. 'It was more through dumb luck than judgment. I went to my pocket when Rory walked in, but I wasn't absolutely sure I'd activated the panic button. I could tell from the way Rory walked towards me there was something serious going on.'

'When did you know about Rory being compromised?' Poole asked. This met with a frown from Harry, so Poole continued.

'I mean, when did you know Rory was being blackmailed?'

'Oh, right, well I thought something was wrong with Rory back at York in late May, at the Dante meeting. Doyle was already threatening him and insisted he lose on his mount in the maiden, so Rory manufactured a slow start. I knew what he'd done straight away; he's far too experienced in the saddle to allow that to happen.

'So you had it out with him?'

'Yeah, I spoke with Rory after the race and discovered the truth about the threats he'd received. But I waited until July before I got Gwent involved.' Harry explained.

'She told us to keep things quiet until we could get evidence against Manton and that's when she set me up with a mobile phone which would call her and record everything once I pressed one button. Do you want it back by the way?'

'No, no, you keep it,' Gwent replied. She raised an eyebrow 'It wasn't the first time he'd pressed it you know, Poole. I got to listen to an eye watering conversation Harry had with his vet. I'm glad I didn't send the blues and two's out to investigate that little story.'

'Yeah,' Harry admitted with a broad grin. 'I had to start keeping the phone in my jacket pocket instead of my tight trousers after that!'

Gwent, shivering slightly, said, 'By the way Harry, I would like you to explain to Poole how you knew the syringe wasn't going to kill you. He's not heard that one yet.' Harry noticed the skin on the Inspector's arms starting to wrinkle in the cold and decided to try and keep his answer short.

'Rory and I have been friends since junior school. We've never been in trouble with your lot, but we did get into a few, er... *situations*. For a bit of fun in our teens we worked out a signaling system for use with teachers, parents... and girls.'

Harry scratched the back of his neck, slightly embarrassed.

'You know the sort of thing; rubbing your nose tells your mate 'Leave me alone, all's well', scratching an eyebrow means 'Help, I need you to get me out of this!' and when Rory walked toward me in the yard that morning he was rubbing his earlobe, which meant, 'Whatever I say, back me up and go with the flow.'

'So you didn't know explicitly there wasn't insulin in that syringe?' Poole asked, a little in awe.

'Nope, but I knew Rory would have it covered... somehow. We trust each other, we always have.'

Harry could see Poole still wasn't fully grasping the order of events so he continued.

'Doyle phoned Rory on the Malton gallops that morning and threatened to kill Jill if Rory didn't meet up with him and follow his instructions. Rory flew down the gallop to meet Doyle, who gave him the syringe full of insulin and told him to stick it in me or he'd kill her. Doyle must have found out Jill went to do her weekly shop each Thursday morning. Doyle was constantly monitoring everything on the video call but Rory managed to squirt the insulin out of the syringe when Doyle got distracted following Jill's car in the Malton traffic. He re-filled it with water from the trough in the bottom yard. I guess we were lucky insulin is colourless. So, I got good old trough water injected into me...'

'Your death throes must have been pretty convincing,' Poole persisted, clearly enjoying the story.

Harry seemed to lose focus for a moment, something which wasn't lost on Gwent. She crossed her arms and shifted uncomfortably.

'Well, I have seen someone die of insulin poisoning before,' he told Poole sadly.

'Never mind that Harry!' said Gwent, attempting to move the conversation on, but not before shooting a contemptuous look at Poole. 'I see there's been a general thawing in your relationship with your brother Andrew. Annie would be pleased.'

'Yes, I suppose you're right. He's invited us over on Boxing Day, to his yard for Christmas,' Harry said, brightening somewhat. 'I think the Gimcrack day was the catalyst, it stopped us... well, he pretty much saved my bacon when he bowled that champagne bottle across the room at Doyle when he was about to shoot me at point blank range, and it made us both think, I guess.'

Harry noticed Gwent was feeling the cold properly now, stamping her feet and rubbing her arms.

'Thanks for the information about Doyle,' Harry said, meeting Gwent's eyes. 'I think Jill will sleep a bit easier when I tell her. Anything else you wanted from me?'

Gwent bit her lip, shivered and then shook her head. 'Nope, apart from thanking you Harry'. She tried to smile, but it seemed her facial muscles were unable to curl her features in the right direction in the cold air.

Harry gave a modest shrug and smiled weakly. 'Can you answer one question for me before we go back inside?'

'Of course, if we can.'

'George... er... William Redblood and Rory. They've been grilled a few times in the last fortnight. Are you going to charge them with anything, it's just they did both ask me whether I could find out, as...'

Gwent cut in. 'I doubt it. There's a possibility George could have been aiding and abetting his brother's disappearance, but frankly I doubt the Crown Prosecution Service will feel they have enough evidence to press charges. It seems to me the poor man has had twenty years with his life on hold. Mind you, if we get hold of his brother and something else comes to light...'

Gwent left her reply hanging, but gave a tight smile.

'As for Rory, as far as I'm concerned everything he's done was under duress. I suppose the racing authorities might want a word with him, but I'm not about to encourage that particular line of enquiry.'

Gwent didn't wink, but Harry felt she was on the verge. She had a sort of amused twinkle in her eyes and Harry read it as benevolence rather than anything more sinister.

'Of course,' she noted thoughtfully. 'You must realise I can't promise anything?'

Harry passed an acknowledging look to Gwent and gestured toward the entrance to the party room, indicating the conversation was over as far as he was concerned.

They entered the party once more and the warm embrace of light, heat, people drinking, laughing, talking, and for Harry, a waiting piano stool.

Gwent waved and promised to catch him later and disappeared toward the bar. Once she had melted into the crowd, Poole unexpectedly placed a hand on Harry's arm.

'One thing I have to ask,' Poole said. 'What did Manton and Doyle have on Rory that meant he had to act on their behalf? Was it the offer of money?'

Harry laughed, but abruptly cut it short to save embarrassing Poole.

'No, nothing remotely like that. He did those things out of love.'

Harry watched Poole's stupefied features contort as he tried to work this out. After a pause, which Harry allowed to continue far too long, he released the man from his torture.

'He has all the money he'd ever want, the perfect job and he's honest, so, I guess Doyle found the one thing which would force Rory to act. He threatened to harm people he loves, my wife and son.'

Poole's mouth opened, hung there slack jawed as he mulled this information over, and then snapped it shut when he noticed Harry examining him.

'I didn't get the reason out of him until a few days after the May meeting, but I'd already guessed. We agreed to keep giving him rides so that Manton wouldn't suspect I knew. Rory was protecting Jill and Will.'

'I'm pretty lucky,' Harry added, looking over to the table where Rory, George and Mike were now in animated story telling mode, hands whirling, exaggerated expressions and lots of laughing.

'I've a best friend who loves my wife as much as I do and who is willing to risk his livelihood and his life for my family. There's nothing more to it than that. I guess we're like brothers.'

Poole whistled and Harry took a step to leave but Poole hadn't finished.

'Sorry Harry, quickly, one more question. I'm quite a fan of racing. Tell me, in confidence, did Rory lose the race at York on purpose, you know, the Gimcrack itself. I've watched that race so many times. He must have been under orders from Manton to throw the race?'

'Ah, there are some things which are best left unanswered,' Harry said enigmatically. He smiled once more and moved off into the room.

Emma and Pascal were already in their places on stage, preparing for their second set of the night. Harry waved to them and indicated with a hand gesture that he'd be there in a couple of minutes before taking a circuitous route to the stage via his staff's table.

He gave an anxious looking George Plant a thumbs up and watched amused as the fifty year old flopped animatedly back in his seat with relief. Harry whispered something quickly to Rory, who thanked him and immediately called for more drinks. Harry gave Bunt a friendly slap on his shoulder as he passed on his way to his primary target, planting a kiss on Jill's forehead before heading for the stage.

Sitting on his cushioned barrel which formed his piano seat, Harry cast his gaze around the room of well oiled Yorkshiremen and women. The room was buzzing, anticipating a cracking end to a Christmas Eve night of dancing and singing. He unconsciously tapped a few keys on his piano, allowing his mind to travel back over the last fourteen months, staring unfocused out over the heads of his audience. He had a wonderful family. The Redblood cheque had cleared, so they had money. He had quality horses in his yard and he had great, no, *brilliant* staff and friends… and he could play piano. He smiled inwardly, what else did he really need?

Filled with a sudden rush of joy, Harry snapped back into the moment. Anticipation was gripping the audience. Shouts and calls of encouragement crossed each from all sides of the room as he remained at his piano but made no move to play. Finally Harry gave in and produced a wry smile. He nodded to Emma who picked up a beat, Pascal joined in and Harry's hands leapt onto the piano keys. The dance floor erupted.

Forty

The quayside path was deserted when Findlay Morrison stepped onto the Millennium Bridge. Given it was seven thirty in the morning on Christmas Day, a lack of footfall on the bridge was to be expected. He pensively scanned the opposite bank of the River Tyne. Once his second foot had hit the surface of the metallic 'Winking Eye', he saw the red laser spot appear on his chest. It travelled up his body and back down before drawing a circle on his stomach. He tilted his head up and smiled across the river into the direction he imagined the sniper was located.

It wasn't a day for being cool or making an impression. For a start it was close to zero centigrade and there was a cruel wind whipping up small crests on the river. Icy pinpricks of spray peppered his face when he faced west. The bridge was empty, so he waited.

Presently a figure emerged from the south side of the river and aped his actions, stepping tentatively onto the footbridge and waiting. Findlay casually thumped one gloved hand into another as he stared intently at the rather rigid figure now waving a hand, presumably at his own sniper in the flats behind him. He's in possession of a sense of humour Findlay noted. This is going to be interesting.

The two men set off across the footbridge's famed ellipse. Findlay arrived at the centre first and cursed at having to turn his back to the handrail and face the wind; he had to ensure he provided a clear target. His host arrived and again, copied him, leaning with both hands on the opposite handrail, his back to the Tyne Bridge. Both men wore heavy winter coats, gloves, and their heads were covered against the icy blast of wind. Two red laser dots floated across both of them.

'Good morning, Mr Morrison,' said Thomas Redblood, the hint of a smile on his lips. He pushed back a heavily furred hood and revealed a head of sparse brown hair with silver streaks, which immediately started to whip around in the wind. Findlay did the same, although his own short-cropped hair stayed rigid when he removed his designer flat cap.

'Mr Redblood, it's a privilege to finally meet you,' replied Findlay, with what he hoped was the correct amount of reverence. He held out his hand.

Redblood looked at the gloved hand, then into the young man's face. He looked vigorous, vibrant, good looking even.

'Put it away, Mr Morrison. A handshake denotes trust. You shouldn't trust me or anyone else in this business.'

Findlay retracted his hand and beamed at the older man, showing no outward signs of displeasure at the rebuke.

'So, why me?' Findlay asked, displaying genuine curiosity.

Redblood shrugged and gave a tired smile. 'Can we dispense with the mutually assured destruction first?' he suggested, gestured to the laser spot still wavering on both of them, and then twirled a finger. The red spot disappeared from Findlay's chest.

'Of course,' Findlay responded, giving his own signal.

Redblood waited for his own laser light to wink out before continuing.

'I've been following your progress for a number of years, Mr Morrison. Your rise through the criminal fraternity neatly coincided with my plans to retire. I suppose if I wanted to bolster your ego I could say you remind me of myself when I was in my twenties; however that's simply not true, I was better than you.'

Findlay remained silent, his face an unmoving mask.

Redblood sniffed. 'It may sound prosaic, but you were in the right place at the right time.'

Findlay lifted an eyebrow, nodding sagely without any sign of rancour.

'I'm fifty years old, Mr Morrison, and I intend to retire with a small pension. However, a half a billion pounds international laundering business isn't something you can advertise on ebay; I needed to manufacture an exit. You'll discover this for yourself in about twenty year's time, if you're still around.'

Findlay crossed his arms and gave Redblood a quizzical look, pausing for several seconds to ensure he would be taken seriously.

'I'm intrigued to know how much of what's transpired was down to you. The horses, the Gimcrack dinner and the... disposal of your staff.'

Findlay paused, hopeful a reply might be on its way, but when Redblood offered nothing he continued unperturbed.

'As you would expect, I have researched you and kept a close eye on everything connected with Halo, Mr Bolt, and Mr Manton. I guess I'm keen to know the game the Master played.'

Redblood studied the young man's features closely for signs of petulance or insincerity and instead found an insurmountable fervour shining back at him. He smiled inwardly; he had chosen well. The boy was eager to learn but still retained respect; he wasn't *just* a cold, calculating killer.

Findlay continued, 'Besides, I'm paying you fifty million pounds in pension payments over the next decade and I severely doubt we will meet again, so please... indulge me.'

Redblood cocked his head to one side and looked Findlay up and down. 'How much do you already know, Mr Morrison?'

'Please, it's Fin. You can call me Fin.'

'No, it isn't,' Redblood fired back, a momentary flash of anger in his eyes. 'You don't have friends in this business, Mr Morrison. Allow your lover or your children to address you as Fin and no one else. Morrison is a fine name, use it exclusively for business.'

Findlay bit his lip, considering the reprimand.

'I understand,' he replied resolutely, quashing the feeling of chastisement which had started to bubble up within him.

Redblood read the look in the young man's eyes and reacted quickly.

'Look, I'm not the perfect villain,' he offered, delivering a quick roll of his eyes. 'Come on, join me,' he said, flicking a couple of fingers toward his side of the bridge. Findlay stepped across and the two men turned to lean on the handrail, shoulder to shoulder, looking west, toward the Tyne Bridge.

The bridge's Christmas lighting twinkled in front of them, although the deeply red sun which was starting to lift above the skyline behind them made the display less impressive with each passing moment.

'As you discovered when we picked you off that street in Sunderland, the quality of the people around you is of paramount importance,' Redblood began.

'I was lucky in that respect. I had the core of my team in place before I left secondary school. Benny Manton was the front man, Pete Warren and Charlie Doyle did the dirty work and I set the business up and directed it. I created the Money Tree when I realised my electronic laundering system was more effective than the best alternative in the country, and we needed a secure base for our technology. We evolved, moving out of frontline criminality and into servicing other criminal gangs. I also liked the idea of being out of the firing line; being linked to the illegal business on the street is dangerous, and I would recommend you find a suitable replacement for your current activities too.'

Redblood's deep voice changed timbre for a moment. 'I assume you have my hardware, software, and people securely relocated?'

'Of course, we're up and running again,' Findlay confirmed.

'They are decent people,' Redblood continued. 'I brought in Deacon to manage the technical side in the late nineties and watched the percentages roll in for the next decade, adding new clients once they had displayed the right characteristics.'

'Which are?' Findlay prompted.

Redblood blew out a derisive snort and lifted his eyes from the swirling black depths of the River Tyne. 'I think you already know, Mr Morrison. Your relentless growth can be attributed to more than sheer brute force. You are driven by a thirst for power and shrewd, which is why I spoke with you all those months ago and made my offer. Mind you, your cock-up at Wolverhampton races in February almost killed my belief in you.'

Findlay wore a slightly embarrassed expression. He wondered for a moment whether he was about to be cut loose. Could he have been yet another pawn in the game Redblood was playing? Again, Redblood read the warning signs in his protégé's face.

'Listen, there are parts of this story you *do* need to know. Let me finish and we can get off this freezing bridge,' Redblood added quickly, effectively subduing Findlay's fears.

'I decided to retire three years ago, but the issue was how I was going to hand the business over to a suitable candidate. I needed to re-align the business, as my colleagues were unfit to run Halo. I had been manipulating Doyle and Manton far too long and they simply weren't up to the job. They had increasingly become of the opinion that they were the most important cogs in the wheel, when in fact they were simply being played. I needed to dissolve Halo, remove the old staff, and place myself in such a light with the authorities that they wouldn't spend too long looking for me. I like England, and intend to stay here.'

Redblood had been peering ahead as he spoke, but took a quick glance round to make sure Findlay was listening before he continued.

'Manton was a horse racing fan and I'd indulged him by allowing him to buy a few horses each year; enough to make him appear to be an entrepreneur enjoying his passion. It helped with his image as a law-abiding citizen, as did his appearance on that dreadful television series. He was the public face of Halo. Anyway, I knew about the Gimcrack race because Manton had been desperate to speak at the dinner for years and wouldn't shut up about it. However, I realised it was the perfect platform to set up Manton and Doyle, because it dovetailed beautifully with their one serious error, the death of Laya Bolt.'

'At that time in the early nineties I needed to cut my brother loose. He had started to question whether I was involved in criminal activities. Billy could have been a part of the business; he's intelligent, reliable, and loyal but he has one major failing – an incurable honesty. I needed to rid myself of this distraction, and I suppose, keep him safely out of my world.'

'It was when we were still running the drugs supply and protection business in the East Riding. Manton, Doyle, and Warren were supposed to take my brother out one night to implicate him in a small crime, enough to scare him into running. I'd found a suitable girl, and set her up to play her part; to wait on the roadside and feign an assault. But the idiots picked the first black girl they came across on the Norton road. They were supposed to pretend to intimidate her, she would then report the crime and beef it up, but Doyle not only got the wrong girl, he inadvertently killed her by trying to be too clever. However, it did provide the right reaction from Billy; I was able to keep him at arm's length for the next sixteen years. I paid off a policeman to fudge the Laya Bolt investigation and we moved on.'

Findlay was listening like an attentive schoolboy, enraptured by his mentor. He provided encouragement for Redblood to continue with a wide-eyed expression.

'I have no real interest in horseracing, Harry Bolt or if I'm honest, my brother for that matter. They were simply assets,' admitted Redblood.

'They were pieces to be moved around the imaginary chess board that lives in my head. So, I set up a convenient death by paying off a doctor we had entrapped, got a dying man to play my corpse, and then managed the rest of the exit plan with the odd personal appearance where necessary. It was all a matter of applying pressure to each of the players at the right time and in the right way.'

Redblood paused. He glanced up and caught Findlay's rapt expression and continued after dropping is gaze to the river once more.

'For example, I needed to keep Manton away from Bolt's stables for a few months, so my people poisoned the water at the stables on a day where it couldn't go unnoticed. It had to be executed with a light touch; with just enough poison to cause a scene, but without any long-term effects. The authorities were bound to show an interest, and sure enough, the police started to poke around, which kept Manton at bay for a useful length of time.'

Still staring into the swirling depths of the river, Redblood continued in a matter of fact manner, 'Oh, and by the way, owning a building which you then lease to a business like a high street bank, is always useful. Most people will assume a business like a bank owns its premises, but it's hardly ever the case. I've used those rooms at the bank in Malton for hundreds of business transactions over the years.'

'Manipulating events is frighteningly easy,' Redblood pointed out, an odd hint of sadness in the older man's voice. 'I pushed Manton into ransacking the Bolt farmhouse and stables, as I was placing extreme pressure on his laundering business. This allowed me to put in a personal appearance at the stables with someone they already trusted, my brother, and paint myself as the injured party of the piece, which set up the Gimcrack dinner day. In order to get Bolt back onside I simply needed to tell my story and rebuild his home. One way or another I manipulated the players in my little plot to ensure Manton would attend the Gimcrack dinner and produce the chance for me to expose him in public.'

'Yes, the dinner was rather eventful!' Findlay exclaimed, 'And somewhat risky?'

Redblood paused, debating how much to relate to his youthful counterpart.

'Perhaps, if it hadn't been planned correctly,' he answered with a wry smile. 'However, it was necessary to consolidate my innocence in the minds of the police. The key was to get Manton into a public place and get him speaking. I knew I could push the right buttons once he was all set up. The Gimcrack at York was perfect; plenty of reporters, a smattering of national press coverage, and even better, a live video link on the internet. Manton loved the idea of addressing the top brass in the racing industry as it gave him the chance to bask in his success and be recognised as belonging to that exclusive little club. In Manton's world, the class system was still there to be climbed. I suppose speaking at the dinner also appealed to his twisted side, allowing him to address the great and good of the racing fraternity, when in fact he was laughing at them and sending a message of strength to his laundering clients.'

'That didn't last long,' Redblood added with smirk.

'Prompting Manton into a contest against me to win the race, even though I was supposedly dead, was even more enticing for him. He always felt threatened by me. All I needed was either one of my own horses or Manton's to win, and with eighty percent of the field between us we managed it easily. Win or lose, his pomposity would ensure he would attend the dinner. Then it was just a case of pricking his bubble in public so he would react. Of course, exposing Warren and Manton as Lara Bolt's killers whilst the lad was standing on stage in front of them was...' he gave a dry laugh, '...priceless.'

'I read the reports about your part in the incident at York, but no one seemed to know how you got out?' Findlay queried.

Redblood gave a generous smile which warmed his face.

'I went down to the floor as soon as I saw Doyle draw his gun. I had a two-man team waiting in the serving area that immediately shot out of the kitchen and bundled me to the back of the room, dodging behind the projection screen. They clicked a rope and harness onto me and dropped me over the edge of the viewing gantry, making sure I landed lightly two floors down on the concourse below. From there I dived into a car waiting just outside the racecourse. The whole exit took less than fifty seconds.'

'It did work rather well,' Redblood admitted, his chest swelling with a large intake of pride. 'My brother gets a new lease of life, Bolt gets the media attention instead of me, and I get to disappear without too much fuss, hand over my business, and take an annual stipend. Manton and Doyle's deaths were an unexpected bonus.'

Findlay produced a flicker of a smile which left one manicured eyebrow raised in an incredulous pose. 'Wasn't that a lot of work, just to...' He left his query hanging.

'I did consider just killing them,' Redblood admitted. 'But Manton's public image had become too high profile and our clients would not have as readily allowed you to take over.'

Redblood turned once more and locked eyes with Findlay. 'And you, Mr Morrison, have received the chance of a lifetime as a result. Please don't muck it up.'

Findlay nodded, engaging an expression serious once more. 'I've already met most of the clients. They are satisfied the business is running smoothly and will soon be back to full capacity.'

Redblood grunted his approval.

There was a short pause in their conversation where the wind and gurgle of the river flowing beneath them were the only sounds. Findlay took the opportunity to change tack. 'What about Mr Smith and your female colleague?'

'Ah, of course,' Redblood cackled happily. 'Well, David Smith and I are more than business associates. He became my husband last year and we will be retiring together.'

He arched an eyebrow and waited for a reaction. Pleased when Findlay responded with nothing more than a minor shrug, he added, 'Lisa will be in touch with you. She is a freelance operator and you will find her a useful addition to your team.'

Findlay nodded appreciatively and mouthed, 'Thank you,' in return.

Redblood squinted into the teeth of the icy breeze. 'Now, that is us done. I've revealed as much as you need to know. All that is left is for you to take this from me.'

Redblood removed his right glove and making sure to move slowly for any itchy-fingered gunmen watching, dipped into his coat pocket, and removed a packet of Marlboro cigarettes.

'Smoke?' he asked, before going on to explain: 'I always find a packet of cigarettes an excellent storage medium. The person receiving will trust something they recognise, the power of brands I suppose, and they don't tend to lose a box, whereas a memory stick or a piece of paper is easily misplaced. It also has the benefit of appearing very normal to an onlooker, even these days with smoking being frowned upon.'

Findlay removed his own glove, carefully took the packet, and popped the lid open. A memory stick was wedged between the remaining sixteen cigarettes.

'I don't mind if I do, Mr Redblood,' replied Findlay, taking the packet and removing one of the long American cigarettes and rolling it between his fingers. He slipped the red and white packet into his own pocket.

'The security decryption key,' Redblood stated, turning to look out over the river. 'Deacon will know what to do. It will release the full potential of the laundering system. As I'm sure you are already aware, the system has a back door. I'm also sure Deacon will find it eventually, but his time will be better spent on building you a new system. I assume you already have Deacon and his two young protégé's working on one, but for now the back door is my little insurance policy.'

Findlay had to hand it to the old man. He was a true pro. He directed an amused smirk into the river and shook his head.

'I understand, but tell me, that bloodstock business Manton described, was it just fantasy or was the plan to use it to launder money?'

Redblood chuckled. 'Any business which relies on the passing of huge amounts of money around the globe is perfect for laundering. You should take the time to speak with Deacon, it will be illuminating. But creating a new system wasn't the goal, *this time*. Besides, Manton's dream of the perfectly bred racehorse was a naïve fantasy.'

The older man pushed himself away from the rails and took half a dozen strides toward the deserted south bank of the river. Findlay turned his head to watch Redblood depart, noticing he walked straight, tall and without a cane. The master launderer seemed to have shed a decade of age during their conversation. He watched him for a few seconds more, and spun round intending to set off for the north bank. However, a soft voice called his surname and he looked back. Redblood was standing with his hands in his pockets, his long coat being blown sideways. A burst of dawn sun gave his outline a warming glow.

'By the way, Mr Morrison,' Redblood shouted above the sound of the wind. 'It goes without saying that if my pension isn't paid on time and in full, I will kill you.'

Findlay remained solemn, however his eyes were dancing. 'I would be disappointed if you didn't, Mr Redblood.'

Redblood aimed a quick, tight smile at Findlay and the two criminals turned on their heels in unison. Thirty seconds later the winking eye was devoid of pedestrians and Halo had a new man at its helm.

Author's Note

The Gimcrack is a real race, run at York racecourse each year in August and the Gimcrack dinner is usually held in December. It will celebrate its 150th year in 2020.

The race is unique. The winning owner is invited to address the racing industry at the Gimcrack dinner, which is attended by many luminaries of the sport. In the past the winning owner was expected to supply six dozen bottles of champagne for the dinner guests, although this tradition has apparently been allowed to lapse in recent years.

I hope you enjoyed Gimcrack. If you did, please visit Amazon's website and provide a rating and a short review – it really does help my stories reach a wider audience. Many thanks.

Richard Laws
February 2019